SM

"Hurry, Rachel. The fire is spreading over the roof."

The sound of his voice calmed the fear rising in her even as she climbed to the window and grabbed Jake's hands to hold tight. With her arms hanging out the window and her upper chest lying on the bottom of it, her legs dangled in midair in the bathroom. She tried to move forward, but something sharp scraped her side.

"There must be some glass on my right, but don't stop."

"Sorry, I thought I got all the glass out of the frame."

Another crash sounded behind her. Time was running out.

Rachel managed to shift a bit while Jake said, "I'll be right back. I remember there was a blanket in the shed." Jake raced toward the small building.

The scent of smoke and burning wood bombarded Rachel. Someone wanted to destroy the house, and Rachel and her aunt with it. But why? Coughs racked her while Jake rushed back. He took the blanket and put it between her and the window frame.

"This should help you move easier." Then he grabbed her arms and yanked.

"Just get me out." She imagined the flames eating away at the door and any second bursting into the room…

USA TODAY Bestselling Authors

Margaret Daley
Valerie Hansen
Laura Scott

Yuletide Threat

Previously published as *Standoff at Christmas*
and *Military K-9 Unit Christmas*

⟨H⟩HARLEQUIN®LOVE INSPIRED®CLASSICS

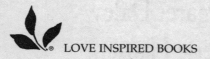

LOVE INSPIRED BOOKS

Recycling programs for this product may not exist in your area.

ISBN-13: 978-1-335-14309-9

Yuletide Threat

Copyright © 2019 by Harlequin Books S.A.

Standoff at Christmas
First published in 2015. This edition published in 2019.
Copyright © 2015 by Margaret Daley

Military K-9 Unit Christmas
(Christmas Escape and Yuletide Target)
First published in 2018. This edition published in 2019.
Copyright © 2018 by Harlequin Books S.A.

Special thanks and acknowledgment are given to Valerie Hansen and Laura Scott for their contribution to the Military K-9 Unit miniseries.

CONTENTS

STANDOFF AT CHRISTMAS 7
Margaret Daley

CHRISTMAS ESCAPE 215
Valerie Hansen

YULETIDE TARGET 329
Laura Scott

Margaret Daley, an award-winning author of ninety books (five million sold worldwide), has been married for over forty years and is a firm believer in romance and love. When she isn't traveling, she's writing love stories, often with a suspense thread, and corralling her three cats, who think they rule her household. To find out more about Margaret, visit her website at margaretdaley.com.

Books by Margaret Daley

Love Inspired Suspense

Lone Star Justice

High-Risk Reunion
Lone Star Christmas Rescue
Texas Ranger Showdown
Texas Baby Pursuit
Lone Star Christmas Witness
Lone Star Standoff

Alaskan Search and Rescue

The Yuletide Rescue
To Save Her Child
The Protector's Mission
Standoff at Christmas

Visit the Author Profile page
at Harlequin.com for more titles.

STANDOFF
AT CHRISTMAS

Margaret Daley

Who gave Himself for our sins, that He might deliver us from this present evil world, according to the will of God and our Father.

—*Galatians* 1:4

For Helen, who introduced me to Alaska

ONE

Rachel Hart left the warmth of her office building to trudge through the snow toward the processing center at the Port Aurora Fishery. The lights on in the building beckoned her in the predawn morning. The sun was just rising to the east in Port Aurora, Alaska, and then it would set by three in the afternoon.

She was used to the winters, having lived most of her twenty-eight years in the town, but today she wished the sun would shine for more than six hours. She looked up at the dark clouds rolling in and quickened her pace. An omen?

She lifted her cell phone and listened again to the message from Aunt Betty. "Rachel, I've got to talk to you. Today. Alone. Something's wrong. I don't know what to do. I'm taking my break at nine this morning." Luckily, today was payday, so Rachel could use her position as bookkeeper as an excuse to visit the processing center.

The urgency in her aunt's voice shivered down Rachel's spine. *What's wrong? Aunt Betty is always so cheerful and calm.* She must have called earlier while Rachel was away from her office.

Entering the building, Rachel walked down the hallway that led to the mail room for the employees who worked in the processing center. It was part of the large break room next to the office where Sean O'Hara managed this part of the company.

When she popped into the break room, Aunt Betty sat at the table with one of the newer employees. "I've got your paychecks." Rachel covered the distance to the two women and handed Betty and Ingrid their checks. "The next one will come with a bonus right before we close down for Christmas." She wanted to pull her aunt out in the hallway and find out what was wrong, but when she looked at the older woman with touches of gray hair around her face, her brown eyes widened and she shook her head slightly.

"I'm just thankful for the extra hours." Aunt Betty opened the envelope, looked at the amount and forced a grin, the corners of her mouth twitching.

In past years the fishery had closed down during the winter months, and the crabs were sent to another plant. Rachel had been thrilled about that part of the fishery's expansion in the last year. So had everyone else, especially Aunt Betty.

"But I'm also excited to have a few weeks off for the holidays." Her hand shaking, Aunt Betty stuck her paycheck in her pocket.

Rachel wanted to ask the other employee to leave but swallowed those words and instead said, "Me, too. Jake Nichols got in late last night for the holidays." She should be excited, but a lot had happened between them since they were teenagers. Jake had been her best friend while growing up, but when he left town eight years ago, they lost touch.

"I know Lawrence is glad to see Jake here, especially after what happened in Anchorage in August." Aunt Betty finished off her coffee.

"What happened?" Ingrid asked, having only recently been hired.

Rachel moved to the mailboxes and began stuffing the envelopes into them, hoping Ingrid left soon. "There was a serial bomber. Jake, a K-9 officer in Anchorage, was working one of the crime sites, searching for survivors or missing people, when the building collapsed on him. He nearly died." And he had made it clear he didn't want her to come see him while he was recovering. That hurt—still did.

Ingrid hugged her arms. "Oh my. Search and rescue is dangerous, but I'm finding out it's even more so here in Alaska with so much wilderness."

"Where are you from?" Rachel asked as she finished her task.

"Seattle."

"That's where Brad Howard's new partner is from."

"Who?"

Rachel paused at the exit. "Peter Rodin. Have you heard of him?"

"He was on the news from time to time," Ingrid said.

Aunt Betty's eyebrows rose. "About what?"

"His foundation gives money to various projects for the city." Ingrid rose and headed toward Rachel. "My break is over."

Relieved the woman was leaving, she moved to the side to let Ingrid pass, while her aunt's expression morphed into the apprehensive look she'd worn when Rachel first came into the break room.

When Aunt Betty remained in her seat, Ingrid said from the hallway, "Aren't you going back to work?"

Her aunt blinked several times. "Yes, I just want Rachel to pass a message on to my sister about this weekend."

Ingrid started toward the end of the hallway but much slower than her usual brisk pace.

As soon as Ingrid turned the corner and disappeared, Rachel moved toward her aunt. "What's going on? I got your message."

Waving to Rachel to come closer, Betty pushed to her feet. "I'm glad Jake is home. He's a police officer. He might know what's going on and help. I need some…" Her aunt's voice faded into the silence.

Rachel heard footsteps and glanced toward the door. Sean O'Hara came into the break room.

"Hello, ladies." Sean's eyes brightened as they took in Rachel. "Ah, payday. That's always a good day around here."

"Yes, it is. I need to get back to work." As a pallor crossed her features, Aunt Betty took her paper cup, crushed it and tossed it into the trash can by the door as she left.

Her concern growing, Rachel watched her leave as though a grizzly bear was hot on her tail. This wasn't like her aunt. What did she want with Jake? What had her scared? She'd get in touch with her later. Maybe she would swing by her house on the way home today. Aunt Betty only lived a mile away from Aunt Linda's, the older of her two aunts, and the one she lived with.

"I saw Jake down the hall. I told him I'd give him the grand tour. I know you two were good friends growing up. You're welcome to come along."

"Jake is here?" He and Sean had been friends in high school, too, so it wasn't that odd.

"Yeah, he couldn't believe all the changes around here. He wants to see the new vessels, processing center and shipping warehouse."

Rachel couldn't shake the worried expression on Aunt Betty's face. This might be her chance to see if she could talk to her on the floor, rather than wait until later. "Make it the short tour. I need to get back to work. Everyone will want their checks."

"I just came inside. It started snowing."

"Right on time, for a change."

Sean chuckled. "Predicting the weather isn't an exact science. But I'll be glad to get home before the hard stuff hits, which shouldn't be until tonight."

Jake Nichols turned as they approached him at the entrance into the large processing room. She took in his tall, muscular build, blue eyes and short black hair—the same and yet something had changed in the last couple of years since she'd visited Anchorage. It had to be the accident that nearly took his life in August.

Jake's look warmed when he saw her. Maybe in the next month they would be able to renew their friendship, and he would come back to Port Aurora more frequently.

"Rachel was in the break room. She thought she would join us like old times." Sean opened the wide double doors into the cavernous space where the fish and shellfish were processed for shipping to the rest of the United States.

Sean began pointing out some of the additional machines and the areas that were expanded this year. Rachel stepped away and glimpsed Aunt Betty decked out

in her protective clothing with white hat and long gloves
at the end of a conveyor belt. While Sean strolled with
Jake to various stations, Rachel hurried toward her aunt.
Out of the corner of her eye, Rachel spied Ingrid approaching Aunt Betty. Her aunt locked eyes with Rachel
and shook her head. She came to a halt. Suddenly, she
felt like she was in the middle of a spy movie, which
was ridiculous. Aunt Betty could be melodramatic at
times, but usually she was levelheaded.

Ingrid paused next to her aunt and said something.
Aunt Betty nodded. Rachel would have to wait to ap-
pease her curiosity. She released a long breath and pivoted, searching for Jake and Sean.

She caught up with them near the freezers. "I need to
get back to headquarters. It was great seeing you again,
Jake. You and your grandfather are supposed to come
to dinner tonight. A welcome-home party."

"I'll come with you." Jake slanted his glance briefly
toward Aunt Betty.

Did he see that nonverbal exchange between her aunt
and her? Jake had always been perceptive, which probably made him a good police officer. Rachel gave Jake
a smile, waiting until he shook hands with Sean and
joined her before heading out of the processing room.
In the hallway leading to the exit, she asked, "What do
you think of the new additions to the fishery?"

"Impressive what has been done in a short time.
Gramps told me things were automated and upgraded
where they could be. What's in the building next to this
one? That's new."

"The shipping warehouse. Everything going by boat
to Anchorage is loaded easily when the vessel docks

right outside. They even dredged the harbor to allow for bigger ships."

"How much is flown out?"

"Maybe a third—more in the warmer months. Ready?" She peered at Jake as he reached to open the main door. His strong profile had been shaped by the recent events in his life—the lines sharper, adding a hard edge to his features.

His hand on the knob, he peered sideways at her. For a few seconds his gaze trapped hers, and she didn't want to look away.

"Is something wrong with your aunt?"

"I don't know. She called upset, but we haven't had a chance to talk alone yet. I'll stop by after work to see what's going on."

"When she went into the processing room, I said hi to her and she didn't even acknowledge it. She just kept going. I know I've been gone, but that's not like her. She's the first to want to know everything about a person."

"I agree she isn't acting normal." Rachel headed into the lightly falling snow and made her way toward the office building.

She'd make sure Aunt Betty came to dinner. She'd been invited. The storm shouldn't hit full force until after midnight, and if she had to, Aunt Betty could stay at her sister's.

"Why were you at the processing center? I was surprised to see you there."

Jake smiled. "To see you. I saw you entering the building and came to say hi. I hear you were promoted to bookkeeper."

"Yes, which reminds me, I have to finish my rounds and give out the payroll checks. I'll see you tonight."

Midway through the afternoon, Rachel called Sean's office to see if she could talk with Aunt Betty. His secretary told her that her aunt had clocked out early and gone home. Rachel tried Aunt Betty's home number. No answer. She might not be home yet.

When Rachel was ready to leave two hours later, she made the call to her aunt's again, and the phone still rang and rang. Rachel's worry mounted. What if she was sick and couldn't answer it? She had looked pale earlier. And why had she wanted Jake's help?

Rachel hurried to her Jeep and navigated the snow-packed streets to the outskirts of Port Aurora. Aunt Betty's house was on the same road out of town but before Aunt Linda's house. Both her aunts and Lawrence Nichols, Jake's grandfather, loved living a little out from town.

When she reached Aunt Betty's drive, she drove down it and parked in front of the cabin, not far from the shed where her aunt's truck was. She was home.

Rachel made her way to the covered front porch, the wind beginning to pick up and blow the snow around as it fell. Rachel knocked. A minute later she did again.

When Betty didn't come to answer the door, Rachel stepped to the side and peeked into the living room window. She froze at the sight of the chaos inside.

Jake finished getting the supplies for Gramps and strolled toward the checkout at the Port Aurora General Store. It had been good to see Rachel again. Talking to her this morning made him realize he missed their conversations. While in Anchorage, he'd kept himself busy, and he'd let their friendship slip. He should have come back to town before this. Port Aurora had been his home for years until... He shook the image of Celeste from his thoughts and put the items on the counter. Marge, the owner's wife, began ringing up his purchases.

A bell rang, announcing yet another customer coming into the popular store near the harbor. Jake glanced toward the person entering. He stiffened. He'd known he would see Celeste Howard—the woman who broke off their engagement eight years ago—during his extended stay at Gramps's, but he'd hoped not the first day in town.

Their gazes clashed. He gritted his teeth and swiveled his attention to Marge to pay for his supplies.

Marge's eyes twinkled. "She always comes in right before Brad leaves work and gets a drink at the café. She usually picks him up." Marge, one of the best gossipers in Port Aurora, waited for his response.

He smiled and said, "Thanks. Merry Christmas," then grabbed his bag and started for the exit of the store, which was dripping with Christmas decorations.

Celeste intercepted his departure. "Hi, Jake. It's good to see you again. I heard about your injury. How are you?"

She had meant everything to him at one time, but when he looked at her now, a cold rock hardened in his gut. "I'm fine, as you can see." Then he continued his trek toward the door, welcoming the blast of icy wind as he stepped onto the porch.

The heartache and humiliation of their breakup, done in front of a large audience at their engagement party, still fueled his anger. After his mother had left him with

Gramps and gone on her merry way, he'd been wary of forming any deep relationship. First losing his father in a fishing accident and then his mom because she didn't want to be a mother anymore, had left its mark. Rachel's friendship had helped him through those hard times because she had gone through something similar with her own mom. Then when he'd fallen in love with Celeste, it felt so right. But the whole time, she'd been making a play for Brad Howard, the son of the richest man in town, using Jake to make Brad jealous.

Jake climbed into his grandfather's SUV and headed home. He was glad to have gotten that inevitable meeting over with. The earth didn't shake and swallow him because he'd seen her today. He was a different man than the one who had naively fallen for Celeste eight years ago.

In the dark of a winter day, Jake turned down the long drive that led to a cluster of several homes, one being his grandfather's on a few acres. He shouldn't have stayed in town so long. Although dinner at Linda's wasn't for a few hours, he wanted to spend time with Gramps and help him as much as he could around his place. Gramps, at seventy-three, moved slower and wasn't as energetic as he once was.

When Jake entered his childhood home, Mitch, his black and brown German shepherd, greeted him at the door, his tail wagging. He hadn't been sure how his dog would do, flying in a small plane, but he had been great. He would miss working every day with Mitch when he returned to the Anchorage Police Department. Mitch had been retired early because he'd lost one of his legs in the accident at the bomb site they had been searching.

"Did you miss me?" Jake rubbed him behind his ears.

Mitch barked.

The noise brought Gramps into the entry hall. "Every sound sent Mitch to the window to see if you were coming home."

"I stayed a little longer than I planned. I'm surprised at how much Port Aurora has grown, changed."

"Yes, it's been a harbor of busyness for the past year. Lots of construction in the summer. The roads still okay?"

"Yes. Five or six hours from now they might not be."

"If the storm blows through quickly, they'll have the roads plowed by tomorrow afternoon."

"All the way out here?" They didn't when he lived here as a child, but Port Aurora's population had been only twenty-eight hundred in the winter. With its growth came more needs for the residents.

"Yep, that's called progress. They don't plow the long drive, but I'll get out there and do that tomorrow morning."

"I can."

"No, you're on vacation."

"I've been on vacation for months, and frankly I can't wait to get back to work."

Gramps turned and ambled toward the great room where he spent a lot of his time. "Then let's pray your doctor says you're ready to go back to work at the first of January. Did you see any old friends?"

"Rachel and Sean." Since Celeste wasn't a friend, he left her name out. Whenever she was mentioned, Gramps always got angry.

"How's Rachel?"

"Fine." Jake sat on the couch while his grandfather took his place in his special lounger. "We really didn't talk long. Aunt Betty was upset about something, and Rachel was focused on that."

"Really? Betty is one lady that goes with the flow. She doesn't let much of anything get to her. I should learn something from her."

The landline rang, and Jake reached toward the end table and snatched up the receiver. "Hello."

"Jake, I'm so glad you're home." The relief in Rachel's voice came through loud and clear.

"What's wrong?"

"I stopped by Aunt Betty's house on the way home, and no one answered the door, but her car is here. I just looked into the living room window and someone has tossed her place. It's a mess."

"Call the police, stay outside and I'll be right there."

"I'm already inside. My cell doesn't work this far from town. The first thing I did was call you."

"Make the call to the police and then get out. Okay?"

"Yes." The urgency in Jake's voice heightened her concern for her aunt.

TWO

After reporting to the police about the trashed living room, Rachel hung up her aunt's phone not far from the front door and started edging back. Her heart pounded against her rib cage, her breathing shallow. She should get out like Jake said, but what if Aunt Betty was knocked out on the floor? She didn't think an intruder was still there since there was no sign of a vehicle other than Aunt Betty's. But if someone robbed her, and from the disarray of drawers emptied and cushions tossed on the floor, it was obvious that was what happened, then her aunt could be hurt, tied up or even...

No, she wouldn't consider that. She wouldn't leave until she found her aunt. The least she could do until Jake came was walk through her cabin and search. Rachel had first-aid training because of all the hiking and camping she did in the warmer months. If Aunt Betty was hurt, she might need medical attention right away.

She moved through the clutter, careful not to step on anything. Maybe this was the only room involved. Maybe her aunt had been looking for something in the living room and...

When Rachel entered the kitchen, it was worse. Everything was out of the cabinets and refrigerator. If someone had been looking for something, they probably found it, but Aunt Betty had little in the way of money. Rachel noticed the television was still in place as well as the small appliances. There was a walk-in pantry near the arctic entry at the back. The wooden floors were littered with flour, sugar, cereal. She would disturb the kitchen if she walked across it. Instead, she'd check the rest of the house first. By then, she hoped that Jake had arrived, and he would know how to proceed.

She walked several feet into her aunt's bedroom before she couldn't go any farther because of the mess on the floor, but from that point she could look into the open closet. No Aunt Betty.

A sound from the living room sent a wave of panic through her. It was probably Jake, but just in case, she flattened herself behind the open door.

"Rachel, where are you?"

Jake's deep baritone voice pushed the panic away, and she came out from behind the bedroom door. "I'm in Aunt Betty's bedroom."

"I should have known you wouldn't listen to me," Jake mumbled as he came into the short hallway.

"You brought Mitch." Rachel knelt next to the leashed German shepherd and petted him. "He looks good."

"I thought if we needed to search for your aunt he could help. He loves tracking. Have you found anything?"

"A mess, as you can see for yourself, but no sign of Aunt Betty. I haven't looked in the bathroom or the second bedroom, though."

"I'll check them and then we'll wait for the police.

You stay here with Mitch. This will only take a minute." After handing her the German shepherd's leash, Jake walked toward the open bathroom door and peered inside. "The same thing here but no Betty."

The door to the second bedroom was ajar but not open. Jake shouldered his way into the room but stayed by the entrance. "She must not be here. Could she have gone somewhere with anyone?"

"Maybe. I suppose she could have fled when she saw the chaos, but she most likely would have contacted her sister or me."

"Have you called Linda?"

"No, I didn't want to alarm her if I didn't have to. If anything happened to Aunt Betty, we would be devastated." Like when Jake had left Port Aurora years ago. His departure had stunned her, as if he'd taken part of her with him. She cared about the town and its people, but her family and Jake had been the most important people in her life. "I'll call her, then we can stay inside by the front door."

While Rachel placed a call to Aunt Linda, Jake picked his way through the mess in the living room to look into the kitchen. When she answered, Rachel said, "I'm at Aunt Betty's house. Her car is here, but she isn't. She was upset today, and I wanted to make sure she was all right. Do you know anything?"

"Well, that explains the weird message from her at lunchtime. I was waiting until she got home to call her. Her car is there?"

"Yes, where she parks it in the shed." Rachel glanced at the chaos and hated to tell Aunt Linda, but she continued. "Someone tore her house apart as though they were looking for something. For all I know, they could have found it."

Her aunt gasped. "I'll be right there."

"No, stay put. The police are on the way. What did the message say?"

"That she should never have taken those pictures."

"What pictures?" Rachel asked as Jake returned to her side.

"I'm not sure. You know how she's always snapping pictures. She was excited about some new project and was going to show us this weekend. She told me one day the town might want to even display the photos."

Maybe that had been what she'd wanted to talk to Rachel about. But then if that were the case, why had someone searched her house? Strange. "Display what?"

"She was being secretive. You know how she is about the big reveal when she gets an idea. Why would anyone try to steal from her? The only things worth taking are the TV and her camera, although it isn't a digital one like most people use today. Are they still there?"

"The TV is. I didn't check for the camera in her darkroom, but Jake said that second bedroom was trashed like the rest of the house."

"Really, I can't see someone taking it. It's old. Not something that someone would steal. How about her food processor I gave her for her birthday?"

Rachel remembered seeing it in the kitchen, in pieces. "It's here."

A long pause from her aunt, then in a tight, low tone, she said, "Then something has happened to her." Her voice sounded thick.

Rachel peered out the front window, seeing head-lights piercing the snowy darkness. "The police have arrived. I've got to go. I'll be home as soon as I can. We're probably overreacting." At least she prayed she was.

"Rachel, let me know what's going on. If you need my help, call. Are you sure I shouldn't come over?"

"Yes, she might call you. Someone needs to be there. Besides, the police are here, and they'll probably kick us out while they check the house. When we find Aunt Betty, she'll need you and me to help her clean this mess up." *If they find Aunt Betty.* She couldn't rid her mind of that thought.

Jake opened the door for the two police officers from town—the older man, Police Chief Randall Quay, and the younger one, Officer Steve Bates.

The chief shook Jake's hand. "It's good to see you back home. What do you think?" He gestured toward the trashed living room.

"I've searched the house as much as I could without disturbing anything, but there are some places I didn't get to check. The closet in the second bedroom, the pantry and the back arctic entry."

"Aunt Betty used the closet in the second bedroom as a darkroom."

The chief nodded once, then turned back to Jake. "Can you help me? Since you're here, I'd like to send Officer Bates on up the road. We are shorthanded with this storm that moved in early. It seems to bring the crazies out."

"Sure, I can help. Mitch here can track if we need that."

"Betty is a special lady. She taught me in Sunday school." Chief Quay moved farther into the room while his officer left. He frowned, his gaze fixed on a broken vase. "She didn't deserve this." He pulled out a camera and started taking pictures of the living room.

"I can cover the kitchen." Jake started forward.

"I appreciate it. We need to find Betty." The chief turned to Rachel. "Can you make some calls to people she may know and see if she's with them?"

"I already called Aunt Linda, and she's not with her. But I know a few others she's close with at the fishery. I'll give them a call." Rachel pulled out her cell to use the list of phone numbers stored in it. She was relieved to be able to help and needed to stay busy to keep from fixating on what might have happened to her aunt. She picked up the phone and began dialing.

Jake carefully started on one side of the kitchen and made his way around it. Behind the island in the center in the midst of the emptied flour on the floor, he found footprints—one set, too big to be Betty's, more like a man's size eleven. He took a photo with his cell of that and anything else of interest. He refrained from touching anything in case the chief wanted to dust for latent prints.

So far no evidence that Betty had been here when this happened—except her car parked in the shed. That would need to be searched, too. In fact, after he went through the kitchen he would go out the back arctic entry and check Betty's old pickup.

When he reached the pantry, he used a gloved hand to open the door. His gaze riveted to the spots of blood on the wooden floor about six inches inside. He lifted his eyes and scanned the disarray, homing in on bloody fingerprints on a shelf as if someone tried to hold on to it. Maybe trying to get up? Whatever went on in here, a fight occurred in this walk-in pantry. Did the intruder find Betty hiding?

The question still persisted. *Then where is Betty?*

He took more photos, then proceeded to the arctic entry. A pair of boots and a woman's heavy coat hanging on a peg were the only things in the small room. He took the coat and let Mitch sniff it, then kept hold of it in case he needed it again. His dog smelled the floor and paused by the exit outside. This was probably the way Betty came into her house since this was closer than the front entrance to the shed. Jake returned to the kitchen and grabbed a flashlight on the wall by the door.

On the stoop, Jake took in the area. The snow falling had filled in any footsteps, but that wouldn't stop Mitch. His German shepherd sniffed the air and started down the three steps, then headed toward Betty's pickup.

As he approached the driver side of the vehicle, he spied a bloody print on the metal handle. Not a good sign. Mitch barked at the door.

Jake said, "Stay," then skirted the rear of the old truck and opened the passenger door. The seat was empty.

Then he investigated under the tarp over the bed of the Ford F-150, using the interior light from the cab. Nothing.

"Where is she?" Rachel asked as she approached, carrying a flashlight. "I called at least twenty women she knew from church and the fishery, and no one knows where she is. One lady said she got ill after lunch and left. That would mean she should have gotten home by one. What happened in those three hours?"

Something not good.

"Is the chief through in the house?"

"He didn't find anything in the second bedroom but was going to go through Betty's. Did you find anything?"

He hated to tell her. Rachel had always been close to both of her aunts. "Blood in the pantry and on the driver's door handle."

"Do you think someone attacked her in the house and—" Rachel swallowed hard "—somehow she got away? Did she try to leave and that person caught up with her?" Her large brown eyes shone with unshed tears.

"I didn't see any blood inside on the seat. I don't think she ever opened the door."

Rachel blinked once, and a tear ran down her face. She swung around in a full circle, the flashlight sending an arc of illumination across the yard. "Then where is she? Why would anyone want to hurt Aunt Betty?"

Jake moved to his dog and let him inhale her scent on the coat again. "Find." While Mitch smelled around, Jake said to Rachel, "Let's see if he can pick up a trail going away from the house or shed."

Blond hair peeking out from under her beanie, Rachel swept her arm to indicate the yard outside the shed. "She could have decided to hide out here because she didn't have her truck keys on her."

"Maybe."

"But then why didn't she come forward when we arrived?" Rachel took one look at his sober expression and added, "Never mind. She would if she could..." Her gaze locked with his. "Could have."

Mitch picked up a scent, barked, then headed out of the shed across the field toward a stand of spruce and other evergreens. Giving his dog a long leash, Jake followed with Rachel beside him. Mitch plowed his way through four or five inches of snow.

At a place his German shepherd had disturbed, Jake yelled, "Halt," then stooped to examine a couple of drops of blood in the white snow with his flashlight.

Rachel's gasp sounded above the noise of the wind. He glanced over his shoulder at her face, white like the snow. He wished he could erase the fear in her eyes.

"You should return to the house and let the chief know."

Rachel shook her head. "I started this. I want to find her. I've been praying she's still alive and only hurt. Time is of the essence. She could freeze to death."

He rose, commanded Mitch to continue his search, then took her gloved hand in his. "We'll do this together." He felt better having her by his side rather than trekking back to the house alone about five hundred yards away.

As they trailed behind Mitch, Jake prepared himself. Betty could have been out here without a coat for hours. He stopped again a couple of times when more blood became visible in the glow of his light. Mitch was following Betty's path closely. If anyone could find her, his dog could.

Among the trees, the snow on the ground wasn't as thick because the top branches were heavy with it. They saw evidence of more blood, and Rachel's expression lost all hope her aunt was still alive. Tears returned to glisten in her eyes.

Mitch's bark echoed through the woods. He stopped about twenty feet away. Jake spotted a shadowy lump in the snow and blocked Rachel's path. "Go back and get Chief Quay."

Rachel tried to look around Jake.

"Please, Rachel. I think Mitch found Betty."

"Then I need to see if I can help her."

"If she's alive, I can. I trained as a paramedic when I first went to Anchorage." He'd been debating whether to continue his career of being a police officer in the big city or wanting to try something else before making that decision.

She looked into his face, snowflakes catching on her long eyelashes. She blinked, trying to conquer the tears welling in her eyes.

"Please, Rachel."

She whirled about and hurried back, following the path already cut. When she'd cleared the trees, Jake quickened his pace toward Mitch. Betty, stiff as if totally frozen with a bloodied head wound, leaned against a tree trunk facing away from the house. Had she been trying to hide? Her lower body was covered with a white blanket of snow while she hugged her sweater-clad arms to her chest. She stared off into space.

Betty was dead, but Jake knelt next to her and felt for a pulse to make sure. He said a silent prayer, something he hadn't done in a long while. She was with the Lord.

He would find whoever did this.

THREE

"Aunt Linda, I can call Lawrence and Jake and re-schedule this dinner for another night." Rachel stood in the entrance to the kitchen where her aunt was cooking a beef stew and putting some rolls in the oven to bake.

"All I have to do is the bread. The stew has been simmering half the day." She turned from the stove, her eyes red from crying for the past hour. Aunt Linda held the baking sheet in her hands like a shield, her fingertips red from her tight grip on it. "I know Randall asked you to come home, but Jake stayed and I want to know what they found out about Betty's death. Murder! I still can't believe it." She slammed the cookie sheet on the countertop and placed the rolls on it. "My sister was one of the sweetest people in Port Aurora. She never hurt a soul. I've got to make some sense out of this."

"I don't know if we'll ever be able to do that."

"They should have been here five minutes ago. Call them to make sure they're coming," her aunt, a petite woman with short blond hair, said in a determined voice.

Aunt Linda was always where she was supposed to be on time, if not early. "I will," Rachel said before her aunt decided to do it instead. Since she'd returned home an hour ago, Aunt Linda had fluctuated between tears and anger, much like what Rachel had been experiencing since she glimpsed Aunt Betty leaning against the tree. Stiff. Snow covering her.

As Rachel made her way into the living room, she heard the doorbell. She continued into the arctic entry and let Jake and his grandfather into the house. They removed their snowshoes and stomped their feet to shake off what snow they could.

"You two walked?"

"The wind has died down some." Jake removed his beanie.

"But the snow is still coming down a lot." Rachel had been looking forward to seeing him and spending time with her best friend from childhood. A few months ago, he'd almost died, and now her aunt had been murdered.

"With what happened this afternoon, I needed to walk some of my stress off." Jake hung his coat and his grandfather's on two pegs in the arctic entry and headed into the living room.

Lawrence looked around. "Where's Linda?"

"In the kitchen. Dinner will be soon."

"I'll go see how she's coping. I still can't believe someone would kill Betty." Lawrence strode from the room.

The second he was gone, Rachel pivoted toward Jake. "Tell me what happened after I left."

"How's Linda doing?"

"Mad one minute, emotional the next. She wants to find the person responsible and..." Rachel's mouth twisted. "I'm not sure what she would do, but she wants the murderer caught. She's trying to make some sense of what happened to her sister."

"Have her come in here, and I'll tell both of you before dinner. Although I can't say any of it makes sense."

Rachel headed toward the kitchen, but Lawrence and Aunt Linda were already at the doorway.

"I turned the oven on to warm so the rolls ought to be fine while Jake tells us what happened." Aunt Linda took a seat on the couch with Lawrence next to her, his arm around her shoulder. Her aunt leaned against Jake's grandfather as though she couldn't hold herself upright without him.

Jake stood by the roaring fireplace, while Rachel sat down and told her part of the story. "When I went back to Betty's house, Officer Bates had returned and was trying to pull fingerprints while the chief finished with photos, especially of the kitchen and pantry. When I told him what we found, he left his officer processing evidence and told me to go home, then he started toward the woods." The sight of Aunt Betty on the ground haunted her. Rachel shut the memory down and shifted her attention to Jake. "Your turn."

With his hands behind his back, he drew in a deep breath. "The chief took photos of Betty, then we carried her to the house. When I left, he was waiting for Doc to come take her. It appeared she died either from the head wound from someone hitting her with some kind of round object—possibly a can from the pantry—or she succumbed to the cold. Either way, the police chief is looking at the case as a murder."

Aunt Linda dropped her head, tears falling on her lap. "I can't believe this."

Lawrence cupped Aunt Linda's hand in her lap. "We

haven't had a murder here in years. A couple of deadly bar fights. That's all."

"Do you know if they found what they were looking for?" Aunt Linda lifted her gaze, her eyes red.

"No. The police don't know what she had of value at her house." Jake stepped away from the fire and took the last seat in the living room. "Was the TV the only thing of value that a robber would steal?"

Her aunt shook her head. "She had a few pieces of jewelry, but nothing to kill over, a state-of-the-art food processor and an old Kodak camera. Do you think Chief Quay would like for me to go through the house and see if I can find anything?"

"I'll call him tomorrow. It might help to know if that was the motive for the break-in. Knowing the motive might help find the killer."

Rachel remembered her brief encounters with Aunt Betty earlier that day. "I don't think it's a robbery. I think Aunt Betty discovered something that concerned her. She asked about talking to you, Jake, because you were a police officer in Anchorage. Aunt Linda, do you know of any place she uses for hiding valuable items? I can't think of any."

Her head lowered, Aunt Linda stared at her folded hands, the thumbs twirling around each other. "She had a cubbyhole in her kitchen. If you didn't know about it, you wouldn't see it. It's where the two cabinets form an L-shape near the sink. But it only can hide small objects. She kept her spare key to the truck in there. A diamond ring our mother passed on to her. I'm not sure what else."

"Then that should be checked." Rachel glanced at Jake, who nodded. "We can do that tomorrow."

Her teeth digging into her lower lip, Aunt Linda rose. "Since we're her only living relatives, it's our responsibility to see to her—" she swallowed several times "—belongings. Now, I'm going to set the table, and dinner will be in about ten minutes."

Lawrence also stood. "I'll help."

After they left the room, Jake leaned across the end table that separated their chairs and said in a low voice, "Is something going on between your aunt and my grandfather?"

"Good friends. That's all. Over the years, they've helped each other, and their friendship has grown. It kind of reminds me of us when we were kids. Not that I'm saying theirs is childish. Aunt Linda told me a few years ago that she'd had a wonderful marriage she would always cherish in her memory, but she didn't want to get married again."

"How about you? I thought by now you'd be married. You have so much to offer a man."

But not you. When they had been friends, before Celeste, Rachel had wondered if Jake and she would fall in love, and whether the marriage would work—unlike her mother's six marriages—because she knew Jake so well. Her mother would date a man for a couple of months, marry him, then discard him in a few years. "I don't have a lot of faith in marriage—at least what I've seen of it."

"You might be right. A successful marriage is becoming rarer."

"Is my cynicism rubbing off on you?"

He grinned. "I've been around you for a day, and look what happened." His gaze shifted to the Christmas tree in front of the living room window. "Your lights were what we focused on. Even with it snowing, we could see them from our front porch. Of course, it's not snowing as hard as earlier."

"We always decorate the day after Thanksgiving. Aunt Betty comes over…" Thinking about how her aunt died churned her stomach. She needed to forget the last few hours for a while or she wouldn't be able to help Aunt Linda. "Is Lawrence going to put a tree up this year? He usually doesn't because he visits you in Anchorage."

"He hasn't said. Maybe I should go cut one down like we used to, and then he'd have no choice. He always insists we do when he comes to visit, so turnaround is fair play. He's really a kid at heart."

Rachel took in the hard edge to Jake's expression and the reserve he didn't have as a teen. She missed who he'd been. "But you aren't. From what he's told me, you're very serious and focused."

"Being a police officer in a large town colors your perception. Sadly, I have covered murders. I'd forgotten the charm of Port Aurora and the lack of what I call *real crime*."

"You should come home more often." This exchange brought memories of how they were as teenagers. They used to tell each other everything—until Celeste. She changed Jake. He became closed, and in the end he left because she married Brad Howard. That hurt her more than she cared to acknowledge.

"We'll see."

"Have you seen Celeste yet?"

His shoulders tensed. "I've only been here less than a day."

"But you were in town for hours, and it's a small place. She and Brad don't live far from the main street."

"I've seen that big house overlooking the harbor."

"You mean the audacious home looming over the town," she said with a forced chuckle.

Jake pushed to his feet. "I can smell the dinner, and I'm starving. Let's eat." He held out his hand to her.

Celeste was still a sore subject with him. That broke her heart. Rachel wanted him to be happy and move on from Celeste. Rachel placed her hand in his, and he tugged her up. For a few seconds they were only inches apart, his spicy scent—or maybe the Christmas tree nearby—teased her senses and blended with the aromas of the bread and beef stew.

At least he loved someone once. You don't even want to take that chance.

The next morning, after Gramps plowed the long drive from the road to the cluster of houses, Jake headed for town to talk with the police chief, a man he'd worked with for over a year, before he moved away. Randall had taught him a lot, but his real police training came when he went to Anchorage.

Jake parked in front of the police station, a small building, nothing like where he worked. When he entered, he saw the chief coming out of his office and putting a paper down in front of the dispatcher/secretary. From what he understood, only seven officers worked for the department besides Randall, three more than when he had been an officer on this force. That wasn't too bad in the winter months when the year-round population was a little over four thousand, but in the warmer months there was an influx of tourists, mostly hunters and fishermen.

Randall came toward Jake and shook his hand. "I'm sure glad you could help out yesterday. I have one officer on vacation, and with the storm yesterday, there are always more wrecks."

"While I'm here, I'd be glad to help out, if needed. I wanted to know what the cause of Betty's death was."

"The verdict was she passed out and froze to death. It was estimated by body temperature she was outside close to three hours."

"Are you calling it a murder?"

The chief nodded. "She wouldn't have been outside with a head wound if someone hadn't intruded in her house and hit her."

"Did you find the weapon?"

"Yes, a can of soup. I think the attacker left her in the pantry where she had probably been hiding and continued his search. She must have awakened and fled outside."

"How many people do you think it is?"

"We have two different sets of footprints in the house that weren't Betty's." Randall half leaned, half sat on his dispatcher's desk as Officers Bates and Clark walked from the back of the station, talking.

"Any latent prints that you could match?"

Randall signaled for Bates to join them. "Yes, one, but the print isn't in our system. Did Linda know what might have been taken from Betty's? If someone wanted to steal, I could think of many better off than her."

"No, but Linda and Rachel are going to start cleaning up since I checked with one of your officers this morning. He said you're through with the crime scene."

Randall glanced toward Bates. "We were there until late, processing the scene. Finished about ten o'clock. If Linda or Rachel find anything missing, please let me know."

Jake shifted slightly toward the young officer. "I'll leave you to talk business. I'm going by the general store for some cleaning supplies they might need at Betty's house, then to Port Aurora's Community Church. Linda couldn't get hold of the pastor this morning, so she wanted me to tell him Betty only wanted a small memorial service at church."

"That sounds like Betty, but it won't be small. I don't see how the church will be big enough for the service. She worked at the processing center at the fishery and was a moving force at church. I figure at least half the town will want to come." Randall reached behind him for a piece of paper and handed it to Bates. "Red Cunningham had his cell phone stolen. Check it out."

"Yes, sir. On it."

"Was Betty's cell on her?" Jake asked.

"From what I understand, she only had a landline at her house." Randall straightened. "I can't imagine not having a cell."

"Me, either. It's hard enough that it doesn't always work here." They nodded goodbye, and Jake left the police station and drove the half a mile to the general store, which was close to the harbor on the main street.

He decided to grab a cup of coffee, because no one made it as good as Marge, then get the cleaning supplies. As he entered the store, his gaze almost immediately went to Brad and Celeste sitting at a table talking. Neither saw him, and he hoped it stayed that way.

He stood in line a couple of people behind Sean

O'Hara. They had been in the same class in high school. If he had been spending time with Rachel growing up, usually Sean was with him. Sean placed his order, then turned away from the counter.

"I just heard about Betty this morning," Sean said when he glimpsed Jake. "She was such a good employee. I should have realized something was wrong when she went home early yesterday."

Jake moved up in the line. "Linda and Rachel are planning a memorial service for her next week. Police Chief Quay said the church wouldn't even be able to accommodate most of the people who would attend. If that's the case, is there anything at the fishery that could be used?"

Sean rubbed the back of his neck. "Don't know. I'd have to talk with Brad about it. I'm sure he would want to do something. Betty worked at the fishery for most of her life."

Jake leaned toward Sean. "Yeah, I can hardly believe she's dead. Murdered."

Sean's eyes widened. "Betty? Why?"

"You haven't heard—a robbery gone bad."

"I tried to stay away from the rumor mill. Betty doesn't have that much."

"That's what Linda said. She and Rachel are at her house, trying to figure out what was stolen. I have a few errands, and then I'm going to help them later." Jake stepped up to the counter to buy his coffee.

"I'll let you know what Brad says about a bigger place for the memorial service." Sean made his way toward the exit.

After Jake ordered his drink, he grabbed a basket and

found the aisle for cleaning supplies, staying away from the café section where Brad and Celeste sat.

Jake finished his coffee and paid for the items he bought. When he stepped outside, the chill made him think about what had happened to Betty. Anger swelled in his gut. Why did bad things happen to good people? He'd asked the Lord that many times. Maybe life as a police officer in Anchorage wasn't really for him? And yet, he'd only been home one day and a murder occurred in this usually peaceful town.

He walked around the corner of the large store. When he reached his grandfather's SUV, the rear driver's side tire was flat. He stuck the sack of supplies in the back and got out what he needed to replace it with a spare. As he knelt to fix the jack under the car, he glanced at the front tire—flat like the back one. Jake examined it and found a large slit in it.

This wasn't an accident. Someone did this on purpose.

Carrying a sack of supplies, Rachel stepped into Betty's house, drew in a fortifying breath and said, "Remember this place was trashed."

"I've seen trashed before. Your dad was the messiest guy." Hands full with a mop, broom and garbage bags, Aunt Linda entered a few paces behind Rachel. She glanced at the living room and blew out a rush of air. "Okay. This tops anything your dad did."

"Probably more than one person did this. Going through everything takes time. Jake was stopping by the police station to talk to Chief Quay."

Aunt Linda shook her head as her gaze skimmed over the piles of items on the floor. "I hope Betty didn't see this. Everything in her house had a place, and she kept it that way. Very organized. It will take days to go through, but I'm determined to see if anything is missing. I have a good idea what she has of value that a burglar might want."

"I can't see this as a robbery gone bad. Everyone knows her in town. They know she has limited funds and just makes it every month."

"Where do we start?" Aunt Linda leaned the mop and broom against the wall.

"In here. If we can get this room and her bedroom done today, I'll consider it good, then after church tomorrow, we can come work on the kitchen. It's the worst."

"Sounds like a plan."

"But first, we should check to see if her valuables are still in the hidey-hole in the kitchen."

"Yes, I'm sure the police chief would like to know if anything was taken as soon as possible. It might help him find who did this." Aunt Linda crossed the living room to the kitchen entrance and halted. "This looks like a tornado went through here. Why were they emptying food boxes? What in the world were they looking for?"

"Some people have hidden cash in cereal, flour, whatever."

Aunt Linda harrumphed. "That gives me the willies. What about the germs?"

"Usually they have them in something plastic." Over her aunt's shoulder, Rachel gestured to the open freezer, a puddle of water on the floor nearby. "People have been known to hide money and stuff like that in the freezer."

"Obviously, it didn't work. They checked it. But really, the intruders couldn't have known Betty very well, or they wouldn't have wasted their time."

Rachel thought back to the panicked look on Aunt Betty's face the day before. She could still hear the scared desperation in Aunt Betty's voice in the break room. Why didn't she talk to the local police?

Aunt Linda stepped over the worst of the mess on the floor and covered the distance to the counter area she'd described last night. With her foot, she brushed some empty boxes and cans away, then knelt. She reached into the cubbyhole at the junction of the cabinets. "Got something."

Rachel stooped down behind her aunt. "Do we have anything like this at our house?"

"Nope." Aunt Linda slid out a plastic bag with a few pieces of jewelry and another with several keys and gave them to Rachel, then she stuck her hand back inside. "There's something else. Feels like one of her photos—actually several."

When her aunt drew them out and examined them, Rachel looked over Aunt Linda's shoulder. "That's the shipping room at the fishery. Why would she take a picture of that? She didn't work in that department."

"I don't know. Maybe there are more in her darkroom." Linda glanced back at Rachel. "The camera she used was old—one she had for years. She still used film. That was probably her one luxury. Buying film and what she needed to process her own photos."

"Three pictures are all that's in the cubbyhole?"

"Let me check to make sure. It goes back to the wall." Her aunt rechecked and came up empty-handed. "Before we start cleaning, let's see what's left of her darkroom.

Most of her photos are of nature. She is… I mean, she was good. Photography made her happy."

Rachel clasped her shoulder, hearing the pain in her aunt's voice. She leaned over and hugged her. "She's with God now."

Aunt Linda cleared her throat. "I know. But…" She gave her head one hard shake, then pulled herself to her feet. "This isn't getting her house cleaned. Betty would have hated her house this way."

As they made their way to the second bedroom closet, Rachel slipped the items from the hidey-hole into her pocket.

"I remember it took Betty a year to save up for her camera. She was so excited when she finally got it. I bought her enough film that I think it lasted six months, even though she went out every weekend and took pictures of things that interested her."

Rachel dragged the door open, so that Aunt Linda and she could peer into the darkroom side by side in the entrance.

"I don't see her camera," her aunt mumbled, then crouched down and began moving the clutter to see what was under it. "She keeps it in here on the hook by the door. It's not there, and whatever she was processing was destroyed. Could that be the reason someone came to her house?"

The scent of the chemicals still lingered in the air, but something else invaded and began to overpower that odor. Rachel swiveled around and went to the entrance into the bedroom. As she took in a deep breath away from the closet, a whiff of smoke grew stronger.

Rachel hurried into the living room, her gaze riveting to flames licking up the drapes on the front and side of the house.

FOUR

Jake paced the reception area of Max's Garage while Max changed his second slashed tire and replaced it with a new one. He'd tried calling Rachel at Linda's and then at Betty's house but got no answer. He'd even called his grandfather to send him over to Betty's, but he must still be outside plowing some of the roads for people near them. Why would anyone slash his tires unless they wanted him delayed in town?

The hairs on his nape stood up. Something was wrong, and the only thing he could think about was Rachel and Linda over at Betty's. What if the intruders hadn't found what they were looking for and came back?

He snatched up the receiver to call the police. When the dispatcher answered, he asked, "Is Chief Quay in?"

"No, he's out on a call. In fact, everyone is busy. May I help you?"

"This is Jake Nichols. I was in there earlier. Ask him to go to Betty Marshal's house as soon as possible." Maybe he was overreacting. He hoped he was.

"That was so sad about her being killed yesterday. Is something wrong at her house?"

"Rachel Hart and Linda Thomas were going to Betty's house to clean it up and see if they could discover if anything had been stolen. My tires were slashed when I was parked at the general store, and now no one is answering at Betty's house. I think something could be wrong." Jake looked toward the counter and saw Max with his keys. Jake rose. "I'll be heading there now."

"I'll call the chief and let him know. In the meantime, Officer Bates is nearer. I'll see if he can drive by."

"Thanks." Jake hung up and headed toward Max. "I appreciate the rush."

"I put the new spare in the back. Someone wasn't happy with you. Do you think it's somehow connected to what happened at Betty's?"

Jake shrugged and grabbed his keys. "I don't know, but I don't want to take the chance." Then he started for the car in the bay area in the back.

He pushed his SUV as much as he could without ending up in a ditch. The unsettled feeling in his gut wouldn't go away. In fact, it grew stronger the closer he got to Betty's house.

His heartbeat kicked up several notches when he spied a plume of smoke billowing in the cloudy sky in the direction where he was heading. He pressed down the accelerator.

"Aunt Linda," Rachel screamed over the crackling of the fire as she raced back to the second bedroom. "We've got to get out of here."

Her aunt rushed out of the darkroom, her eyes round like the full moon a few nights ago. "Why?"

"The living room is on fire."

Aunt Linda hurried past Rachel, and when she

reached the end of the hallway, smoke invaded the corridor. Putting her hand over her mouth, her aunt stopped and peered into the living room, a thick gray cloud filling the whole area.

"We can't get out the front door," Rachel said as the fire consumed that part of the house. She swiveled her attention toward the kitchen and noticed smoke mushrooming through the doorway. Grabbing her aunt's arm, she tugged her away. "We can't get out that way, either. We'll climb out a window." But when she hastened into the first bedroom, her gaze fixed on the high windows that allowed sunlight inside but would be hard to climb out of.

"There's a bigger one in the bathroom. The other bedroom is just like this—a set of high, narrow windows." Aunt Linda pivoted and raced to the bathroom.

When Rachel rushed inside behind her, she nearly ran into her aunt, who stood still in front of the frosted pane. "It's smaller than I thought, and the glass is thicker than normal."

Aunt Linda whirled around, looking for anything to break the window. Nothing. Rachel hurried back to Betty's bedroom to find something while her aunt checked the second one. In the midst of the clutter on the floor, Rachel didn't see anything that would break the glass.

Smoke snaked into the room. Rachel pulled her turtleneck over her mouth and continued her search. Her gaze fell on a metal flashlight that might work. She had to try it. She snatched it up and raced back to the bathroom. After putting the toilet seat down, she climbed on top of it and swung the flashlight toward the thick, frosted glass. It bounced off, not even cracking the window.

* * *

Jake pulled into the long driveway to Betty's house, spying Rachel's Jeep. Flames mixed with blackened smoke shot up from the roof of the cabin. He pulled out his cell phone and prayed he had reception. A dead zone. His throat tightened with the thought of what Rachel and Linda must be going through—if they were even still alive. The idea of not seeing Rachel again stole his breath.

That's not going to happen if I can help it.

He slammed his SUV into park and jumped from it. The front door blazed as fire ate at the wood around it. He raced to the side of the house, then the back entrance. The same sight greeted him as though someone started the fire at the points of entry. He hurried to the left where the bedrooms were. When his gaze latched on to the long, slender windows at the top of the bedroom, the thundering of his heartbeat vied with the roar of the fire. Then he remembered the other bedroom was the same.

He moved toward the bathroom, trying to imagine what the window was like. Frosted and thick, but he could see movement behind the pane. Someone was still alive. It would be hard, but he thought both Rachel and Linda could fit through the opening.

He swept around, trying to find something to break the glass with. He ran to the shed and found a sledgehammer in the tool closet. When he hurried back to the house, he stood near and shouted, "Get back. I'm going to break the glass."

He lifted the sledgehammer onto his shoulder, praying that whoever was in the bathroom had moved back, but he had no choice. Getting cut was better than dying in a fire. He swung the tool toward the window with all the strength he could muster.

Rachel had tried several more times with the flashlight, then discarded it. Needing something else she climbed down from the toilet. Fingers of smoke crept into the room.

Coughing, her aunt scurried into the bathroom with a shotgun and gave it to Rachel. Then Aunt Linda closed the door and stuffed some towels under it. "We don't have much time. Maybe we could use the gun like a bat or shoot at the glass."

Rachel checked to see if the weapon was loaded. "If shooting doesn't work, we can try the other way." She lifted the shotgun and aimed. Her ears pounded with the beating of her heart. With the noise of the crackling fire coming down the hallway, she put her finger on the trigger.

"Wait. Listen." Aunt Linda grabbed Rachel's arm. "That sounds like Jake."

Something slammed into the window. Her aunt shoved her into the bathtub as the glass exploded into the room. The backs of her legs hit the edge of the tub, and Rachel tumbled backward, her aunt following her. A few shards pierced Rachel's arm as she put it up to block her face. Her body crashed against the hard white acrylic, knocking the breath from her.

"Rachel. Linda," Jake shouted as he appeared in the smashed window.

Aunt Linda rolled off Rachel and replied, "We're okay."

With a sledgehammer, Jake began knocking the rest of the glass out of the frame. "Grab some towels to lay on the ledge. You need to hurry. The fire is working its way to this side."

Her aunt scrambled from the bathtub and held her hand out for Rachel to take. Still trying to catch a decent breath, she gripped her aunt's hand and let her haul her to her feet. Aunt Linda helped her out of the tub and removed the towels from under the door. Smoke poured into the room from every crack around the door seal. It tickled Rachel's throat, and she coughed. She pulled her turtleneck over her month again, but the smoke stung her watering eyes.

"Ready?" Jake took the towels that Aunt Linda gave him and placed them on the ledge. "I'll help you from this side."

"You go first." Rachel helped her aunt up onto the closed toilet seat. She couldn't lose her other aunt. Please, Lord.

The cuts on Rachel's arms hurt, and blood dripped onto the tile floor. She took a washcloth to help stem the flow while Aunt Linda leaned into the window. Rachel helped her out the hole. Her aunt was petite, and she barely made it.

A loud boom shook the house. Rachel glanced back at the door.

"Hurry, Rachel. The fire is spreading over the roof." Urgency filled Jake's voice.

The sound of his voice calmed the fear rising in her even as she climbed onto her perch, leaped to the window and grabbed Jake's hands to hold tight. Her legs dangled in midair in the bathroom. She wriggled her body, trying to move forward, while Jake pulled her toward him. Her side rubbed against the frame, and something sharp scraped her.

She groaned.

"Okay?"

"There must be some glass on my right, but don't stop."

"Sorry, I thought I got all the glass out of the frame."

"Pull harder. My shoulders are barely through, but my hips are bigger."

"Scoot as much to the left as you can. I'll find something to put between you and the frame on the right."

Another crash sounded behind her. Time was running out.

Rachel managed to shift a tad bit while Jake said, "I'll be right back. I remember a piece of flashing in the shed." Jake raced toward the small building.

Without Jake to block the wind, it bombarded Rachel with cold and the scent of smoke and burning wood. Coughs racked her while Jake rushed back. He took the flashing and put it between her and the window frame.

"This should help you move easier." Then he grabbed her arms and yanked.

"Just get me out." She imagined the flames eating away at the door, any second bursting into the room.

He pulled slowly at first, and then the second her hips cleared, she slipped out easily, almost toppling into him.

After moving away from the house, he gathered her into his embrace and held her for a few seconds. "I thought I'd lost you when I saw the house on fire."

She nestled against him, relishing the warmth of him and the sense of safety she felt. In that moment she never wanted to leave the shelter of his arms.

"Are you okay?" he murmured against the top of her head.

She nodded against his chest, then turned within his

arms and looked at the cabin nearly consumed totally by the flames. "This was no accident. The fire was at the back and front exits. Even the windows we could have easily been able to escape through were consumed with flames."

Her face ashen and wearing Jake's coat, Aunt Linda stepped closer. "Someone wanted to destroy Betty's house. Why?"

"Good question and one I intend to find out. No one goes after you two without answering to me." Jake's arms cuddled Rachel even closer. "I don't want to go through that again."

"Neither do I," Rachel whispered, her throat raw.

"I'm taking you to town to report this to the police and see the doctor."

Not wanting to leave his arms, Rachel glanced over her shoulder. "Take us home. We'll call the police and report the fire."

"Nope. You need to have Doc look at your injuries." He released her and examined her right side. "You're bleeding. Let's get to Gramps's car. He has some towels you can place over the wound." Jake looked at her aunt. "Are you okay? I didn't see bleeding."

She nodded.

As flames engulfed the cabin, they hurried to the SUV, the sound of sirens filling the air.

A police car came down the long drive followed by the fire department. There wasn't anything that could be done for the cabin. With only a light breeze and a snow-covered ground, hopefully the blaze wouldn't spread.

"See? Now we don't have to go to town." Rachel took the clean towel from Jake and pressed it into her side.

"You're still going to see Doc." Jake started the car

and turned the heater on, then he climbed from the vehicle.

"Wait," Aunt Linda said. "Take this." She shed his coat and tossed it toward him.

He caught it and walked toward Chief Quay as he got out of his cruiser.

Rachel watched the conversation between them with Jake gesturing toward the house, anger creasing his forehead as he spoke to the chief.

"Jake saved us," her aunt murmured.

"I know." Since he'd come home, she felt as though she'd been on a tilt-a-whirl, spinning out of control. And yet, seeing him again renewed feelings she'd kept buried—conflicting emotions from anger at him leaving to happiness he was here.

As Jake returned to the SUV, the firefighters hooked up their equipment. "Let's go. Randall will come out to see you later after you've seen Doc."

"How did he find out about the fire since we couldn't call it in?"

"Gramps saw the black smoke when he returned from plowing the Andersons' drive down the road. He went home, placed the call and then was going to come over. Randall told him that he just received a report from another neighbor and he would take care of it." Jake backed up, then made a turn and headed for the highway.

Jake opened Linda's door to greet his grandfather and Mitch. "Thanks for bringing him over. Randall should be here soon to interview Rachel and Linda."

"The cabin must have gone up quickly." Gramps entered while Jake petted Mitch.

"Probably an accelerant was used. One of the fire-fighters has experience in determining arson."

"That makes sense." Gramps sat on the couch. "Where are Linda and Rachel?"

"Changing. Doc had to sew up Rachel's right side where some glass sliced her good. The rest of her cuts were small. Neither of them have smoke inhalation problems." As Jake rattled off the list of injuries, a part of him was back at the cabin, frantically trying to get Rachel free. If something had happened to her, he would have blamed himself. He'd rescued many people while working for the Northern Frontier Search and Rescue Organization and the police, so he should be able to save someone he really cared about.

"That's a relief. I should have gone with them this morning."

"And what? From what they told me it happened fast, and there wasn't anything that could be done, except to get out. Besides, you wouldn't have fit through the window."

"True. I never thought something like that would happen."

"Neither did I or I would have been there."

Gramps's wrinkled face cracked a big grin. "Do I need to say if you had, you wouldn't have gotten out? We have the same build. Most of the Nichols men are tall and have broad shoulders."

Jake chuckled. "Touché."

"It's good to hear some laughter after the day I've had," Rachel said as she walked slowly into the living room.

Jake turned toward her, remembering how close he'd come to losing her. That thought left his gut roiling, and he was even more determined to find out what was going on in Port Aurora. "Are you all right?" He took in her pale face and tired eyes—a beautiful sight to see. It could have gone so wrong today.

"My side hurts, but it felt great to take a shower and get that smoke smell out of my hair. I think I washed it three times."

When Rachel moved past him to the chair across from Gramps, Jake drew in a deep breath of the apple-scented shampoo. She still used the same one from when she was a child. He associated apples with Rachel because of that.

She eased down, wincing once. "When is the chief arriving?"

"I see his car coming down the road." Linda crossed the room and opened the door to the arctic entry.

After shaking Randall's hand, Jake sat next to Rachel's aunt on the couch while the chief took the last chair. His grim expression fit Jake's mood. Every alarm bell was going off in his head. The fire only reinforced his belief that Betty's death wasn't due to a robbery gone bad. What had Betty gotten herself into?

"Are you two all right now?" the chief asked, withdrawing a pad and pen from his pocket.

"As well as could be expected." Linda pressed her lips together.

Randall shifted his attention to Rachel. "I understand Doc had to see you."

"I'll be okay. Do you have any idea what happened?"

"No, other than there were footprints leading to the house from the woods on the left side. I followed them to tire tracks—probably a truck. I'm treating this fire as arson at this time. Did either of you see anything?"

Linda shook her head while Rachel said, "We were in the back bedroom, looking for Aunt Betty's camera."

"Why?"

"Although I don't think it is worth much except to her, someone could have taken it," Linda answered Randall.

"Did you find it?"

"No, but I didn't check the darkroom thoroughly. It was trashed like the whole place was. The camera usually hangs on the peg by the door, but it wasn't there."

The chief wrote on his pad. "So it's possible that a camera was stolen. Anything else you know of?"

"We found her few pieces of jewelry that were worth something, although not that much." Rachel withdrew the ring and two sets of earrings still in the plastic bag. "And as you know, the television and small appliances like the food processor were still in the house, so truthfully I don't think anything else was missing, but we'll never know for sure."

"I wonder if the camera might be the reason the cabin was torched." Randall wrote something else on the paper, then glanced at Linda, then Rachel.

"It was a ten-year-old Kodak that was special to Betty, but I couldn't see it bringing much money for anyone who stole it. It wasn't even digital." Linda combed her fingers through her wet, short blond hair.

"Anything else?" Randall asked.

Her gaze trained on Rachel, Linda furrowed her brow but remained quiet. Rachel shook her head slightly. Was there more that Rachel wasn't saying? Randall didn't seem to pick up the exchanged looks between them, but when he left, Jake would be asking them about it.

"If I think of anything, I'll call you," Rachel finally

said. "Please let us know the progress on the case. Aunt Betty never had any enemies in town. She was always one of the first to help others."

Randall stood and pocketed his pad and pen. "It's most disturbing to me. She is the last person I would expect to be murdered."

"So you're ruling her death a murder for sure?" Jake rose to escort the police chief to the door.

"Yes, we are. And we're taking the investigation very seriously."

Jake opened the door for Randall. "I'd like to check the cabin site after it cools. Is that okay?"

"Sure, after the firefighters give the go-ahead." Randall tipped his head toward the ladies. "I'm glad you're both okay. Good day."

At the window Jake watched Randall climb into his car before he swung around and asked, "What are you two keeping from the police chief?"

FIVE

Rachel sat forward. "How did you know?"

"I may have been gone for a while, but I know when you're holding something back."

Rachel stared at her aunt. "We don't know who to trust. We don't believe Aunt Betty's murder was done by a person passing through town. It's not like Port Aurora is on the beaten path. If this had been summer, it might be different."

Lawrence narrowed his gaze on Aunt Linda. "You think we have something to do with Betty's murder?"

"Of course not. That's why Rachel is telling you two. We also found three photos of the fishery in Betty's special cubbyhole. That was why I was looking in the darkroom, but there was no sign of other pictures being processed or the camera. If more photos were being developed, they were either ruined when the intruders trashed the house or taken by them."

Rachel sat on the edge of her chair. "Why would she keep in her hidey-hole three pictures, one of the Tundra King and the Alaskan King next to each other, the Blue Runner and the shipping warehouse?"

"Where are they?" Jake asked in a no-nonsense tone.

"On my dresser." Rachel pushed to her feet. "I'll get them. Maybe you can explain why these were special to her that she hid them with her valuables."

"In the meantime, I'm starving. I'm going to make some sandwiches. Anyone else want one?" Aunt Linda strolled toward the kitchen.

"I do, and I'll help you." Lawrence followed her aunt while Jake accepted the offer of food.

"Me, too, Aunt Linda. Escaping a fire wore me out." Rachel retrieved the photos and returned to the living room to find Jake standing next to the decorated Christmas tree, staring out the window. She came up beside him. "It's starting to get dark. No wonder I'm hungry. I haven't eaten since seven this morning." She held out the pictures.

Jake took them and studied each one. "I'm familiar with the Tundra King. Is the Alaskan King a new boat to Port Aurora?"

"Yes, it's a new addition from Seattle. When Brad acquired a silent partner, he purchased a couple of trawlers that belonged to the fishery as well as overhauling the Tundra King. That brings his fleet up to ten boats. The rest are independently owned but sell their catches to us."

"Who captains the Blue Runner?"

"Still Tom Payne. He was sweet on Aunt Betty. She thought of him as a friend. After her abusive husband died, she didn't want to get serious with anyone else. Tom understood that. But that reminds me, I need to talk to him. Maybe Aunt Betty said something to him about what she wanted to talk to me about. His boat is due back Monday. He and his crew went out crabbing on Wednesday."

"So they were good friends?"

"Yes." Rachel took the picture of both the Tundra King and Alaskan King and the Blue Runner and studied them. "That might be when Aunt Betty took this photo. It looks like the Tundra King just arrived at the pier while the Blue Runner is getting ready to leave. That coincides with the date on the back of the pictures. It's daylight and Aunt Betty might have taken them on her lunch hour."

"If she was worried about something, why didn't she say anything to Linda? Or you at that time? You all are family."

"I don't know. Maybe it was something she didn't think Aunt Linda should know, or she was going to tell her sister and me when we finally talked. We may never know."

"Hey, you two. Are you hungry? Dinner—or whatever you want to call a meal at three in the afternoon—is ready in the kitchen."

After they were all seated and Lawrence blessed the food, silence fell over them for five minutes while they satisfied their hunger.

Eventually, Rachel broke the quiet. "Do you think I should give the police chief these photos? They really don't show anything but three boats and the shipping warehouse, and I think Tom would love to have the one of the Blue Runner."

Jake's intense regard took her in for a long moment while her aunt and Lawrence discussed what the photos meant. Finally, Jake said, "I think you should give them to Randall. I know the man, and he was a good pick to run the department. I worked under him, and I never had a reason to question his integrity."

"So you think I should tell him that Aunt Betty wanted to talk to you and me?" Rachel asked, still trapped by his penetrating gaze as though no one else was in the kitchen but them. Her heartbeat accelerated, and she wiped her sweaty palms on her pants.

"Yes. He can't do his job if he doesn't have all the pieces." Jake glanced at the photos in the center of the table, releasing her from the invisible tether connecting them.

Her stomach tightened. What was going on with her? Granted, she hadn't seen Jake in a few years, but she shouldn't be reacting to him like this. Their lives were on different paths.

"I'm not sure they have any significance to Betty's murder, but he needs to rule them out. The first one is of the Tundra King and Alaskan King unloading their catch at the loading dock. The second is Blue Runner in its slip. The third is boxes stacked in a room, which you said looked like part of the new shipping warehouse." Jake picked it up and flipped it over to show the date. "Since these may have been the last photos Betty took, maybe they will help Randall."

"Son, we haven't talked about someone slashing your tires earlier. If they hadn't, you'd have seen the fire much earlier or even come upon the persons who set it." Gramps took another bite of his turkey and Swiss sandwich.

Jake frowned. "To tell you the truth, with all that has happened, I haven't had time to think about it, but you're right. I only went to the police to find out what progress had been made on the case, then to the general store for the supplies. I came out and my tires were slashed."

"Did you say anything about what happened at Betty's cabin to anyone?" Rachel finished the last of her sandwich and relaxed back, trying to ease the tension gripping her, not just from nearly dying in the fire but from Jake, too.

"I mentioned it to Randall at the police station and told Sean that you and Linda were at the house cleaning it up. Anyone in earshot could have overheard that I was getting supplies and going to Betty's cabin to help you. When I couldn't get hold of you two at Betty's or your house, I left Max's Garage and headed that way."

Lawrence slapped his hand on the table. "That's it. Someone heard and didn't want you to go. You need to make a list of who was at the store and station besides Randall."

"Well, except for Randall, Officers Bates and Clark were at the station. It was just the people at the store and frankly, I can't remember all of them. There were some who I couldn't even tell you their names. Marge was behind the counter, and I saw Celeste and Brad."

He saw Celeste? Why didn't he say something to me? Rachel balled her hands in her lap. *How did he feel? Is he still in love with her? I hate being shut out of that part of his life.*

"Linda, I was going to stop at the church on the way back to Betty's, but forgot all about that after my tires were slashed." He looked toward her aunt. "Sorry about that. But I did talk to Sean in the store about using a larger venue at the fishery for the memorial service. He reminded me how many people Betty had known and would want to pay their respects. The church won't be able to hold all of them."

Aunt Linda began taking the empty dishes to the sink. "Thanks for letting me know about the church. I'll call our pastor this evening and get his take on where to hold the memorial service. Betty wanted to be cremated. We can sprinkle her remains in Bristol Bay. I think Tom would let us use the Blue Runner. In fact, I'm sure he would insist."

"What did Celeste have to say?" Rachel finally asked, not wanting to talk about her but wanting to know how it went with Jake. At one time she and Celeste had been friends, but after Jake, that had all changed.

"Nothing. She and Brad were eating. I'm not even sure they saw me."

Lawrence rose and headed for the sink. "I'll help you clean up, then you might offer me some of that pie left over from last night."

"Anyone else want a piece?" Aunt Linda asked as she handed Lawrence a dish to dry.

Rachel groaned. "I think I'll pass."

Her aunt gave her a puzzled look. "But it's your favorite. I was counting on your helping me finish it today."

"I need to go on a diet after today, trying to squeeze out of that window."

"I'll take an extra big piece," Jake said.

Rachel leaned closer to him and whispered, "Are you okay with seeing Celeste?"

He lifted one shoulder in a shrug. "I knew I would see her eventually. She doesn't mean anything to me."

Rachel wasn't convinced by his casual tone. He'd walked away from Port Aurora, his grandfather—her—all because of Celeste. "I'm here if you need to talk to anyone about her."

"She's my past. Let's leave her there."

But are you over your past? Rachel gritted her teeth

to keep from replying. An uncomfortable silence fell between her and Jake. She took the last sip of her cold coffee and stood. "Do you want a refill?"

"Yes, thanks."

She grabbed Jake's mug and headed for the stove when her aunt stepped back from the sink, put her hands on her hips and said to Lawrence, "Jake is going to do what?" Her voice rose.

Rachel's gaze flew to Jake.

He stood. "Gramps, what did you say to her?"

"I told her what you and I talked about. Somebody's got to protect these gals. What if the people who burned Betty's house come after them? Remember that conversation we had a couple of hours ago?"

Jake glanced between Aunt Linda and her. "I was going to bring it up and see what you thought." He swiveled his attention back to his grandfather. "Nothing was settled between Gramps and me."

Lawrence waved his hand in the air. "They are both sensible, practical women. They will see it's for their own good."

Aunt Linda's eyes flared. "Our own good?" She tossed the wet dishcloth at Lawrence's chest. "I answer to no man. I've done just fine for fifteen years since my husband died."

Rachel grabbed hold of Jake's hand and dragged him from the kitchen as her aunt became worked up. "What are you and your grandfather scheming?"

"It's possible that whoever killed Betty thinks you know something about her murder. If you're in danger, we need to protect you."

"But I don't know anything."

"You might not realize what you know. Something

is going on in Port Aurora. I don't know what, but two people went to a lot of trouble to shut up Betty. I'd feel better if you let me stay here with Mitch. He's a great watchdog on top of everything else."

"What if you're in danger? Your tires were slashed today. People know how close we once were. They might think you also know whatever it is that I'm supposed to know."

"I was trained to take care of myself. I'd like to take you to and from work. You're too important to me to have anything happen to you. And in case you haven't noticed, my grandfather is as he says *sweet on* Linda."

"But she only thinks of him as a friend."

Jake stepped into her personal space and grasped her upper arms. "Do you know what would happen if you and your aunt were hurt? Gramps and I would be devastated. Being a friend to you means a lot to me. Gramps feels the same way about Linda."

Over the loud conversation coming from the kitchen, Rachel asked what she'd wanted to for years. "Then why did you leave and not come back until now?"

"I needed to get out of the city. As soon as I was released from physical therapy, I came home, and I'm staying until the new year."

"Eight years is a long time to be apart."

"I saw you several times, and we talked on the phone."

"Not the same thing. Remember when we were teenagers and something would go wrong with one of us at school? We would talk about it all the way home that very day."

Jake released her arms and put some distance between them. "When Celeste called off our engagement,

I'd felt like I'd been abandoned. It was my mother all over again. I didn't process it well."

"That's what having a friend means. I could have helped you."

"I couldn't stick around and be constantly reminded of what she did. See her all the time. This is a small town."

"So you're still in love with her." Acid burned in her stomach, threatening to send her meal back up. She'd always felt when Jake finally made a commitment it would be forever.

"No!" His face hardened into sharp angles. "When I saw them together, I didn't care. I felt nothing."

She wanted to believe that was the case, but he'd stayed away for eight years. That didn't sound like a man who was over Celeste. She didn't want to be dragged back into his life, then have him leave in four weeks.

"Why are we wasting time talking about her? She's married. I don't love her, and she has nothing to do with someone trying to kill you."

"We don't know someone's trying to kill me. Maybe the killers came back today to burn the house because they didn't find everything they wanted, and Aunt Linda and I just happened to be inside at that time."

"Do you want to take the chance with your life and your aunt's?"

He was right. She had no problem with a man protecting her. Her aunt might, but she could talk her into it. And an added bonus would be having a watchdog. "Fine. You can stay and be my chauffeur, starting with tomorrow when I go to church."

"I'll drop you off and—"

"Jake Nichols, you always went to church when you lived here. But then maybe it's best you don't."

His forehead crunched. "Why?"

"Brad and Celeste usually attend every Sunday."

He glared at her. "I know what you're doing."

She batted her eyelashes. "What am I doing?"

"Challenging me. You know how I am. We'll both go to church tomorrow. Then you and I can go see Randall with the photos."

"He might not be working on Sunday."

"Then we'll go to his house. If someone's after those pictures, you giving them to the police ends the threat on your life. In fact, we should go right now."

"But there's nothing suspicious on those photos, and no one knows I have them. After the horrible day I've had, all I want is to go to bed early."

"Maybe there is and we can't see it, or maybe the arsonists thought there was more than what was in the darkroom. You said that Betty takes tons of pictures to get the right one she wants to use."

"I've convinced Lawrence to stay here tonight, too," her aunt announced from the entrance into the kitchen. "I don't like the idea of him being alone with all that's going on."

Lawrence snorted behind her. "I know how to take care of myself. I have for seventy-three years."

Aunt Linda shot him a glare. "I think we should stick together until the police find who murdered Betty and torched her house."

Jake came up and laid his hands on Rachel's shoulders, then he leaned close to her ear. "I think your aunt has a thing for my grandfather, too." His chuckles slid deliciously down her spine.

Rachel was beginning to wonder if she had *a thing* for Jake.

* * *

Monday morning Jake drove into town with Rachel. "You have some time to grab a cup of coffee at the general store? I could use another one before I meet Randall at Betty's house."

"That sounds good. This was one weekend I didn't rest. I'm more exhausted this morning than I was Friday when I left work."

"Nearly dying can do that to a person." He slanted a look at her. "Take it from me."

"I still wish you'd let your grandfather call me in August. Finding out after you were out of danger robbed me of praying for you when you needed it the most."

"I was in a dark place. I thought I'd lost Mitch and might not walk again. I had no words for anyone." Jake pulled into a parking spot in front of the store, remembering the last time he was here and his tires were slashed.

After they purchased their coffees at the counter, Jake found a table, one of the last in the crowded café, and sat with his back to the wall. "If I see anyone I recognize was here on Saturday morning, I'll tell you. I knew the town had grown, but there are a lot of people I don't know. I discovered that yesterday at church."

"I've been here the whole time, and I feel that way sometimes. In the summer the tourist season nearly doubles the town's population, and there are more fishing boats going out then, too."

Jake sipped his coffee. "I'm meeting Sean for lunch at the harbor restaurant. I hope to find out what Betty was like the few days before she was murdered."

"I'm going to see Tom on the Blue Runner. I know he's been told about Aunt Betty over the radio, but that's no way to learn about it. All he knows is she's dead. Since Chief Quay is letting me give him the photo she took of his boat, I thought I would also use the time to make sure he's all right and see if she said anything to him that concerned her."

"What time are you meeting him?"

"He'll unload his catch, then be in his slip around twelve."

"I can't be there, but hearing the details of what happened to Betty is better coming from you than a police officer." He covered her hand on the table. "Remember, leave the detecting to me or Randall. Tell him about Betty but no snooping."

"He's one of the people we know didn't kill Aunt Betty. He was at sea with his crew."

"True, but he could have hired someone."

"Do you always think that way?"

"I look at all the angles. I've seen a lot of stuff that people do to each other, even ones who are supposed to be in love."

Rachel shook her head. "I've seen how Tom was with Aunt Betty. He cherished her."

"I've broken up many couples who supposedly loved each other." After his own experience and some of the people he encountered as a police officer, he didn't know if love between a man and woman really existed. "Can you get me the names of the boats and crews not in harbor? That should help us eliminate them or at least move them to the bottom of the list of suspects."

"Yes. I know some because I deliver their paychecks on Fridays. I'll make a list, then you should get with Charlie, the harbormaster, to make sure I have everyone."

"So Charlie Moore is doing that job now. If anyone knows who was there or not, it would be him."

"He may have a bum leg that keeps him from working on a trawler, but he gets around and keeps an eye on all the boats. You should see him in the summer. He seems to always be around in the daylight, which means he puts in a lot of hours."

"Does he get any rest in the winter?"

"You'd think." Rachel chuckled. "I guess he does, but he still knows what's going on."

"I'll have to stop by and talk to Charlie myself." Jake caught sight of a familiar face. "The big guy coming into the store. Who is he? He was here on Saturday."

Rachel scanned the people coming inside. "That's Beau Cohen. He works on the Tundra King. They're going out in a few hours. His brother, Kirk, is the captain."

"Ah, a crewman from one of the boats in the photos. Who is he talking to?"

"Ingrid. I'm surprised she isn't at work by now. She works in the processing center. So many of the people new to Port Aurora are connected to the fishery. At least I know their names and most of their faces."

"When do you think the memorial service will be held for Betty?"

"Now that Brad has offered the large hall in the fishery, Aunt Linda told me she and the pastor were planning it for Wednesday late afternoon. Then later is the Christmas tree lighting at the harbor. Aunt Betty always loved that, and Aunt Linda thought that would be a nice way to end the service. Most of the boats will be in harbor, and many of the crew members knew Aunt Betty. She worked at the fishery for years."

"Since when does the fishery have a large hall?"

"It's temporary until the spring when the processing plant will be expanded, which means more workers. That's the last part of the expansion. It should be up and running by June." Rachel glanced at her watch. "Oh, no. I'm going to be late."

"If I don't see you, when do you want me to pick you up?"

"Five."

"I'll be at your office then."

"I can meet you outside." She rose.

"I'd like to see where you work." Jake started to get up, but Rachel waved him down.

"I only have to go a block. I think I can do that. Enjoy the warmth and the coffee. See you later."

As she left the store, stopping several times to speak to someone, Jake realized he'd missed her. It hadn't taken long for them to get back into the groove of sharing and talking. He had friends in Anchorage, but no one like Rachel. She was special. In all the years he'd known her, she'd always been there for him. What would have happened if he hadn't left Port Aurora eight years ago?

He'd thought being in Anchorage would be the change of pace he needed to get over Celeste. But now he was back because he'd needed the quiet of the town—and if he was honest with himself, Rachel. She'd always had a way of helping him to see things in a clearer light.

He sighed and headed for the counter to get a cup of coffee to go. When he pulled in to Betty's driveway later, he saw the fire captain shake hands with Randall, then walk to his vehicle. From the grim lines on both men's faces, Jake knew the verdict was arson, which didn't surprise him at all. He finished the last few sips of his coffee, then climbed from the SUV and strode toward the burned remains of the cabin, the scent of charred wood filling his nostrils.

"Captain found three places where an accelerant was used to start the fire. By the front door and window, on one side by the kitchen window and by the back door. It's obvious they didn't want anyone getting out." Randall pointed toward the first area.

"Yeah, I agree. The bedroom windows would have been impossible, and the bathroom one was iffy. I think when they searched the place the day before they either found some of what they wanted or nothing and decided to come back the next morning and burn it to destroy whatever was inside. Did the captain okay the site to be examined?"

"Yes. In this weather, it doesn't take long for the ashes to cool. I've walked the perimeter and seen little evidence that anything survived. I especially looked at the place where Betty's cubbyhole would have been."

Jake walked toward the crime scene. "I agree, but I still would like to see if anything that looked like a camera was in the darkroom area. It might not have been in its usual place on the hook."

"Or the killers took it the day before. I have to meet with the mayor. If you find anything, let me know. So you really think Betty stumbled across something and took pictures of it? I don't see anything on the photos I looked at yesterday."

"Honestly, I don't know what to think, but if it had been a robbery gone bad, why would they come back the next day to burn the cabin? They knew someone was inside because Rachel's Jeep was out front."

"I agree." Randall started for his cruiser. "I appreciate any help you can give me. As I mentioned, we're an officer short and will be through Christmas."

As the police chief drove away, Jake carefully picked his way through the burned rubble to the place where he estimated the darkroom had been. After sifting through the remains in a ten-foot radius, he straightened and stretched to work the kinks out of his muscles from bending and squatting. He found nothing but the overpowering scent of charred wood.

The hairs on the nape of his neck tingled. He rotated in a full circle, searching the woods that edged Betty's property. A movement in the midst of the spruce trees riveted his attention. He started for the woods, glad he had brought his Glock. Suddenly, the sound of an ATV filled the quiet. Knowing he couldn't outrun a vehicle, he stopped and studied the trees. Nothing. Had someone been watching him?

SIX

"I'll see you at the memorial service on Wednesday."
Rachel waved goodbye to Charlie at the harbormaster's office and stepped outside into the bright sunlight.

Although a chilly wind blew off the water, the rays warmed her. She paused at the railing and scanned the various sizes of boats in port. Spying the Blue Runner tying up to its slip, she strolled toward the trawler. She was not looking forward to talking to Tom Payne. She'd gone over what she was going to say, only to discard it. Tom had made no bones that he loved Aunt Betty, whereas she wasn't eager to marry again. Rachel certainly understood not wanting to marry after having an abusive husband. She didn't want to marry after seeing her mother go from one husband to the next, as though she were sampling an array. She'd seen few examples of a loving marriage.

As she neared the Blue Runner slip, she felt eyes boring into her. She looked around, her gaze skipping from one boat to the next. Finally, it lit upon the Tundra King maneuvering out of the harbor. On the deck she caught sight of Beau dressed in the common yellow outerwear that protected fishermen from the bitter cold wind and water. He brought the binoculars he'd been using down to his side, but she still felt the singe of his perusal. She shuddered.

Rachel shook off her apprehension about Beau. He'd once asked her out on a date, and she had turned him down. Ever since then, he'd been standoffish and almost hostile, which only confirmed he wasn't the type of man she wanted to go out with. She rarely dated, even though there were over twice as many men in Port Aurora as women, but if she did, it wouldn't be someone like Beau.

She stepped down onto the Blue Runner and called out, "Captain Payne?"

A tall man with bright red hair poked his head out the back door into the cabin. "Good to see you, Rachel. If you hadn't been here, I was going to find you at your office. Come in. While the men are finishing up, let's talk in the wheelhouse. It'll be quiet there."

When she entered, Tom's stoic expression evolved into a look of sorrow. "I almost came in early, but that wouldn't be right for the crew. They count on the money they get, and that depends on the catch." He indicated the captain's chair. "Take a seat. I'm too agitated to stay still. What happened to Betty? She was fine on Wednesday when I left."

As Tom paced the length of the wheelhouse and back, Rachel told him about Friday and finding Aunt Betty's body in the woods. "The police are investigating it as a murder. What you might not know is that the next day someone set fire to her cabin. Aunt Linda and I were over at her place trying to straighten it."

"Yeah, Betty…" His voice faded, and he swallowed hard several times. "She would have hated the mess." He stopped at the front window and stared outside. "What I don't understand is why anyone would kill one of the sweetest women in Port Aurora."

"I agree. We don't understand why, either. Earlier that day she'd told me she needed to talk to me. She looked afraid. She'd wanted to talk to Jake, too. I tried to get her to tell me what was wrong when I saw her at the processing center after she left me a message on my phone, but she just said 'later.' I figured she didn't want to talk until we were alone, so that was why I stopped by on the way home from work. Do you have an idea why she would put this photo—" she passed him the one of the Blue Runner "—along with photos of the Tundra King and Alaskan King and a storage area in the shipping warehouse in her hiding place, or why she would be afraid?"

He shook his head, tears welling into his eyes. "I didn't know she had a hiding place. At the house?"

"Yes, in the kitchen, but the cabin was nearly burned to the ground."

"Then how did you get this?"

"The police chief wanted to know what, if anything, was stolen. The TV and other items a robber might steal were still there. But we never found her camera. We checked the cubbyhole for the few pieces of jewelry that are worth something. They were there, along with these photos. We were in the process of examining the darkroom when I smelled smoke and discovered the fire in the living room and kitchen."

"When I left last Wednesday, she was excited. She was starting to work on her photos of the harbor, the boats and the fishery. She'd had pictures of the fishery before the expansion, and she wanted some after."

"So she wasn't upset?"

He plowed his fingers through his red hair, then massaged his nape. "No, the opposite. She said she would have some to show me when I returned." He blinked, and a tear rolled down his tan cheek.

Rachel gestured toward the photo he still held. "Chief Quay said you could keep that. He made a copy of it, but he didn't see how it was tied to her murder."

"I remember when she took it. She'd been on the boat and had left to go back to work. She shared her lunch with me on…" He closed his eyes. "I'm sorry. I need time alone."

Rachel stood and gave Tom a hug. "I understand. If you remember anything that might have upset her on Friday, please let me know."

"I will," he said in a thick voice.

"I can find my own way out."

"Thanks for giving me this photo." His chest rose and fell as he expelled a long breath.

Rachel climbed onto the dock and started back toward the fishery headquarters. She still had a lot of work to do this afternoon before Jake picked her up. She needed to catch up on the paperwork that was put on hold because of last Friday's payroll, especially since she would be taking off half a day on Wednesday to help set up Aunt Betty's memorial service.

When she entered the building, Brad walked into the lobby with his wife, Celeste. Rachel greeted them. She received a cool reception from Celeste, but Brad was always polite and gentlemanly. She wondered if Celeste ever felt bad about how she'd treated Jake. Calling off an engagement in front of half the town wasn't the best way to do it.

"Rachel, wait a sec," Brad said as he opened the front door for Celeste and gave her a quick kiss on the cheek. When his wife left, he turned toward Rachel. "What can I do for the memorial service?"

"You've already done it by letting us use the hall. It will hold twice what the church will."

"Did you talk with Tom yet?"

"Yes, and he didn't take it well."

"I'm not surprised. He proposed to Betty the weekend before last." Only five feet eight inches, Brad always seemed taller by the way he carried himself, but at the moment his shoulders were hunched. "I didn't think Tom would ever marry."

"The same with Aunt Betty. She never said anything about the proposal."

"She told Tom she had to think about it. She was going to give him her answer when he returned from this last fishing trip." Brad began strolling down the main hall toward his office.

"Oh," was all Rachel could think to say. Why didn't Aunt Betty say anything to her and Aunt Linda? Most unusual. Was that what Aunt Betty wanted to talk to her about on Friday? Then why did she want to talk to Jake, too?

"Tell Linda I can contribute money for the food, whatever she needs."

"I will. Thanks." Rachel rounded the corner and hurried toward her office at the back of the building.

Once there, she started working her way through the pile of papers on her desk while she ate her sandwich. The hours flew by and before she knew it, Jake stood in her doorway, watching her, with Mitch on a leash next to him.

"It's five already?" She glanced behind her at the dark landscape out the window.

"Afraid so. I can wait a while in the lobby if you want." Jake moved to her desk. "I brought Mitch. He wanted to get out of the house."

"Oh, he told you that?"

"Yes, he did. He brought me his leash."

Rachel laughed. "I like a dog that knows his own mind." She reached toward the German shepherd and began to rub his head.

Mitch stepped back and sniffed her hand, then sat and barked twice.

Not sure what just happened, Rachel glanced toward Jake. His frown unnerved her. "What's wrong with him?"

"That's his signal when he smells illegal drugs."

"On me?" Rachel stared at the hand Mitch smelled. "I haven't been handling any drugs. Just papers all afternoon."

"What kind of papers?"

"Lists from each boat of the crewmen and hours they worked. Also shipping notices and orders. The typical paperwork that needs to be put in the books."

"Where are they?"

Rachel waved to a foot-tall stack on the table behind her.

"Step out in the hall and let me see what has triggered his response."

Rachel moved to the corridor and leaned against the wall while Jake released Mitch by the entrance and commanded him to find the drugs. Starting on his right, the German shepherd sniffed around the room until he came to the pile of paper she'd been recording. He sat and barked again.

When Rachel came back into her office, she asked, "Could this be what Aunt Betty found out?"

"Possibly. Can you take this stack home with you without being detected? Then I can spread them out and see which sheets have the strongest scent on them."

"Yes, but I shuffled them into different piles before putting them in that stack. If it could transfer to my hands, then why not to other pieces of paper?"

"It could. But maybe I can narrow it down some. If I take Mitch through all the boats and the fishery, we could scare off whoever is handling drugs. It could be something as simple as a worker dealing or taking drugs or a bigger problem than that."

Rachel grabbed a canvas bag and stuffed the papers into it. "Bigger problem?"

"That the fishery is being used by someone to smuggle drugs."

"I've worked with most of these people for years. Your grandfather worked for the company up until five years ago. I…" What happened to Aunt Betty made more sense if large amounts of money were involved.

"As a police officer I've seen a lot of illegal drugs on the streets. It's a big business."

Rachel stared down at her hands. "I hope I can get this smell off me." She wondered how many times in the past she'd handled something that had the same scent. She grabbed her coat and purse. "Let's go."

"We can't tell anyone about this except Linda and Gramps."

"Not the police?"

A hard edge entered his blue eyes, darkened to a

stormy sea color. "No, not even the chief, at least for the time being. If I could keep this from Linda and Gramps, I would, but I don't see how we can since they are already involved with Betty's murder. Not much gets past my grandfather."

"Nor my aunt. She'll probably be wondering why I'm scrubbing my hands over and over."

"Not much gets past a dog. One trained to smell blood can find where a drop of blood has been cleaned up."

"That's amazing."

"K-9s are being used more and more for various jobs. Their sense of smell is much keener than ours." Jake held the door open for Rachel.

When she stepped outside into the dark of night, the lights from the harbor and the fishery taunted her. How pervasive was this problem in Port Aurora? Now murder and drugs? What was happening in her small, peaceful hometown?

That night Jake stood outside while Mitch sniffed around. The air was crisp and cold, but clear, too. The silence surrounding Jake helped him to relax after a day spent running down leads that hadn't gone anywhere. He'd searched the woods by Betty's cabin and sure enough there were ATV tracks coming from the main road and going back that way. Someone had been in the trees watching. A curious person or one involved with what happened to Betty?

He heard the door open and glanced back. Rachel came outside, carrying two mugs. The colored lights from the Christmas tree and on the house reflected on the snow and bathed her in their glow.

She gave him a cup. "Hot chocolate with one big marshmallow."

"You remembered?"

"Of course. In the cold months that was our drink." They used to do almost everything together—until Celeste came along and he thought he could have it all. The woman. Marriage. The career he wanted. Why hadn't he seen through Celeste's charade? Now he didn't know what he wanted.

Rachel took a sip of her drink, ending up with marshmallow on her upper lip. "Do I have a mustache?"

"Yes, and that hasn't changed, either."

"It's because I like three marshmallows in my hot chocolate." She licked her tongue over the area. "Did I get it all?"

"Yes, but you might as well wait until you're finished with your drink."

"Good advice as always." She released a long sigh and stared up at the sky. "It's gorgeous. Not a cloud around and a million stars."

"I forget how clear the view is away from the city."

"I should have turned off the Christmas lights. It would have been perfect."

"Nah. I like them. They're welcoming."

She angled toward him. "I thought you were going to tell Aunt Linda and Lawrence about the drugs."

"Since they both were exhausted with planning the memorial service and went to bed, I think we can get away with them not knowing anything until we know more."

"That sounds fine. How long is Mitch going to take?"

"He finished five minutes ago. I just like the quiet."

"And I came out and ruined it."

"No, you came out and joined me. We're sharing the stars." That thought eased the tension thinking about Celeste had caused. In the years he'd been gone, he'd been sure he had dealt with the betrayal and the bitterness his relationship with Celeste had produced. Was Rachel right? Was he not over her? No, when he saw Celeste, he'd felt nothing.

He slung his arm over Rachel's shoulder and looked again at the black sky overhead. Their closeness brought back fond memories, something he'd needed after the past months. Peace wove its way through him, and he didn't want this moment to end. Rachel snuggled closer, sending his pulse zipping through him.

"I've missed this," he murmured, not realizing how much until he said it out loud. Rachel had always been the bright spot in his life. Every birthday and Christmas when he wouldn't receive a call or present from his mother, Rachel had cheered him up and given him her gift.

Suddenly, Mitch became alert, emitting a low growl.

Jake dropped his arm from around Rachel and straightened, handing her his mug. "Stay here." All his police training coming to the foreground, he moved toward Mitch, twenty feet away.

He approached Mitch. "Stay."

His dog did, but he pointed at attention at an area on the west side of the house. Jake wished he had his weapon, but it was in the house.

Then he noticed the huge moose in the moonlight, and relief replaced the stress. Although he had a healthy respect for the damage a moose could cause, he wasn't worried about this one. He was sure the animal knew they were there, and yet he ignored them.

He started back toward Rachel. "Come, Mitch. Time to go in."

"What was it?" she asked in a shaky voice.

"A moose."

"Oh, that's Fred. He comes around once or twice a week. Sometimes during the day. Sometimes at night."

"How do you know it was Fred?"

"Was he missing part of his antler?"

"Yes."

"Then it's him. He's been around for years. He started coming not long after you left Port Aurora."

"Good to know." Jake held the door open and let Rachel and Mitch go inside, then he gave one last look across the snow-covered ground to the line of evergreens about thirty yards away. Darkness loomed in the depth of the forest.

"I'll get the canvas bag. Let's get this over with." Rachel headed for her bedroom and returned in half a minute. "I think I should handle the papers. You don't need to get the smell on you."

"Fine." Jake sat on the couch where he slept at night while Gramps took the third bedroom. He called Mitch to his side, and they watched while Rachel laid the papers in a row across a blanket on the floor. He'd suggested that way earlier, so if the drug scent got on anything, it would only be the blanket.

She went through that same routine three times with a different set of papers before Mitch indicated the scent of drugs and barked. Rachel glanced in the direction of the bedrooms. "I'm not sure we won't wake them up if there's more than this one."

By the time Mitch had checked all the papers in the bag, Rachel had collected ten different sheets. "They're all different. A couple of time sheets for the boat crews. Some are shipping notices and a few are orders."

"The paper most likely was touched by someone who had been handling drugs, and some of those sheets were contaminated by the original one or two."

"Which doesn't narrow it down a lot. I'll write these down, and then we can look at the boats in the harbor for the past week since all these papers are from that time frame." Rachel jotted down the information and then collected everything and stuck it in the canvas bag. "I feel like a criminal having to sneak these in and out of the fishery."

"If something fishy is going on, we need to find out and let Randall know. I don't want to accuse anyone without evidence, but the police chief did say he needed my help. They're shorthanded."

Rachel chuckled. "Definitely something fishy is going on. That's the nature of the business." She sat next to Jake on the couch. "Here is the list of boats in the harbor the past week with when they came and when they left, if they're gone."

Jake lounged back and read the forty names. "Is anyone who works for the fishery not on this list because they've been out over a week?"

Rachel leaned toward him and reread the list. "There are three due back soon. There are some boats in the harbor that have nothing to do with the fishery."

The apple scent from her shampoo teased his nostrils. He'd come to associate that smell with warmth and caring. She'd always had a calming effect on him. "We'll concentrate on the boats that work for the company. Let me see the list of contaminated sheets."

She handed it to him. "They are all from people on

the list of boats in the harbor, but I would expect that. So how does this help us?"

"Not sure yet. I'm going to start taking Mitch for walks on the pier and see if anything catches his attention. I'll concentrate on the four boats on this second list. Who handles the crew time sheets?"

"Everyone writes down their own hours, then the captain verifies it and turns it in. I can't see the Blue Runner having anything to do with Aunt Betty's death. They were out of the harbor on Friday and Saturday. The other three were tied up in their slips."

"I can't rule them out concerning the drugs, but you're right about Aunt Betty's death. So tell me about Tundra King, Alaskan King and Sundance." The brush of her arm against his threatened to steal his concentration on the task at hand.

"Tundra King and Alaskan King are owned by the company. As I told you before, the Alaskan King is a new trawler. Captain Martin of the Sundance sells his catches to the fishery."

While he looked over the lists, Jake asked, "Who is in port right now?"

"Alaskan King and the Blue Runner. Tundra King left today and Sundance is due back tomorrow. We're closed for two weeks during the holidays, then we start back up with crabbing. What do you want me to do to help?"

He dipped his head and turned toward her, her glance trapping him in a snare. For a moment he didn't say anything until she dropped her gaze to the papers. "You've done it. Leave the rest to me. This is my job."

"But you don't have access to the fishery like I do."

After nearly losing her in the fire, he didn't want

to take the risk. "I'll find a way. Remember Sean and I were good friends in high school, and I was over in the processing center with him today before we went to lunch. Gramps and I know many of the men who work there."

"I thought we were in this together. I want to find who did this to Aunt Betty. She was family. She doesn't deserve this."

And I want to keep you safe. If anything happened to her…he shuddered at the thought. "We're a team. We've always been one."

"But that wasn't enough to keep you here or let me know about the injury you suffered in August until much later." Rachel pushed to her feet and walked to the Christmas tree. After turning off the lights, she shut the drapes. "I have to be at work by seven thirty. Good night." She started for the hallway.

"Rachel," Jake called out and rose. When she stopped, he bridged the distance between them. "I'm sorry. I promise I'll be around so much in the future you're going to get tired of me, but my job is in Anchorage. I make a difference. I'm good at working with a K-9."

She spun around, her teeth digging into her lower lip. She did that when she wanted to remain quiet and was fighting the urge to talk.

"I've seen Celeste on a number of occasions, and my life hasn't fallen apart. She doesn't have any power over me anymore."

She inched closer and lifted her hands to cup his jaw. "Good. I hated seeing what she did to you. I wish you'd come to that decision years ago."

"What can I say, I'm stubborn."

She leaned toward him and kissed his mouth lightly, then dropped her arms to her sides and rushed from the living room.

His lips tingled from the contact with hers. Suddenly, he wanted more than just a brief kiss. He watched her disappear into her bedroom and wondered why in the world it had taken him so long to see her as more than a friend. He shook his head and pivoted. But that was crazy. Neither of them wanted a long-term commitment.

On Wednesday Rachel stood next to Jake. Halfway through the memorial service for Betty, she grasped his hand, needing that connection, or she might break down. Then her aunt would start crying, and she was to speak at the end.

When Aunt Linda finished paying tribute to Aunt Betty, the church choir sang "Amazing Grace" and then her aunt announced that after the Christmas tree lighting everyone was invited to come back to the hall for refreshments provided by the Port Aurora Community Church's women.

Jake bent to her ear and whispered, "Are you ready? Do you need to stay?"

His breath on her neck tickled, making her think about the kiss she'd given him the other day. She'd wanted more, but she was afraid of these feelings his presence was generating in her. She'd always thought they had been best friends, but now she wondered if she hadn't taken it further and felt rejected when he fell in love with Celeste instead of her.

"Rachel, are you okay?"

She closed her eyes for a few seconds. "I'm all right. Aunt Betty used to come with us to the ceremony at the harbor when all the lights were turned on officially. The part I love is the lights in the harbor are turned off for a few minutes while the mayor gives a little speech then flips the switch. Then for a while the only lights are on the Christmas tree. It's like a ray of hope at the end of the pier, that Port Aurora is welcoming any lost soul." And now someone had tainted their small town.

"I never thought of it like that. I see Gramps is with your aunt. If we're going to get a good place, we better leave."

"The best places are reserved for the children at the front. Remember when we would push our way through the crowd so we were in the first row?"

"Yes, but they always tolerated us doing that. Does the mayor still toss out candy to the kids?"

"Yes, and I wouldn't mind something chocolate right about now." When Rachel stepped outside, she lifted her hood since the wind off the water could be freezing cold.

"Remember that year the harbor iced over? Thankfully, that doesn't happen every year."

"But the water feels like it could turn to ice at any moment. I've never been into the polar bear plunge some people do."

Jake laughed. "Neither have I, but I have navigated some cold rivers and streams before that almost felt like that's what I was doing."

Again she felt like years of separation had slipped away, and their relationship had returned to what it was before Celeste. But he would be leaving again in a few weeks. Would he stay away as long as he had before? She had to remind herself even though he might come home two or three times a year, their friendship wouldn't be the same. She wished he would work for the Port Aurora Police Department like he had before going to Anchorage. What was the lure of a big city? A place with too many people and not enough open space wasn't for her.

Jake maneuvered them to where they could see the tree well but at the back of the crowd and off to the side on one of the docks. "So much for hurrying. We're going to be at the back, anyway. Want me to put you on my shoulders? Maybe the mayor will take pity on you and toss you a piece of chocolate."

"I know where there is some chocolate at Aunt Betty's reception afterward."

Jake saw Lawrence and Aunt Linda and waved to them. They headed in their direction.

"Being back here is probably the best since we have to get to the hall to serve the food and refreshments." Aunt Linda took the place next to Rachel while Lawrence and Jake began talking.

Then the lights in the harbor and surrounding area went out. With a cloudy night Rachel couldn't see anything around her. She touched her aunt beside her. "Now for the mayor's long-winded speech. It gets longer every year."

"That's because he's always running for mayor at any ceremony he officiates."

Someone moved into Rachel's faint line of sight, so she sidestepped a couple of feet away from her aunt and snuggled in her heavy parka. "When we get home a roaring fire in the fireplace would be great."

"I know what you mean," her aunt's voice came from the dark nearby.

Rachel opened her mouth to say something to Aunt Linda when a large body rammed into her and she went flying backward...into the freezing water.

SEVEN

When Rachel hit the frigid water, she gasped as if she'd been submerged in a bucket of ice. She plunged totally under, taking in a mouth full of salty water. Instinct kicked in, and she fought to the surface, her heavy parka like a boulder dragging her down.

Have to scream. Only minutes before I begin shutting down. The thought sent panic surging through her, and she thrashed, barely keeping her head above water.

Calm down.

In her mind she could hear Jake talking to her in a soothing voice. *Stay still. I'm coming.*

No, don't. I can't lose you, too. She tried to say those words aloud, but her heartbeat raced at a dizzying speed, and her body started shivering from head to toe.

Behind Jake, a woman screamed, the blood-curdling sound vying with a loud splash as if someone hit the water. He swung around, so dark he could only see about a foot in front of him.

He headed toward where Rachel was a few feet away. "Rachel, what's wrong?"

Linda used her cell phone like a flashlight and gasped. "Someone pushed her into the water!"

His heartbeat galloping, Jake quickened his step, removing his cell and using it to illuminate his path. "Gramps, we need light."

People around them began doing the same with their phones while he glimpsed his grandfather shoving his way through the crowd. The fear on Linda's face scared Jake. As he reached her, she grabbed his arm and pointed toward the water.

The faint light from their cells barely showed a head bobbing in the water, arms thrashing. Rachel looked so far away when in reality she wasn't.

"Stay calm. I'm coming." Struggling could make the situation a lot worse. The movement would lower her body temperature faster.

Jake searched the pier and saw a lifebuoy against a piling. He rushed to it, grabbed it and hurried back. "Rachel, I'm going to toss this life buoy to you. Hold on and get as much of yourself above water as possible."

Coughing followed a weak, quavering voice saying, "I will."

Suddenly, the harbor lights flooded the area, and Jake could make out Rachel better as he threw the life buoy to her. She grasped it and hung on.

Now he had to get her out of the water—over four yards below the pier. Too bad it was low tide.

Tom appeared behind him. "My boat isn't far. I have a skiff on it. It would be easier to haul her out of the water from it."

He and Tom raced to the Blue Runner with a skiff attached. Tom lowered it to the water. Each minute they took, Rachel's body temperature was dropping. In less than fifteen minutes, hypothermia could set in. That didn't leave much time to get to her.

Bright light illuminated the harbor and hurt her eyes. Rachel closed them and tried to latch on to a single thought, but her mind raced with nonsense.

She couldn't feel her arms and legs. Were they moving? Shivers consumed her body.

The sound of concerned voices reached her. Jake? Aunt Linda?

Help, Lord.

A loud noise penetrated the haze that gripped her. She eased her eyes open, comforted to see she was still holding the life buoy. If she let go, she was sure she would sink to the bottom of the harbor. Then she saw a skiff coming toward her with Jake in the front of it.

"Hang on, Rachel. Almost there," he shouted over the racket of the motor.

She tried tightening her hold on the life preserver but couldn't feel if she had or not. It seemed like ice had replaced the marrow in her bones.

Stay calm and still. She repeated those words she remembered Lawrence telling her and Jake once about falling through the ice. Her eyelids slid closed again.

The sound of the motor stopped—nearby. But she couldn't find the strength to open her eyes.

"Rachel! Rachel!"

She turned her head slightly and looked at Jake leaning over the side of the boat. "You're here," she said while her teeth chattered so much she wasn't sure he heard her.

He scooped down and hooked his arms under hers,

then lifted her from the water. The second she was in the skiff, it started moving toward a larger boat.

"You'll feel much better once you get out of your wet clothes." Jake used his body to block the wind that knifed through her while he stripped off her gloves and heavy parka and then wrapped her in a blanket. "This is only until Tom gets you back to the Blue Runner. I see your aunt. She'll help you then."

Rachel caught the gist of what he said, but pain took hold of her from her feet to her head. And cold still had its icy talon around her.

When they reached the Blue Runner, hands grabbed at her. She pushed them away and pressed herself closer to Jake. The memory slammed her. Someone had pushed her into the water. *Who?*

"I've got her." Jake swung her up into his embrace and leaped to the trawler.

The motion made her sick to her stomach. She buried her face against him. As he walked then descended some stairs, she knew she would be safe with him.

When he set her feet on the floor of the boat, she began to sink down, but Jake's arm clamped around her and steadied her.

"Have her sit, then leave. I'll get her clothes off. I need a warm blanket. Some warm sweet tea," a familiar female voice said.

Rachel met her aunt's worried expression. "I'll be okay."

Aunt Linda helped her undress, then wrapped blankets around her. She towel-dried Rachel's wet hair and pulled a wool beanie down over her head, followed by a scarf around her neck. "Doc is on his way."

* * *

Even though her feet and hands tingled as though tiny needles were being stuck in her, Rachel hated Aunt Linda missing the rest of the evening's events held in Aunt Betty's honor. "I want you to go to the memorial service reception. I'm going to be fine. Doc said so. Tom, you loved Aunt Betty. You need to go and take my aunt and Lawrence." Rachel lay on a bunk bundled up like a baby with everyone standing around waiting for something to happen.

"I agree Linda and Tom need to attend, but I'm staying with Jake and Rachel. I'll keep watch. No one is gonna hurt Rachel." The fierce expression on Lawrence's face matched Jake's earlier one when he had been determined to haul her out of the frigid water.

Her aunt and Tom looked at each other, then Tom replied, "I'm only going to be there an hour. Is that okay with you, Linda?" When her aunt nodded, Tom grabbed his heavy coat and shrugged into it. "Rachel, you need to stay on my boat and rest for the time being. When you think you are capable, you should get up and walk some. Get your blood pumping. I'm just thankful you were only in the water fifteen minutes. I've pulled a few guys from the Bering Sea and believe me it isn't fun. Ready, Linda?"

Her aunt leaned down and kissed Rachel's cheek. "Are you sure you're okay?"

"Believe me. The feeling is definitely returning to my limbs. I'm not shivering as much. Go."

Jake moved to Lawrence and murmured something to him. The older man frowned but gave a nod.

"I'm coming with you." Lawrence slipped into his parka.

After the trio left, Rachel peered at Jake, standing at the back door they'd left through, staring at the harbor through the window. She glimpsed the bright lights of the Christmas tree. They blended with the other illuminations on the pier. "The man who pushed me in was waiting for the right time. It would have been hard to get away unseen if the lights had been on at the harbor."

Jake turned, his forehead creased, the look in his eyes thoughtful. But she could see the worry in them.

"I'm fine now, Jake." She wasn't so sure an hour ago she could have said that.

He closed the space between them and sat in the chair next to the bunk. "You came close to dying for the second time in less than a week. I don't..." He cleared his throat. "I don't know what I would do if anything happened to you."

She brought her hand out from under the blankets and laid it over his, drawn to the warmth radiating from him. "Obviously, someone thinks I know what's going on, so we'll take precautions. They may be sending a message not to dig any deeper, which means we're on the right track. My aunt was murdered. Something bad is going down in the town I love. I can't ignore that."

"That's what I'm supposed to say. I'm a police officer. You aren't."

"But I'm in the middle of this, and that's not going to change. We need to be sneakier. Don't give them anything to worry about."

One corner of his mouth quirked. "I think we're beyond that. You have to promise me you'll be careful wherever you go and to assess each situation as though someone was out to kill you."

"What did Chief Quay say about the incident?"

"One lady late to the lighting of the tree saw a tall man running away. Another felt a jostle as someone went through the crowd. Nothing clear-cut."

"What did you say to Lawrence?" Rachel finally realized that he had captured her free hand and had it cupped between his. She savored the warmth of his skin against hers.

"I want him to go Betty's reception because they were friends, and I also want him to listen to what people were talking about. Sometimes a person will witness a crime but not step forward because they're afraid. If there is a witness that saw something who isn't coming forward, maybe I can at least talk to him in private."

"Are you always thinking like a cop?"

He grinned. "Pretty much. Except if I get my hands on the guy who did this, I might forget I'm a police officer and take matters into my own hands."

"In situations like this one and what happened with Betty, I find it difficult to forgive the person who caused them."

"I've continued to wrestle with that since I became a police officer. I haven't forgiven the bomber, and I don't know if I can. He hurt a lot of people and changed many lives—not for the better."

"How about your mother?"

His smile faded, and he released her hand, pulling back. "I didn't think much about her in Anchorage. I can't change the fact that she didn't want to be a mother. At least in your case it was your mom's new husband who didn't want children, and later she asked you if you wanted to come live with her."

"Only after she divorced and married husband number four. I think my mom leaving me with Aunt Linda was the best thing she could do for me. In her own way she loved me, but my aunt has really been my mother."

"So you've forgiven her?"

Rachel thought a moment, searching her heart to make sure of her answer. "Yes. I like the stability I've had here. This is home." *I wish you saw it that way.* The words were there in her mind, but she couldn't say them to him. Although both of their mothers left them in Port Aurora, his situation was much different, and he still hadn't dealt with it.

Jake rose. "Tom said to get you up and walking around. I don't want him to come back and have to tell him I didn't." He offered her his hand.

Again she put hers in his, and he helped her to stand. Her body ached, and her muscles were stiff, but she shed her blankets, wearing clothes borrowed from the general store. A chill hung in the cabin, even though the heater was on, but it was much warmer than outside in the cold and wind.

Jake retrieved his coat and slung it over her shoulders, then he held her arm and took a step. Once she began walking, she loosened up. She felt safe next to him. In less than a week she'd come to depend on him being in Port Aurora. She had to work on that because he was leaving at the end of the month, and she didn't want to go through the hurt she had when he left eight years ago.

"When they return, I want to go home. I can walk to the car now."

"But your shoes are still wet and all you have are the socks from the general store. You can't walk. I'll carry you."

She started to protest, but he was right. And she

knew she'd enjoy being in his arms. That thought surprised her, but her feelings for Jake had always been deep, so she shouldn't be. She cared about him beyond friendship, feelings that were doomed to cause nothing but heartache.

Rachel and Linda's house was quiet—too quiet for Jake. He sat up on the couch and swung his legs to the floor. He probably slept no more than three or four hours. He couldn't shake the image of Rachel bobbing in the harbor's ice-cold water. When he'd stuck his hand in the water to hoist her up into the skiff, he'd gotten enough of a feel of what she'd been in. Hypothermia could strike quick in Alaska.

He switched on a lamp and checked his watch. Five in the morning. He might as well get up and make the coffee and then use the time to go over what they knew so far about Betty's murder. What if he couldn't find the killer? How could he leave knowing Rachel was in danger? For that matter, Gramps and Linda? Worse, if a drug-smuggling ring was working out of Port Aurora, it would be a big blow to the town. If drugs were tied up in Betty's case, that heightened the danger even more. He would call a buddy he knew who was a state trooper and specialized in apprehending illegal drugs. Maybe he'd heard something.

Jake headed into the kitchen and put on a pot of coffee to brew. Then he began to pace while he waited for it to perk. An unsettling restlessness dominated him, and he didn't know if he would get a good night's sleep until the case was solved.

But he wasn't sure the feeling was totally caused by the murder. Ever since he'd returned to Port Aurora, he had been fighting mixed emotions. Being home was what he needed, and yet Celeste's appearance had churned up all he'd gone through years ago. He'd honestly thought he'd gotten over her, but maybe it was because he'd never really resolved things with her.

Last night Rachel had asked him about forgiving his mother. But it wasn't only her he needed to deal with, but Celeste, too. When he'd started dating her, he'd had such hopes that Celeste could banish the feelings of abandonment his mother had caused. Instead, she'd added to them. That was why he wouldn't commit to another.

"That coffee smells great."

Jake spun around and faced Rachel dressed in the same sweats from the night before. The color had returned to her cheeks, and as she walked into the kitchen, she wasn't stiff. Seeing her alive and all right was the most beautiful sight. "You should be sleeping."

"Then you shouldn't have made coffee. That's all that keeps me going some days."

"Me, too. Do you think it will wake up your aunt? I know she was really tired when she went to bed."

"She usually drinks tea, so it shouldn't. How about Lawrence?"

"Probably not, but if we fried bacon he would be in here instantly."

Rachel went to the cabinet and took two mugs from it. "That would draw me, too. That and baking bread. Maybe later I'll make some biscuits, bacon and gravy. I feel bad about staying home today."

"But according to your aunt, Brad was adamant you not come into work. I think he's right. You might be okay now, but your body went through an ordeal. I have a feeling you'll be taking a long nap by midmorning."

Rachel sat at the table. "Oh, you think so."

"Take it from me, I know a little about traumas." Jake filled the mugs, then put her coffee in front of her and took the chair next to her.

"How long were you trapped in the debris?"

"They told me three hours before they dug me out. Part of that time I was unconscious. The worst thing was I couldn't get to Mitch, but I heard him whining. It broke my heart to listen. Maybe it was good I passed out. We both broke a leg. They could fix mine but not his."

Rachel looked around. "Where is Mitch?"

"Sleeping on the bed next to Gramps. He knows I won't let him, but Gramps did."

Rachel laughed. "I don't blame Mitch. I'd rather sleep there than on the floor."

"I brought his bedding."

"Not the same thing. I hope the couch isn't the reason you aren't sleeping."

The picture of Rachel trying to escape the fire followed by being in the water invaded his mind again. He couldn't lose her. "No, you're the reason."

"Me?" She pointed to herself. "I'm all right."

"Just to make sure, Doc is coming back today to check on you. Also, Randall will be coming."

Rachel took a sip of her drink. "How am I supposed to rest with everyone parading through here?"

"Oh, I don't think that will be a problem. Your body will tell you. Take it from me. I had visions when I was in the hospital of being up and around, even going to work, within a month. As you see, that didn't happen. I still have a slight limp when I'm tired, and the weather can make my leg ache."

"I don't understand why you didn't want me to come to visit you then."

He thought back to those first few weeks and shook that image from his mind. "I didn't want you to see me bitter and angry. Especially at God. There were people still missing. I was trying to save others. Instead, I ended up hurt. Mitch did, too."

"It's hard not to feel that way, but everything happens for a reason. We don't always know what it is. Faith is what gets us through it."

"You sound like Gramps. He wouldn't let me wallow for long."

"Did they find the missing people?"

"One was found alive, but the other was dead." Jake finished off his last few sips of the lukewarm coffee. "So what are you going to do on your day off?"

One of her eyebrows hiked up. "Day off? Didn't you remind me that I needed to rest?"

"Good. Just checking to make sure you know what you should do. I thought I might return to find you gone and taking your car to work. More than ever I need to be with you. I don't want to go through a third attempt on your life."

"And neither do I." She rose. "Do you want some more coffee?"

He came to his feet and put his hands on her shoulders. "What part of resting did you not get? I can refill our cups."

"I hope Lawrence was as relentless with you as you are with me."

The laughter in her gaze twisted the knot in his gut

that had yet to unravel from the events of the evening before. It transformed her pretty face into a beautiful one and made her brown eyes come to life. He sometimes felt trapped by them, as he was now.

He almost lost her last night. For a moment a bone-cold chill encased him. He cradled her head and leaned toward her lips. When his mouth covered hers, for the first time in a long while, he felt at peace.

EIGHT

On Friday Rachel stared out the window of her Jeep as Jake drove her to work. The snow-layered landscape passed by, but she really wasn't seeing the beauty before her. Most of her thoughts for the past day had been centered on the kiss Jake gave her yesterday morning. He had taken her by surprise—a very pleasant one, and afterward she'd walked around the house in a daze. She wanted him to kiss her again, and yet she didn't. He didn't want to make a long-term commitment to a woman—not after his mother and Celeste—but that was the only kind she would have, and there was no way to guarantee that.

"Rachel, we're here." Jake cut into her musing with Mitch barking from the backseat.

She blinked and focused on the fishery headquarters in front of the car. "Sorry, I was thinking."

"Dangerous. Aren't you sick of the case after spending most of yesterday going over and over what little we know?"

"Solving a crime is different than on TV. They have it done in an hour, and it looks so easy, especially when the suspect confesses."

Jake laughed, a deep belly kind. "If only that were the case. My detective friend, Thomas, would actually have normal hours if it were."

She loved hearing him laugh like that. She'd gotten the impression he hadn't done much of that in the past four months. "Is he the guy you're going to call today?"

"No, he works for the Anchorage Police Department. He worked on the bomber case. I don't think he had a life during that time. Actually, most police officers didn't. A lot were working double shifts and overtime."

"Are you going to stop in to see Chief Quay?"

"Maybe, if my walk on the pier proves profitable."

"Who knows what kind of dog Mitch is?"

"A few people here in Port Aurora—Randall, Gramps, your aunt. I don't think anyone else."

"With his missing limb, that ought to throw anyone off."

Jake's eyes widened. "I never thought that his injury would be a blessing, but you're right. What boats are coming in today?"

"Only two that the company owns, the Alaskan King and Tundra King. There may be one other that contracts with the fishery. They should be in before dusk."

"I'll probably wait until after lunch to take a walk with Mitch on the pier. I'll pick you up, and we can go to the café at twelve."

"You don't have to escort me to lunch. This is your vacation. You should spend some time with your grandfather."

"We did, yesterday. This morning I'm going to observe the fishery operations. Gramps is coming into town in a couple of hours to explain what's going on in each area. His friend who owns the bait shop near the harbor is visiting relatives in the lower forty-eight. We're going to use that as our base of operation. It has windows on three sides, so we'll be able to see most of the fishery and harbor."

"But what about the inside of the fishery?"

"I want to narrow down my search. If I went everywhere, that would make someone suspicious with all that's happened so far. Gramps might take Mitch with him to visit a friend. I can also go to the processing center. After lunch the other day, Sean and I talked about getting together."

"And I can go anywhere."

"No. You are *not* to do anything. Someone has gone after you two times. Stay in your office."

"But—"

"There's no but to it. Stay or I'm going to glue myself to you."

Rachel bit her bottom lip rather than protest. She had to do her job, or that would raise more questions and suspicions. "If I go anywhere in the fishery, it will be during the daylight hours."

His glare bored into her. "I'm probably going to have to spend all my time at the bait shop just keeping an eye on you gallivanting around the fishery and harbor. I'll bring you coffee from the café before I head that way."

"Thanks. I'd better go. I'm already late." Rachel climbed from her Jeep and hurried toward the building. Since they'd gotten a late start, she didn't have the time to stop at the café before work, so she would appreciate the coffee later.

Inside, Rachel stashed her purse in a locked drawer of her desk, then proceeded to Brad's office to get his final amounts for the employee bonuses going out today.

He'd been dragging his feet for some reason. His secretary was gone, so Rachel headed toward his door. It stood slightly ajar, and she lifted her hand to knock.

"The shipment will be ready to go on time," Sean said in his deeply raspy voice. "Even with holiday leave coming up, we'll finish processing the Tundra King and Alaskan King's catches that are coming in today. It sounds like they had a good haul. I understand there will be a couple of boats going out during the two weeks most are on vacation. I can run a skeleton crew during that time. There are some without families that don't care. Now that we've expanded we should look at running all the way through December, except for Christmas and Christmas Eve."

"I don't want to change that policy. I've already cut down the time we're gone drastically to accommodate the expansion. There's more to life than work."

"But Ivan and I can handle…"

Rachel backed away, not wanting to eavesdrop. Brad was in a meeting with Sean. She'd talk with her employer later today about the bonuses. As she turned to leave, she came face-to-face with Eva Cohen, Brad's secretary and the wife of the Tundra King's captain. The older woman's shoulders were thrust back, and she was so stiff that a light breeze could snap her in two.

"What are you doing?" The secretary's terse tone cut through Rachel.

"Brad and I are supposed to speak sometime this morning. I thought I would catch him before the day starts, but he's busy, so I'll come back."

"I'll inform *Mr. Howard* you are at work, and let you know when he can see you." Mrs. Cohen raised her chin and peered at Rachel from the bottom of her glasses.

"He's a busy man, and you should always call ahead to see if he's available."

In the past, Brad had an open-door policy, but everything changed with Mrs. Cohen's arrival last summer. She guarded access to him like a mama bear did her cubs. "I'll try to remember that," she muttered, clenching her hands as she left and hurried back to her office.

Brad had better let her know about the bonuses this morning. She would be passing out the checks early since most of the people went on vacation after Wednesday. That was supposed to be everyone's last day until after the New Year. But according to Sean, there would be a skeleton crew working over part of the holidays, at least if he had his way. Since when? Why didn't anyone tell her? She would have to note that so she could pay them at the end of the month.

She worked on the early checks for next week and would add the bonuses in when her employer let her know. When someone cleared their throat, she looked up and found Jake, leaning against her doorjamb, a paper coffee cup in each hand.

"I come bearing gifts." Jake walked to her desk and set the drinks on it, then went back out into the hallway and brought in a sack with the scent of freshly baked glazed donuts, something she loved from the café but rarely indulged in. "I figure you would be starved with only a piece of toast for breakfast."

"You must have heard my stomach rumbling all the way to the café. Where's Lawrence?"

"He went on to the bait shop. I told him I wouldn't be long, and he said for me to take my time."

"Then he has Mitch."

"Yep. I think Mitch has bonded with Gramps. It must

be the soft bed he gets to sleep in. Could you see me with two big dogs trying to sleep in a double bed? I'd probably end up on the floor while they ruled the bed."

"Mitch has worked hard. He deserves a few luxuries."

Jake chuckled. "My dog has gotten to you, too."

Rachel dug into the sack and pulled out one fluffy donut, dripping with glaze. "He's a sweetie."

"Shh. Don't say that to him. He may be officially retired, but I intend at least to keep him involved in search-and-rescue missions where he doesn't have to chase after bad guys."

Jake took the chair in front of her desk and plucked a donut from the bag. "I brought you two. I know how much you love them."

"You didn't eat much more than I did this morning."

"But I already had two donuts with Gramps."

"So where's my third one?"

He smiled from ear to ear. "I told Gramps you would say something like that." He rose and went into the hallway again. A half a minute later he set another sack on her desk.

Her eyes grew round. "I was half kidding. I can't eat three right now."

Jake retook his seat. "Save it for later and have a midafternoon treat."

"I overheard an interesting conversation—"

Jake put his forefinger over his mouth.

That was when she heard footsteps coming down the hall. She took a bite of her donut, then a sip of her coffee.

Brad poked his head around the door frame. "I thought I heard voices. It's good to see you again, Jake."

Her employer came into her office and passed her a
sheet of paper. "Those are the amounts for the bonuses
according to what they do. I've singled out a few that
have gone above and beyond their duties to see the fishery do well this year."

"Thanks. I wanted to work on payroll today because
there is paperwork that needs to be done by the end of
the year before I go on vacation."

Brad started for the door and glanced back. "By the
way, Mrs. Cohen is right. Call before you come to the
office. That way you don't waste your time. Have a
good weekend."

As the sound of the footsteps receded, Jake said,
"Tell me at lunch. We're going to have a picnic at the
bait shop. I'll stop by and get you."

"You don't have—"

"When are you going to learn not to argue with me?"

"Probably never," she said with a laugh.

"See you at twelve."

When Jake left, she sipped her coffee and nibbled
on the donut while looking over the list of bonuses.
She stared at the amount for her and nearly dropped
the sheet of paper. One month's salary! Twice as much
as most of the people at the fishery. Why? She hadn't
worked any harder than the others. She needed to check
with Brad. That he hadn't added an extra zero by mistake.

She started to get up and head for his office when
she remembered what her employer said right before he
left. Instead, she picked up her phone and called him.

"Mr. Howard's office, Mrs. Cohen speaking."

Just to irritate the prim and proper secretary, Rachel

said, "Eva, this is Rachel. I need to talk with Brad about the list he gave me a few minutes ago."

"Just a minute." A hard edge sharpened each word.

A long pause and Brad answered his phone. "Is there a problem, Rachel?"

"No, but I'm confused about my bonus numbers. You're giving me a month's salary instead of two weeks' pay."

"You're important to this fishery, and this company is vital to the economy of Port Aurora. I'd hate to think what would happen if the company went under."

"Okay." She drew that word out; for some reason it wasn't really okay. "Thank you, Brad."

"You're welcome. Have a nice weekend." Then he hung up.

Rachel started when she heard a click on the phone. Was Mrs. Cohen listening to our conversation? Why would she? Should she tell Brad? But she really didn't know. Maybe she had imagined it.

Her eyes glued to the paper before her, she stared at the thousands of dollars she would receive.

Why did she feel she was being paid off?

When Jake arrived at Rachel's office at twelve, he found her prowling her domain as though restless energy had been bottled up in her and she was trying to release it. He took one look at her face and knew something was wrong. He gave her a quizzical look.

"Later. At lunch."

Not a word was spoken until they had walked away from the building. "Okay, what's wrong?" Jake asked, wondering if Rachel had done any work since he'd left her that morning.

She told him about the bonus that was two or three times more than she ever had received. "Plus, I think Brad's secretary, Mrs. Cohen, might have been listening to my conversation with him."

"Why would she do that?" Jake asked, making a note to investigate this woman.

"If I didn't know better, I would think she ran this place. Everything has to go through her to Brad. It was never like that before she came."

"Maybe she does. How did she get the job?"

"When her husband was hired as the captain of the Tundra King, she was given the job as Brad's secretary shortly afterward. Brad's previous one got another offer and moved away. It happened fast, and I guess Brad was grateful that Mrs. Cohen could fill in quickly. Celeste did the job temporarily until Mrs. Cohen came. Celeste left it a mess, so I can understand Brad's desire to keep Mrs. Cohen happy, but still…" Rachel twisted her mouth as she did when she was in deep thought. "Do you think Mrs. Cohen might be involved in what's going on?"

"I'm suspecting everyone until proven otherwise. If drug smuggling is taking place, we're dealing with ruthless people." Jake scanned the surroundings, then opened the door to the bait shop.

"All I have to do is think about Aunt Betty to know what kind of people they are." Rachel went inside first, greeting Gramps and Mitch.

"Anything happen while I was gone?" Jake asked his grandfather while rubbing his dog's back.

"The Alaskan King is unloading their catch." Gramps stepped away from the window that afforded a great view of the harbor and passed the binoculars to

Jake. "It looks like the Tundra King is a few miles out so all the trawlers have returned. They'll be either shutting down or slowing way down until the first of the year."

Rachel frowned. "That may make it harder to find out what's going on if no drugs are coming through the fishery."

"Not necessarily. The scent of drugs will stay on an object for a while. Without so many people around, I might be able to investigate with Mitch inside the buildings, but because I'm a law-enforcement officer, our search has to be able to hold up in court."

"In plain sight?" Rachel asked as she stared out the window facing the processing center.

Jake lifted the binoculars to his eyes. "Yes, unless we get a warrant, which will need evidence of probable cause. We think someone is touching the drugs, testing or cutting them, to the point that the scent ended up on your paperwork, but that won't be enough to convince a judge."

Rachel's forehead furrowed. "Not even because Mitch discovered it? He's a drug dog."

"We need to search everywhere because we don't know what's going on, so no. We'll have to have more evidence. If we went to a judge now with what little we know, it would get out what our intention is, and the smuggling ring would shut down until we go away."

"This operation must involve more than a few people? These are people who have lived here and been our friends." His shoulders slumped, Gramps shuffled to the lunch sack and laid out the containers and wrapped sandwiches on the counter.

"Not all of them, Lawrence. We've had an influx of

new people due to the expansion at the fishery. Many have been here less than a year."

"Yeah, but the ones in a position of authority are people from Port Aurora except Ivan Verdin. Could this go on without their knowledge?" Gramps took a bite of his fish sandwich, then drained the last of an old cup of coffee.

"My friend in state police is coming the first of next week. We'll gather what information we can and give it to him."

"But what about Aunt Betty's murderer? What if her death had nothing to do with the suspicious stuff going on at the fishery?" Rachel brought Jake his lunch while he stood guard at the window.

"I think they are tied together. Why else would someone have murdered her? She could have taken some pictures that showed something. Maybe the intruders who searched her house took the photos. We may never know, but she must have made someone very uncomfortable for them to risk killing her." Jake's gaze seized hers and held it. "You said that she was afraid. What made her act like that? Most likely, she stumbled upon something to do with the drug smuggling."

"If some people at the fishery are involved, how far is their reach in Port Aurora? Remember, Aunt Betty was interested in talking to you because you were a police officer. Why didn't she go to the police here?" Rachel sat on a tall stool at the window with a view of the processing center. "What if she wandered around where she worked and discovered something? The catches are processed, then boxed up and shipped out."

"Who handles the boxing and shipping at the fishery?" Jake leaned closer to the window where a few of the slats in the blinds opened at a slant, while the rest were closed.

"Ivan Verdin, another transplant from Seattle, runs the shipping warehouse." Rachel popped a couple of chips into her mouth.

"Have I met him?" There was a time Jake knew everyone who worked at the fishery because Gramps used to do Sean's job. This visit had shown him how much he'd lost touch with the town he grew up in.

"Maybe. I can pull up a picture of him on my computer at my office."

"When I walk you back, I need you to do that. I want to know what all the players in this look like."

"I'll take over watching, Jake. Enjoy your lunch with Rachel," his grandfather murmured, too low for her to hear.

"Don't go there, Gramps." But Jake took him up on the offer. He'd rediscovered how much he loved Rachel's company and planned to enjoy it until he had to return to Anchorage. Jake sat on the other side of the counter from her and plopped his sandwich on the glass top. "I forgot to ask you if you like their fish sandwich."

"It's good. Really nothing at the café is bad."

"At least that's one thing that hasn't changed."

"We have gone through a lot of changes in the past year. If you'd come back this time last year, it wouldn't have been that different."

"When you think of your hometown, you always remember how it was when you were living there. I'm glad you haven't changed. There is one constant in Port Aurora—well, two with Gramps."

"Do you feel you've changed?"

He nodded. "I'm not naive anymore. Growing up here sheltered me from a lot of evil in this world."

"But you were a police officer here, too."

"Not the same thing."

"Are you happy in Anchorage?"

He didn't have a ready answer for her because he'd been avoiding asking himself that question. But if he said yes, he would be admitting it out loud. But he couldn't say no, either. So much had happened in the past four months. It might be different in another four. "I don't know."

Her forehead scrunched, and she pressed her lips together—lips he would like to kiss again and again. "That in itself tells me a lot. You are either happy or not."

"Not everything is black-and-white. In fact, most things aren't."

She finished her sandwich, then said, "I realize you were in the hospital for a couple of weeks and have faced a long rehabilitation, but—"

"Okay, I was fine until I came home. I'd forgotten how much this place meant to me. I promise you I'll come home more from now on."

"Alaskan King is still unloading. Tundra King has come into the harbor. It will be docking soon. I think this is a good time to go for a walk, Jake."

He looked at Gramps. "You're right. I guess it's back to surveillance mode. I'll walk you to your office, then I need to take Mitch on a hunt. Afterward, I'll stop to talk to Charlie. As harbormaster, he might have seen something and not realized it."

"Charlie is a good friend, but son, I wouldn't trust anyone, not even Randall after all that has happened."

Jake rose and grabbed his dog's leash. Mitch immediately climbed to his feet, but not quite as quickly as he used to, which brought sorrow to Jake. "Let's go, Rachel. This may be the last time for a while that a boat is returning."

"So you think if there are drugs going through the fishery, they're coming in by boat?" Rachel headed for the exit.

"It's the most logical answer. One or more of the trawlers could be meeting another boat in the Bering Sea. US ships aren't the only ones there, and the Coast Guard can only patrol so much area at a time."

"I know."

Five minutes later Jake entered Rachel's office and closed the door. He didn't want someone overhearing them as she pulled up Verdin's photo. "You should lock your door every time you leave during the day."

"The important file cabinets are locked, so I only lock the door when I leave at night."

"Still, I would feel better."

"Okay." She sat behind the computer and brought up a list of personnel. She clicked on Verdin's folder, and his picture popped up on the screen.

"I've seen him. Last Saturday he was two people back from me while I was talking with Sean, so Verdin could have overheard."

"When you have time, you should wade through everyone's picture on here."

"Will it seem strange you are accessing those files?"

"I do from time to time. Generally not all at once, but it would be good to know who else was at the general store that morning."

"Then I'll be back after my stroll around the harbor."

Jake left and made his way down the incline to the pier. He gave Mitch the command to search for drugs, then strolled the length to the right, also going down the docks attached to the pier where the boats were moored. When he saw Tom, he waved and stopped to talk for a few minutes, while keeping an eye on the activity by the pier that ended at the processing and shipping buildings.

"So Rachel is at work today?" Tom asked, winding a long length of rope.

"Yes. It was all I could do to keep her home yesterday, but by the middle of the day she was glad she didn't come in. She took a three-hour nap."

"The cold water saps your strength. I'm just glad she's all right."

Jake gestured toward the two boats tied up. "It looks like the Alaskan King is finishing unloading. They must have had a big catch. They've been at it for quite a while."

"Yeah. That's always good for business."

"I think I'll take a closer look. I see Sean with someone else on the pier, supervising the unloading."

"That's Ivan Verdin. He oversees the shipping department."

"I haven't met him yet. Now's a good time to." Jake strode away.

Five minutes later Jake slowed his gait and headed toward Sean and Ivan, who stood holding clipboards, talking.

"Hi, Sean. I'm glad I caught you. I was going to stop by your office and see if you would like to go to the Harbor Bar and Grill this evening. We haven't had much time to catch up."

His friend glanced at Ivan, then shifted toward Jake. "That sounds nice. Have you met Ivan Verdin? He manages our growing shipping department. Ivan, this is Jake Nichols. We hung around together when we were teens."

Jake shook the man's gloved hand. "Nice to meet you. How long have you been in Port Aurora?" he asked, although he already knew the answer.

"Since June. I'll be right back. I need to talk to the captain of the Alaskan King."

When the tall, thin man left, Sean watched him walk away while Jake tried to see what was on his clipboard, but it was clasped against his coat. "I'm surprised Brad didn't promote within the workers at the fishery. That's what he did for you and Rachel."

"Ivan comes with experience from another fishery in Seattle. He's had great ideas about the packaging and shipping."

"So he's from Seattle like Brad's new partner?"

Sean's eyes popped wide. "I guess he is. I never thought about it."

"Want to give me a tour of this part of the new fishery?"

"I wish I could. I'm going to be really busy for the next few hours."

Jake had given Mitch a long leash, and he'd gone as far as he could, sniffing everything around him. Jake caught Ivan glancing back at him, a scowl on his face. This wasn't the time to look around. "See you at six at the grill."

Jake didn't go to the bait shop because when he looked back a couple of times, he found Ivan watching him. Jake headed to Rachel's office to go through the rest of the employee files. He'd have Gramps take

Rachel and Mitch home tonight while he met his friend to pump him for information.

Almost nine o'clock and the Harbor Bar and Grill was finally beginning to thin out. Jake had drunk three cups of coffee while Sean had ordered one beer after another. He'd never seen his friend drink so much alcohol. Thankfully, he lived near the harbor so he could walk to and from his job. What had made Sean change? When other teens were experimenting with alcohol, Sean never had. He prayed that Sean wasn't involved in the drug smuggling. The guy he grew up with wouldn't have been.

"I'm going to have to head home," Jake said when the bartender rang a boat bell nine times.

"Don't. We haven't had a chance to talk about your job. I think you know everything that has gone on since you left, but you're awfully closemouthed about Anchorage." Sean slurped the last of his drink and set the mug on the table with a loud thud.

"There's little to tell."

"You were injured searching a bombed building. What about that?"

He hated talking about it, but he didn't say that to Sean. Instead, he replied, "We'll get together again, and I'll tell you all the gory details. Let me drop you off at your house before I head home."

Sean waved his hand in the air. "I'm not drunk. I can walk. You go on and leave."

"I don't mind taking you home."

"I know. But I'm gonna stick around and escort our waitress Bev home. She lives down the street from me."

He tapped his temple. "I've got my eye on her. She's interested in me."

Reluctantly, Jake left the restaurant and limped to Gramps's SUV. It was long days like this one that reinforced he'd been injured only four months ago and nearly died. Sean could take care of himself.

He climbed in and started the car. He hadn't learned much tonight, but he did get the feeling Sean really didn't care for Ivan and that the man was difficult to work with.

After looking through the photos of the employees, Jake couldn't remember anyone else that stood out to him that Saturday at the general store. What if one of the police officers was involved? After all, he'd been talking with Randall about where else he was going on that day. They might have alerted the arsonists to go to Betty's cabin. So many questions, so few answers.

The roads were much better since the last snowfall, but Jake focused his full attention on the highway. In the dark, he didn't have a lot of time to react if there was a slick spot that had developed that day.

In the distance across a field, he spied the Christmas lights on Linda's house. That meant he was only a mile away. Suddenly, someone stepped out of the brush on the side of the road and aimed a rifle at Jake.

NINE

Rachel circled the living room for the tenth time and glanced at her watch. Nine thirty. Where was Jake? She paused at the front window and stared into the night, hoping to see two headlights coming. Nothing but darkness.

Mitch came up beside her and sat, looking up at her.

"I know, boy. Something doesn't feel right. He should have been home by now."

"Child, my grandson can take care of himself. He was meeting with Sean. You three used to hang out together in high school. You know how those two will get to talking and forget the time."

"You're right. But if anything happened to him because of me, I don't know what..." Emotions crowded into her throat, stopping her words. She swallowed hard but couldn't continue. She didn't want to lose him again, especially now that he was back in her life. This time she hoped he would visit Port Aurora more often, and she would go to Anchorage to see him. And maybe in time they—

Lawrence wedged himself between the Christmas tree and her. "I know how you feel. You love him."

"Of course I love him. He's my best friend. I'm not letting him disappear from my life for the next eight years." He'd hurt her when he'd left and she'd mostly stayed away, nursing her wounds.

Lawrence angled his head toward her. "I think it's more than friendship, but you two are too busy running away from commitment to see it."

Was that true? In the past week so many feelings had surfaced. Anger at him for keeping his distance. Relief that he was here to help with Aunt Betty's case. And then she thought of the kiss they'd shared—not anything like two good friends would. But Lawrence had a point. They both had commitment issues.

"Tell you what, Rachel. We'll give him another half an hour, and then I'll drive you to town. We'll take Mitch and hunt him down."

"He's at the Harbor Bar and Grill. I could call them and see if he's still there."

"Give him some time. I know a lot has been happening in Port Aurora, but the town is still essentially the same."

She turned toward Lawrence. "Is it? This past year we have added over five hundred to our population. With growth can come more crime, and if there is drug smuggling going down in the town, then it will only get worse."

"We still don't know that for sure."

"Both Jake and I strongly suspect it. We'll find the evidence to prove it if it's there. We can't ignore the scent of drugs on those papers in my office."

"Let me call the grill." Lawrence covered the space to the phone sitting on an end table in the living room, and dialed the number.

Rachel went back to her vigilance at the window. *Is this the way wives of police officers are when their husbands are late?*

Lawrence hung up and approached Rachel. "He's been gone for over half an hour. We're less than fifteen minutes from town."

"Then we have to go out looking for him." She headed for her purse and snatched up her keys to the Jeep.

A shot rang out, and the bullet hit the SUV's windshield. Jake ducked, and the car swerved toward the shooter. Another blast pierced a second hole into the glass, followed by a third.

Jake steered blind with one hand while fumbling for the glove compartment where his gun was. He grasped it as the SUV went into a spin. He rose, catching a glimpse of a figure fleeing right before Jake crashed into the thicket at the side of the road, the airbag exploding against his chest.

The hard impact into the ditch tossed him back then forward. A fine white powder choked him, and he coughed. Stunned and pinned against the seat, he closed his eyes to still the swirling sensation.

For a few seconds he couldn't remember what happened, then it all slammed back into his mind. As he shoved at the deflated airbag, he searched for his seat belt release. He pushed down on it.

It's stuck.

He fought rising panic, sucking in shallow gasps. Scenes from the bombing threatened to overtake his senses. Then he felt his weapon still clutched in his hand. Even if the man came to finish him off, he could protect himself. He jammed his thumb against the release once. Twice. Finally, the latch popped out, and the strap slackened across his chest.

His heartbeat racing, he began dragging in deeper breaths and searching the terrain around him. His headlights gave off illumination, enough that he didn't think the assailant was near. But how long would he remain away?

After he retrieved the flashlight in the glove compartment, Jake groped for the car handle, found it and shoved the door open. It creaked. The sound seemed to magnify and echo through the air, sending out a signal he was getting out of the car. All he had was a foot to squeeze out of the SUV. He pushed on the door, but it wouldn't budge any more.

After wiggling out of his bulky overcoat, he transferred his Glock to his left hand and clutched the parka in his right one. When he sucked in his breath, his bruised body protested. He gritted his teeth and squirmed out of the car.

When he stood, his legs started to give way. He gripped the door, leaning into it as he got his bearings. Then he noticed the cold boring into him and remembered to put on his coat.

He didn't want to stay around the SUV or walk home using the road. If the assailant came back, he would easily find him. He started across the field, using the lights in the distance as his guide to his destination. It had been years since he had walked over this ground. He tried to remember what obstacles were in his path.

Trudging slowly through the snow, he would head behind Betty's house and avoid the woods near where she'd lived. It would be a little longer but safer. He didn't want to use his flashlight unless absolutely necessary. If his assailant was looking for him, he wasn't going to make it easy.

The wind whipping across the flatland drove the cold deeper into him. Every sound heightened his alertness. About halfway home, Jake paused, turned his back to the wind and inhaled frigid air. His healing leg throbbed. His knee must have hit against the console. Every muscle screamed for him to sit and rest, but after a minute he scanned his dark-shrouded surroundings, then kept going toward the Christmas lights. The first thing he would do when he reached Linda's house was kiss them for stringing so many.

Then in the distance to his left came the sound of howls. A pack of wolves. He pressed on, trying to increase his speed to keep distance between them, but each time he lifted his leg out of the foot-deep snow, his steps shortened.

The howling continued. Jake's grip tightened around the gun handle. He pushed himself even more. Out of the corner of his eye, he saw a movement, but he couldn't tell what was there. From the well of what energy was left, he poured everything into his speed.

Suddenly, the ground beneath him fell away, and he tumbled downward.

"That's your car!" Rachel pointed toward the Jeep's front windshield. "He's been in a wreck." The words rushed out so fast she could hardly understand herself.

Heartbeat pounding against her rib cage, Rachel pulled over to the side of the road and put the Jeep's flashers on while Lawrence hopped from the car. They both converged on the driver's-side door, the headlights from her Jeep glowing into the SUV's dark interior.

Rachel straightened and turned toward Lawrence. "He's gone. I didn't see him walking home."

He leaned around her and examined the front seat. When he lifted his head toward the windshield, he tensed.

Slightly behind him, Rachel asked, "What's wrong?"

"There are three bullet holes in the windshield."

Rachel squeezed around Lawrence and bent forward, glancing at the holes then the seat. "I don't see any blood. The keys are gone. Maybe he's okay, and we just missed him on the road." But as she said that, she didn't believe it.

Lawrence rounded the back of his car and opened the passenger door, then checked the glove compartment. "The flashlight is gone. Do you have one in your car?"

"Yes, the same place."

While Lawrence retrieved it, Rachel inspected the ground illuminated by the Jeep lights. "There are a lot of footprints here. I'm not sure which ones are ours."

Lawrence shone the flashlight a few feet from the SUV where there were two sets, not theirs. "There was someone else here. No doubt the shooter. One of these went southwest toward town and the other into the field."

Rachel followed the footsteps leading to a huge meadow near her house with the woods bordering part of it. "All I see is our Christmas lights. Nothing like a flashlight."

"Maybe that's why he went that way. It's the shortest way to our houses."

"What if he's hurt?" Rachel pointed to the tracks.

"He's dragging the leg he injured in Anchorage. Isn't that what it looks like?"

Lawrence focused the flashlight on the drag marks in the snow. "He crashed into the side of the ditch. He was going fast enough for the air bags to deploy. At the least he would have some bumps and bruises."

"Then we need to follow the tracks. What if he hit his head and isn't fully himself? He could have internal bleeding or…" Her throat jammed closed. She fought the tears welling inside her.

"He's a survivor. It was hours before he was safely rescued from the building rubble. He made it."

He had to be okay. He was hurt because of her. *Please, Lord, be with him. Show us where he is.*

Lawrence went first, illuminating the path, while Rachel trailed close behind him.

After walking ten minutes, she said, "Shine the light toward my house. We might catch his silhouette." She *needed* to see he was all right.

But when Lawrence swept the flashlight across the meadow, no one was there. Rachel's heart sank. "We've got to keep going. He may be in trouble."

Jake's feet went out from under him, and he slid downward. He slammed against the bottom of a snow-crusted crevice, his body wedged between the narrow walls. Pinned down. Stuck.

The only thing he could move was his right arm. His left one was trapped between his chest and the jagged stone. His weapon had jerked from his fingers as he fell, but lay within reach of his good arm.

He switched on his flashlight to see if he could fig-ure a way out of the crevice. On both sides of him the walls were closer together. Until he'd fallen into the gap, he'd forgotten about there being a few in this meadow. He could have avoided or stepped over if he'd seen the fissure in time.

He turned off his light. He didn't want to call attention to his location. Hopefully, Gramps would find his SUV and figure out where he was going before anyone else. This was a time he was glad his grandfather was an expert shot, having been a sniper in the US Marines. He should be able to take care of himself if his assailant returned.

Since he couldn't see the wolves getting at him, all he had to worry about now was keeping himself warm when he could hardly move his limbs. The wind whipping through the crevice cut right through him. With his free hand, he pulled his hood, bunched around his neck, over his beanie. Occasionally, he stomped his feet and moved his right arm to keep the blood circulating, but the sting of needles pricked his trapped one.

As time ticked away, the cold snaked through his body like fog slowly creeping over the landscape until it was everywhere.

Lord, I know I've been a stranger lately, but I need You. Gramps and Rachel say You are always with us. Help me get out of this.

His teeth chattered, and he shivered. He needed to stay awake, but his eyelids drooped. Then his head dropped forward, hitting against the side of the ice-encased rocky surface. He didn't care. Maybe if he rested for a while...

Growls and yelps ricocheted through his tired mind. Jake jerked his head up and aimed the flashlight above.

Amber eyes stared down at him.

* * *

"Did you see that?" Rachel pointed to an area about three hundred yards in front of them and to the right. "I saw a light. It's gone now, but it was coming from the ground. That could be Jake."

"That's near those fissures in this meadow."

"He could have fallen into one."

"Let's go." Rachel charged out in front of Lawrence.

He grabbed her arm. "Wait. Look." He gestured toward the area they were heading to.

Rachel froze, her gaze riveted on a pack of four wolves, all standing around and peering down. At Jake? Hurt? "What do we do?"

Gramps handed her the flashlight and grabbed the rifle he'd slung over his shoulder before leaving the Jeep. "That's why I always come prepared."

"You're going to kill them?" Because she went hiking and camping, she knew how to use a gun, but one of the things she loved about her home was all the beautiful creatures that lived in Alaska.

"Not if I can help it. I had my fill of killing in the Vietnam War." His gruff voice softened and thickened when he mentioned being a soldier. Jake had once told her he would never talk about being in that war.

Lawrence crept forward. "Shine the light on them."

When Rachel did, a shot rang out in the night.

When the gunshot sounded, the wolves yelped, turning away from Jake, their attention on someone else. Had the assailant decided to see if Jake was hurt or dead? Had he brought reinforcements?

Sweat popped out on his forehead and rolled down his face. He was a sitting duck, but at least he still had some rounds in his weapon. He wouldn't go down without a fight.

Another blast echoed through the darkness, followed by a third one. Suddenly, the wolves jumped over the crevice and ran off, leaving Jake to face whoever was out there.

He lifted his Glock and prepared for the worst. With each second that passed, his heart rate increased until all he heard was its thundering beat against his skull. More sweat stung his eyes, and he blinked several times so he could see his assailant. He wouldn't have much time to make a decision. He pointed the barrel upward.

"Jake! Jake!"

Rachel's sweet voice, followed by Gramps's deeper one, took a few seconds to register and for him to drop his arm to his side. As he saw her peer over the edge, relief sagged his tensed shoulders, and he smiled.

Thank You, Lord.

Then his grandfather appeared next to Rachel. "You've gotten yourself into a predicament, son."

"Nothing you two can't handle, but before I turn into a block of ice, you might get some help. I'm going to have to be hauled out of here."

Three hours later, Jake lay on the couch in Linda's house while Rachel let the police chief out. Finally, some quiet after a very long and exhausting day. He closed his eyes, tired but not sleepy. He hurt, over his whole body, but he was too wired to get some rest.

When he heard Rachel's footsteps return from seeing Doc and Randall out, he shifted his head and looked at her—a welcome sight after the long evening he'd had.

"I think we should ask Doc to move in since he's been here so much this past week."

Rachel laughed. "His wife might have a problem with that. Randall says he'll have the SUV towed into the garage and have it fixed, but it's going to take a while. Bodywork needs to be done as well as a windshield, not to mention the seat cushions with bullet holes in them. One only missed you by an inch."

"I wish you would leave Port Aurora until this case is solved," Jake said in a determined voice.

"I can't. I have to work through part of next week, and I'm the best way into the fishery. You might not be able to snoop around, but I can. I have keys to most of the places."

Jake sat straight up, groaning as he swung his feet to the floor. "You will not do any investigating on your own. Do you understand?"

"Yes, I do."

A gleam in her eyes made him ask, "Do you understand and promise not to look into it by yourself?"

The corners of her mouth drooped. "I'm not answering that question."

"Rachel." Jake started to rise but sank back onto the cushion. "I can't be worrying about you while trying to figure out what's going on."

She lifted her chin a few inches. "And I can't be worrying about you, either. The assailant wasn't after me this time."

"Don't you think I know that? I'm going to call Chance O'Malley, my friend who is a state trooper, and ask him to come before Monday, if he can. The drug smugglers obviously are aware we're looking into the fishery."

Rachel sat on the coffee table near Jake while Linda and Gramps came into the living room. "Then use that fact to work against them."

Gramps covered the distance to the lounge chair next to the couch. Linda poised on its arm and glanced at his grandfather. "Son, we overheard your conversation and think we have a plan that might help bring everything to a head."

Linda clasped Gramps's shoulder. "The problem is we need to figure out if it is drug smuggling or something else, and the only way to find that out is to get inside the shipping center and see what's going out. They will be processing two big catches tomorrow and Monday, then sending them to their destination on Tuesday and Wednesday. After that, most of the fishery will shut down for two weeks."

Gramps patted Linda's leg. "That doesn't leave a lot of time. I know all of us want this settled before Christmas. The alternative to not figuring out what's going on is to be a target for weeks and then try again after the first of the year. But then you have to return to Anchorage."

Jake slanted a look at Rachel, meeting her intense gaze. "Have you been talking to them while I was gone this evening?"

She smiled. "Maybe."

He frowned and turned his glare back on Gramps and Linda. "You are not police officers."

Rachel leaned forward, her apple scent swirling about him. "That's just it. But you are and can't investigate inside without an invitation or a good reason to be there. I work there, and Gramps is a concerned citizen, not an officer of the law. You need evidence to get a warrant."

"Right." Jake stood, anger sharpening his features into cold stone. "You and Linda are going to decorate for the fishery's annual Christmas party Sunday afternoon. While you're doing that, I'll walk on the pier again, and see how close I can get to those two boats that came in today. Also, I'll see what Chance has to say. If he can come earlier, he can walk with me."

"But you can't—"

"Rachel, that's it. I'm not going to put you in harm's way." Jake limped toward the hallway and escaped into the bathroom.

Leaning onto the counter, he took in the scrapes and bruises starting to appear on his face. He looked like he'd been in a fight and lost, but he wasn't giving up. His feelings toward Rachel were changing, and he wasn't sure what to do about them. But he did know that he wasn't going to let anything happen to her or the others.

Sunday afternoon, Rachel worked beside her aunt, setting up the tables and putting decorations on each one. Celeste was in charge of getting the large hall ready for the Christmas buffet and party. At one time they had been good friends, but ever since the incident with Jake, she had kept her distance from Rachel. She'd been so mad at Celeste at first that she didn't try to repair the rift, even after Jake left for Anchorage.

Celeste went all out for this event every year, and this one even more so. Once, Rachel had discovered Celeste made all the centerpieces for the tables throughout the year. She heard through the grapevine that Brad wouldn't let her work, and since they didn't have any children, what did she do all day? Their house on the hill was always beautiful and spotless, even when the fishery was going through hard times.

"I need to get a few more centerpieces. Be right back, Aunt Linda."

Rachel made her way to Celeste to see where the rest of the table decorations were. There were still six more to set up. Rachel waited until Celeste was finished talking with Eva Cohen, who stormed away with a pursed mouth and a tic twitching in her cheek.

"What's wrong with Mrs. Cohen?" Rachel said when she approached Celeste.

"She can be so difficult. She is Brad's secretary, but you would think she runs the whole fishery with that attitude of hers. I don't know how my husband puts up with her."

"She definitely runs a tight ship. Maybe he should make her a captain of a boat, and she'd be gone most of the time."

Celeste chuckled. "Not a bad idea, but Brad raves about her, so I don't dare make that suggestion." She glanced toward Eva, who snatched up her coat and left the hall. "I'm glad Jake is okay after his wreck. He looked beat up this morning in church."

"That can happen when you fall into a fissure."

"When did he do that?"

"Friday night. When his car went off the road, he thought it would be faster to hike across the meadow not far from where we live."

"I remember when I used to pick wildflowers in that field with you...before Jake and I started dating. Is he still angry with me?"

"You need to ask him that." Before the conversation

turned to a subject Rachel didn't want to discuss, she said, "I need six more centerpieces."

"I still have some in my car. Will you help me bring them in?"

"Sure. Let me get my coat. After my dunk in the harbor, it doesn't take much to get me cold."

"I was so sorry to hear that. Probably some drunk ran into you and didn't even realize what he'd done. Did Chief Quay ever find the guy?"

"No."

Celeste looked toward the main door. "Brad's here. I need to talk to him for a minute."

"Where's your car? I can get the centerpieces."

"Between the processing and shipping buildings."

Bundled in her warm coat, Rachel left the hall through the back door, which was closer to the shipping warehouse. She wasn't going to waste this opportunity to check it out. The only day of the week it was shut down was Sunday, so no one would be around. Her master key should get her inside. When she became part of management, she'd been given a set.

She glanced around for anyone watching her. The parking lot was deserted as well as the field that led to the water. Perfect time to see if she could get in. Then she could come back when it was dark. She'd even let Jake keep guard outside. At the door she inserted the key, then turned it. It didn't work. Why? It should. She examined the lock. It was new, not the weathered one she noticed a couple of weeks ago.

She started for Celeste's car, her step nearly faltering when she glimpsed Ivan coming toward her. Where had he been? She prayed he didn't see her trying to unlock the door. With a nod toward him, she cut across the parking lot, determined not to glance back at him. At Celeste's Lexus SUV, she opened the back door and reached for two of the centerpieces. When she pivoted to leave, she ran right into Ivan.

She started to say something, but no words came out. Why was he here? All she could focus on was the man's dark eyes, intense, narrowed on her. A movement behind him snagged Rachel's attention.

Rachel called out, "Celeste, I love your new car. I've seen you driving it around. It still has that new car smell."

"It drives great on snow." Celeste paused next to Ivan. "It's good to see you, Ivan. With your help, Rachel and I will only have to make one trip."

Rachel sidled toward the rear of the silver-gray SUV while Celeste retrieved two centerpieces from the backseat and gave them to Ivan without the man saying a word. By the time she picked up the last two, the man's expression evened out into a bland look.

As he strolled with them toward the large hall, he said, "I'm glad I can be of service to women in distress." Finally, he grinned at Celeste and held the door open for them to go inside first.

Rachel shivered. When Jake smiled, she always felt the caring and warmth behind it. When Ivan did, she felt a chill, although he would be considered a classically good-looking man, tall, with a muscular build and raven-colored hair and eyes.

After Ivan set the two centerpieces on an empty table, he left. Celeste watched him leave, her lips pinched together. "I don't like that man," she murmured.

"Before you arrived at your car, he seemed..." Rachel realized she shouldn't say any more. Celeste was married to the owner.

"He seemed intense?"

"Yes. I don't have a lot to do with him." Mainly because Ivan usually sent his assistant with the shipping information and billing to Rachel's office. "Is he always like that?"

"Afraid so. Brad insists he's indispensable. But a lot of the workers give him a wide berth."

In the next hour, the hall was transformed into a winter wonderland of white, red and green. Rachel stood with her aunt on the perimeter and surveyed the decorations.

"Celeste is quite talented. The centerpieces of different Christmas scenes are fascinating. I found myself examining each one I put on a table." Aunt Linda swept her arm toward a round table on the edge at the back. "I want to sit there tonight. Celeste's creation reminds me of the time you, her and some other kids in Sunday school put on the nativity scene for the church."

"I remember that. Jake was Joseph. Celeste played Mary while I was the angel." Rachel fixed her gaze on the table across the room and near the rear door. "That does remind me of that."

"Are you two ready to head home?" Lawrence asked from behind them.

Rachel half turned. "Where are Jake and Mitch?"

"He's coming. He's walking Mitch down to the loading dock, then circling the building." Lawrence threw a long glance toward Aunt Linda and winked at her.

"Isn't that being obvious, especially after what happened Friday night?" Rachel asked as her aunt's cheeks reddened.

"That's the great part about it. He met Brad in the parking lot, and they started talking about the expansion. They decided to tour the outside with Brad explaining what had happened and what will."

"That's odd. Brad and Jake were a couple of years apart and never that close."

"You know what I think? Brad feels threatened with Jake in town."

Aunt Linda shook her head. "Lawrence, where in the world did you come up with that?"

"I saw Jake and Celeste talking before church. So did Brad."

"They did?" Rachel searched the room to find Celeste. "I didn't know that." Why didn't Jake say anything? They used to share almost everything.

"We'd better go if we're going to turn around and come back in a couple of hours," Aunt Linda said as she grabbed her parka. Lawrence helped her into it.

At her Jeep, Rachel spied Brad and Jake shake hands, and then he and Mitch made their way to her. "Did you discover anything interesting?"

"Nope, except that Brad's silent partner has deep pockets. Brad has all kinds of ideas for expanding the business and town. He has a point. The town is located between the sea and mountains. It's perfect to grow the recreational fishing, camping and hiking industry. I have a friend in Anchorage who owns a chain of sporting goods stores in Alaska. Josiah and his twin sister, Alex, are always looking for ways to expand. Alaska has something to offer that other states don't. It's the last frontier in the United States with parts still rugged and hard to get to."

Rachel slipped behind the steering wheel, started

the Jeep to get it warm and waited for the other two to climb in. "If the town continues to grow like it has the past year, we'll need more than the general store and the few restaurants to cater to the townspeople and the tourists."

As she drove out of the parking lot, Brad and Celeste emerged from the meeting hall. The expressions on both their faces made Rachel wonder if they'd had a fight. Did Celeste tell Brad about Ivan?

When Rachel parked at her house, she grabbed Jake and held his arm to keep him inside the Jeep while Lawrence and Aunt Linda headed indoors. They took Mitch.

Jake assessed Rachel. "Did something happen today?"

"Why don't you tell me?"

"What?"

"Your grandfather said you had a conversation with Celeste before church. What did you two talk about?" She had no right to ask him that question, but she was the one who tried to help him piece his life together after Celeste broke off the engagement. She couldn't do it again.

"She was asking how I felt after the wreck on Friday."

There was curiosity in his tone. Staring out the windshield, she gritted her teeth to keep from saying anything. She wasn't going to force him to confide in her. If he wanted to get hurt again, then—

"But mostly we talked about what happened eight years ago. She actually apologized for what she did."

"What did you say?" *What did you do?*

"I told her in the end it was for the best. I just didn't know it at the time. Coming back here has made that clear to me. As we talked, I realized that I don't hold any grudges against her. That surprised me at first."

Me, too. But Rachel kept that to herself. "What's different?"

"I'm different. I'm not the same heartbroken guy who left for Anchorage. I should have come home years ago, and I would have realized Celeste and I wouldn't have worked."

"That's good because all I can say is you'd better not be a stranger to Port Aurora ever again. I missed you." The last word caught in her throat.

Jake edged closer and clasped her hand. "I've missed you, too. I don't know what's happening between us, but I want to see where it goes."

She touched his lips with her fingertips, wanting to say so much but settling on, "I like the idea of getting reacquainted with each other." She was falling in love with Jake—that was the only thing that explained the feelings she was having. But how would she know for sure? She'd never been in love—had purposely avoided it. Maybe she was wrong. Confused thoughts raced through her mind.

He stared at her for a long moment, then released her hand as he put his on the car door handle. "Is everything set for tonight?"

"Yes. I'd hoped that you and I could check out the shipping warehouse tonight while everyone was partying, but I discovered that my master key no longer works. They've changed the locks."

Jake rotated toward her, thunder in his expression. "You did what?"

Rachel flinched at the fury in his voice. She needed to do something to help, but all Jake wanted to do was protect her.

TEN

Rachel pressed back against the driver's-side door. "I didn't really plan to do it. I saw an opportunity while going to get the centerpieces from Celeste's car to try my key in the door. I looked around, and no one was there. I wasn't at the door more than half a minute."

Jake curled his hands and squeezed them so tight they ached. "What part of *don't investigate the building* do you not understand?"

"I wasn't going to. But if my key had worked, and it should have, I was going to suggest I go back with you and Mitch later tonight. I know you shouldn't search the warehouse without a warrant, but I can. I could take Mitch and see if he found anything. You could keep watch. Well, at least that had been my plan, until the key didn't work."

Her explanation flowed nonstop from her, which indicated to Jake she was nervous. She should be. "I don't think you grasp the seriousness of this situation."

"I've seen TV shows about—"

"Stop right there. Real life crimes aren't wrapped up in an hour or two with a happy ending. These people mean business. Chance talked with a DEA agent who said recently their office in Seattle has become alerted about Peter Rodin's recent activities."

"What activities?"

"His association to a big-time Russian mafia boss."

"Do you think because we are so close to Russia, someone at the fishery is smuggling in drugs from there?"

"It's at the top of my list of theories."

"I can't believe Brad would condone that."

He loved how she always looked at the good in people. She'd lived a sheltered life. Probably the first time crime touched her was Betty's murder. "He might not know. It's only recently that law-enforcement agencies discovered a link between Rodin and the Russian mafia. If I were going to look at boats involved, it would be the ones added after Rodin became a silent partner. Also, there are a lot of new employees since the expansion. Any number of them could be involved."

"So they could be using the fishery without Brad's knowledge?"

"Yes."

"Then we need to get Mitch onto the Alaskan King and maybe even the Tundra King since it was overhauled in Seattle."

"There could be a scent, but without the drugs actually on the boat, it would be hard to use that as evidence. They would move the drugs off the trawler as soon as possible."

"During unloading?"

Jake nodded. "Have any shipments gone out since the last boats came in?"

"Not until the first of next week."

"I'll need a list of the shipments. Where they're

going. When. How." He hoped to turn this investigation over to Chance O'Malley and the DEA, so all he needed to do was protect Rachel, Linda and Gramps.

"I usually get the information after the fact for billing purposes."

"Who has it?"

"Ivan Verdin. His department readies the fish for shipping after processing, schedules the deliveries and moves them to the ship or plane."

"That's where the drugs will be, in shipping, then on some transport to their destination." He spied Gramps standing at the front window by the Christmas tree, trying not to look at them in the Jeep. "We probably need to go in."

"I'll go see Ivan tomorrow about the shipments. I'll tell him I want to wrap everything up before vacation starts on Wednesday."

Jake's gut tightened. "No. Gramps, Chance and I will keep our surveillance on the shipment warehouse to find out when the shipments go out. I want you as far away from there as possible. You are not involved in this anymore."

"Are you going to be at the bait shop again?"

"No, I have a room for Chance at the bed-and-breakfast that has a great view of the harbor. He's flying in tomorrow morning. I'll pick him up at the airport and make a big deal that a friend is visiting. That will give us a reason for going in and out of his room."

"I'll stay away from shipping if you promise you'll be careful. Someone came after you on Friday, not me."

He held out his hand. "A deal."

She fit hers within his. "Yes. I want my town back."

He'd never forgive himself if something happened

to her. She meant too much to him. She'd always been there for him, and he was the one who had let her down. He left rather than dealt with his feelings after Celeste called off the wedding. Then he poured his life into his work, focusing on helping others in his job and spare time. He never really came to terms with his mother leaving or Celeste breaking their engagement. He'd been running away from his feelings for years. Maybe that was why he felt so strongly about returning to Port Aurora.

"Jake, are you all right?"

He blinked, orienting himself to the present. He still held Rachel's hand, and in the dim light he saw worry lining her face. When neither of them was at risk, he needed to have a long talk with Rachel. He wanted to make sense out of all these feelings swirling around inside him.

"I don't know about you, but it's cold out here. Let's get inside before Gramps sends out a search party." He grinned, released her hand and opened the door.

When Jake entered Linda's house right behind Rachel, Gramps gave Rachel then Jake a mug of coffee. "I figure you need it to thaw out. I could have thought of warmer places to talk."

A blush tinted Rachel's cheeks as she made her way to the fire. She put her drink on the mantel and held her hands out near the blaze, rubbing them together. "This feels good."

Linda came from the kitchen with a plate of cookies. "This can tide us over until dinner tonight. Celeste told me fish would *not* be on the menu. The main course will be prime rib."

Gramps patted his stomach. "What a treat! Although without fish to catch, Port Aurora would be an extremely small community."

Jake moved closer to the fire. What was going to happen to the town if the fishery was involved in drug smuggling? If Rodin was behind it, how would the fishery keep going without its major backer? Thousands of people would be affected if the main industry failed. If he had a hand in taking it down, Jake needed to figure out a solution.

Rachel scanned the crowd crammed into the huge hall at the fishery. This year the Christmas party had been opened to a lot more people besides the workers. In addition to the elaborate buffet tables featuring many side dishes, freshly baked bread, salads and desserts, she counted four different stations for prime rib, ham and chicken. At the front of the room stood a fifteen-foot Christmas tree, decorated in different fish ornaments interspersed among glittering balls of silver and gold.

"Brad and Celeste outdid themselves this year," Lawrence said over the noise in the hall.

Jake put his hand at the small of her back. "Speaking of Brad, I need to talk to him. He said something today about giving me a tour inside the fishery, and I'm going to see if he can tomorrow. Do you see him?"

Rachel leaned toward him and whispered, "I thought you were turning the investigation over to your friend tomorrow."

"I am, but I'll help where I can. Chance wouldn't likely get a tour of the shipping warehouse, but I can."

Rachel took Jake's hand and pulled him toward the right side of the room along the wall. "So it's okay if you keep putting yourself in danger, but not me." Jake was only involved because of her.

He inched close to her. "Yes. I'm a police officer. I've been trained for this. You haven't."

For years she'd worried about him in Anchorage, especially when she'd heard of a serious crime committed there. The serial bomber had heightened her fear something would happen to Jake. And it had. "You don't want me in danger. I don't want you to be, either."

"It's part of the job. Before I left for Anchorage, I was a police officer here, and you never said a word."

"Because crime here wasn't anything like a serial bomber, gangs, murder. With all that has happened, it just makes me realize how dangerous your job is."

He boxed her in, hands placed on the wall by the side of her face. "There's nowhere totally safe. Stay out of this."

She stared at his mouth, set in a firm line. "I'm going to, but what will happen if we can't get proof?"

"There is no more *we* in this investigation." He frowned. "But to answer your question, until that moment comes, let's think positive. When I was injured and had a lot of downtime in Anchorage, Jesse Hunt, another canine officer, kept me informed of what was going on for a while. I sank deeper into depression. I was stuck on medical leave and couldn't do a thing about a case, and yet it consumed me. About a month later something had to give. I needed to focus on my recovery, or the feeling of helplessness I was experiencing would grow. I've learned to concentrate on the moment—not the future."

She'd remembered how he had been when he first came home and saw Celeste. "How about the past?"

He cocked one corner of his mouth. "I'm working on that. It helped to talk to Celeste this morning. But when you come home after being gone so long, the past hits you square in the face. I can forgive Celeste, but I don't know if…" He heaved a sigh.

"You can forgive your mother?"

"It's one thing to be rejected by Celeste and totally different by the woman who gave birth to you."

Rachel cupped his face. "I know, and you've had a constant reminder of that while you've been here. I'm surprised you put Chance in the bed-and-breakfast."

"It was the best solution. It isn't the same place as when I lived there as a child with my mother."

Chief Quay stepped into her peripheral vision, and all thought of continuing this conversation vanished.

"What are you two concocting?" the police chief said with a chuckle.

Without missing a beat, Jake replied, "She's trying to pry information about her gift from me."

"Yeah, I hate surprises." Rachel placed her hand on Jake's arm. "Nobody is waiting to eat. If we don't get our food, there's not going to be any left for us."

"Leave it to Rachel to worry about dinner." Jake threaded his fingers through hers. "Any news about Friday night?"

"Nothing. The other set of footprints near the SUV went toward town for about two hundred yards, then crossed the road and went down a turnoff. There were tire tracks, most likely from a big truck. That must have been his transportation, but there are tons of trucks in Port Aurora. We're matching the tire tracks with a database, but what we've found doesn't narrow the hunt down much. Don't worry. I'll let you know if anything worthwhile comes up."

"Thanks, Randall."

Rachel watched the exchange between the men. Jake didn't feel the police chief was involved, but he couldn't rule him out, either. How entrenched was the drug-smuggling ring in the town? The thought that the police might be part of it nauseated her. For Jake it would be devastating. He knew some of the officers—worked with half of them. But she couldn't deny Aunt Betty's warning, either.

Jake panned the crowd, his gaze pausing on the other side of the room. "I see Brad is in line. Let's hurry and get behind him and Celeste. I want to finagle that tour out of him after I get Chance settled. It will be interesting to see if he says yes."

"What will you do if he says no?"

"Go to the next plan."

"And what's that?"

His roguish grin appeared, his dimples and bright eyes enthralling her. "I could say Plan B, but that's cliché, and I don't have a Plan B at this moment."

"You think you can charm a tour out of Brad?"

"No, but I could out of Celeste, especially after her apology this morning. She'll want to make amends."

Celeste might have apologized, but Rachel didn't want her escorting Jake anywhere.

He slung his arm over her shoulder and weaved their way through the throng of people until they arrived at the buffet tables set up on the left side. Jake walked down the line until he reached Brad, who was second from last.

Jake held out his hand. "This is some party you've thrown."

Brad pumped Jake's arm vigorously, then draped his arm over Celeste's shoulders as though staking claim to her. "You clean up nice."

Jake swept his arm down his body. "Oh, this old suit? I was told I needed to dress up or stay behind, then I heard there would be prime rib and I put on a tie. Not my favorite piece of clothing."

Brad laughed. "I know what you mean. Most days at the fishery it's informal. This town doesn't have too many reasons to dress up. Celeste wanted this to be one of them. We're having a DJ play music after dinner. Has your dancing improved over the years you were away?"

Jake looked him straight in the face. "Not one bit, so I won't be taking part in that activity."

Brad swiveled his attention to Rachel as the line moved forward. "Then if you need a partner, just come get me." He switched his gaze to Celeste. "That is, if my wife is okay with me dancing with another woman."

"Please do. After all the decorating today, I'm exhausted. I'm going to sit back and watch everyone." Celeste smiled at someone behind Rachel. "Captain Martin, I heard you had a great catch."

The captain of the Sundance, a short man with a full black beard, paused. "I'm impressed with all you managed to do today. When I helped bring in the tables, I never thought the hall would be decorated so lavishly, Mrs. Howard."

"A hobby of mine to keep me busy."

"You've outdone last year," the Sundance's captain said, then continued to the back of the line.

"I have to agree, Celeste. You had to be working for

months on these decorations." Rachel picked up her plate at the beginning of the long table. "Brad, I've been telling Jake all about the changes you're making. I wanted to show him around, but I have to get the next payroll out by Wednesday instead of Friday."

Jake squeezed Rachel's hand. "That's okay. Brad said something about giving me a tour when we talked earlier." He looked right at the owner. "Maybe you have some time tomorrow."

"Sure. I'd been thinking about it since we talked earlier. How about eleven thirty?"

"That's good." Jake filled his plate with potato casserole, green beans with almond slices, mandarin pasta salad and bread. To Rachel he asked, "Do you think carrying two big plates might be uncouth?"

Rachel nodded her head toward Brad. "You'll be in good company."

By the time they sat at the table Aunt Linda had saved for them, Rachel's stomach was rumbling loud enough that Jake chuckled. "You should have gotten a second plate."

She grinned at him. "That's okay. I'll go back for seconds, then you and I need to dance the calories off afterward."

"Weren't you listening? My ability to dance hasn't improved one bit from high school."

"It doesn't take a brain surgeon to figure out how to slow dance. You just rock back and forth to the music."

"If he doesn't, Rachel, I would be glad to," Gramps said as he cut a big piece of the prime rib and slid it into his mouth.

But hours later as the crowd dwindled to half the

guests, Jake came up behind her chair, bent over and murmured, "If you still want to dance, I will."

She turned her head and peered over her shoulder, Jake's mouth inches from hers. She leaned back, her pulse racing. "You don't have to."

"No way am I going to let my grandfather put me to shame. Look at him dance." Jake gestured toward Lawrence and Aunt Linda on the floor with the other couples. "I must have inherited some of his genes." He held out his hand for her.

She took it and rose, and ten seconds later he whisked her into his arms and swept her out into the middle of the other dancers. "I thought you didn't know how to."

"I don't, but I've been watching. I'm a quick study."

When he suddenly dipped her and twirled her around, she stopped. "Who have you been watching?"

"Gramps, who else?"

"You might follow someone younger."

His forehead crunched, and he scanned the couples around them. "Oh, you mean like this." He dropped her hand he held out straight and clasped his arms around her middle, slowed his pace and began swaying. "Is this better?"

"Much," she said as she laid her head on his shoulder, the day's activities catching up with her, her heartbeat thumping against her rib cage. But in the midst of her possible assailants, she felt safe with Jake.

With his scent swirling around her, she closed her eyes, imagining them alone—no drug smugglers, attempts on their lives or a murder victim. If only it were that way.

As Rachel stared out the window on the passenger's side of her Jeep, she wanted to dwell on last night when, for a short time, she could believe all was well with her world. But all she had to do was look at Jake's scrapes and bruises on his face to know otherwise.

Jake pulled in front of the fishery's headquarters and parked. Rachel turned toward him. The next couple of days would be the best chance to catch the drug smugglers as they sent out their last shipments of the year—at least they hoped they would. After the holidays, Jake would be gone, and she hated the idea of going to work and wondering who to trust at the fishery—or in town, for that matter. If Brad's silent partner in Seattle was behind this, the blow to Port Aurora could be devastating. But the town's revival shouldn't be from illegal activities.

"Remember, go about your duties and no more snooping. Gramps, Chance and I will take care of that. Okay?"

"Yes, I have a lot to do today. The checks go out two days early, but no one remembers to send me the paperwork I need. Also, since this is the end of the year, there's a lot to do with the books, information to track down." She started to get out, stopped and glanced at Jake, taking in his face she'd known for years but seeing so much more there than when they had been teenagers. "By the way, I poked around in the accounts and can't find any unusual amounts coming in or going out."

"Probably a second set of books to keep this from you."

She smiled, watching his expression, set in determination as if his mind was already on the task of catching the drug smugglers. "Be careful. I don't want to have to worry about you."

As she turned away, Jake clasped her arm and tugged

her back to him. He laid his lips over hers and drew her as close to him as he could with a console in between them. The sensations she'd been trying to suppress came to the foreground. No other man ever made her feel as Jake did.

When he pulled back, he cupped her face, and his gaze locked with hers. "And I don't want to have to worry about you. We're gonna talk when things are settled down in Port Aurora."

The intensity in his voice sent flutters through her stomach. "About what?"

"Us."

"About being friends?"

"No, we're past that. I'm not sure where we're headed, but I know I care more for you than just a friend."

"You're right, this is different. We aren't the two teenagers who hung out together and were best friends." She ran her finger across his lips, wishing they weren't sitting in the parking lot of the fishery. "I guess I'd better go to work." Although at the moment she didn't want to leave the car.

"Stay safe."

"I intend to. Only my duties, no extracurricular activities. I feel better with Chance O'Malley coming in this morning."

"Yeah, while we're at the airport, we're going to take a look around. We'll have to be quick so I can go on that tour with Brad."

She opened the door. "Come see me after the tour. Maybe we can catch a late lunch."

"Sounds good."

The grin that spread across his face radiated charm,

making her want to stay, to be with him, to discover everything that happened to him during their eight-year separation. When she was inside the building, she had a bounce to her step as she walked to her office. Then she spied the work on her desk, and reality came crashing down.

She hung her parka on the peg behind the door and locked her purse in her bottom drawer, then sat. All she wanted to do was think about Jake's kiss and the fact he wanted to talk about their relationship, but the ringing of the phone jolted her back to the present, and she answered it.

"This is Mrs. Cohen. I received a call from Captain Martin. He had an emergency and won't be able to run the time cards to you this morning. He said just go on his boat and into his cabin. They're on the table by his bunk."

"Is there something wrong?"

"He's taking his wife to the doctor. She was up all night sick." Even over the phone, Eva Cohen's formality and strict discipline came across in her tone.

"I will. Thanks for letting me know."

Brad's secretary hung up without saying goodbye or giving Rachel a chance to.

Before leaving for the harbor, she checked all the necessary paperwork she needed from each boat and wrote the few names of the ones who still hadn't sent theirs. She might as well go by each one and pick up what she needed if the captain was there. This was one of her biggest headaches—getting what she needed to do her job, especially with the growth in the number of boats the fishery utilized.

After bundling up because the wind was strong coming off the bay, Rachel strolled to the pier. Dawn was sneaking into the night sky with a few splashes of yellow and rose to the east. She hadn't heard if a storm was brewing out in the Bering Sea. That body of water could be treacherous, especially in the winter months, even without bad weather.

Her first stop was the Tundra King. She rang the bell the captain had posted on the dock to signal someone wanted to come aboard. When no one appeared on deck, she was tempted to climb onto the boat and take a look around. Then she remembered her promise to Jake and clanged the clapper against the bronze with more force.

She'd come by at the end and see if anyone was on the boat by then. She turned to leave when Captain Kirk Cohen came out of the wheelhouse.

"Sorry. I saw you and knew what you wanted. Here are the time sheets and catch info." The captain walked along the side of the trawler until he reached where she was on the dock and handed her the papers.

She nearly lost them in the exchange as the wind whipped between vessels. "Thanks."

As she left, she nodded toward Beau Cohen and another member of the Tundra King's crew as they passed her on the dock to hop on board. Before disappearing inside the boat, Beau winked at her, the gesture startling her. What was he up to?

She visited three more trawlers before she arrived at the Sundance, her last stop before returning to the warmth of her office. She went on board and made her way to the captain's quarters on the deck level. His cabin was to the fore and through the galley and salon for the crew while at sea.

She knocked on the closed door in case Captain Mar-

tin was able to return to the boat earlier than he antici-
pated. When no one answered, she eased it open and
stepped into his quarters with a view of the harbor out
the bank of windows. The choppy water rocked the
ninety-foot boat. The fishermen were used to walking
in rough seas. She wasn't. The papers she needed were
right where Mrs. Cohen said they were. She walked
from one piece of furniture to the next, scooped up the
manila envelope with her name on it and started back
toward the door.

Standing just inside, Beau and Captain Martin blocked
her only means of escape. Danger emanated from both
men from their clenched fists to their scowling faces.

ELEVEN

In the reception area of the small building attached to a hangar at the Port Aurora Airport, Jake waited while Chance's plane landed. He was thankful it was able to land since the crosswinds were getting stronger. The twin-engine Cessna fought them and made it—barely. Jake released a long-held breath as the door opened and his friend exited.

Jake, with Mitch on a leash by his side, left the building to meet the state trooper partway. They shook hands, then hurried inside, stomping the snow off their boots.

"Glad you're here." Jake closed the door.

"I wasn't sure we were going to land. It was shaky, and I'm used to going to out-of-the-way places in Alaska." Chance leaned over and petted Mitch. "He's looking great. Retirement agrees with him." Chance slid Jake an assessing look. "How are you doing?"

"I'm managing. Although this trip back home hasn't been what I thought it would be." Jake pointed at his single duffel bag. "Any other luggage?"

"Nope. I brought only what was necessary."

Jake went to the counter, leaning against it. "Will you let us know if any planes will land or take off tomorrow? My friend, Chance O'Malley, may have to go back to Anchorage earlier than planned." He slipped her a card with his cell and the bed-and-breakfast's number.

The woman behind the counter smiled. "Yes. There's one scheduled tomorrow at ten, weather permitting. Mostly flying in supplies and taking a big shipment from the fishery, but he might be able to tag along as a passenger. There is another flight right before sundown, too, if he needs to leave later."

"How about Wednesday?"

"The same schedule as Tuesday."

"Thanks, Toni." Jake smiled at the lady, then headed for the door. "Let's go, Chance."

Outside, Jake quickened his pace to the Jeep parked at the side of the building. When they were both inside, he angled toward his friend. "I went to school with Toni, who runs this airport with her husband. I had no trouble looking around before you arrived. No shipments for the fishery in the hangar. The flight you were on is the only one today. It isn't taking back much cargo except letters and packages, although it did bring in the mail and some supplies for the general store. I think the drugs will be shipped tomorrow or Wednesday."

"How about by boat?"

"Gramps has paid the harbormaster a visit. They're friends. He thought he would play some dominoes with Charlie. They usually end up doing more talking than making moves." Jake drove toward town.

"So we're going to the harbor?"

"No, I'm taking you to the bed-and-breakfast. Your room has a great view of the buildings and the harbor. I thought we could use it for surveillance purposes. The owner of Port Aurora Fishery is giving me a tour at eleven thirty. I want to see what's going on in the ship-ping warehouse. I think the drugs are probably going from the boats to there." Jake withdrew a diagram of the harbor and buildings and handed it to Chance. "Then I'll be back, and we all can have lunch and talk strategy."

"Sounds good. I might take a walk to familiarize myself with the town."

"I should be back around one, and you'll get to meet my friend, Rachel."

"The lady that started all of this?"

Jake laughed. "Yep. Gramps is supposed to head here when he's through pumping his friend for information."

Jake left Chance at the bed-and-breakfast and hur-ried across the street and toward the harbor. He was to meet Brad at his office. Inside, he decided to stop by Rachel's first and tell her Chance made it.

As he approached the open door, he remembered the night before. She felt right in his arms as they slow danced. For a while all he thought about was her—not the drugs, attempts on them or Betty's murder. Then at the end, when everyone lit a candle and the lights went out in the hall, he held her hand as they sang "Si-lent Night." In that moment he missed being home. He missed being with Rachel more. His life in Anchorage wouldn't be the same unless he could persuade Rachel to move there.

When he stepped into the doorway, he opened his mouth to say hi, but the empty office mocked him. Where was she? He walked in and looked around. Her coat was gone. For a few seconds concern nibbled at him. Then he remembered all she said she had to do.

He wrote her a brief note about lunch and stuck it on her computer screen, then went in search of Brad.

When he met Mrs. Cohen, Brad's secretary, he immediately understood Rachel's misgivings about the woman. An iceberg might be warmer than that lady. She stood when he came in and looked at him out the lower part of her glasses. He didn't let her demeanor stop him from saying, "I'm here to see Mr. Howard."

"Does he have an appointment with you?"

"Yes, eleven thirty. Jake Nichols." Mitch, standing beside him, made a low growl. Jake stroked him, but his dog remained tense though quiet.

A brief frown descended, directed at Mitch, before she replaced it with her haughty look. "I'll let him know."

He decided to rattle her. "That's okay. I can." With Mitch next to him, Jake strode toward the door and thrust it open.

Mrs. Cohen charged past him into Brad's office. "I—I... He says he has an appointment with you, but I don't have it down."

Brad waved his hand. "Sorry. I forgot to tell you. We made it last night at the party."

She heaved a deep breath, then spun on her heel and left.

Jake started to make a comment, but Brad held his palm up and he mouthed the word, "Wait."

Brad pushed back his chair and said, "I'm eager to show you all that has been done this year," then grabbed his overcoat and shrugged into it. "We'll start with the plans I have for an additional processing center."

Jake wanted to steer him to shipping, but if Brad was involved in the drug smuggling, he didn't want to be too obvious. It bothered him that a friend he'd known as a child could be caught up in the illegal activities, but

Brad had always had rich tastes, so it really wouldn't surprise him if he was having financial problems.

When Jake reached the hall, remnants of the Christmas party had been cleaned up, except the tables and chairs. "If I didn't know better, I wouldn't believe such a wonderful celebration went on last night in this place."

"That's Celeste. She put it on and made sure it was taken care of this morning. She loves doing stuff like that." He swept his arm to indicate the large area. "Some men are going to come in late this afternoon and remove the tables and chairs, and then this will be one big empty room. Celeste is a great organizer."

As Brad talked about Celeste, his comments didn't bother Jake. His feelings for Celeste were gone. During the party as he watched her move among the guests, decked out in an expensive red dress, not a hair out of place, he realized her leaving him before they were to be married was the best thing in the long run. He'd been dazzled by her beauty, and although she was gracious and kind to the townspeople, she always held herself apart as though she were playing a role. He didn't think he'd really known the person behind the facade.

Whereas with Rachel, he used to be able to predict her next move. She knew him better than even Gramps when they were growing up. Everything she was thinking was right there in the open. No guessing. A person knew where he stood with Rachel.

"Everyone enjoyed themselves, and the prime rib was a big hit." Jake also didn't hold a grudge against Brad because he moved in on Celeste when she was engaged. Letting go of the anger freed him. Now he understood what Gramps and Rachel had said about forgiveness. Being mad at Brad and Celeste really only hurt him in the long run. He was the one who stayed away from Port Aurora and let any relationship he had with Rachel dwindle to almost nothing.

Brad stopped in the middle of the cavernous room and slowly rotated all the way around. "I need to talk to you without people seeing or listening."

His hushed tones drew Jake's full attention and Brad's action, rubbing his palms together, looking from side to side, held Jake's concentration. He slipped his hand into his parka and grasped his gun. Had Brad lured him here to kill him? Every nerve ending sharpened its awareness.

Finally, as though satisfied they were alone, Brad stepped closer and expelled a deep breath. "Some strange things have been going on at the fishery. I think Ivan is doing something illegal behind my back. On Sunday I was going to go into shipping and do some checking, but the lock had been changed. I didn't authorize that."

"Did you ask him about the new lock?" Jake held up his hand for a few seconds while he stuck his other hand into the top shirt pocket and showed Brad he was recording their conversation using his cell phone.

Brad gave him a slight nod. "Yes. He said he just did it and had forgotten to tell me. He would have a new key for me this week."

"What was wrong with the old one?"

"Nothing. But it was old and could be picked easily according to Ivan."

"Is that true?"

Brad combed his fingers through his hair. "I guess so. Up until Betty's murder, serious crimes didn't happen in Port Aurora. I suppose I've let security go lax because our town has been relatively untouched by crime, especially in the winter months." He sighed. "But with the expansion, more people are coming to Port Aurora, and crime is increasing."

Was Brad playing him? Was he really innocent of the drug smuggling? "What do you think is going on?"

"It's got to be some kind of smuggling. Maybe drugs. I don't know. I've looked at Rachel's accounting, and everything seems on the up and up, but have you ever had a gut feeling something is wrong and it is?"

"Yes. I've learned to trust my gut. Who do you think is working with Ivan? If he's smuggling something in, he has to have coconspirators. Where is he getting the drugs from, if it is drugs?"

"That's why I'm talking to you. I don't know. There are parts of this fishery I don't have access to. I'm the owner. I've always gone freely anywhere around my company. Now doors are locked in buildings and to buildings."

"What doors in which buildings?"

"I went into shipping this morning to talk to Ivan, and then I walked around. One freezer was locked and a small storage room."

"What did Ivan say about that?" Jake asked, studying Brad for any signs of lying.

"Nothing. I couldn't find him."

Still not sure if he could trust Brad, Jake asked, "What do you want me to do?"

"You're a police officer."

"Not here in town."

"Okay, I don't know if I can trust ours. Ivan and Officer Steve Bates are good friends. I've seen them hanging out together at night."

Jake thought back to Friday night and recalled seeing Bates come into the Harbor Bar and Grill and sit at the bar. Ivan sat next to him for part of the night before the officer left. They talked occasionally during that time but also to others. That fit with what Betty said to Rachel about not trusting anyone.

"What do you want to do?" Jake wasn't going to say anything about a state police officer staying at the bed-and-breakfast until he felt Brad wasn't playing him.

"Contact some people you trust. I'll give them permission to search the whole fishery. If there isn't a problem, then I've overreacted, but I'll be relieved that the company is doing only legal business."

"Let's go, then." Jake started for the exit.

The sound of a shot cracked the air.

Rachel gulped and backed up against the table. As she gripped its edge, strength flowed from her legs, but somehow she managed to keep herself upright as Beau came toward her and Captain Martin shut the door.

She fought the fear attacking every part of her. Beau was muscular and huge. *Is he the one who hit Aunt Betty so hard she died?* Trembling followed the fear and encompassed her whole body.

Beau gripped her upper arms and jerked her toward the bunk nearby. After he shoved her down, he took out a rope and yanked her hands together, then bound them in front of her. When he produced a second length of rough twine, he knelt, removed her boots and tied her ankles together so tight she didn't think blood would circulate to her feet.

"Too bad you had to be so nosy. Now we have a

mess to clean up," Captain Martin said, still standing by the exit.

"I came in to get the payroll papers," she said in a quavering voice. "As Mrs. Cohen told me."

"Don't take us for fools." Beau stepped back from the bunk.

"Just ask her."

"I know she did because I told her to. It's all the other snooping you've been doing." Captain Martin glared at her.

"What are you going to do with me?"

"Why, kill you, my dear. Didn't you get the message that snoops end up dead like Betty?" The captain shook his head and put his hand on the door handle. "You don't cross the Russian mafia."

As Captain Martin left, Rachel peered at Beau. "I don't know anything."

"We know a state trooper flew in this morning. That ain't a coincidence."

"I don't know a state trooper."

Beau backed away from the bunk, his cackles sending goose bumps down her body. "You might not but your boyfriend does. Don't worry, he'll get his due soon enough."

"You don't need to kill me. Use me as a hostage."

His hideous laughter filled the cabin. "We don't need you. When the rest of the crew is here, we're putting out to sea. When we're far enough out, I'm going to kill you, then dump your body over. The current will take you where no one will find you. Frankly, after the fish take care of you, you won't be recognizable. You know it might be fun just to toss you into the water alive and let nature take its course."

As Beau turned toward the door, Rachel sent a prayer to God. *I need Your help. Anything is possible through You.* There was still time that Jake could save her.

"Oh, just in case you think your boyfriend is going to come to your rescue, he won't. He's being taken care of as well as the state trooper. Then people in Port Aurora will learn who really runs the town." Beau slammed the door as he left, the lock clicking into place.

Leaving Rachel alone.

Devastated.

Hopeless.

A bullet whizzed by Jake and struck Brad, who cried out. As he collapsed to the floor, Jake dropped down and knocked a metal table onto its side to use as a shield, rolling it to also protect Brad. The shooter was behind a concrete pillar about fifteen yards away.

Mitch jerked on his leash, wanting to do what he had for years. Jake couldn't risk him, even though his K-9's heart was in it. He pointed to Brad and said to Mitch in a low voice, "Lie down. Stay." When his dog was stretched out beside Brad, guarding him, Jake asked his friend, "Where are you hit?" as he cased out their chances of getting out alive.

Brad moaned. "Ch—est."

Another shot blasted and splintered the corner of the table by Jake's head, a fragment piercing his cheek. He hoped the assailant was counting on Jake being unarmed since he was on vacation. He contemplated returning fire but wanted to see if the man would do something foolish like rush him.

He peeked around the table and saw a man dressed in a black ski mask dart to the next pillar. Jake still didn't shoot when the assailant came out from behind that protection and raced to the nearest concrete support, forcing Jake to roll the table to the side to shelter Brad, Mitch and him.

Minutes ticked away with only silence from the shooter. Was he playing his own mind game? Jake sneaked a look and noticed a door behind where the assailant was. Did he escape? Would he be coming in another door to take him by surprise?

He needed to know. Jake popped up, taunting the guy to shoot him.

Nothing.

Jake had to get medical help for Brad—fast. He took out his cell and called Randall. Although not totally sure how involved the police were in the drug-smuggling ring, it was a risk he had to take. He needed assistance, or Brad would bleed out. The red splotch on his coat was growing quickly.

"Randall, this is Jake. I'm at the hall at the fishery where the party was last night. Someone shot Brad, and he's bleeding a lot. The shooter may or may not still be here. He was behind the third support pillar from the back on the left side."

"Be there."

They needed more protection in case the assailant had escaped and was coming in another door. Jake placed the table where he could rush to the next one and lift it onto its side to be a second shield. He dragged Brad closer to the back exit with Mitch moving beside the fishery owner. As Jake upturned a third table, the shooter leaned out from the pillar and fired several rounds at them. The last bullet grazed his arm. He winced. Ignoring the pain, he focused totally on what he had to do to get them out alive.

This time Jake shot back, and the guy ducked behind the concrete support. After positioning the third table, Jake pulled Brad even closer to the door. Adrenaline pumping, Jake was deciding if he should go for a fourth one when the door on the assailant's side burst open, and the police chief and an officer rushed into the building. While they pinned the shooter down, Jake tugged Brad to the back exit with Mitch beside them. Brad had passed out, and Jake prayed the one ambulance in town was there.

His arm throbbing, Jake opened the door and used his leg to hold it ajar while he hauled Brad the rest of the way out of the building. When Jake straightened, an officer ran toward him, gesturing at the ambulance speeding into the parking lot. The two paramedics jumped out, and one hurried to Brad while the other retrieved the gurney from the back.

Once the paramedics took over, Jake said to Mitch, "Stay," then headed toward the door, intending to help the police inside.

The officer stopped him. "You're hurt. You need to go with the paramedics, too."

Jake glanced at his arm, blood on his coat sleeve, but nothing like Brad's. "Not until I'm sure Randall is all right. Who is with him?"

"Officer Bates."

When the engine started on the *Sundance*, Rachel knew her time was ticking down quickly. Once they were away from the harbor and out of sight of land, she would be killed and tossed into the sea. If she didn't die from the bullet, the frigid water would kill her.

The boat began moving. Rachel wiggled off the bunk until she could stand up. She looked out the bank of windows at the front of the trawler. She wasn't giving up. If she could get to the window, maybe somehow she could signal for help. The only way was to hop the ten feet.

Slowly, she jumped toward the windows, but when she was only two feet away, the trawler picked up speed close to the mouth of the harbor. The sudden jerk forward sent her to the floor, her left shoulder slamming into the wooden planks, her head bouncing up then down.

Pain radiated from her arm. She rolled onto her back and stared up at the ceiling as the boat accelerated even more. *I was too late.* The thought taunted her with despair.

No, you aren't going to win. I'm in God's hands. He's with me.

She pushed herself to a sitting position and scanned the cabin for any kind of tool to help her untie herself. Once freed she would find a weapon to use. She wasn't going down without a fight.

Using her knees to bear her weight, she bridged the distance to the bunk and plopped her tied hands onto it to assist her up. When she straightened to a stand, she scanned the cabin for anything to help her untie her hands. All she saw was a glass in a holder on the desk. She inched along the bunk toward it, steadying herself when the boat pitched. Her stomach roiled like the waves did. Fighting the nausea, she reached the edge of the desk and used it to move down its length.

The Sundance veered to the right, and Rachel flung herself across the desktop to keep herself upright. Sucking in shallow breaths, she tried to calm her racing heartbeat. The glass was inches away. She rolled partway on her side and reached for it. Her fingertips grasped the lip of the drinking cup and she lifted it from its holder, barely clutched between her two hands, the coarse rope chafing her wrists.

Her chest burned with lack of adequate oxygen. Again the trawler lurched, this time to the left. Rachel slid to the floor, the back of her head hitting the leg of the desk. She heard the glass hit the wooden floor and shatter. For a few seconds she closed her eyes, the nausea rising into her throat.

Lord, I need You.

Slowly, she opened her eyes to the swaying room. She found the shards of glass and plucked up the largest one to slice her ropes. Back and forth she maneuvered the jagged piece, occasionally its sharp edge slashing into her wrist. The blood flowing from the wounds made it harder to hold the slippery piece of glass, but she couldn't stop.

They were going to kill her if she didn't do something. As she repeated that over and over, she kept working on cutting the ropes about her hands while listening for anyone approaching.

Then the sound of footsteps echoed the warning one of the thugs was coming for her. Were they already far enough from land to kill her? Frantically, she sawed the last part of the twine binding her hands. It fell away, and she hurriedly went to work on the ropes around her ankles. The door handle rattled as though a key were being inserted.

* * *

His Glock in his grip, Jake eased the back door into the hall open and used the rolled tables to sneak forward. The sound of a gunshot reverberated through the cold air. Peeping around his barrier, he assessed the situation, needing to know where the police chief, Officer Bates and the man in the ski mask were. Jake glimpsed Bates coming into the room from the side door near the rear while Randall stood at the far end. In between lay a still body with a black ski mask on, probably shot by the police chief. Bates hurried to the downed perpetrator and felt his pulse.

"Is he alive?" Randall walked toward the shooter on the floor and his officer.

Bates took the gun on the concrete and rose. "Yes." Then he lifted the assailant's gun and aimed it toward the police chief. Randall halted, his eyes widening.

Jake stood and squeezed off a shot a second before Bates did. The blast resounded through the hall as Randall dove to the left and Bates collapsed to the floor, the gun skidding across the concrete. Jake rushed him as the officer fumbled for his gun holstered at his side.

He made it to Bates a few steps ahead of the police chief. "Don't force me to shoot again." Jake pointed his Glock at the officer's head.

The ski-masked man on the floor groaned and tried to get up. Randall pushed him down, then rolled him over and removed his black covering. Sean's eyes glared up at the police chief, then connected with Jake's.

Although Jake had told Rachel he suspected everyone until proven innocent, seeing Sean lying on the floor stunned him. Jake felt like he'd been punched in the gut, all air rushing from his lungs. He clenched his jaws together so tightly that pain streaked down his neck.

Sean looked away. "You're gonna regret this," Sean said through gritted teeth as he clutched the side of his stomach, blood leaking through his fingers.

"I'll call the ambulance to come back for these two and have your officer Clark come in to help you. Then I've got to make sure Rachel, Gramps and Chance are okay. Chance is a state police officer who can assist you in searching the shipping warehouse and processing center." Jake kept his voice low so no one could overhear him. He was still concerned. Where was Ivan?

Randall frowned. "Why didn't you let me know he was coming?"

Jake pointedly looked at Officer Bates. "I wasn't sure who to trust." He hurried toward the back door, hoping that Officer Clark was nearby.

The police chief called out, "I've got another man coming. He was on a call outside town."

As Jake exited the building, the ambulance pulled away with Officer Clark coming toward him. "I need you to call the ambulance back as soon as Brad is dropped off."

"I heard gunshots, but Chief asked me to stay with Brad until he was safely away from here. Who's hurt?"

"Sean O'Hara and Bates." Jake refused to acknowledge Bates as part of law enforcement.

Officer Clark tensed. "Is Chief Quay all right? How bad is Bates?"

Jake signaled Mitch to come to him. "Randall is okay, and Bates was hit in the left thigh. He'll survive and go to jail." The police chief needed help. Jake hoped the rest weren't on the payroll of the drug-smuggling ring.

"What do you mean?" A scowl grooved deep lines in Clark's forehead.

"He tried to kill Chief Quay. I'll let him explain it. How is Brad?"

"The paramedics said it was a through and through in his shoulder. He should be all right once he gets to the clinic."

"Good. I've got to find Rachel."

Jake took off in a jog toward the fishery head-quarters, hoping she was back in her office. When he reached her office, the vacant room goaded him into searching the whole building. No one he saw knew where Rachel was. Jake, with Mitch beside him, ended his hunt at Brad's office.

His secretary rose when he came into the room. "May I help you?"

"Have you seen Rachel? It's urgent."

"No. I haven't talked with her this morning."

"Any suggestions where she could be?"

"She could be anywhere. She flits from one place to the next." Disapproval dripped from the secretary's words.

"Thanks." He started to turn away when he heard Mrs. Cohen pull a drawer open. He stopped and swung back as the older woman raised a gun.

As the lock clicked open, Rachel dove across the bunk for the nearest weapon she could see, binoculars, which she gripped while she scrambled to hide behind the door.

When Captain Martin came into the cabin, Rachel used all her strength and brought the improvised weapon down on the back of his head. For a couple of seconds, he remained standing, and Rachel started to hit him again, but he crumbled to the floor. She quickly closed the door and then checked to see if he was alive. Blood oozed from his wound.

The only rope not cut up was the one around her ankles. She took it and brought his hands behind his back and tied him up. Then she spied a smelly rag and stuffed it into his mouth. She searched his pockets for the key to the cabin, found it and grabbed her boots. After slipping them on and snatching her coat from a chair, she hurried to the door and peeked out into the short hallway. Clear.

Without another thought, she quickly left, locking the cabin, then hurrying to the end of the corridor. If she could get to the life raft on the side of the trawler without being seen, she hoped she could lower it to the water and somehow escape. It was that or remain and be killed. It wasn't the best plan, but she didn't even know if Jake thought she was missing. She would take her chances with the Bering Sea. The water felt calmer than before, but when she emerged outside, she still saw whitecaps from the waves.

She snuck toward the life raft in its white container on the side, keeping an eye on the door to the wheelhouse, where Beau and whoever else was on board probably were. She'd seen a demonstration once a year ago and prayed she remembered how to do it. With one line tied to the railing, she tossed the canister overboard, and when it hit the water, she jerked the painter line two times to inflate the life raft. As it filled with air,

Rachel had to wait a couple of minutes, the whole time scanning her surroundings.

From inside she heard a shout. Did someone see her out here? She had to jump now even though the raft wasn't quite blown up. More loud voices came from the wheelhouse, and the door began to open. Her heartbeat thundering in her ears, she leaped over the side, hoping she hit her mark, rather than the ice-cold water. The second she landed in the life raft, she untied the rope and looked up.

Beau poked his head over the railing, saw her and pulled his gun from his waist. She ducked inside the covered boat as a shot rang out.

"Don't," Jake said in a tight voice over the sound of Mitch's growls, his Glock aimed at Mrs. Cohen's chest. "I won't hesitate to use this if I have to."

Her arm stopped in midlift, anger hardening her features.

No doubt Mrs. Cohen heard the gunshots at the fishery. "So you are involved in the drug-smuggling ring." Every muscle in Jake locked, ready to react at the slightest movement from the woman.

She pressed her lips together.

"Put the gun down and walk from behind the desk." Jake took several steps toward her. "Mitch might have only three legs, but he can attack. He can still perform his police dog duties."

Her narrowed gaze stabbing into Jake, Mrs. Cohen slowly laid the gun down, then skirted the desk.

He stood behind the older woman, wishing he had a set of handcuffs. "Mitch, guard." Then he urged Mrs. Cohen forward. "Where's Rachel?"

"I don't know what you're talking about. I have no idea what you think I'm guilty of, but I have a permit to carry that gun. I was defending myself against a man waving a gun at me."

He ground his teeth to keep from replying. Outside, he headed with Mrs. Cohen toward Randall talking to two of his officers near the shipping warehouse.

The police chief saw him and came toward him. "What happened?"

Before Jake could answer Randall, Mrs. Cohen said, "I want this man arrested for pulling a gun on me."

"She's involved, possibly the ringleader. She refuses to tell me where Rachel is, and I don't have time to wait for her to smarten up."

"I'll take her from here. Can I use Mitch in the shipping warehouse? We haven't found Ivan, but while my men are searching for him, I want to see if your dog can detect where the drugs are."

"Brad gave his okay to search the whole fishery, although in this case you don't need it since we were ambushed." Jake passed his K-9's leash to the police chief and gave a signal for Mitch to go with Randall. Then Jake headed for the bed-and-breakfast. He needed help finding Rachel and prayed he was overreacting.

When he reached the house and walked down the hallway toward Chance's room, a cold lump in the pit of his stomach spread its icy fingers. He entered and came to a halt, standing over a prone body, gagged and bound on the floor. Gramps sat on the bed with his rifle pointed at the stocky, unfamiliar man. Hatred in his blue eyes drilled into his grandfather, then shifted to Jake.

Before he could find out what happened, the door to the bathroom opened and Chance came out, sporting the beginnings of a black eye. "You'll have to fill me in later. Have either of you seen Rachel in the past hour leaving the fishery headquarters?"

Gramps shook his head.

"What's she wearing?" Chance asked.

"A powder-blue parka with fur around the hood. Black pants and boots. She's about five feet five."

"I saw a woman of that description heading for the pier about forty minutes ago. She stopped at a boat, and a man handed her a manila envelope, then she moved on to another one."

"That was the time I was at the café grabbing coffee for us while we staked out the shipping warehouse. I didn't see her, son."

"Brad and I were ambushed in the hall by Sean. Officer Bates tried to shoot Chief Quay. Obviously, this one was sent to take care of you two."

"There was another—Ivan Verdin. He got away and is sporting a limp." Gramps frowned. "I ain't as spry as I used to be, or he would be hogtied like this one." He shoved to his feet. "Let's go find Rachel while you tell me the details about your ambush."

"I'll take this one to a police cruiser, then check in with Chief Quay and let him know about Ivan. I've already called in reinforcements." Chance hoisted the captured assailant to his feet.

Jake followed his grandfather to the door, paused in the doorway and said to Chance, "Brad gave his permission to search the fishery, and the police chief is using Mitch to help him."

Then he left. As they approached the port facilities overlooking the harbor, Jake told Gramps about the shootout in the hall.

Charlie grinned when he saw Gramps coming inside. "You just can't stay away. Once a fisherman always…" His voice trailed off into silence as he took in their serious expressions. "I'm pretty isolated over here. Were you two involved in the commotion at the fishery?"

"Yes, we're looking for Rachel Hart. Have you seen her lately at the pier?" Jake asked.

"About thirty minutes ago."

"Where?" Jake's gut solidified into a hard knot.

"She was going on the Sundance."

Why? "Did you see her get off or go anywhere else?"

"She went by several boats. She does that a few times a week."

"Which boats?"

Charlie rubbed his nape. "Let's see. The Alaskan King was one." He snapped his fingers. "And the Tundra King as well as Bering's Folly."

Jake walked to the large glass plate window that overlooked the harbor from the right side, opposite the fishery. "I see the Alaskan King and Bering's Folly in port. Were the Tundra King and Sundance going back out?"

Charlie's thick gray eyebrows slashed together. "I've been in the back eating lunch so I didn't see them leaving. They weren't supposed to be. Tundra King was delivering a shipment to Seattle but not until tomorrow." He crossed the harbormaster's office and stood next to Jake.

Jake pivoted toward Gramps. "I'm going to the pier to see if anyone has seen Rachel. I don't have a good feeling about this, especially with someone going after Brad."

Gramps frowned. "Why did they try to kill Brad?"

"Because he knew something was going on and wanted my help."

"Son, I'm coming with you."

"Gramps, you have to go back to Chance and have him alert the Coast Guard. They need to check those boats and hunt for Ivan. I hope that Chance can get Sean, Bates or the other thug to talk." Jake strode to the door and left.

He quickened his pace toward the pier. Seeing the flags flapping in the wind, he realized its force had died down. He hoped the storm forming had diminished. Jake started with the first boat and worked his way toward where Tundra King and Sundance were moored. Either no one was around or they saw Rachel coming to the docks but didn't see her leave. The wind didn't have to blow to send a chill down his spine. One of those boats took Rachel out to sea.

He couldn't shake that thought as he approached the Blue Runner and stepped on board. "Tom, are you here?" he called out when he opened the back door that led into the living quarters.

The captain came out of the galley, took one look at Jake's face and said, "I thought I heard gunshots. What happened? I was just grabbing a cup of coffee. Want any?"

"No, have you seen Rachel this morning?"

"Sure. She stopped by and checked to see how I was doing about an hour ago. Why?"

"She's missing. Why was she down at the docks?"

Tom sipped his coffee and looked out the window. "Getting time sheets and paperwork for payroll. I turned mine in. Others don't always. It's been a frustration for her, especially the new captains."

"Did you see where she went after talking to you?"

"Yeah, the Tundra King."

A tightness constricted Jake's chest. "Did she go on board?"

"No, she rang the bell the captain set up for visitors. Finally, he came out and gave her a manila envelope. Then she went to the Sundance, the dock over." Tom pointed in the right direction.

"Did you see her leave the Sundance?"

"No, but I wasn't watching all the time. I was working on a maintenance schedule."

"Did you see either boat leave the harbor?" All he could drag into his lungs were shallow breaths as his heart rate increased.

"The Tundra King. Suddenly, the crew appeared not long after Rachel had left and prepared to go to sea."

"But you didn't see the Sundance leave?"

"They must have in the last fifteen or twenty minutes while I was getting coffee and a sandwich."

"Thanks."

After Jake hopped off the Blue Runner, he hurried to the other dock, examining the wooden planks for a sign of what happened to Rachel. But there wasn't anything out of the ordinary. He stopped by each boat on that dock, but there was only one fisherman around, and he never saw Rachel get off the Sundance, but again he said he wasn't watching for it so she could have.

Enough wasted time. He hoped that Chance had alerted the Coast Guard, stationed at Port Aurora, by now because he didn't think Rachel had much time left. Their cutter was the best boat to go after the Sundance, especially with its head start. Jake prayed that Rachel was alive when they caught up with the boat.

TWELVE

Huddled beneath the canopy, Rachel sent up yet another prayer. More gunshots sounded, several striking her life raft. But the waves were carrying her farther away from the trawler. She peered around the opening and saw Beau hurrying toward the wheelhouse, no doubt to come after her while a Sundance crewman continued firing at her.

She ducked back under the canopy and moved from the opening. As she crawled away, a bullet struck the raft on the side near her. She heard the hissing of air leaking out.

Jake gripped the railing on the Coast Guard cutter at sea, heading toward the Sundance. The boat had been spotted. *Is she still alive? Or what if I have it wrong, and she's on the Tundra King?* A second Coast Guard ship had been dispatched from another station and would intercept the trawler on its course toward Seattle. But if she was on that boat, it could be too late by then.

Chance came up beside him. "Everything is set to stop the Tundra King."

"That's good." The icy wind whipped at him, but

Jake wouldn't go inside. He could see the Sundance in the distance and had been praying that they would rescue Rachel in time.

"We're making good time. I was told the Coast Guard would board first, then we could."

"What if they tossed her overboard before we get there?"

"There are spotters keeping an eye on the vessel. Smuggling is one thing. Murder is a bigger crime. Let's hope they decide to take the lesser of the charges."

Jake half turned toward his friend. "I'm a cop. I want to be at the front of the assault."

"Not your jurisdiction, but we wouldn't be here if it weren't for you."

"Still, we might not be in time. We don't even know if we have the right boat."

Chance clasped his shoulder. "We will. We're due a break."

Jake stayed at the railing while Chance went inside to go over the boarding with the crew. Little by little the cutter shrank the distance between them and the Sundance.

When the Coast Guard was near enough, the captain of the cutter announced over a PA system, "Halt. Prepare to be boarded."

The Sundance increased its speed. The cutter followed suit, and the captain again demanded they stop. When they didn't, the Coast Guard fired a warning shot near the vessel. Finally, the Sundance slowed and then stopped.

As the boarding party jumped onto the trawler, Jake waited until the last man had, then he and Chance hopped on to the boat, following behind the Coast

Guard crew. The sound of a blast cracked the air, and everyone dropped behind cover. More gunfire rained down on them. They weren't going to give up easily.

Jake was close to the side that led to the wheelhouse, while three shooters were at the back of the main cabin. He signaled to Chance to cover him while he ran forward, hoping he could come in behind the kidnappers. As the boat rocked back and forth in the increasing wind and waves, Jake raced toward the wheelhouse, low running past the side windows of the salon. He peeped into the wheelhouse. Empty.

When he eased the door open and snuck inside, he half expected someone to jump out. But it was clear. He headed for the galley and eating area between the wheelhouse and the main cabin. As he crept forward into the dining space, Beau popped up from behind the counter in the galley and fired at the same time Jake did, then dived into a nook that partially hid him. He immediately flattened himself against the wall as a crashing sound reverberated through the air.

Adrenaline pounding through him, he stole a quick glance into the galley. Jake spied an arm flung out on the floor, as though Beau had been hit and had gone down. He thought he might have hit him, but being cautious, he rushed forward, alert, his nerves on edge. When he found Beau down, he felt for a pulse. He was alive, but with a bleeding wound in his left shoulder. As Jake moved around him, he switched his attention between Beau and the main cabin.

There was a loud volley of gunshots, another thump to the floor, then someone shouted from the cabin, "I surrender."

While the four kidnappers were rounded up, Jake and

Chance searched the boat, going down below to check the two cabins before coming to the captain's. When Jake burst into the room, he hoped to find Rachel. Instead, Captain Martin lay on the floor, moaning behind a rag stuffed in his mouth.

While Chance checked the injured man, Jake moved to the bunk and picked up the pieces of cut rope. Anger swelled in Jake, and he threw them back on the mattress. She had to be here.

"He's coming around. I'll take care of him while you continue looking for Rachel." Chance pulled out his handcuffs.

As Jake began to leave, the captain murmured, "She's not here."

"I won't believe that until I search every inch of this vessel. She's here. I know it." *She has to be, Lord.*

The inside of the boat had been covered so he went aft to inspect the containers they put their catch in. As Jake passed through the salon where the Coast Guard had the two men handcuffed and a medic treating Beau, it was all Jake could do not to grab him and beat Rachel's location out of him. What if she had already been thrown overboard before they even spotted them?

Outside by the back of the boat, he flipped the lid on the first insulated box. Nothing. The second one was the same, but when he lifted the third top he found fish. Strange. He started to move on to the next container, stopped and went back to the last one. He plunged his arm into the box, his fingers grazing a metal bottom. Only the fish.

Straightening, he looked around. What was he missing?

The head of the boarding party joined Jake. "Did you find your lady friend?"

Rachel was more than that, but he might never have a chance to tell her how important she was to him. No, he wasn't giving up. "No. Chance and I looked everywhere. Any idea?"

"I'll have a couple of my men look around, too, while we interrogate the crew."

Jake trailed the lieutenant into the salon, glancing back at the sky starting to darken. Night would fall soon, which would make finding Rachel even harder.

The lieutenant conferred with one of his men guarding the three crew members, then he returned to Jake. "They haven't said anything, but he thinks the tall one at the end might say something. He looked afraid while the others were cocky."

"Then let's talk to them separately. We can start with that tall—"

"Lieutenant, the life raft is missing."

Jake watched the tall crew member's reaction. Flinching, he ducked his head and stared at his lap.

Jake lowered his voice and said, "I think the tall guy knows something."

"Then let's see what he has to say."

Jake and the lieutenant escorted the tall crewman to the wheelhouse. Before the guy could sit, Jake was in his face. "Where is Rachel? In the life raft?"

The crew member looked down at his feet.

"Do you know how serious the trouble you are in? Kidnapping. Attempted murder. Drug smuggling. If she dies, murder. You will never get out of prison. I'll personally see to that." Jake paused and drew in a fortifying breath. "The first person who helps will get a deal."

The tall guy raised his head and stared at Jake. "Yes,

the lady got into the life raft, but Beau shot at it and hit it several times. It has to be losing air."

"Was she injured?" It took all Jake's willpower to refrain from grabbing the man's shirt and yanking him close and shaking him.

The guy shrugged.

Jake started to come at the tall crewman, but the lieutenant grasped his arm and kept him still. "We'll find her. I'll call for a helicopter to help us look. It'll be dark soon and that will make it harder."

Jake left out the side where the life raft would have been stored and gazed out to sea, rough whitecaps everywhere. Was she shot and in pain? Was the raft intact?

Where are you, Rachel? I need you.

Freezing, Rachel peered out the opening in the protective canopy. The sun neared the horizon to the west. She looked around to see if she saw the Sundance or any boat. Nothing but the waves, which carried her farther away from the trawler, getting rougher and bigger.

Hugging her arms to her chest, she sat near the opening, the wind pushing the life raft—toward land or farther out to sea? What did she know about the life raft? The ones the company bought were double-tubed and had an Emergency Position Indicating Radio Beacon. But the Sundance wasn't part of the company's fleet. Did it have an emergency system? She crept around the six-person raft looking for the EPIRB. When she found it, relief swept through her. She pulled it from its bracket and flipped the switch, praying a rescue vessel reached her before the Sundance did. And before her raft was compromised by the bullet holes in it.

She huddled away from the opening with a flashlight

she grabbed near the EPIRB to use when she needed it. Shivers attacked her body like when she'd been pushed into the ice-cold water. Panic quickly followed.

God, anything is possible through You. Please send rescuers—send Jake. I have so much I need to say to him.

Slowly, her rapid heartbeat calmed as she thought of the Lord watching over her. As she thought of Jake. She'd loved him for years but hadn't realized the depth of her feelings. Could she bear a long-distance relationship?

As all light vanished, the waves attacked the life raft, tossing it about even with the ballasts on the bottom of the craft to keep it as steady as possible. She crawled toward the opening and glanced out. The raft was perched at the top of a large wave, then plunged down, icy water splashing into her face.

Back on the cutter, Jake paced as the Coast Guard tried to figure out the best place to look for the raft. The three wounded kidnappers were being treated. Chance was with some Coast Guard crewmen, guarding the kidnappers.

Darkness finally set in and increased the danger Rachel faced. If only he were with her...

The commander of the cutter approached Jake in the pilothouse. "An emergency signal was received from a beacon in our general location. We are headed toward it and hope that it's from the raft. My XO is talking to the captain of the vessel to see if they had an EPIRB on the life raft. A helicopter is also heading toward the coordinates from the beacon."

"Do you have a pair of infrared binoculars I could

use? I'd like to go on deck and search. I've got to do something."

"I understand." He gave him the pair around his neck. "Take this. It's getting rougher, especially the farther away from land we go."

Jake descended to the lower deck, gripping the railing with one hand while holding the binoculars with the other. The wind cut right through him, even when he was heavily clothed. Was Rachel? Again he sent up a prayer for her to be rescued in time. The Bering Sea could be treacherous.

As he scanned the vast darkness beyond the cutter, he felt as though he were looking for a white rabbit in a sea of snow. He'd been in search and rescues where they were too late to save the person. He couldn't be this time.

A yell went up toward the front. A crewman spotted something in the water. As he hurried toward the coast guarder, his heartbeat slammed against his rib cage, his breathing shallow gasps.

"Did you find her?" Jake shouted over the roar of the wind and sea. "Where?"

The man pointed to the southwest while relaying the news to his CO. Jake scoured the area and saw a small raft raise to the top of a wave, then disappear down the other side.

"What's next?" Jake asked the crewman who started for the back.

"We'll launch our rescue boat at the back when we get nearer. We're closer than the helicopter."

At the back Jake turned to the XO and said, "I'd like to go with them. She needs to see a familiar face after all that has happened. Please." He threw in the last sentences because he couldn't have the man tell him no.

"You'll have to gear up and stay out of the way of the crewmen."

"I'll do anything you say." *Just be alive, Rachel.*

Five minutes later Jake climbed into the craft that launched from the rear of the cutter. They bounced over the choppy sea toward the life raft. Using the infrared binoculars, Jake kept his eye on it, hoping to see Rachel. Nothing.

What if she wasn't on the raft?

What if she'd been tossed into the rough sea?

Those questions flittered through his mind as they came up beside the raft. A crewman jumped onto the raft through the opening in the canopy.

An eternity passed before he emerged, carrying Rachel. As he gave her to another crewman, Jake made his way toward them.

The man saw Jake and handed him Rachel, her parka soaking wet. In the dim lights from the boat, he looked into her face, her teeth chattering, her eyes barely opened. Hypothermia was setting in again, but at least she was alive and in his arms.

THIRTEEN

Jake held Rachel against his chest while she slept. The paramedic on the Coast Guard cutter checked her out and said she would be fine. Hypothermia hadn't gotten a good grip on her yet. He kept the blankets covering her even when she stirred and pushed them off.

Chance poked his head into the room. "We're nearing the harbor. How's she doing?"

"Getting restless. That's got to be a good sign. Did any of them talk?"

"Not a word. But I think I can crack Captain Martin."

Jake clenched his jaws together, pain radiating down his neck. He hadn't been able to keep her out of harm's way. That was his job: to protect.

"She's safe. Don't beat yourself up over this. As a police officer you know you can't always anticipate every scenario. I'll be back when we dock."

With Rachel in his arms, at least safe now, he leaned back against the wall and closed his eyes. *Thank You, Lord. You protected her. I don't know what I would have done if she had died.*

Her eyelashes fluttered.

"Rachel," he whispered, stroking her face.

She nestled closer, cushioning her cheek against his shoulder. Her eyes opened and locked with his. "I'm so tired."

He held her tighter, never wanting to let her go.

"I think every inch of me hurts. I feel like I was put in a dryer and it was turned on high."

He grinned. "Are you telling me you are hot?"

"No, but I've been bounced around so much, bruises must be covering me."

He combed his fingers through her still-wet hair. "But you're alive. That's the most important thing right now."

"Did we catch the drug-smuggling ring?"

"Didn't I tell you that there is no *we* in this?"

She tried to sit up, but he didn't want to let her go. "I didn't go looking for trouble. I was sent to the Sundance on the pretext of my job. I think Mrs. Cohen is in on the drug ring."

"And she is in custody. She pulled a gun on me. I was faster."

"Is everyone in custody?" Worry coated each word.

He assisted her until they both sat on the bunk, their backs against the wall. He grasped her hand between them. "Don't know. It'll probably be a crazy few days when we get back. And until the whole smuggling ring is rounded up, you are not safe."

Rachel stared out the window as the sun came up on Wednesday morning. In thirty-six hours so much had changed. The drug smugglers were being arrested. If all went well today, Jake and Lawrence would return to their house for the rest of the time that Jake would be here. The thought saddened her. She'd loved having

Jake back in Port Aurora. If he hadn't been here, she'd probably be dead right now.

A shudder zipped down her body when she remembered the men who would have thrown her into the Bering Sea to disappear forever. She'd seen the concrete block and chain they were going to use to weigh her down so there was no chance she'd be found.

All yesterday Jake and Chance had been investigating into who else had been in the drug-smuggling ring. Lawrence and a police officer had been guarding her when Jake wasn't there. They've not had any time really alone, and there was something she wanted to find out.

She'd missed Jake being around but understood why he wanted to be involved in the criminals being rounded up. He wanted to make sure she was safe before he left. Then they needed to talk. She just wasn't sure what she should say. She loved him, but she didn't want to live in Anchorage. It was bad enough being a police officer in a small town, but in a city like Anchorage, would she ever see him? He had admitted his work was his life, and because of that, she couldn't take him away from it.

She saw Jake walking with Mitch across the yard after visiting his grandfather's house. They were both expected in town at the police station before she went to work later. Brad had insisted she take Wednesday off, too. Her employer would be recovering at home himself for a few days. But she had the payroll to get out. The people who worked for the Port Aurora Fishery were depending on those checks, especially with it being right before Christmas.

Jake noticed her and waved. She smiled and watched him trudge through the new snow that fell the night before. It left a pristine white blanket over the terrain and reminded her how the Lord could change anything—the landscape, a bad situation into a good one, people's hearts.

As Jake stomped up the steps to the porch, Rachel made her way into the arctic entryway. He came into the house, shaking off the snow that clung to his clothes. Mitch did the same, then wanted her attention while Jake hung up his coat.

"I'm not sure why I'm even bothering. We need to leave for town soon. There's been a change in plan—they want you there for the meeting with the DEA. They also want you in the room when I interrogate Captain Martin. Do you think you can handle that?"

Rachel swallowed hard and nodded. She'd do anything that would help put this case to rest.

"Where are Gramps and Linda?"

"In the kitchen playing dominoes."

"When did they start that?"

"About a year ago. Lawrence taught Aunt Linda how to play dominoes, and she showed him how to play chess. He has yet to win a game, though."

Jake grinned. "So that's why he's been reading that book about chess. Are they going into town with us?"

"No. Lawrence wants to go cut down a tree for Christmas. She's going with him since he helped us with ours."

"When he came for the holidays in Anchorage, by the second day I'd come home from work to find a tree standing in my living room, ready to decorate."

"You wouldn't have it otherwise, I'm sure."

"Nope. If Gramps hadn't been there, I would have worked extra to give some of the guys with families time off during Christmas. I've never taken longer than a week for a vacation, so these past few months have been hard on me."

"And the last couple of weeks?"

"I have mixed feelings about that time. It was good to return to Port Aurora, and I can't say that I've been idle much. Of course, nearly dying isn't a great way to spend a holiday. But if I hadn't been here, I hate to think of what could have happened to you and Linda."

Visions of the burning house paraded across Rachel's mind. "It all started because Aunt Betty asked for help. It's mind-boggling to think how one incident had such a rippling effect."

Jake covered the small space between them and clasped her arms. "We're going to the police station, but when we leave, I'd like to put the drug-smuggling ring behind us at least for the last two weeks of my vacation. Randall and Chance have been interviewing the employees of the fishery while I covered every inch of it with Mitch. They think they have everyone. A couple of them are talking."

"Yes, let's wrap this up so you can actually have a vacation, and I'll stop looking over my shoulder."

"I like that."

She relished his hands rubbing up and down her upper arms as though trying to warm her. "The new year is going to bring a lot of changes around town, but I want to wait until then to worry about what will happen to the fishery now that we know about the involvement with the Russian mafia."

"I told you about my friends who own Outdoor Alaska. This afternoon we're going to talk about opening a store here and investing in the fishery. Brad approved the meeting."

"I'm going to refill my coffee, then I'm ready to go." Rachel walked into the kitchen as Lawrence pulled out the chessboard. "We're leaving. Do you need anything from town?"

He shook his head while her aunt said, "Lawrence says he needs more ornaments for his tree."

"I'll have Jake pick some out at the general store."

"I personally don't want him leaving your side until you are assured by Chief Quay everyone has been rounded up." Lawrence set his pieces up. "And I'm going on record that I think we should stay until we know one hundred percent you two will be all right."

"Know one hundred percent we're safe? That will never be, Lawrence. You know that. There comes a time we simply have to put our trust in the Lord." Aunt Linda moved a pawn.

He harrumphed as he stared at the board.

Rachel hurried and filled her travel mug, then escaped before they started arguing. Lawrence knew how independent her aunt was, but it frustrated him because he'd been good friends with her aunt's husband. He once told Aunt Linda that it was his duty to watch out for them. He made a promise to her husband. But it was much more than that. Rachel was sure he loved her aunt, but she wouldn't marry again.

"Let's get out of here before the fighting starts over the game." Rachel headed for the arctic entry. "My aunt threatened him the last time with bringing out her timer."

"That's the way he is with dominoes. He carefully considers every move and its consequences."

"Not really a bad trait." Rachel donned her heavy

coat, gloves and hat, then tossed the keys to Jake. "You drive. I'm going to enjoy this coffee."

On the ride to town, Rachel brought up a subject she'd wondered about since he had returned. "Are you happy in Anchorage? With your job?"

"Why are you asking?"

"With Officer Bates arrested, there will be an opening at the Port Aurora Police Department. I know we don't have the same type of crime as in—"

"With the past couple of weeks, that has changed."

"And it will continue to as more people come to live here. I don't know what will happen with the fishery, but the business was successful this past year. The drug money didn't go to pay people's salaries. It went to fatten a few criminals' pockets. The expansion was needed to compete with other ports and fisheries. Everything has been done except the additional processing center." Rachel rubbed her sweaty palms on her jeans. "Chief Quay will be retiring in a few years. You could take over his job easily. I know he would recommend you to the city council."

He slowed and glanced at her. "Why do you want me to stay?"

"Lawrence is lonely. He has missed you. I've missed you."

Jake stopped in the middle of the road leading into town. "You have?"

"Well, of course. I think that's obvious the last couple of weeks. We've picked right up where we left off."

"Not exactly. We're eight years older. A lot has happened in that time."

Rachel thought about her life, and up until recently,

it had been the same old thing. "Speak for yourself. You had a near-death experience a few months ago."

"And you don't call getting trapped in a burning house a near-death experience? Or being hauled out to sea to be dumped?"

"Those things just happened. It hasn't shaped me yet. Your experiences have changed you, as well as your job. Again, I'm asking you, are you happy in Anchorage?" She held her breath, waiting for his answer. She wanted to tell him how she really felt, that she loved him, but didn't want to pressure him. He had to want to stay, or it wouldn't work.

"I have my job, my friends and I volunteer with Northern Frontier Search and Rescue, which has been fulfilling." Jake resumed the drive to town.

"We have our share of search and rescues here, especially during tourist season. The big, bad world has intruded on Port Aurora. I want someone like you protecting this town." That was the last she would say about it. He had to make up his own mind.

He pulled into a parking space in front of the police station. "I will think about it. I always wanted to make a difference in people's lives."

"I'd say you've accomplished that in a short time here. You don't have to be in a big city to do that. I didn't like the feeling we couldn't go to the police." She opened the door. "People trust you. I trust you." She climbed from the Jeep and walked toward the police station, aware Jake was probably trying to understand why she brought up the subject.

Inside the building, people were crammed into the small space, which only had one interview room and the chief of police's office. Otherwise, it was open with a counter in front where the dispatch answered the phones and questions from anyone who walked in. The jail was at the back of the building. Officer Clark talked with a DEA agent while Chief Quay signaled for them to join him in his office with Chance and another man.

She peered back at Jake. "We've stirred up a hornet's nest."

"I have a feeling the three cells are full. I see two DEA agents are here."

"The only agency we're missing is the FBI."

"They're coming, but Chance is taking the lead on this case for the state. The FBI and DEA agencies are working together to round up Peter Rodin and his employees in Seattle." Jake reached around and pushed the swinging half door open.

When she entered the police chief's office, enough chairs for everyone filled the whole room. She squeezed over to the far one by the wall, figuring she wouldn't have much role in this meeting other than to answer a few questions. Jake sat in the one beside her and took her hand for a moment while his gaze captured hers. Through this whole ordeal, he'd been there for her. She couldn't have asked for more.

Chief Quay took his chair behind his desk and said, "I wanted to review what we've done so far and make sure all the loose ends are tied up. I don't want one of these people to get away because something wasn't done right. They came into my town and nearly destroyed it. We have never had a shootout in the middle of town, let alone murder, multiple assaults and kidnapping in such a short space of time. Jake, I understand you have worked with DEA agent Daniel Porter before."

"Yes. I'm glad to see you here representing the DEA.

The lady sitting beside me is Rachel Hart, the one responsible for uncovering this drug-smuggling ring." Jake squeezed her hand, then leaned forward. "Who has been arrested?"

"The crews of the Sundance and Tundra King as well as their captains. Along with them, we also have Ivan Verdin and four other coworkers from the shipping department, Sean O'Hara and Eva Cohen." Chief Quay scowled. "And then there is my officer, Steve Bates. He kept them informed about anything going on with the police and Coast Guard, since his girlfriend was a yeoman at the station here."

"We are checking financial records for each person, especially in connection to Peter Rodin. As we follow the money trail, it's leading us to him," Daniel said, remaining standing by the door. "I believe Captain Martin will help us on this end once you talk to him, Miss Hart."

"We'll be transporting the suspects to Anchorage, where the facilities are more secure. Several more state troopers are coming in on a special plane tomorrow and will take them back. We're working with the DEA to see if this drug-smuggling ring has any other operations in Alaska. Our preliminary findings are leading to the conclusion this was a test run. Peter Rodin hasn't invested in any other businesses in the state." Chance shot a glance at the DEA agent. "I'll be here for the next week helping the DEA comb every inch of the fishery, but there are no financial records indicating Brad Howard is involved. It appears that Eva Cohen ran the operation as his secretary, controlling what he saw or heard."

Rachel thought of her last contact with the woman. "She's the one who sent me to the Sundance. She called and said Captain Martin had left all the papers I needed on his boat."

The police chief relaxed back in his chair. "The injured assailants have been airlifted to the hospital in Anchorage. They will be under guard until they are released to be transported to jail. Are there any questions?"

"Will the fishery be able to open after the first of the year?" Rachel hated seeing the town suffer for a few greedy people.

"I've told Brad Howard probably or shortly after that. The investigation will have to be completed before life can go back to normal. The owner realizes he will be under scrutiny from the Coast Guard, DEA and the state for a while." Daniel put his hand on the knob. "Unless you need me, I'm going to take another crack at Verdin's second-in-command."

Chance rose from his seat, turning toward Jake. "We'll bring in a few dogs to check all the boats. They should be here shortly. Give Mitch an extra treat for all his work."

"I will."

After both Chance and Daniel left, Jake shook hands with Chief Quay. "Thanks for keeping us informed. Do you think it's safe now for Rachel?"

"Yes, but if that changes, I'll let you know. Go enjoy your Christmas vacation. You deserve it, Jake, and if you ever decide to come back to Port Aurora, there's a job for you here. If the drug-smuggling ring had gotten its hooks into the town any more than this, I hate to think of the crime rate. This is a good reason to keep the police staffed adequately."

As Rachel followed Jake toward the door, she threw a smile at the police chief. "Thanks."

"Officer Clark is bringing Captain Martin to the interview room. Anything he tells you about the smuggling ring will make our case stronger."

"I'll try."

As they left the police chief's office, Jake escorted her to the interview room. "I'll be with you, and he'll be handcuffed to the table. You'll be safe."

As she entered and her gaze fell on Captain Martin, she hadn't realized how hard this would be. She'd known him for years. Most of the people in the drug-smuggling ring were new to Port Aurora. So why did the captain take part in the illegal activities? He was going to stand by and watch her be murdered. The thought shivered through her. But she sat across from the man, trying to forgive him as the Lord wanted her to do.

"Why did you do this?" Rachel asked, needing to make some sense from all that had happened.

"First, thank you for agreeing to talk to me. I got caught…" Tears glistened in the captain's eyes.

She still ached, and her wrists and ankles were chafed red from the ropes. Jake had stitches in his arm from where he'd been grazed by a bullet. And this man had been in the middle of it all. "Why did you do it?"

Captain Martin cleared his throat. "My son lives in Seattle and owes this group a hundred thousand dollars. If I didn't help them, they'd have killed him and his family."

"A hundred thousand dollars? How?"

"Trying to keep his business solvent, he got in over his head with the wrong people."

"Where are your son and his family?"

"In hiding with the US Marshals. I wouldn't talk to you until they did that."

"What boats were working for them?"

The captain frowned. "The Tundra King is all I know of. We took turns meeting the Russian trawler with the drugs. I can give the authorities all that information."

"So everyone in your crew is involved?"

With sadness in his blue eyes, Captain Martin nodded. "I will testify. I'll do anything they want, but first I needed to ask for your forgiveness, Rachel. I never meant for someone I knew to be hurt. That tough show on the boat was for Beau Cohen's benefit. I don't know if I could have let them kill you and throw you overboard. I was coming to see you to talk to you. To see if there was a way to get you out of the situation alive. I deserved what you did."

Jake covered her hand in her lap. She slanted a glance at him and knew when they left she had to tell him she loved him, no matter where Jake ended up living. If Captain Martin had gone to the authorities when he was first contacted, this might never have happened in Port Aurora. But he held the truth inside him. She wouldn't anymore.

"I forgive you," she finally murmured, meaning every word. She shoved her chair back and rose. "Now, I need to get to the fishery, so the employees will be paid today."

As she left, Jake put his arm around her, and they walked side by side to the exit. She didn't say anything until they reached the fishery headquarters. "Are you coming in?"

"Yes. I'm still not one hundred percent sure you're safe, so I'm sticking with you until I'm satisfied."

"I like the sound of that. Let's go to my office."

When she arrived there, she hung up her coat and took Jake's to do the same. Then she shut the door and turned toward him, the words she wanted to say to him on the tip of her tongue.

He pulled her to him. "Alone, finally. I've wanted to talk to you ever since you were found, but so much had to be wrapped up, and I had to make sure it was done correctly." He plastered her against him, his arms locking around her. "When I didn't know if you were alive or not, I knew without a shadow of doubt that you've always been the woman for me. We got so hung up on being friends that we suppressed our growing attraction for each other when we were teens. I love you. I want to marry you."

She laid her cheek against his shoulder, nestling into the crook of his arm. "Good thing we're smart as adults."

"Are you saying you'll accept my proposal?"

"You're right. I've been in love with you for years but kept denying it. I didn't want to be like my mother going from one man to the next. All I had was time to think while I waited on that boat, praying you knew where I was. But you found me, and deep in my heart I knew you would. We're connected—two halves of a whole. How can I deny my other half? I would be denying myself. I love you, Jake, and if you want to live in Anchorage…" Emotions swelled into her throat. She never wanted to leave, but she would for Jake. After swallowing hard, she continued. "I will make it work. But I'm warning you, I'll want to come back to Port Aurora *a lot.*"

He brushed his lips across hers. Once. Twice before he pressed his mouth against hers in a deep kiss that spoke of his love for her.

EPILOGUE

Christmas morning, a knock sounded at Aunt Linda's house in Port Aurora. Rachel hurried to answer it because her aunt was still asleep. They had attended a late-night service with Lawrence and Jake, and none of them had gone to sleep until two in the morning. She peered outside and saw Jake on the porch. It wasn't even eight yet.

She answered the door, throwing her arms around him and kissing him before he was even inside. "I've missed you."

"Soon, we'll be married, and I won't have to go home."

She stepped to the side and let him in. "I'm glad they have rounded up everyone in the ring including Peter Rodin, but I did like the fact you had to be with me all the time. I kinda got used to it."

After hanging up his coat, he backed her into the living room and pushed her gently onto the couch, then settled next to her. "I know what you mean. That's why I want to marry you as soon as possible."

"So do I. I wish Aunt Betty could be here to see us. Who do you think killed Betty?"

"What little evidence there was indicates that Sean did. The other with him was Ivan. Their size and tread of a pair of their shoes match what was taken at the scene, and there was one set of latent prints in the pantry. That matches Sean's."

She really hadn't known Sean, but she couldn't say that about Jake. Over the years, they had been through so much. "Now I want to put it behind us. I don't want to talk about the smuggling ring. At least for today."

"Sounds fine to me. I came early because I wanted to give you my Christmas present alone."

"Where is it?"

He rose and walked into the arctic entry. When he returned a few seconds later, he had a wrapped box in his hand. "I hope you like it."

She tore into the red-foiled paper and removed the lid to reveal a Port Aurora police badge. She stared at it for a few seconds, then lifted her gaze to his. "Does this mean you're going to work for them and we'll live here?"

He nodded. "Working with Randall these past weeks, I realized this was a good compromise. My job will be different, but I can still use Mitch. Brad wants me to go through the fishery at random times to make sure there are no more drugs. The police department is going to apply for a grant for a trained K-9, and if we get it, I'll be its handler. Josiah mentioned doing that when he met with Brad this week about being a partner in the fishery."

"Do we know if he and his sister are going to invest in the fishery?"

Jake grinned. "I'm supposed to keep this a secret until the first of January."

The twinkle gleaming in his eyes told her every-thing she needed to know. "They are! I could kiss you."

"Go right ahead. I won't complain."

She held his head between her hands and planted her lips on his. "Thank you, Jake. I know you had a lot to do with it."

"Not really. What Brad did expanding the fishery was on the right track, but you can't tell your aunt anything."

"I won't. I'll go make us some coffee. When is Lawrence coming over?" She started to rise, but Jake grabbed her arm.

"In two hours. Didn't you forget something?"

"What?"

"My present."

"Oh, about that." She gave him a quick kiss, then stood. "You'll have to wait until after Christmas. I'm taking back the gift I had for you."

Jake arched an eyebrow. "Why?"

She retrieved a flat box from under the tree. "You'll see."

He carefully unwrapped it and peeked inside, then started laughing. "I guess I see why. These Anchorage employment applications won't be needed now, but I appreciate the gesture."

"I meant it. I would move to Anchorage if that was the only way we could be together. I don't want to be separated ever again."

He tugged her to him and whispered against her lips, "Nothing is going to stop us from being together."

* * * * *

Valerie Hansen was thirty when she awoke to the presence of the Lord in her life and turned to Jesus. She now lives in a renovated farmhouse on the breathtakingly beautiful Ozark Plateau of Arkansas and is privileged to share her personal faith by telling the stories of her heart for Love Inspired. Life doesn't get much better than that!

Books by Valerie Hansen

Love Inspired Suspense

Emergency Responders

Fatal Threat
Marked for Revenge

Military K-9 Unit

Bound by Duty
Military K-9 Unit Christmas
"Christmas Escape"

Classified K-9 Unit

Special Agent

Rookie K-9 Unit

Search and Rescue
Rookie K-9 Unit Christmas
"Surviving Christmas"

Visit the Author Profile page
at Harlequin.com for more titles.

CHRISTMAS ESCAPE

Valerie Hansen

And the light shineth in darkness...
—*John* 1:5

May God bless the men and women serving in our current military and those whose sacrifices in the past have kept us free. We are grateful beyond words.

ONE

"I love my job," Rachel Fielding murmured, smiling. "Who wouldn't? I help brave members of the military and get all the free kisses from them I want." She chuckled and blushed, checking her surroundings to make sure no one had overheard her silly musings.

Her patients might have four paws and wagging tails, but they were the dearest part of her job as a veterinary assistant. Sure, some could be hard to handle, but very few had proved impossible in the years she'd worked at Canyon Air Force Base in Texas. Since a blissful marriage and raising her own children didn't seem to be in her future, she'd fill that void via her job. Thankfully, any time she got in a bind trying to tend to a sick or injured dog she could always count on fellow techs or Captain Kyle Roark, DVM, her boss for two of the past four years.

Rachel knelt to hug Stryker, a three-legged German shepherd who had had his front leg amputated after being wounded overseas. For a tough K-9 soldier who had taken down the worst of the worst in battle, he sure was a sweetie—once you gained his trust as she had.

The abrupt opening of a nearby door made them

both jump. "Easy, boy," Rachel said to soothe the dog. She smiled up at her boss. "I'll be in soon. I was just socializing Stryker a little on my break."

Captain Kyle Roark shook his head. "It's not that, Fielding. There's a personal call for you. They say it's important."

"Sorry." Rachel got to her feet. Since her K-9 buddy immediately started leaning against her, looking up and pleading with his beautiful brown eyes, she asked, "Can I bring Stryker with me? You said he needs more casual exposure."

"Fine." Roark held the door open for them. "Take your call on the phone in my office."

"Thanks." Barking echoed in waves along the corridors when Rachel and the big shepherd passed by. Now that winter had brought a cooldown, the dogs housed at the training facility and animal hospital were more active as well as vocal. "Did the caller say what this was about?"

The captain paused at the entrance to his small office and gestured instead of replying. To Rachel's surprise he followed her and the dog in, pulled out a chair and said, "Sit," as he handed her the portable telephone from his desk. "Please."

Both she and the obedient K-9 complied. Rachel was getting uneasy. Captain Roark had always been a perfect gentleman with all the enlisted personnel but he had never, in her memory, acted so solicitous. Her hands were trembling and she used them both to grip the phone.

"This is Airman Fielding speaking."

A woman's voice captured and held her attention. "I'm with Patient Services at Municipal Hospital in San

Antonio. I have had a terrible time locating you, Ms. Fielding. Is your first name Rachel and do you have a sister, Angela?"

"Yes. But I haven't seen…"

"Angela is here with us. She's asking for you, Ms. Fielding."

The unspoken meaning behind that statement weighed on Rachel's heart as if a boulder lay atop her chest, making it hard to breathe. Stryker sensed her tension and pressed his good shoulder to her knee. "My sister? Are you sure?"

"Yes, ma'am. If it's at all possible, I urge you to get here immediately."

"Angela's sick?"

"She's been injured. I'm not authorized to go into detail. Everything will be clear once you've visited and spoken with her. You are coming?"

"Of course." Rachel's stomach knotted, and she tasted bile on her tongue. If her sister had been hurt in an accident there would be no reason to keep that information private. Therefore, there was a very good chance Angie's live-in boyfriend was to blame. The mere thought of having to face that horrible man again gave Rachel discernible tremors. She had to ask, "Is her, I mean, is a guy named Peter VanHoven with her?"

"I'm sorry, I have no idea. I was told to contact you and relay your sister's message, that's all."

"All right. Where do I need to go?"

The patient services spokesperson was in the middle of giving directions when Rachel realized she hadn't taken in anything. "Wait. Please. I need…" With that she passed the phone to her captain.

Kyle Roark rose from his perch on the edge of his

desk and circled it, picked up a pen and made notes. "Yes, I have it. Thank you. When are visiting hours?"

Although Rachel couldn't hear the other end of the conversation, she read empathy and concern in the veterinarian's expression. His dark eyes were resting on her as he nodded and said, "Yes. I see. All right. Tell her sister that Rachel is on her way." He glanced at his wristwatch. "We should be there before fifteen hundred hours. Thank you."

She stood as he ended the call, using the arm of the chair for added balance. "I'll need to get permission to leave the base and be gone for who knows how long. And I'll need to borrow a car."

"Leave that to me. When you put Stryker back in his kennel, tell Sylvia to cover your duties while I make a few calls and adjust staffing." He was stripping off his white lab coat to reveal a light blue shirt beneath.

Rachel was almost to the door when Roark stopped her by calling out, "Fielding. Change into the civvies you keep in your locker and grab a warm jacket in case we're still gone after sunset. I'm going to contact my commanding officer, Lieutenant General Hall, and explain the emergency situation so there won't be any misunderstandings about both of us being away."

"Are you sure you want to do this?"

"Absolutely. You're clearly in no shape to drive and I'm escorting you to the hospital to see your sister. Period."

"It's very kind of you to offer, Captain."

"You're welcome, Rachel. And please remember to call me Kyle while we're away from the base."

"Of course... Kyle."

"Get going. We need to hit the road in minutes, not hours."

"On my way." So many poignant memories were whirling through Rachel's mind as she changed into jeans, a T-shirt and a lightweight jacket that she hardly gave thought to anything but her sister.

Angela. Dear, sweet, clueless Angela. What a waste her life had been after she'd fallen for Peter. He'd been bad news from the beginning but Angie would never listen, never see him for what he really was: a mean, ruthless bully with a temper to match.

The difference between that man's psyche and that of the trained attack dogs in their program was self-control. A K-9 could be called off by his handler. Once Peter lost his temper and began to inflict suffering, there was no stopping him until he was physically spent. She knew him well. She'd been on the receiving end of his wild temper and vindictive actions more than once.

The price she'd paid had been high. He had cost her the only family she had left in the world.

Kyle drove his military SUV as fast as the speed limit allowed, plus a tad more. The caller from the hospital had not minced words once Rachel had handed him the phone. Her sister was in critical condition with broken bones and a damaged heart and might not live long. He knew what it was like to be cheated of a chance to say goodbye. To express love and devotion one last time. He'd been too late to kiss his wife or his little girl and it still galled him, especially at this time of the year. Sadly, the anniversary of their deaths coincided with Christmas celebrations that were supposed to be joyous.

Well, they sure weren't happy times for him. Not

anymore. He didn't try to fake it, either. There was no sense pretending to be having a good time when he wasn't. He didn't expect others to stop enjoying themselves, but he made it clear he did not want to be included. When Christmas Day arrived he was more than willing to take over kennel duties and give most of his enlisted staff the day off. No longer having a family of his own hurt worse on that particular day than at any other time.

Rachel said very little as they drove. Kyle saw her tense against the seat belt and pull her purse into her lap as he wheeled into the hospital parking lot and stopped. Before he could walk around to open the passenger-side door, she was out and jogging toward the front entrance. "Wait."

Rachel didn't even bother to shake her head; she simply kept going, making Kyle wonder if she'd heard him. He'd seen plenty of shocked reactions demonstrated by both humans and K-9s who had been traumatized in battle, and that was exactly how his vet tech was behaving. She was trapped in a zone between fight and flight, determination and panic, and that conflict had rendered her temporarily deaf and mute.

Catching up as she passed through the automatic-entry doors into the lobby, Kyle caught hold of her arm. She wheeled, wild-eyed, as if his touch was an attack.

He immediately released her, palms facing out, hands raised. "Simmer down. They told me your sister is in the ICU on the fourth floor." He pointed. "Elevators are over there."

Rachel stared at him for a moment before he saw recognition light her blue eyes. "O-okay. Hurry."

"You need to act calm even if you don't feel it. The

last thing your sister needs is to see you in hysterics."
Kyle pushed the up button for the elevators. "Take some
slow, deep breaths and get it together. What's got you
so spooked?"

"You wouldn't understand." The elevator doors
swished open. Rachel jumped on ahead of him, faced
front and repeatedly punched the button for the fourth
floor.

"Try me." He noticed she was focused not on him,
but on the narrow slice of lobby she could see behind
him. Worry masked her usually sweet expression, and
panic dampened the spark in her eyes.

When she slammed the heel of her hand against the
control panel, Kyle cautioned again. "Whoa. Beating
those buttons to death won't make them work any faster,
you know."

"We have to go! Now." She was leaning to one side
for a final glimpse as the doors slid smoothly closed.
"I think I just spotted Peter."

Whirling, Kyle took a defensive stance, but it was
too late. The elevator was moving. "The guy you asked
about on the phone? Why didn't you say so?"

"It was just for a second. This guy was wearing a
black T-shirt, jacket and a baseball cap so I couldn't see
if his long hair was pulled back, but everything about
him fit what I remember."

Her lower lip quivered when her gaze met Kyle's.
"What am I going to do? I want to be brave for Angie's
sake but the thought of facing that man makes me sick
to my stomach. She must be in terrible shape to take
the chance of sending for me."

Take the chance? The more he learned, the less he
liked it. "Why were you and your sister estranged?"

"It's complicated. We don't have time for the whole story."

"Okay, fill me in later. Right now, the important thing is your reunion. Obviously, she wants to make peace or she wouldn't have asked for you. So, make the best of it."

The shiny metal doors slid open on their floor. Rachel stepped into the hallway, looked around and froze.

Kyle placed his hand lightly at her waist. "You can do this. Come on. ICU is this way."

She didn't move. "What if...? What if I was right and I did see Peter? He can be violent and he could be right behind us."

"If he is, I'll take care of him."

"You'll watch my back?"

"Of course. When you and your sister want privacy, just say the word and I'll step outside."

"Outside the room, maybe. Not outside the hospital. Not that far away. Promise?"

"I promise," Kyle said, frowning.

Rachel blinked back tears. "I wish we had brought Stryker or another K-9 for self-defense. Peter VanHoven is more than Angela's significant other. He's also a sadist with a hair-trigger temper. I'm positive he's the reason she's in intensive care. If he is around here we won't want to cross his path."

"You're that scared of him?"

"Let's just say I've experienced Peter's foul moods firsthand. And I have the scars to prove it."

"I'll stick close." Kyle had already been entertaining an urge to protect and shelter her. Now, it blossomed. It had been a long time since he'd allowed himself to feel proprietary toward any woman, let alone a beautiful one. Why had he failed to notice how truly attractive this vet tech was before?

Kyle's cheeks flamed. That kind of thinking made him decidedly uncomfortable. Rachel Fielding had always acted as if she was just as determined as he was to remain unattached. That constant standoffishness had puzzled him from time to time, but he hadn't questioned her because he was comfortable with it. Now that he'd seen how afraid she was to face her sister's boyfriend, her attitude was beginning to make perfect sense. The man had physically and emotionally injured Rachel in the past and now her poor sister was hurt, too. That was totally unacceptable.

Confounded by his innermost thoughts, Kyle clenched his fists as they made their way down the hallway. A part of him was wishing they would run into this Peter guy so he could tell him off—or more. It wasn't an exemplary Christian attitude, but it certainly was human.

On alert, Kyle stood taller and braced himself to repel the unknown. No low-life abuser was going to get his hands on Rachel without going through him first.

TWO

Keeping watch behind and to the sides, Rachel let Kyle request admittance to the sealed-off ward via the intercom. Automatic doors swished open and her senses were assailed by pungent medicinal smells, beeping machines and an atmosphere so hushed, so heavy, it seemed tangible. If she had not yearned so strongly to be reunited with Angela, she would have turned and fled.

Up ahead, a woman wearing a mask, gloves and a long-sleeved disposable smock gestured to them and pointed. "Ms. Fielding is in the last bed in this row. Behind that curtain. We don't usually allow more than one visitor at a time and a neighbor brought her daughter to see her, but under these circumstances you can go ahead, too."

The extra strength Rachel needed came from the man beside her. She took a deep breath, steeled herself for what she might see and started forward. Off on her left and right, other patients were clearly struggling to survive. Most were elderly, but not all. Angela was barely thirty. This was so unfair.

As they drew closer, Rachel could hear a woman

speaking to a child behind the partially drawn curtain next to Angela's bed. When Rachel reached out and pulled it aside with a trembling hand, the sight of her sister's swollen, bruised face and emaciated arms made her gasp. Tears immediately blurred her vision. She rushed forward as an older woman carrying a little girl backed away to make room.

"You came," Angela whispered.

"Of course I did."

"I was afraid you might not."

Previously unshed tears began to slide silently down Rachel's cheeks and she noted that her sister was also weeping. What could she do or say to help? Fond memories made her revert to a long-unused quip. "I had to see my favorite sister."

To Rachel's delight, the comment brought a slight smile to the badly beaten face. "I'm your only sister."

"Picky, picky." Rachel's hands were clasping Angela's on the side of the bed opposite the IV, and she could feel bones inside the painfully thin fingers. Beeping from a nearby machine increased in frequency, and she realized she was hearing her sister's racing pulse.

Slowly, tenderly, Rachel reached to smooth Angela's damp hair off her forehead. "Take it easy, sis. You need to rest so you can get better and take care of your daughter. This pretty little girl must be Natalie."

"Yes. Natalie, this is your aunt Rachel. Maria Alvarez is my neighbor. She's the one who called the police when I couldn't."

Not only did Angela's weeping continue, she looked past Rachel and the others to focus on Kyle. "You're her friend?"

"Kyle Roark. We work together," he said.

"But you are friends, too?" She kept struggling to control her emotions enough to speak.

Rachel answered for him. "Yes. Kyle and I are friends. He drove me here."

"He'll stay?"

That question made Rachel stiffen and peer behind her. "I thought I saw Peter downstairs. Is he…?"

Attempting to shake her head, Angela winced in pain. "He's in jail. The police arrested him for doing this to me."

"Thank God for answered prayers," Rachel confessed. "He's the last person I want to run into. Ever."

"That makes two of us," her older sister admitted, sniffling and struggling to go on. "I'm so sorry, sis. I should have listened to you and left him years ago."

"That's all in the past." Rachel stroked Angela's forehead again. "Right now, you need to worry about getting better."

Again, Angela focused on Kyle, then looked to Mrs. Alvarez. "Maria, can you and this gentleman take Natalie for ice cream or something? Please? I want to talk to my sister. Alone."

"Sí." The full-bodied woman lowered the child to the ground and clasped one of Angela's hands. "Hold on to Senor Kyle, too, Natalie. We don't want him to get lost."

The child complied, slipping her small hand into Kyle's and holding tight, then looking up at him in awe. "He's real big."

Rachel smiled and almost chuckled until her niece added, "I think he could beat up my daddy if he had to."

Rachel's heart clenched. *Of course.* Angela wouldn't be the only victim of her live-in's temper. Peter would have lashed out at anyone who displeased him. The way he had at Angela. And the way he had at her when he'd driven her out of her sister's life that last time.

Returning her full attention to her weeping sibling, Rachel tried to apologize. "I'm so sorry. I should have found the courage to stay with you."

"Nonsense." Sniffle. "You begged me to go away with you and I was too stubborn and stupid to listen. That's not your fault."

"I wrote. You never answered."

"I couldn't. I just couldn't admit what a horrible mistake I'd made. By the time I thought I was ready to leave Peter I'd lost touch with you."

"You knew I was close by."

"Not for sure. I'd had your unlisted cell number in my phone but Peter took it away. When your letters stopped coming I figured you had washed your hands of me."

"No way. I didn't stop trying to keep in touch," Rachel vowed. "He must have intercepted my letters. I was only writing once a month or so after the first year. It would have gotten easier for him to destroy your personal mail before you saw it."

Falling silent, Angela seemed to struggle to breathe.

"Do you want me to call a nurse?"

"No. No. Just give me a second." She inhaled a little more deeply, wincing and groaning as her chest expanded. "I want you to promise me something."

Rachel leaned closer. "Of course. Anything."

"I want you to take Natalie, look after her and tell her about me so she remembers and knows I loved her."

"I'll be glad to babysit. You can tell her you love her, yourself."

"Promise."

"All right. I promise."

Shuddering, Angela tightened her grip on Rachel's hand. "Don't let Peter get his hands on her, whatever you do."

"How can I prevent it? He's her father."

"Not legally. I never put a father's name on her birth certificate, and we never married. Besides, I have high hopes he'll rot in jail after doing this to me."

"From your lips to God's ears," Rachel quoted, meaning every word. "Is it all right if I take her to the base with me while you're recuperating? I can't be away from my duties too long, and there's a good preschool there for when I'm working."

"Did you take that veterinary aide course you kept dreaming about?"

"Yes. Kyle's the head vet in the military K-9 training program at Canyon Air Force Base and I'm one of his techs. That's what he meant when he said we worked together, although actually I work for him."

Angela managed a lopsided smile. "Wonderful. You'll be with all those protective dogs they train. Couldn't be better."

"And when you get well we'll find you an apartment close to Canyon so we can see each other all the time."

The dreamy, weary expression on her sister's face comforted Rachel. When Angela closed her eyes and sighed, she did the same. Hands still clasped together, Rachel began to pray with her and for her. "Thank you, Father, for healing old wounds in our hearts and for the healing You are about to do in Angela's body. Amen."

Rachel watched Angela's eyelids flutter. Her breathing had been noisy all along but now it began to sound labored even though the beeping machines kept up their even cadence. Rachel wanted to tell Angela how much she loved her but was hesitant to disturb her further. Time ticked past so slowly that every second felt as if it lasted minutes.

Praying silently, Rachel listened to the mechanical manifestations of her sister's life until suddenly Angela was squeezing her hand. Rachel met her gaze, mirrored Angela's smile and felt her heart breaking. An amazing peace and release settled over the bruised face. Angie's pain and suffering were over. Her sister was finally free. Peter couldn't hurt her anymore.

But what about Natalie? The little girl had never met her aunt Rachel before today and now she was going to have to take her away from the only home she'd ever known. How could she possibly make a child understand and accept the situation when she hardly could herself?

Three ICU nurses and a doctor had finished confirming Rachel's fears and had left by the time she heard the sound of boots on the bare floor. Kyle was back. And Natalie was undoubtedly with him. Angela was positioned as if asleep, but Maria Alvarez guessed what had happened in their absence and gasped, beginning to mutter a prayer as she stepped ahead to block Natalie's view.

Kyle, too, quickly closed the distance. He stopped behind Rachel and laid a hand of comfort on her shoulder. "I'm so sorry."

Without hesitation she accepted his condolences by placing one of her hands atop his and saying, "Thank you."

"I wanna see my mama," the little girl whined. She was trying to wiggle past the adults.

"Let her come closer," Rachel said, surprised at how calm and in control she felt despite everything. She held out her hands and Natalie let her pick her up. The urge to kiss the child's hair and stroke her back as a mother would surged through Rachel and squeezed her heart. "I'll take care of you now, honey. You can come and live with me."

The big blue eyes, lashes wet with tears, looked up at Rachel as if she had just promised the world. "I—I don't have to go back to Peter?"

Rachel pulled her close again and dried her cheeks. "No, baby, no. We're not going to have anything more to do with Peter. I promise."

As she comforted her niece and glanced at the others, she saw concern in Maria's expression and disbelief in Kyle's.

"What else can I do?" she asked him aside. "If I send Natalie with Maria, Peter will know how to find her and try to take her back. I have as much legal right to her as he does."

"How do you figure?"

"Angela said they never married and his name is not on the birth certificate. He'd have to go to court to prove he actually is her father, and I'm sure a background check will show him as an unsuitable parent."

"Then we should call the authorities and do this the right way, the legal way," Kyle warned. "You can get in a lot of trouble if you just walk off with her."

"I know, but..." Rachel looked to Maria for moral support and found the older woman staring out the window at the parking lot below. Nobody could blame her for turning away. She'd been sucked into this mess by being a Good Samaritan and probably feared and hated Peter VanHoven almost as much as Angela had.

"Ai-yi-yi." Hands clamped over her mouth, Maria whirled.

Rachel tensed. "What is it? What's wrong?"

"It's him! Look. He's coming!"

"Who? Peter? Where?" Rachel asked, joining her. "Angie said he was in jail. Are you sure?"

Kyle crowded closer, too. "Which one is he?"

Maria pointed. "There. Getting out of the old red truck. See?"

"Maybe he's out on bail. If he's the guy I think you mean, he's good and mad. Look at his body language."

"Yeah." Putting Natalie down, Rachel began to gather up the few personal items Maria had brought for the child.

Kyle frowned. "What are you doing?"

She paused only long enough to glance his way and say, "Running. Far and fast."

"That's wrong." Arms folded across his broad chest, Kyle stood like a sentinel, apparently ready to enforce his opinion.

"I don't care if you go with us or not. Natalie and I are leaving."

"Get a grip and think," Kyle urged. "Where will you go?"

"Back to the base if we're welcome to ride with you," Rachel shot back. "Out the door and into hiding if you don't help us. I'm not staying here where VanHoven can get his filthy hands on me or anybody else." She glanced at the still figure on the bed. "He's done enough damage for a lifetime."

Rachel was ready to abandon Kyle and carry out her

threat, and she would have, if Natalie had not grabbed a bedraggled baby doll in one hand and Kyle's index finger in the other. The man's expression froze for an instant, then melted in a way Rachel had not seen in the two years she'd worked for him.

He was going to help them escape. She could tell that as surely as if he had spoken.

One final peek out the window was all she allowed herself. No sign of Peter! He must already be passing beneath the entrance canopy, on his way to berate Angie for his arrest when she was the true victim. Rachel had seen it before, plenty of times. It was his excuse for normal.

And since Angie was not going to be available to listen to his tirade, he was sure to turn his wrath on whoever happened to be close by, such as his daughter. Or Rachel. As much as she would like to see someone give him a taste of his own medicine, she knew better than to place Kyle in such a tenuous situation when a confrontation could be avoided.

What she must do is grab her niece and run. Now.

THREE

Rachel sidled through the door from the ICU into the hallway. She had shouldered Natalie's small bag along with her own purse and was towing the child by the hand. Kyle brought up the rear.

Suddenly, Natalie was pulled away. Rachel whirled, ready to do battle, when she realized that her companion had picked up the little girl and was headed in a different direction. For a few seconds she wondered if his plan was to return the child to her father. Then, he allayed her fears.

"Not the elevator, Rachel. He'll probably come up that way. We'll take the stairs. Follow me."

That logic was unquestionable. She fell in behind him. He shouldered through the stairway exit door and cradled Natalie while he waited for Rachel to pass. Her body was trembling, her legs unsteady. Each downward step brought her closer to escape, closer to the parked SUV that would carry them all away before it was too late.

Would they make it? They had to, for Natalie's sake if for no other reason. Rachel had vowed to protect her niece, and that was exactly what she intended to do.

Peter was never going to get his hands on her as long as one Fielding sister was left.

She heard the measured thuds of Kyle's boots on the stairs behind her. He was sticking close. Praise the Lord she hadn't made this trip to see Angela alone! A sense of divine presence and peace flooded through her. The fear she had defined as a personal weakness her heavenly Father had used for her good. If her pride hadn't gotten in the way, she might have recognized the hidden blessing sooner.

Their path took them to a side door. Rachel glanced over her shoulder to ask, "Now what?"

"We can circle around or I can bring the truck to you, depending on whether or not this Peter guy spots you. If he came inside the way I suspect, we can make a run for it together."

"Okay."

She started to lean on the push bar to the exterior door as she heard Kyle shout, "No!"

It was too late. A claxon horn was blasting and warning bells sounded. Rachel immediately realized her error. That door was supposed to stay closed and she'd triggered an alarm.

Frustrated, fearful and more angry with herself than anyone else, Rachel faced him with a grimace. "You said we were going to circle around so I thought..."

"Inside, not out there," he shot back. "Come on. Follow me before the guards catch us."

Rachel didn't argue. They turned back into the hallway. Curious employees and patients glanced at them in passing, but nobody approached with questions.

"Walk calmly and slowly," Kyle ordered. "Don't

hurry and don't look back. Pretend you think that noise is a nuisance the way everybody else does."

"Okay."

"And stay close. We want to look like a normal family."

Rachel could see wisdom in his suggestion even if heeding it did place her in an awkward position. Putting aside her personal misgivings, she moved to Kyle's side and slipped her hand through the crook of his bent elbow.

That touch was a mistake. His arm was muscular beneath his sleeve, his countenance commanding and sturdy as well as comforting. She knew his hands were especially skillful because she'd watched him do delicate surgeries, but nothing had prepared her for this potent an assault on her senses.

Distracted by the masculine presence beside her, she almost missed spotting a familiar figure fidgeting in front of a bank of elevators.

"Stop," she hissed, giving his arm a tug.

Kyle halted. "What is it?"

"There. Up ahead. See the scruffy man with a ponytail, cutoffs, bomber jacket and flip-flops by the elevators? That's him. We got here too soon."

"It's still better than coming face-to-face when those doors open upstairs."

"Right." Slinking backward into a shallow doorway, Rachel was relieved when Kyle turned and handed her Natalie.

"Hold her tight and stay behind me so he won't spot you if he looks this way."

"Gladly." Rachel couldn't tell whether the elevator

had come and gone until Kyle told her. "The coast is clear. Remember, act normally."

Rachel huffed. "I doubt I'd recognize *normal* if it walked up and bit me in the leg. The only part of my life that ever seemed well ordered was my time in the air force working with K-9s. I can hardly wait to get back on base."

As he ushered her and Natalie toward the automated sliding doors leading to the parking lot, Kyle was shaking his head. "I'm afraid that by the time you get through all the red tape involved in gaining legal custody of your niece, nothing will feel the same. Not even life on Canyon."

A childish, barely audible "What's that?" sounded in Rachel's ear.

"Canyon Air Force Base," she told the child. "That's where I live."

"Do you have toys?" the wan little voice asked right before a big yawn.

"Well, we have what Senora Alvarez brought for you and there's a wonderful store where we can buy more."

"I don't wanna leave my mama," Natalie whined, rubbing her eyes with her little fists.

"I know you don't, sweetheart. I don't want to leave your mom, either, but we have to go before Peter sees us."

Thin arms tightened around Rachel's neck, reminding her that she had just accepted an immense responsibility, one she was far from certain she was ready for. Suppose her efforts at parenting failed? Or suppose Peter won in court and she had to give Natalie back to him?

That possibility was so unacceptable it brought tears

to her eyes. *No, no, no.* She would not fail. She would never give up no matter who or what came against her. She couldn't disappoint her sister—or the frightened child now clinging to her. No matter what happened she was going to stick it out. To win. There was no acceptable alternative.

Glaring sunshine barely warmed the winter day. Kyle loaded the sleepy little girl and her scarce personal belongings into the second seat of the SUV, then began to adjust her seat belt before fastening it. "She should have a booster seat, too, but this will have to do."

"Not if it isn't safe. I hadn't thought about how she was going to ride with us."

Seeing Rachel's tears begin to glisten, Kyle said, "Look. A lot has happened already and I know you're not thinking clearly. That's where I come in. Trust me. I've got this."

Shoulders sagging, Rachel nodded. "I know. I just feel so confused. I'd finally reconciled with my sister and now she's gone again. It's like I was robbed. Twice." She draped her jacket over Natalie to serve as a blanket before sliding into the front passenger seat.

Kyle fought to keep from identifying too closely with Rachel's plight. It was no use. And, considering how bereft she seemed, he figured he owed it to her to commiserate. "I do understand, believe me. It's hard. Any unexpected loss is, especially when it's a younger person."

She sighed. "I really did love my sister even if we hadn't had contact during the past six years. I keep wondering if things would have been different if I'd stayed with her instead of letting Peter scare me off."

"Sure. Maybe he'd have beaten you senseless, instead."

Kyle noted her sidelong glance at the second seat as he started the vehicle, and toned down his responses, beginning with, "Sorry." He started to back out of the parking space. "How much do you know about the whole home situation?"

"Not a lot beyond what I witnessed years ago. Angela managed to tell me some things but it's probably not enough to get him thrown back in jail. At least not until the forensic report is in."

He knew she was purposely being evasive by not mentioning a medical examiner. Surely anyone who had been so severely beaten and had named her attacker on her deathbed would be believed. The problem was whether or not this Peter guy was going to accept any legal edict. Even if he wasn't put in prison for killing Rachel's sister, he should never gain custody of the sweet little girl nodding off in the back seat.

"We can take her home to your apartment and look over what she brought with her. Then I'll go down to the base exchange and buy whatever else she needs."

"You don't have to do that."

"I know." Backing out, he joined a line of cars waiting to leave the lot.

"Then, why?"

"Let's just say it's the right thing for me to do and I don't mind a bit. Okay?"

"Sure. I get it. I have the Christmas spirit, too."

Kyle's head snapped to the side. "Who said anything about Christmas?"

"I'm sorry. I thought, since there are decorations

hanging from every lamppost and store windows are all lit up for the holidays, that was influencing you."

"Well, it isn't." His hands had fisted on the steering wheel so firmly his knuckles were turning white.

Her voice was soft, tender. "I understand completely."

"What do you mean?" There was no way she could know his story without digging into his past. He'd been very careful to keep his history to himself after selling his civilian practice and reenlisting as an air-force veterinarian.

"Holidays can be tough on everybody," Rachel said. "There really are no perfect family gatherings or ideal celebrations. After my parents died, Christmas was never the same, even when Angela and I tried to make it festive." She took another peek at the snoozing little girl before she added, "That was before Peter came on the scene, of course. Once he and Angie were a couple, we didn't even try. And now…"

"Okay. One thing at a time," Kyle said, purposely changing the subject. "Do you have a place for her to sleep? Enough food in the house? Blankets, pillows, that kind of thing?"

"Yes. She'll need some decent clothes for preschool if there isn't anything suitable with her. And probably shoes. Those flip-flops aren't going to be warm enough." Slowly shaking her head, Rachel made a face. "I don't imagine she's used to having much, given the way she looks today."

"According to what Senora Alvarez told me when we went to the cafeteria, your sister had a rough time. So did Natalie."

"Undoubtedly. My biggest concern isn't her past—

it's her future. How am I going to keep Peter away from her?"

"Once we're on the base it will be relatively safe." The line of cars was moving too slowly to suit Kyle, but since it was almost his turn at the exit he tamped down his anxiety.

Rachel cited recent history. "Oh, really? Look what that serial killer Boyd Sullivan did. He sneaked on and off base for months before he was caught. If he could do it, so can Peter."

"Sullivan was a special case. He was a certified nutjob. Those are unpredictable."

"And Peter isn't?" Her volume increased on the final word.

"Shush. You'll wake Sleeping Beauty."

"She is beautiful, isn't she?" Rachel's smile was so tender as she gazed at the napping little girl that Kyle's heart clenched almost as tightly as his fists. Visions of another little girl, of his precious Wendy, melded with the current image of Natalie and gave him a jolt. He hadn't been there for his own daughter or for his wife when they'd needed him, and that failure had eaten away at him for four long years.

Was God giving him a second chance to protect an innocent little girl who had no other champion? Perhaps, but the opportunity was bittersweet. How much better it would have been if his little family had never been torn apart by that drunk driver in the first place.

And how much more he would have trusted in his Christian faith if his prayers for their survival had been answered that awful winter night. He hadn't wanted to let them go, to lose them forever, yet he had. It had been a terrible struggle to go on without them, to accept his loneliness and live with it. He'd made a new life by returning to the air force, where he knew he could do the most good, and had kept his emotional distance from fellow officers as well as the enlisted personnel assigned to him. Until now.

Kyle knew he was entering uncharted territory and his misgivings were almost strong enough to cause him to back off. Almost. But not quite.

His innermost thoughts were directed to God while he continued to fidget and inch the SUV forward in line. *Why, God? And why at Christmastime? You know how this hurts so why a woman and little girl? And why me?*

He didn't need an audible reply to know the answer. The trauma of the past made him particularly suited to this task. He had lost to evil once by not being totally diligent, not making himself available when his gut told him he should. It would not happen again. No matter what developed in regard to his vet tech and her niece, he was going to be there for her. For them.

He would not make the same mistake twice.

A horn honked behind them as the space at the very front of the line was vacated. Rachel jumped at the noise. So did Kyle. Checking for cross traffic on the street, he also glanced toward the hospital and caught his breath.

"Rachel," he said abruptly. "Look over there. Is that…?"

She followed Kyle's gaze, then immediately whirled to face him. Her complexion paled and her lips parted. She didn't have to speak to tell Kyle who they were seeing. Peter VanHoven had somehow figured out what they were up to and was racing for his battered red truck.

Accelerating as much as he dared without drawing undue attention, Kyle angled the black SUV into a spot in front of a slow-moving gray sedan and joined passing traffic.

He saw the red truck come to life and start down the same crammed exit lane that had delayed their departure. Rachel swiveled in the seat to watch so Kyle made it her assignment. "Let me know how long a line he gets stuck in, okay?"

"Oh, no!" Her gasping reply sent a shiver the length of Kyle's spine.

His hands gripped the wheel, his senses on full alert as he angled to check his mirrors. "What? I can't see him anymore. Where did he go?"

"Over the curb," she shouted. "He's already in the street. Ahead of us!"

FOUR

Rachel couldn't breathe. Every muscle in her body knotted, and she felt trapped in the kind of nightmare where she opened her mouth to scream and no sound emerged. The only thing remotely functional was her brain's ability to call out to her heavenly Father. There were no apt words. Just a silent plea for divine help.

Thankfully, she was braced against the dash with one hand, the other on the back of the seat, when Kyle whipped the steering wheel and accelerated. The SUV bumped up over the right-hand curb with a twist of its chassis. All wheels were spinning when they hit the lawn. Grass churned and clumps flew out behind them.

Horns honked. Bystanders put cell phones to their ears. She finally found her voice. "What are you doing?"

"Getting away."

"You're causing a scene. People are staring at us."

"Doesn't matter," he countered. "Peter already knows where we are or he wouldn't have jumped the line to get ahead."

"But..."

"Just hang on. Is Natalie okay?"

"Yes. She's stirring but still asleep. She must be exhausted."

"No doubt." His next turn was so abrupt the rear of the SUV fishtailed. Straightening out the vehicle and dropping its tires back onto the pavement, Kyle asked, "Do you still see him?"

"No, I..." Her breath caught. "Yes! He's turning off like you did. I hear sirens but they sound far away."

"Could be for some other reason," he said. "Keep watching."

She had no intention of doing anything else. The old red pickup was on their tail all right, but it apparently didn't have four-wheel drive, because it was doing a lot of slipping and sliding while digging curved trenches in the turf. That was an unexpected plus.

"He's losing traction on the grass," she shouted. "We're pulling ahead."

"As soon as he hits the asphalt again he'll have power," Kyle yelled back. "I'm going to head for the highway so we don't cause an accident on these city streets."

"Will we be able to outrun him?"

"Temporarily. But the hospital found you, so he'll be able to, too."

"If it was just the two of us I'd say *stop and have it out with him*."

"So would I," Kyle agreed. "We can't take a chance with Natalie. Once you—we—took off with her, we stepped across a line. Involving the police at this point won't help us. And it might help Peter."

Rachel was nodding. "Right. If it was only foster care she faced I wouldn't worry too much. We can't trust Peter to leave her alone. He's likely to kidnap her and disappear."

"My thoughts exactly."

Two more sharp turns and they were starting up the on-ramp to the highway. Rachel spotted a problem. "This is east. We want to go west."

"All I care about is speed and safety," Kyle said flatly. "Keep watching."

"I am, I am." She had swiveled to face forward again so she could peer into the right-hand outside mirror. *Blue car, white car, semi, space, Peter!* She screamed. "He's hiding behind that truck in the far right lane."

"I don't see him."

"Hang on. You will." One of Rachel's hands was fisted around the door handle. The other grasped the edge of her seat. In the mirror's reflection the big truck was falling back. A flash of red swerved out to pass and nearly collided with a second semi. Rachel gasped as that truck driver laid on his horn and barely avoided an accident.

"He's going to get us or somebody else killed," Kyle shouted. "We can't endanger Natalie like this. I'm going to try to lose him."

She refrained from comment because nothing that came to mind lacked sarcasm. They were caught between a rock and a hard place. To stop would put the little girl in ongoing danger and to continue as they were made that threat immediate. Nevertheless, she was glad it was Kyle at the wheel and not her. Defensive driving was not her strongest talent and she was already queasy from riding backward.

"You may want to close your eyes," he yelled as he whipped the wheel at the last instant, cut across two lanes and left Peter trapped on the wrong side of the speeding semis.

Rachel rolled down her window and leaned out, preparing to lose her breakfast, but the gust of cold air shocked the nausea out of her. "You're crazy!"

"I'm successful," Kyle countered with a tight smile. "He won't have a chance to get off until the next ramp. By that time, we'll have a good head start."

Wind whipped her hair, the tendrils stinging her cheeks. Tears filled her eyes. Had he really done it? Were they safe for the time being? After such a harrowing chase, it seemed impossible.

She sagged against the door, her seat belt holding her. They were passing under the highway, ready to start back in the other direction, when she pushed away and closed the window. "I suppose I should thank you for scaring me to death. Would you mind driving like a normal person from now on?"

Kyle turned briefly to flash a smile. He looked elated as well as short of breath. That was comforting. She'd have been really worried if she'd believed he viewed his stunt driving as everyday behavior.

"Right. Normal. Normal is good," he said. "The speed limit here is high. As long as we maintain our lead we'll be fine."

"Do you think Peter will give up?"

"It's possible. I doubt he had time to listen to the whole story about Angela when he got to ICU. He may go back there."

"Wishful thinking?" Rachel managed a slight smile. "He knows enough. He wouldn't have chased us if he hadn't heard we had Natalie."

"That's probably true."

"And speaking of my niece, I suppose, since this is a civilian matter, I'll need to retain private counsel to defend my right to keep and raise her."

"Uh-huh. I have a couple of connections in San Antonio from my days in the regular world. If you'd like, I can contact them for you."

"I'd appreciate it. Thanks." Realizing she was hoarse, Rachel was reminded that an apology was called for. "Sorry I yelled at you, Kyle. Guess I got a little too excited."

"We both did." A gentle smile lifted the corners of his mouth and crinkled the outer edges of his dark eyes as he leaned to study the sleepy child in his mirror. "I don't want to stop if we don't have to. Can you make sure she's okay from up here?"

"Sure." Undoing her seat belt, Rachel got onto her knees and leaned over the back of her seat. "Natalie's breathing evenly and is totally relaxed. I guess she's comfortable being with us even if you do drive like you're competing in the Indy 500."

"I'm better than that," Kyle teased. "All they have to do is keep turning left and going around in circles. I not only go both ways, I sometimes jump the car right off the ground."

"Tell me about it." She rolled her eyes, straightened in her seat and clicked her belt back on before touching his forearm. His muscles twitched but he didn't pull away. "I want to thank you. All kidding aside, that was some great driving."

She saw him eye the placement of her hand before he smiled again and said, "My pleasure."

Rachel chuckled quietly. "It was, wasn't it? You enjoyed every minute of it."

"Not totally. If I'd been alone I would have. With passengers it was different."

"*I* trusted you."

She felt the shaking of his arm before she noticed it came from his shoulders. She gritted her teeth. He was silently laughing! At her. And after she had restrained herself from telling him what she'd really thought of his methods. "What's so funny, *Doctor*?"

"You are." Kyle snorted. "For somebody who trusted me, you sure did a lot of screaming."

Clouds had obscured the sun, and wind had begun to gust across the sandy soil as they neared the air base. They were preparing to enter through the south gate when Kyle saw a dot of red closing the distance behind them.

He quickly rolled down his window, flashed his ID at the guard and jerked a thumb behind him. "There may be a guy in a red pickup coming this way. Whatever you do, don't let him through."

"Yes, sir. Shall I call Security?"

"Not unless he gives you trouble. He hasn't actually done anything to us that we can prove and we'd like to keep it that way."

In the background, Rachel gasped. Kyle held his hand out to signal her silence. As soon as they'd left the guard post, she said plenty. "Hasn't done anything? What about my sister?"

"That's a different case. We can assume he's out on bail. If we start bringing up the reason he's chasing us, that will reveal who our passenger is and stir up a hornet's nest. I doubt Peter will say much because he won't want to call attention to his actions, either."

Slowing, Kyle watched the rearview mirrors until he was satisfied the gate guard had repelled their nemesis. "Done. We should be okay for a little while. I'll drop you and your niece at your place and run over to the base exchange for whatever she needs."

"Start with warm clothes." Rachel leaned to peer up at the sky. "Looks like a storm is brewing."

"That, it does." He wheeled expertly into the driveway of her apartment building and parked behind it. "Want me to walk you in?"

It didn't surprise him a bit when Rachel insisted she was capable of managing Natalie and her belongings all by herself. Matter of fact, she had the child out of the SUV and well in hand by the time he circled and stood next to her. "What about sizes? Shall I guess?"

"When in doubt, go big," Rachel told him. "I'll leave the tags on until we see what fits. We can return the rest." Pausing, she smiled. "Thanks for doing this. We really do appreciate everything."

"You're welcome." Kyle thought of adding *My pleasure* again but restrained himself. He didn't want anyone, especially Rachel Fielding, making too much of his efforts. He'd have done the same for any of his techs. It just so happened that this particular airman was beginning to seem special, which was no problem as long as he didn't break regulations and try to date her. The rules against officers and enlisted personnel getting together for romance had never concerned him before.

"And they don't bother me now," he told himself firmly as he drove toward the BX, base exchange, to go shopping for Natalie. There were good reasons for strictness in regard to separation of ranks. Promotions were earned on merit, not based on who an airman knew or who their family happened to be. Every new enlistee was tested and placed according to skills and aptitude. He, for instance, would have made a lousy pilot because of a childhood injury to his inner ear and thus his balance.

Maybe that was why he'd empathized so readily with Rachel and her sister, Kyle reasoned. It had been a long time since he'd thought about the fights his younger brother, Dave, used to get into. And even longer since he'd remembered being injured sticking up for him. Their older sister, Gloria, had already left home by that time and neither of the boys had told their parents about the beatings Kyle had taken defending Dave. Not that it mattered anymore. Gloria was stationed overseas in the army, and Dave had cut all ties after their parents had relocated to Florida. In a way, his family was no closer than Rachel's had been. He'd hoped to change that pattern with Sue and Wendy until their lives had been snatched away so unfairly.

Mad at himself for allowing such maudlin thoughts, Kyle pulled into the parking lot of the base exchange, climbed out and slammed the door. Cold wind hit him in the face. He zipped his jacket and wished he'd thought to bring a hat. To say he was out of sorts was an understatement. This was just the beginning. Now he was going to have to look at children's clothing and that would make him think about how precious his daughter had been.

The mall entrance was festooned with garlands and blinking colored lights. *Christmas.* A season that was supposed to make him feel joyous. Peaceful. Loved.

He clenched his jaw. Love was overrated. So was the holiday. Oh, he respected the spiritual aspects of it: the celebration of the coming of the Savior. It was the *ho-ho-ho* and all the other folderol that he could do without.

Electronic doors slid open. Kyle stomped in. As long as nobody wished him a *Merry Christmas* he could probably get through this task without too much trouble.

He went straight to the children's-clothing section, then paused in front of a display of warm coats. His Wendy had had a red one a lot like this, with a fake-fur collar and white earmuffs to match. No way could he bring himself to buy that same outfit.

Mumbling to himself, he turned away to look elsewhere. His gut was in knots and he was beginning to perspire. Four long years had passed since his family had been wiped out.

It wasn't supposed to hurt this much anymore.

FIVE

Rachel's bravado faded as she surveyed her apartment and considered her new responsibility. What should she do first? What did kids need? "Are you hungry, Natalie? I'm sure I have the makings of a grilled-cheese sandwich."

The shy child nodded.

"Would you rather have something else?"

"Ice cream."

Rachel smiled. "Of course. Silly me. Tell you what. Let me make you something regular to eat and then we'll talk about dessert. Okay?"

Another nod.

"Besides, didn't you have ice cream with Maria and Kyle?"

"Uh-huh." She brightened. "He got me two scoops."

"Wow, that's great."

"Is he coming back?"

"Of course he is."

"Really truly?"

"Honest." Rachel dropped into a crouch and cupped Natalie's thin shoulders. "Oh, you feel chilly. Would you like to wear one of my sweaters?"

"I had a sweater. A pink one. It's ruined."

"I'm sorry, honey." She stood and held out a hand. "Come on. Let's go look in my room and pick out something you like. It'll be big but warm."

Tears filled the wide blue eyes and Rachel imagined looking into Angela's. "I promise I'll take good care of you, sweetheart."

"I miss Mommy."

Scooping the little girl up, Rachel held her tight and bit back her own sorrow. "I do, too, honey. I do, too."

Natalie's thin arms encircled Rachel's neck. "I'm scared."

"Don't be scared. I'll look after you."

"Peter's mean."

Rachel started to carry Natalie toward the bedroom. "I know. But you're safe here with me. I have lots of friends like Kyle and a whole bunch of wonderful dogs that will protect us both."

"You do?"

"Uh-huh. As soon as Captain Roark—Kyle—gets back, maybe we can go visit the kennels. There's one special dog who's a tripod. I know you'll like him."

"What's a tripod?"

"That means he only has three legs. Stryker is very brave. He was hurt so he got to come home to get better. Kyle is a doctor who fixes injured animals, and he's helping Stryker get well."

"Was he beated like Mommy?"

Rachel pulled the thin body closer to offer more comfort as she said, "No. Not like Mommy. Stryker was in a war a long way away when he got hurt."

The child's voice was thin and reedy when she asked, "Is he gonna die, too?"

"No, baby, no. Stryker is getting better. He's going to be fine. We just have to teach him to walk with a new leg called a prosthesis. But he doesn't have to go back and fight anymore."

"Is he mean?"

"Not at all. You don't have to worry. I won't let you play with any dogs I think are dangerous."

"I wish he was mean," Natalie said. "I'd tell him to go bite Peter real, real hard." With that, she buried her face against Rachel's shoulder.

There was nothing appropriate for rebuttal. Anger was a part of grieving, as was sorrow. Just because Natalie was a five-year-old didn't mean she wouldn't have the same feelings of bereavement that adults suffered. Healing of her wounded spirit would take a while.

For the first time, Rachel realized that she and her niece were probably both suffering from a form of post-traumatic stress. If she understood anything, she understood that. Medical professionals used to refer to it as a disorder, hence the initials *PTSD*. Recently, however, many had begun to see it as more of a syndrome. Semantics aside, she thought it was better to keep from saddling sufferers with a label. Some found post-traumatic stress had to be fought daily. In others, it eventually subsided enough for the patients to carry on normal lives.

Would she ever get over losing her sister? Rachel wondered. Yes, and no. Angela had been a part of her life that she'd never forget. As with the loss of their parents, there would be confusion and undeserved guilt until she was able to accept the inevitable. The same went for Natalie.

Except now they had each other. If that wasn't enough, she'd arrange for counseling. Whatever she had to do, she'd do. There was no maybe about it. She who had despaired of ever having a family had just become an instant mother. And the responsibility scared her witless.

As Kyle had hoped, he didn't encounter anyone from the K-9 unit before he got the child's clothing to his car. He didn't want to have to explain that he had special permission from Lieutenant General Hall to spend so much off-duty time with an enlisted airman. Besides, the next few days and weeks were going to be critical for Rachel and her niece and they didn't need more trouble. If Peter chose to go to the police and claim abduction, as a normal father would, Rachel could end up in jail and the child sent to foster care despite all their efforts.

Kyle huffed, realizing he was almost glad VanHoven was the kind of person likely to avoid the cops. Except that meant he'd be more apt to act on his own, meaning he'd do whatever it took to get even with Rachel and reclaim his daughter. Kyle could actually identify. He'd have done anything to get Wendy back.

He slammed a fist against the steering wheel. "Stop it. Just stop it. They're gone. Get over it."

That was impossible, of course. During the past four years he had mellowed and stopped experiencing sharp pangs of grief that stopped him in his tracks. But the ache lingered. Being mixed up in Rachel Fielding's dilemma was sure not helping, particularly so near to Christmas.

As he climbed out of the SUV with his purchases,

he steeled himself for what he was about to face. A moment's pause was enough for "Father God. Why me? And why now?" Yes, he wanted to be released from the responsibility he felt. And yes, he was ashamed of himself. That didn't keep him from asking.

Sighing, he knocked on Rachel's door. There was no answer. He tried the knob. The door was locked. "Rachel?"

No reply.

Kyle raised his voice. "Rachel! Open up. Let me in."

Still no one called back to him. He dropped the plastic shopping bags, grabbed his cell phone and dialed the private number she'd given him on the way to the hospital.

Instead of the voice on the phone he'd expected, he heard a tentative response through the locked door. "Kyle?"

"Yes. It's me."

"Prove it. What's your rank?"

"Captain. What's going on?"

She threw open the door, grabbed his sleeve and tried to yank him inside before he had a chance to gather up his purchases. Her eyes were so wide they looked surreal. He brought everything in and closed the door. "Why didn't you answer your phone?"

"It's been ringing, but nobody is ever there when I say *hello*."

Kyle heard the ringing again and took the phone from her, not saying anything when he answered. Just as he was about to hang up, a gruff voice said, "You'll be sorry, Rachel," then abruptly broke the connection.

"Was that him? Was it Peter?"

"I assume so, yes."

"What—what did he say?"

"Nothing earth shattering. Just that you'd be sorry."

With a gasp, she was in Kyle's arms before he had a chance to give her back her phone. Not only that—Natalie had grabbed onto his knee and was hanging on as if he were her only lifeline from a sinking ship. "Easy, easy," Kyle said. "Don't panic. He probably got your number from somebody at the hospital."

"No." Speaking with her cheek pressed to his shoulder, Rachel was trembling. "The hospital called the base, not me. Remember? My cell is unlisted. On purpose."

He turned her, encircling her shoulder with one arm after he'd picked up the little girl with the other. "Then he must have gotten it from your sister's old phone. How long has it been since you changed your number?"

"I—I kept it the same so Angie could reach me."

He felt some of the tension leaving her, so he gestured to the sofa. "Sit down and take a deep breath. Empty threats can't hurt you."

"I know Peter, okay? There's nothing *empty* about his threats."

"Okay. I believe you. Now, think. If he'd been able to get on base he would have shown up, not called you. Right?"

"I guess."

"So, he's a nasty piece of work but you're safe here."

"If you say so."

"You don't sound convinced. Tell you what. How about we go get Stryker and see how he does bunking with you? He's been introduced to some of the older children at the base day care and there was no problem, plus you've bonded well. You'll just need to keep an eye on Natalie to make sure she's not too hard on him."

"The doggie Aunt Rachel told me about?" Natalie was almost smiling, something Kyle had not seen her do before.

He crouched in front of the sofa. "That's right. He's kind of big but he's very nice. And he'll bark if anything is wrong so you won't have to be scared when he's being quiet. How does that sound?"

"Maria has a kitty. She scratches."

"Stryker won't scratch you. But you will have to be careful to not bump his shoulder. It's still a little sore."

"He got hurted, huh?"

"He did. But I fixed him."

The child's smile faded. "I wish you could fix my mommy."

Kyle nodded as his heart broke for her. "I wish I could, too, honey. But sometimes, no matter how hard we try, we can't fix everything."

"That's what Maria said when we prayed. I guess God is mad at me."

Rachel spoke up and drew her closer. "No, honey, no. God isn't mad at you. He loves you."

Cuddling against her, Natalie whispered, "I love you, too."

The child's voice was soft, gentle and full of trust. *Just the way Wendy's used to be*, Kyle thought. Children loved without reason or argument. They simply opened up and let it flow.

There was a time when he'd believed his heart had done the same, but those days were over. As a sensible adult he realized that love was far too complex, hard to find and impossible to hang on to. All it did was leave behind painful scars. That was why he'd had no trouble remaining single. No trouble at all.

Sensing that Rachel was staring at him, he stood and turned away. Whatever clues she thought she'd seen on his face were his business, not hers. The sooner he could get in touch with an attorney and set up her defense for taking the child the way she had, the sooner he'd be able to back off and resume their former employer-employee relationship. Yes, he had permission to help her, but he knew he'd be in hot water if the general suspected they were on the verge of becoming romantically involved, as well. Too bad she wasn't also an officer.

That thought struck Kyle a blow that nearly staggered him. If Rachel were an officer, then she and he could date openly. Or more. What in the world was the matter with him? Was he crazy? He hadn't thought about dating anybody in years. Oh, he wasn't brain-dead. He still noticed attractive women. But that didn't mean he made any moves to *court* them.

The difference was the child-mother scenario. It had to be. He was merely equating Rachel and Natalie with the loved ones he'd lost so tragically. Those memories must be coloring his current emotions and throwing off his logic. If he intended to stay in the air force he'd better get a handle on those rampant emotions before he risked his rank and maybe his entire career.

Once in a while there were exceptions made, of course. Even strict rules could be broken with proper permission, such as that which he was currently operating under. It was the possible consequences of carrying things too far that concerned him. And speaking of concerns, there were more immediate ones that needed seeing to.

"I'll leave you two to try on the new clothes," he said flatly, turning to her. "I'll go to the office and do preliminary paperwork on Stryker, then bring him back with me." He started for the door. "Lock everything behind me."

Pausing with his hand on the knob, he added, "And the next time I call you, check the number that comes up on your screen and answer, will you? I almost kicked your door in."

"I don't think I have your cell number," she said, grabbing her phone to page through the contacts file.

He was back to her in three long strides, helped himself to her cell phone and entered his number. "You do now. We'll need to see if we can pull Peter's number off incoming call records when I get back, so don't erase anything."

Rachel stood, her spine straight, her eyes narrowing. "Look, I appreciate everything you've done for me today but despite the mess I happen to be in, I'm not clueless. I took care of myself just fine until Peter showed up and fooled my sister, and I've gotten plenty of commendations for my work in the air force. Don't sell me short. Okay?"

Despite her anger he found himself wanting to smile. With a curt nod he turned away and said, "That's more like it."

Shocked by Kyle's response, Rachel stared at the closing door for a few moments, then hurried to double lock it. When she started back to Natalie she found the child curled into a fetal position on the sofa. Her little arms were pulled in, her hands poking out of the rolled-up sleeves of the bulky borrowed sweater and shielding her head and face. Clearly, that was her typical reaction to adult dissension.

She flinched as Rachel approached and perched on the edge of the cushions next to her. "You don't have to be scared, honey. I'm not mad at you. Neither is Kyle."

When there was no tangible response Rachel began to gently stroke the thin back through the cable knit. "I'm so sorry, Natalie. I didn't mean to sound upset. I just wanted Kyle to stop babying me."

"He—he's nice," the little girl whispered.

"Yes, he is. And I shouldn't have lost my temper with him. I'm sorry for that, too."

"He'll be mad when he comes back."

"No, he won't. He's not like Peter, I promise. And in a lot of ways, I'm not like your mama, either. She let Peter hurt her. I left when he started to hurt me. We don't have to let anybody hurt us. Ever. We can always tell someone, like you probably told Maria. Right?"

A slight nod.

"See? There are lots of nice, friendly people who will be glad to help you if you ask them."

In the back of her mind, Rachel realized she was preparing Natalie for the possibility of being put in foster care, at least temporarily. The more she pondered her dilemma, the more she realized she had few good options. What she'd done at the hospital had been necessary for personal protection and to safeguard the innocent child. What she would have to face in the future to continue doing the same thing was not going to be nearly that easy.

Trying to distract them both, Rachel began to pull clothing out of the shopping bags Kyle had left. He hadn't forgotten a thing. There were even socks and pajamas included. Soft garments. Cute yet serviceable. For a confirmed bachelor he'd done an exemplary job.

Thinking back, she recalled snippets of conversations about his past that she'd ignored at the time. Now, she began to wonder if he'd once had a family. She knew he was presently single because some of the other techs had broken protocol and flirted with him. When they'd gotten nowhere, one or two had blamed a possible traumatic past for his lack of response. Given all the unmistakable masculine vibes she'd picked up by being near him, she wondered if they might be on the right track. Not that it was any of her business. Still, she was curious.

At the bottom of the last bag, Rachel found a stuffed pink bunny. "Hey, look."

Squealing in delight, Natalie hugged it close. "Is this for me, too?"

"Apparently." Rachel was smiling. "It was with your new clothes. Come on. Let's go in the bathroom and clean you up so we can try these things on."

"Why?"

"Because you need a bath."

"I don't like baths."

Instead of stubbornness, Rachel imagined that she was detecting fear. "You don't?"

"No." Her niece was backing away, clutching the bunny and rubbing her cheek against its pink fur.

"Okay. How about a shower? I can help you wash your hair."

Natalie clapped a hand on the top of her head. "Not my hair. That hurts." Tears gathered in her eyes and she looked unduly frightened. "A lot."

"I'll be very gentle, I promise."

Hand in hand they headed for the small bathroom. The more Rachel learned, the worse her opinion of the child's prior home situation got. No telling how much emotional damage had already been done to this sensitive baby.

Rachel was toweling Natalie dry when her phone rang again. A knee-jerk reaction caused her to jump before making a grab for it. Caller ID showed an unknown number. It wasn't Kyle. Nor was it any of her friends on base. She considered not answering, but this time she had something to say. This time, she was going to tell Peter what she thought of his cruel parenting.

"Finish drying and put on clean clothes while I talk on the phone," she told Natalie.

Once in the hallway she slid the green bar to connect and said, "Listen, Peter," leaving her caller no time to respond before she launched into a tirade. Her hands were trembling but her voice stayed strong until she ran out of steam.

Instead of cringing, Peter laughed. "Are you through? Because I can wait out here all night."

Rachel's breath caught. "What do you mean?"

"Exactly what I said. I can see in your back windows but you've pulled the blinds in the front. That's not very welcoming, sister-in-law. After all, we are kin."

Racing to her bedroom window, Rachel lowered the shade, nearly dropping the phone as she ended the call. Was he really out there, watching, or had he guessed about her windows? She couldn't take the chance. She had to leave, to keep running. But where could she go? And how? If she left while still a member of the air force it would be considered desertion!

"He wants to make me a fugitive," Rachel muttered. "If I run, he wins. But if I stay here, I'm a sitting duck."

Taking a couple of quick breaths to try to settle her nerves, she pulled up Kyle's number and called him.

"I'm almost there. Is everything all right?" he answered.

"No!" She had to fight to keep from screeching. "Peter called again. He said he's out there. Watching."

SIX

Kyle would have run full out if he hadn't had to slow down for Stryker's sake. "Heel!"

The German shepherd was panting as he half stepped, half hopped along, but was giving no signs of perceiving danger. "That's it, boy. You can do it. Come on."

Raising his fist to knock on Rachel's door, Kyle was taken aback when she jerked the door open. One hand gripped her cell phone, the other, the doorknob. "Hurry. Come in."

He sidestepped for the sake of the dog. Stryker's tail was wagging a mile a minute, his whole rear end taking part in the joyful greeting. As soon as Rachel slammed and locked the door, he was poking his huge black nose at her hand.

Kyle held him in check. "You heard from Peter again?"

"Yes. Did you see anybody lurking outside?"

"No. Neither did this dog. What made you think Peter was here?"

"He phoned and said he was."

"And you answered? Why?"

"Because I wanted to give him a piece of my mind, that's why."

"Are you sure you can spare it?" Kyle was scowling at her.

"Ha ha. Very funny."

"It wasn't supposed to be. This is no laughing matter."

"I know that. And I think he was bluffing. There's no way he could have gotten onto this base so fast. We've only been home an hour or so."

"Then why were you panicky?"

"I don't know. I guess it hit me harder because I was here alone." Kyle watched her expression morph from one of fear and anger to something more rational. "I'm okay, now that Stryker is here with us."

"Good." He smiled over at Natalie. "I see some of those things I picked out were the right size." He held out his hand. "Come here and meet your new buddy."

Although the child was hesitant, she did obey. Stryker, on the other hand, acted as if he'd forgotten all his training, including company manners, the moment Natalie drew near. He strained at the short leash until Kyle had to correct him. "Stryker, back. Sit."

The dog managed to feign a sit without actually putting his rear on the ground. The tail continued to sweep the floor and excitement made him wiggle all over.

Catching Rachel's eye, Kyle made a face. "I've never seen him quite this eager to meet anybody."

"Neither have I. I gather he was raised around kids before we acquired him for the K-9 program."

"That would be my guess."

Kyle crouched next to the shepherd. "Stryker, meet Natalie. Natalie, this is Stryker. He can't shake hands because he needs his front leg to hold himself up, but if you stick out your hand, I know he'd like to sniff your fingers."

She stayed frozen in place so Kyle purposely grinned at her. "When you're ready, he will be. Here. You can feed him some treats I brought along." To his relief, she slowly extended her hand and accepted the treat.

Stryker, obviously sensing her reluctance, leaned in politely and gave the tips of her fingers a friendly sniff before licking up the tiny morsel.

She pulled back and giggled. "That tickles."

"Would you like to pet him? His fur is really soft, especially his ears. Just be gentle and move slowly. I can see he wants to be your new best friend."

Instead of replying, the little girl reached out and touched the tips of the shepherd's whiskers, then began to stroke the side of his face. He leaned into her hand as if they had been together since he was a pup.

Kyle heard Rachel sigh and felt like echoing that sentiment. This pairing was better than he'd expected. Much better. And, given Peter's continuing harassment, that was more than advantageous. It was an amazing blessing.

In the ensuing minutes, Natalie sat down on the floor and Stryker followed, resting his head on her lap while she continued to pet him. She even ventured to stroke the shoulder above his healing front leg, where short hair had begun to cover the scars, and whisper to him that he was going to be better soon.

It was all Kyle could do to keep from becoming overly emotional. Rachel had already lost that battle and was swiping tears from her cheeks. "Wow."

Kyle cleared his throat. "Yeah. Wow. I don't think

we're going to have any trouble acclimating him to stay-ing with you."

"I was already considering filling out the papers to adopt him. Now I know I will."

"You have other more pressing concerns," he re-minded her. "Like adopting your niece."

"I know." She eased away from the comfortable pair on the floor and motioned to Kyle to follow. "You can help me sort the clothes you bought. I think most of them are perfect and getting three different sizes of the same shoe was genius."

He looked from her to the child and dog. "I think we should keep an eye on these two for a little longer."

"We need to talk privately."

"In the kitchen, then. I can see them from there and you can make us some coffee." He quirked a smile at her. "Unless you want me to do it. I wouldn't want you to think I was relegating you to the kitchen just because you're a woman."

"Were you?"

He raised his hands in surrender. "Guilty. But this is your home. You know where you keep everything so it does make sense."

"Apology accepted."

He suppressed a smile as he followed her. "What apology?"

The arch of her eyebrows told him he was treading on shaky ground, so he sobered. "Okay. Let's hear it. What did Peter say that had you so spooked?"

"Other than hinting that he was watching me through the windows?" She inclined her head back toward her niece. "She was scared to let me wash her hair because she said it always hurt. Maybe I'm imagining things, but chances are that was no accident. It's just the kind of subtle punishment Peter used to dish out—until he'd finally lose his temper completely and start swinging."

"The poor little thing." Anger surged. Kyle clenched his fists. "That's inexcusable."

"At least we agree on something."

"Oh, I think we agree on lots of things," Kyle said, "including the fact that VanHoven is the last person who should parent a child. I can see why you were so determined to get her away from him."

"How can we keep her safe?"

"I'm not sure. Even if she went into foster care that's no guarantee he wouldn't continue to pursue her."

"Exactly."

"However, if he reports her as kidnapped, then we're breaking the law." It didn't escape his notice that they were referring to themselves as *we*. As partners in crime. He didn't like the idea but saw no alternative other than turning the little girl over to the authorities.

"I've never even gotten a parking ticket," Rachel said.

Neither had he. If this situation wasn't resolved quickly, though, they were both likely to get more than a simple ticket.

A whole lot more.

Rachel had busied herself making a fresh pot of coffee and figuring out what to serve for supper. Anything but letting herself dwell on the possibilities facing her regarding Natalie. And, by virtue of his assistance, Kyle Roark, too. If she hadn't been so worried about her niece's future she'd have fixated on Kyle's dilemma. Not only was he pushing against the rules of conduct for an air-force officer by siding with her, but he might be risking his whole career. Yes, he could always go back to practicing veterinary medicine in the private sector, but not if he was serving a prison sentence for kidnapping.

"There has to be a solution," she said as she prepared grilled-cheese sandwiches and a salad.

"If you know of one, feel free to share," Kyle replied. "I'm all ears."

"You never should have gotten involved in my problems."

"Tell me about it."

"I just did."

"Yeah, well, you're a little late."

"And I'm sorry about that." She glanced across the kitchen island to check on Natalie for the hundredth time. "You can still walk away. I'll tell the police that you didn't know what you were getting into. It'll be the truth. Neither one of us had a clue what would happen when we started for the hospital in San Antonio."

"That much is true. But we know now."

"That's the biggest drawback. When we were in the throes of panic—or at least I was—and fleeing from Peter, we could be excused if we claimed fear for the welfare of a minor. Now we have a better idea of what my sister and niece went through but no real proof other than what Natalie said. Any further actions we take will have to be fully justified and even then it might not be enough."

Kyle's lips were pressed into a thin line, telegraphing agreement. Finally, he spoke. "I think I should give General Hall another call and fill him in. If he orders the Security Forces to monitor your apartment, that should keep Peter from getting too close to Natalie."

"What if the general won't? Or suppose he tells you to stop helping me? You're not a cop—you're a veterinarian. The top brass may want you to stay completely away from me, for your own safety. Your skills are much more important to the K-9 unit than mine are."

"You are *not* expendable," Kyle insisted.

"In this instance I am."

"Not to me."

In Rachel's eyes he'd instantly attained superhero status. Yes, she realized there was a wide gap between telling her she was worthwhile and expressing affection. However, she had no intention of questioning his motives and taking the chance she had misinterpreted the importance of those three simple words. It was much more comforting to let her imagination take flight like an F-15 and soar above the clouds of doubt blanketing her heart and mind.

Blushing, she told him, "Thank you," and smiled. She might have continued if Stryker hadn't suddenly raised his head, looked toward the front door and growled.

Rachel froze. Natalie acted surprised and a little frightened. Only Kyle reacted defensively. He crossed the short distance to kneel by the dog and heed his warning. "What is it, boy? What did you hear?"

Despite the slippery floor, Stryker was standing by the time Rachel reached her niece. On full alert, he was more than impressive. He was magnificent. No one in his right mind would knowingly challenge a trained K-9 like him—even one with only three legs.

But *was* Peter in his right mind? she asked herself.

That was a good question, particularly given all she'd learned since being reunited with her poor sister. His ego had always been puffed up and his temper short. Aging had apparently not brought maturity or better coping skills. On the contrary, he'd grown more cruel, not less.

She picked up Natalie and backed away, holding the child close. How long could they go on like this, jumping at shadows or perhaps facing a flesh-and-blood nemesis? This was only the first day of their hazardous journey toward a new life. How could they possibly give this little waif the peace and security she needed when they were constantly on edge?

Kyle checked the hallway with Stryker and quickly returned to report no signs of a prowler, particularly Peter. "It might help if we had something of VanHoven's to give the dog his scent, but for now, we're safe. I don't know what he heard or smelled to make him go on alert. There was nobody out there."

Pacing while carrying her niece, Rachel tried to decide what her next move should be. She stopped and faced Kyle, eyeing him and the K-9 beside him. "Look. Stryker's a comfort because he'll sense trouble long before I do, but his ability to physically defend against an attack is limited." Kyle opened his mouth, evidently intending to refute her conclusion, so she forged on before he could. "I can't stay here. *We* can't stay here. Natalie and I need to go into hiding."

"That's a pretty drastic choice," he countered. "All the guy has done is phone with veiled threats. First he'd have to sneak onto the base for real, assuming he was bluffing before. Somebody's sure to spot him."

"And do what? If he acted normal they might not even pay attention, let alone report him."

"I'll notify the Security Forces office and make sure word is passed to all the units. Lieutenant General Hall seemed quite sympathetic when I asked him for permission to assist you further. I'm sure he'll be glad to assign official protection, too."

"What if he doesn't?"

She could tell Kyle was wrestling with his reply. The supposition of denial was logical on her part. Peter wasn't a terrorist—unless you counted terrorizing his loved ones—so there was really no valid reason to have her watched or monitored now that she was back home on a secure air base.

Kyle checked the time. "It's not very late. I'll give his office a call and leave a voice-mail message. He wanted me to report once we were back on base anyway and I hadn't gotten around to it. Chances are he'll check his messages before he turns in for the night and might even get back to me."

"What's that old saying?" Rachel asked, "'It's better to ask forgiveness afterward than to ask permission before and be denied'?"

"I haven't read that in the regulations," he quipped cynically. "Don't worry. I'll handle Hall."

Rachel took a deep breath and released it in a noisy sigh. "It's not him, or you, I'm worried about. It's Peter. I know what he's capable of, believe me. You should, too, after what you saw in San Antonio. He won't quit just because my sister is gone."

Rachel lowered her niece to the floor and pointed toward the bathroom. "Why don't you go wash your hands before we eat, honey? Our sandwiches are getting cold and I'm hungry. How about you?"

"Uh-huh. Did you make a sammich for Stryker, too?"

"He has regular dog food that Kyle brought," Rachel reminded her. "Go on. Wash up for me, okay? You can take the dog with you."

"Okay." Her small hand grasped the loop of his short leash and he followed obediently, tail flagging.

As soon as Natalie was out of the room, Rachel approached and stopped close to Kyle. Clearly, he was going to take more convincing than just the word of a child. She was ready. Memory of receiving the injuries she was about to show him made her tremble, yet she must. This was necessary. Not pleasant, but necessary.

He was giving her a quizzical look as she stepped in front of him and began to turn to one side. She hooked a thumb in the neckline of her shirt and pulled it just far enough away from her neck and upper shoulder for him to see the grouping of circular scars. As soon as she heard his sharp intake of breath she released the fabric and faced him.

"That's just the tip of the iceberg. Peter was sadistic when I was a teen, and he still is. Now you won't have to take a child's word for it." Swaying in place, she felt Kyle reach out to steady her.

That was all it took. In moments, she was fully in his arms and leaning on his chest while he whispered against her hair. "He burned you?"

Rachel nodded slightly. Kyle bent and placed a tender kiss on her temple, then began to stroke her back through her shirt. How her arms found their way around his waist was a mystery. She hadn't meant to embrace him, yet there they were, holding each other as if they were far more than comrades in arms. She knew she should pull away. Doubtless, Kyle knew it, too. Still, they remained together as she tried to take in every nuance of the special moment, imprinting it in her brain so she would never lose this amazing feeling of belonging. Was this what real love felt like? Or was she imagining that he returned the fondness she was experiencing?

Kyle's heartbeat echoed hers. Their breathing was in sync. He was resting his chin on the top of her head. Neither made a move to step away until they heard a piercing scream from the direction of the bathroom.

Stryker began to bark.

Kyle was a half second ahead of Rachel running down the hall shouting, "Natalie!"

SEVEN

Rachel paid no mind to anything but the frightened little girl. She pulled Natalie into her arms, held tight and flattened her own spine against the wall to get out of the doorway. The dog whirled and tore out of the bathroom with Kyle in pursuit. Barking continued until they reached her bedroom. Then, it stopped abruptly.

Nothing made a sound—not a peep. She didn't hear boots or Stryker's nails on the hard floor for what seemed like an eternity. Finally, footsteps approached. Kyle was coming back.

"The dog was most interested in your bedroom window," he said. "Since you're on the first floor I assume he heard something. There's nobody out there now."

"If you'd been his partner in a war zone would you doubt him?"

"Probably not. But remember, he's been traumatized. We can't send him to a counselor the way we do people."

Rachel made a derisive noise. "I'd sooner trust any of the K-9s in our unit than most people I know."

"Look, there was nothing there. I don't know what scared Natalie or the dog but it wasn't a prowler."

"And you're sure how?"

"Be sensible, Rachel. I know you've had it rough because of your loss and this new development, but you're acting paranoid."

"I'm only paranoid if nobody is after me."

"The guard stopped Peter at the gate. We saw it happen."

Frustrated, she pushed past Kyle and headed for the kitchen with her niece in her arms. The five-year-old was thin for her age but still felt heavy after a while. Lowering Natalie onto a kitchen chair, she proceeded to take the sandwiches from the warming oven and pass them out. When Kyle followed with Stryker, the dog went straight to the child.

A plan was taking shape in Rachel's mind. Because Kyle didn't believe her, she was going to have to play it safe and leave without his knowledge. Then, when he was questioned, he'd be able to truthfully say he had no idea where she'd taken her niece. Destination was the problem. She had no family left and didn't dare use credit cards or the authorities could trace her whereabouts. How far could she hope to get without her own car and with little cash in her purse? Probably not even out of state. Then again, perhaps this was the Lord's way of forcing her to trust more and stay where she was.

That notion did not sit well. Rachel was used to calling the shots and making her own decisions. If the call about her sister had not come as such a shock, she would have traveled to the hospital alone, which, in retrospect, was exactly what she should have done.

As she sat at the kitchen table and picked at her almost-cold sandwich, she sensed that Kyle was studying her. Finally, he spoke. "Okay. What do you want to do?"

"Go back to yesterday and change it," she said flatly. "But since that's impossible, I guess I'm stuck."

"With me?"

She could tell his feelings were hurt, but because she cared what happened to him, she decided that was better than becoming an accomplice to a crime. The longer he stayed with her, the more he'd look guilty when their reckoning came. "You should go. We'll be fine as long as you leave Stryker with us."

"I see." He rose from the table and threw down his napkin.

Noticing that Natalie was wide eyed and cringing, Rachel quickly defused the situation. She inclined her head toward the child and paused long enough for Kyle to get the message. "I'm glad you're not upset," she said cautiously. "We don't want you to be mad."

"I'm not mad at anybody but myself," he countered. "I just thought…"

Empathetic, Rachel watched him slowly circle the table and bend low to place a kiss on the top of the child's head. "You take good care of Stryker for me, okay? I left a bag of his food on the counter. Make sure he always has water to drink. I'll come back to check on him in the morning."

"Okay."

Then, he focused on Rachel. "I'm still going to ask for a Security Forces watch on this apartment whether you approve or not. If the general doesn't see things my way, I'll make other arrangements. I'm not leaving you unguarded. Understand?"

How could she argue with such a sensible plan? "I do. Thank you for everything."

The obvious pain in his expression was nearly her

undoing. There had to be a poignant story behind his emotional response, one she felt compelled to uncover. Following him to the door, she stopped him. "What happened to you in the past, Kyle?"

"I don't know what you're talking about."

"Yes, you do. Tell me. Why is my niece's safety so important to you? Why are you so upset about leaving us?"

"It's the holiday season," he said flatly. "Christmas is always hard for me. Being around you and Natalie at this time of year brought back some strong memories."

"You had a family?" It was a logical guess.

"Once. Long ago. They were killed in a traffic accident on their way home from Christmas shopping."

She laid a hand of consolation on his forearm. "I'm so, so sorry. I didn't know."

"Nobody on base does. It's buried in my file. I never bring it up." His expression hardened. "I'd appreciate it if you kept the information to yourself, as well."

"Of course."

Rachel's heart was breaking for him. She'd caught the poor man at a sensitive moment, and he'd revealed facts he'd been keeping secret. No wonder he was so solicitous to her and Natalie. He was envisioning a second chance, a surrogate family to look after. And the surges of affection she'd detected? Those did not belong to her, but to a woman he had once loved.

Well, so be it. That made her upcoming actions easier. As soon as she could arrange bereavement leave, line up transportation, withdraw some cash from an ATM and buy an untraceable cell phone, she and Natalie would go into hiding. From there she could contact civilian authorities about gaining legal protection, yet keep Peter from knowing where she was. There would be a thin, thin line between what she was doing and what the law dictated, but she'd weather the storm somehow. She had to. A child's welfare depended upon it. And maybe her own survival did, too.

Kyle had little success convincing his commanding officer that extra patrols were necessary for Rachel's sake. He did, however, speak to Westley James, Linc Colson and a few other CAFB K-9 cops and get them to agree to swing by her apartment more often. That helped ease his mind, but not enough to keep him from spending the night parked outside her building, huddled in his warmest jacket while watching for prowlers.

By first light he was exhausted. A shave and a change of clothes were in order, yet he hated to leave his post. Nothing unusual had occurred. The base had been quiet all night except for occasional takeoffs and landings.

He made a fist and wiped condensation from inside the windshield as a vehicle approached. It was Linc Colson. He stopped parallel to Kyle and rolled down his window.

"Morning. I thought I might find you here, Doc. Brought you some coffee."

"Thanks. I can use it. I was about to head back to my quarters and get into uniform."

"You're not on leave?"

Kyle shook his head as he took a tentative sip. Steam was rising through the hole in the lid. "Um, hot. No, not exactly. Hall said I could leave the base to assist Rachel Fielding yesterday and that problem isn't solved yet."

"What's going on?"

"Possible stalking."

"You must think so, or you wouldn't have slept in your car."

"I didn't want to take any chances."

"Okay. Tell you what. I can hang around here for half an hour or so while you go clean up."

Kyle smiled as he drew his fingers down his cheeks to meet his thumb at the point of his chin. "I could use a shave. You're sure you don't mind?"

"It's on my patrol route. Now get going so you'll be back before I have to move on."

"Okay. Thanks."

With one last look at the area surrounding the apartment building, Kyle pulled away. He felt like a fool for worrying so much. After all, CAFB was a secure installation. The chances of a lowlife like VanHoven actually finding a way in were slim. So what had held him there all night, watching, guarding?

He thought back to the night when complacency had cost him his family. Light snow had fallen and he'd warned Sue to drive carefully while he'd finished up at his veterinary hospital in Fort Worth. She and Wendy had planned their outing, claiming they were buying special gifts for him. Something had told him he should have gone along, but he'd ignored the feeling in favor of work. Shortly thereafter he'd gotten the news that a drunk driver had wiped out his loved ones.

Kyle's hands were fisted so tightly on the steering wheel his fingers cramped. He'd never been much of a worrier until he'd lost his family. After that, his practice had floundered almost to the point of bankruptcy, leading him to sell out and return to the air force, where he'd finally found peace.

And now? Now he was beginning to feel almost as anxious as he had four years ago. Only it wasn't just plain concern, was it? He cared too much about Rachel as well as her niece. The comparison to his former family had thrown him for a loop to begin with, but he was beginning to envision more from the experience. He was getting too attached. And despite all the obstacles, he couldn't talk himself out of it.

That was almost as unnerving as admitting his burgeoning feelings in the first place.

Rachel got herself and Natalie dressed, fed and ready to go out. It was comforting to note that one of the Security Force SUVs was idling in the street. As long as Rachel's movements were covered and she had the dog, she felt pretty safe.

"Put your new jacket on, honey. Want me to help you zip it?" she asked.

"I can do it."

"Okay. Come on." She tucked her wallet in a coat pocket. "We need to go shopping and this is a perfect time to leave because there's a base police car right out front."

"Where's Kyle? He said he was coming back."

"Not this early."

"Can Stryker go, too?"

"Only as far as the lawn. We'll exercise him while we wait for a cab, then put him back inside."

"Awww."

"It isn't fair to ask him to walk to the store on three legs, and he can't ride in a cab with us because he doesn't have his official vest and badge," Rachel explained.

"He's gonna be lonesome."

"We'll bring him a treat."

"Ice cream?"

Despite being nervous, Rachel had to laugh. "I had something a little more beefy in mind. Maybe a bone?"

"Yuck."

Continuing to chuckle, Rachel took her niece by the hand, the dog's leash in the other. She'd had enough experience with Stryker to know he'd be well behaved as well as protective. Nevertheless, she wasn't confident enough to turn him loose. She hadn't tested him off lead or around distractions like passing traffic and didn't want to endanger him.

They stepped outside. Rays of sunshine had topped the ridge to the east and were blanketing the base with warmth. Although the overall temperature remained low, the sun felt good on her face. Stryker raised his head, ears perked up, tail flagging happily. Keeping one eye on the black patrol vehicle, Rachel gave the shepherd his head and let him sniff all he wanted. Nose to the ground, he led her and Natalie around the side of the building.

She immediately realized where he was focusing. The dry earth beneath her bedroom window was packed too hard to show footprints, but the dog was certainly interested in something there.

Hair at the nape of her neck prickled like the ruff on an angry animal. She pressed her back to the wall and faced out to scan the neighborhood. A board fence delineated the edge of the property. It was high enough to hide a man. Had it? Was that what the K-9 had been trying to tell her?

Freezing for an instant, she considered the possibility her enemy might have lingered nearby. Reason reminded her that Stryker would be barking if that were the case. No. Whoever had been prowling around the night before and had frightened Natalie was long gone. Her fondest hope was that the dog now had a good idea what he smelled like. If it had been Peter, as she feared, that was even better. All Stryker had to do was remember the scent and react if he ever encountered it again.

As soon as Stryker was safely back in the apartment, Natalie tugged on Rachel's hand. "Carry me?"

Rachel opened her arms and lifted her niece, balancing her weight on one hip. "Okay, I'll carry you to the cab. You have to walk when we get to the store, though."

"Okay." Natalie's arms encircled Rachel's neck and she gave her a squeeze. "You're nice."

"Thank you. I try."

"I'm being good, huh?"

"Of course you are. Why?"

The child tucked her head against Rachel's shoulder, hiding her face when she said, "'Cause I don't want you to give me back to Peter." A shudder punctuated the statement.

"I won't. I already promised." Should she explain further? There might not be a better time. "Sometimes children have to stay in other places for a little while until a judge decides where they should go to live. If that happens to us, that doesn't mean you're bad. It's just how the rules work."

"No!"

Rachel patted her back to try to soothe her. "I promise I'll do the best I can to keep you with me, honey. But I can't break the law and be bad like some people are. The only reason I brought you home with me is because I wanted to keep you safe."

"From Peter?"

"Yes. From Peter." She held her tightly. "I want you to tell me if you see him or any of his friends from your old house, okay?"

"Okay."

The taxi crossed Canyon Boulevard. Rachel remained wary as they arrived at their destination. She took the little girl's hand. "Brrr. Let's go in the mall where it's warmer and look around until the bank opens."

The obedient child let Rachel lead her without a fuss. Perhaps it hadn't been wise to tell her about the legal obstacles she expected to face, but it would have been worse to be separated forcibly without Natalie knowing what was happening or why.

The more Rachel mulled over her predicament, the more foolish it seemed to let fear govern her choices. Kyle was right about the security of the base. And while they were there, they had Stryker on their side, too. It was too bad she couldn't take him with her when she fled or she'd be in even worse trouble than she already was.

Weighed down by reality and the supposition that her situation was getting worse by the minute, she plopped down on a bench inside the mall. Unshed tears filled her eyes. She blinked them back. This situation was untenable. They were doomed and it was all her fault, although in retrospect she didn't see how she could have changed the outcome while still protecting the innocent child.

Natalie crawled up beside her and ducked under Rachel's arm, then took hold of her hand with both of her smaller ones. "Don't be sad, Auntie Rachel."

"I'm sorry, baby. I don't mean to be."

"I miss Mommy, too."

Rachel tucked her closer. "I know you do. I'm sorry I'm not more fun. I just don't know what to do right now to fix everything and I wish I did."

She waited for a reply. When it didn't come, she looked down and saw Natalie's head buried against her coat. Slowly, gently, Rachel lifted Natalie's tearstained face and looked into her Fielding blue eyes, expecting mourning. Instead, she saw raw fear.

Without a word, the child lifted her arm and pointed across the polished stone floor. It took Rachel the space of a heartbeat to realize what she was trying to show. Barely thirty feet away stood a man with his back to them. Instead of wearing camo like most of the others nearby, he was dressed in a red satin bomber jacket with worn elbows, jeans and dirty running shoes. *Peter!*

Rachel gasped, grabbed Natalie and swung her around as she ran for the nearest shop entrance. Inside, she bypassed racks of clothing and headed for the dressing rooms. There had to be a back door. There just had to be.

Natalie was sobbing and attracting too much attention. A clerk eyed them suspiciously. "Can I help you?"

"She's just upset because she wants ice cream," Rachel said, grasping at the first excuse that came to mind. "We'll go out the back so we don't disturb your other customers."

"Sorry. We keep that locked. You understand."

"Sure, sure." Clutching the little girl close, Rachel ducked into an empty dressing room and pulled out her cell phone. There was only one person she trusted enough to summon.

"Hush," she told her niece with a finger to her lips. "You need to be really quiet, sweetie. I'm calling Kyle."

EIGHT

Kyle had decided to check on Stryker, then report to the training center. Traffic was heavy on Canyon Boulevard and around the BX. Many airmen had put in for holiday leave, while others were stocking up to celebrate locally. As far as Kyle was concerned, they were all overdoing it. The last time he'd arranged a special Christmas getaway his plans had died with his loved ones. That remembrance usually brought a tightness in his chest and a lump to his throat. This time, however, his reaction was tempered. Softer. More filled with melancholy acceptance than ever before.

As he drove, Kyle heard his cell phone ringing. "Roark."

Someone was panting, muttering unintelligibly.

"Hello? Who is this?"

"Rachel" he was able to make out. Beyond that, her attempts at conversation were muddled.

"Whoa. I can't understand a word you're saying. Slow down and speak up."

"I can't talk louder. We have to be very quiet."

"Where's Sergeant Colson? He's supposed to be right outside your apartment."

"There was a patrol car there. But I'm not home now. I'm at the BX with Natalie."

Inappropriate responses filled his mind. "Where, exactly?"

"I don't know. Some clothing store. It's near the bank."

He thought he heard her mumble again before she blurted, "It's him. We both saw him. Peter is here."

"Why didn't you say so in the first place?" Kyle whipped the wheel and made a U-turn at the next corner. "Stay put. I'm coming."

Weaving between slower cars, he did his best to rush. The harder he tried, the more obstacles appeared. Frustration built. If he went charging into the base exchange mall he'd attract all sorts of attention. Assuming Rachel and Natalie really had spotted Peter, he knew he had to appear as inconspicuous as possible. That, and locate them before the other man did.

Since he had never gotten a close look at VanHoven it was liable to be difficult to pick him out in a crowd, particularly if he'd assumed a disguise and was dressed in the camo ABU, air-force battle uniform, that most airmen wore.

Kyle slid the last corner on two wheels, cut off another car and slipped into an empty parking place. He was out of the SUV and running toward the main entrance in seconds. A few feet from the automatic doors, he slowed and transformed himself into a normal, casual shopper.

The interior of the mall was crowded, good for hiding but bad for spotting an enemy. As his gaze swept the passing throng, he fixated on one anomaly. The clothing matched what he'd seen at the hospital. And the haircut was far from acceptable for any service member. That had to be Peter.

Kyle faded into the shadow of a doorway and watched. More than nervous, Peter appeared to be under the influence of either drugs or alcohol, maybe both. His mannerisms were jerky and unnatural. He didn't stagger as much as walk with a slight limp.

Edging closer, Kyle got a better look. There was blood on one of the man's ankles and the sleeve of his jacket was torn. Given his grubby condition, it was possible he'd found his way onto the base via one of the washed-out places that occasionally appeared beneath the perimeter fences. If VanHoven had come straight through the woods to the housing area, he might have been able to locate Rachel's apartment, particularly if he'd had help.

At this point, it doesn't matter if he was the prowler Stryker sensed last night or not, Kyle told himself. What he needed to do now was locate Rachel and the child and spirit them away before Peter noticed. Reporting him was out of the question. If VanHoven started screaming for his *daughter*, there would be too much explaining to do. No. First, he needed to rescue Rachel and Natalie. By the time Security picked up Peter, they could be off the base.

Kyle strode past one of the banks that maintained an office in the mall. The next shop featured shoes. After that came one that sold women's clothing.

Taking one last quick peek at Peter, he entered the shop and immediately felt out of place. Why couldn't Rachel have ducked into a sporting-goods store? Pretending to scan the racks of clothes, he worked his way to the rear where the dressing rooms were. Entering was out of the question. So was shouting her name and drawing attention.

"Can I help you, Captain?"

He smiled politely. "I hope so. My wife asked me to meet her down here and she forgot to say which store. I wondered if she might be trying on something."

"Was she alone?" the clerk asked.

"Um, no. Our little girl was with her." He held out a hand, palm down. "About this tall, blond hair, blue eyes."

"Good lungs?" the clerk added with an arch of her brows. "Never mind. I think your wife is here. I'll go get her."

Kyle heard the woman call, "Ma'am, your husband is looking for you. Will you please come out now?"

When Rachel didn't appear he took a chance, leaned in and called, "Hey! Rachel. Are you ready to go?"

She not only came out, she barreled into Kyle's chest and clung to him. Natalie grabbed his knee. "We were afraid it wasn't you."

Instead of asking questions and waiting for her explanation, he lifted Natalie, kept one arm around Rachel's shoulders and started for the door. "Put up the hood on your jacket," he told the child. "We're getting out of here."

All three paused at the store's doorway. Clear glass windows and door gave them no place to hide.

"So far, so good," Kyle said hoarsely. "What were you doing out and about without a bodyguard?"

"I didn't think I'd be allowed to bring Stryker."

"Since when did rules stop you?" he asked cynically.

"I was thinking of the dog, okay? Without his prosthesis it would be harder for him to walk very far."

"What was wrong with staying home?" If he hadn't been looking at her when he'd asked, he might have missed the guilt briefly reflected in her expression. Astonished, he stared. "You were running away from me!"

"What if I was?" Rachel leaned past him to check passersby. "You kept insisting Peter couldn't possibly get on base and he did. What should I have done? Sit at home and wait until he knocked on my door?"

Kyle turned right and headed into the depths of the immense mall, keeping Rachel and Natalie close as he took long, purposeful strides. He had no pat answer for her. Nothing was working out the way he'd imagined. Nevertheless, he did have a few observations.

"First of all," he said with an undertone of anger, "you had no idea that man was actually on the base. Not until you spotted him this morning. So any plans to take off like a fugitive were made before you got here."

She didn't reply. Kyle went on. "Second, if you had intended to tell me what you were up to, you would have phoned before you left your apartment instead of waiting until you were scared to death."

Sensing danger he picked up the pace, making her half jog to keep up. "Third, you'd better hope we can get out of here before Peter spots us and gives chase, because anybody who stops him is going to want to know why he's here and that will point directly to you. And me."

"And Natalie," Rachel finally said.

"Yes. And Natalie. Which is the worst of all three."

"We have to run away. Can't you see that?"

"I'm waiting to hear back from a buddy of mine who's a civilian lawyer. He can probably advise you."

"And in the meantime?"

Kyle could tell she was getting short of breath. Between that and her fear, he wasn't sure how much longer she'd be able to keep up with him. He knew what he should do: call the cops and wait for them to arrive. He also know there were other options, possibilities he'd entertained, then rejected out of hand. He had a place to take her, to hide her, but hadn't been back there in years. Nor was he eager to revisit that part of his past. Why hadn't he sold the tiny cabin long ago? Keeping it up was a useless drain on his finances.

So, why had he hung on to it? *Because it was once a happy place*, Kyle thought with a sigh. A place where his little family had shared holidays and made beautiful memories. Located on an unmarked, forested tract of land, it was so secluded he'd had to convince his late wife, Sue, it was safe to proceed beyond what her GPS could pinpoint.

"My car is parked directly across from the front entrance," Kyle rasped, leaning to speak to Rachel. He pressed a key into her trembling hand. "When we get to the side door, you take Natalie on ahead, get in the SUV and start it. Keep your heads down. I'll be there as soon as I make sure we're not being followed."

Her eyes were wide with fright and glassy with tears. She took a shuddering breath. "Did—did Peter see us?"

"Possibly. I noticed someone moving fast through the crowd. I can't imagine who else it would be."

Panting, Rachel peered past him. "I don't see him."

"That doesn't mean he isn't there."

Wide exit doors slid open. Cold wind rushed in. Kyle set Natalie at Rachel's feet. "Go. Now."

She grabbed her niece's hand, stood on tiptoe and planted a kiss on his cheek. Her lips were warm, her touch gentle yet urgent. Then, without a word, she turned and began to hurry away.

Kyle stared after her. If he'd had any doubt whether to take her to the cabin, that kiss had solidified his decision. He was in this up to his neck and wasn't going to back off.

He stepped aside, stood next to the closing door and waited. If anybody tried to follow Rachel and Natalie, they'd have to take him out first.

Pain sliced through Rachel's lungs and almost doubled her over. She pressed her ribs, hoping that would help. It didn't. She was near the end of her endurance. Intense fright had sapped her strength as much as physical exertion.

Not sure which vehicle was Kyle's, she pushed the button on Kyle's smart key. Flashing yellow lights led her straight to the SUV. She strapped Natalie in the second seat, as before, and climbed behind the wheel.

Shorter than Kyle, she had to scoot forward on the driver's seat to reach the brake and gas pedals. The engine roared to life. Her hands fisted on the wheel. *This* was where she intended to deviate. Prayers for transportation off the base had been answered. No one in his right mind would expect her to just curl up on the seat and sit there like the derelict machinery their fighter pilots used for target practice.

Oh, no. She had wheels. She was going to spin them and "get out of Dodge."

One glance back at Natalie assured her that the child was all right. A second glimpse of the sidewalk outside the door showed Kyle standing alone, apparently braced for attack. This was her chance to escape. So why was her conscience screaming at her to not leave him?

"Please, God," Rachel whispered. "Tell me this is okay."

Partially backing out of the parking space, she was delayed by a passing car. There were blind spots in the SUV mirrors that kept her from being certain the other car was far enough away to allow safe egress, so she inched backward.

By the time she had room to straighten the wheels she was perspiring. Natalie must have sensed her anxiety because her thin voice piped up. "Auntie Rachel? Where's Kyle?"

Where, indeed? She looked back at the place where she'd last seen him. Her breath caught; her pulse leaped. Kyle was down in a blur of male bodies! So was Peter. A couple of airmen had stopped to cheer on the combatants. Nobody seemed inclined to stop the fight. In fact, a third person, in civilian clothes, had just jerked Kyle and Peter to their feet.

For an instant she thought the new arrival was on their side. Then the burly man threw a punch that sent Kyle reeling. That was enough to inspire several airmen to jump into the fray. Fists flew. Men wheeled and staggered, then lunged back into the fight. Where was Kyle? Which one was he? What if they *all* ganged up on him?

Rachel whipped the steering wheel left and floored the gas. Now her decision was easy. She was going to rescue the only real friend she had in the world.

Unarmed, Kyle had made the mistake of assuming Peter was, too. A flash of silver proved otherwise. Kyle knocked the knife aside and closed in, gaining temporary advantage. He barely noticed the gathering spectators—or the wound in his side.

Wiry VanHoven slipped out of his grasp three times before Kyle was able to pin him down. The smaller man fought like a wild animal, or somebody on drugs. Kyle guessed the latter. Superhuman strength was a side effect of meth while it made users unpredictable and irrational. Not the best kind of adversary to face in hand-to-hand combat.

Someone from the crowd wrenched them apart. Fists were flying. He figured the airmen had noticed his captain's insignias and sided with him. That other civilian, however, packed a punch like a mule's kick.

Kyle went down. His jaw ached; his vision blurred. He shook it off and clambered to his feet. Someone slammed him against the outer wall of the building, barely missing the glassed front. In his peripheral vision he glimpsed Peter's jacket. Was he fleeing?

Kyle ducked just in time to avoid another jarring punch from the larger man. Airmen came to his aid and piled on top of the remaining attacker.

Peter was getting away! Kyle yearned to run after him but his image wavered like a desert mirage on a hot Texas afternoon. He staggered. Pressed a hand to his side. Stepped off the curb into the street.

A horn honked. Dizzy, he managed to turn without falling. It was his car! Pulling up right next to him. And Rachel was driving.

The electric window on the passenger side slid smoothly down. She was yelling something but it was drowned out by the noise of the ongoing fight. He reached for the door handle and used it for balance.

"Get in!" she yelled.

Under the circumstances Kyle figured that was a pretty good idea. He pulled himself into place as best he could as she hit the gas. Rapid acceleration threw him back against the seat. He tried to gather his thoughts. Pointed behind them. "Peter is running. He's getting away."

Instead of racing in pursuit as he thought she would, she said, "So are we," and left the parking lot by the farthest opposite exit.

NINE

Rachel's greatest concern was the condition of her companion. "Are you okay? Do we need to go to the hospital?"

Kyle shook his head in what looked like both a reply and an effort to clear his thoughts. "I'm a doctor. I'll take care of myself."

"Not if you pass out. You aren't usually that pale. What's wrong?"

"I'll be fine. Just keep driving."

"Where to?"

"Drive while I think. We can't go back until the cops get their hands on Peter and whoever that man-mountain was he brought with him."

"I thought I saw two guys attacking you but everything happened so fast I wasn't sure."

Kyle winced. "I'm sure. Swing by your place and pick up Stryker. We can't abandon him. Then head for the east gate."

"We're leaving the base after all?"

"Temporarily. I have some calls to make as soon as we're in the clear."

"Who are you going to call?" After what had just

happened she trusted him to do the right thing, but that didn't mean she'd stopped worrying.

"Security, first, so they'll know what the fight was about and won't blame the airmen who jumped in to help me. I'm also going to tell them what VanHoven was wearing and warn them that he has a knife."

She caught a glimpse of him peering down at his side. There was blood on his hand! "You're hurt."

"It's not deep. Keep going."

"To the hospital, you mean." They were approaching her apartment building. "I can turn around here."

"No!"

"You don't have to yell. I can probably stitch you up but I'll have a hard time explaining myself if you aren't conscious."

"I doubt sutures will be required," Kyle told her. Although his jaw was clenching when she pulled to the curb, he sounded convincing. "I'll stay with Natalie while you get the dog."

"We could call somebody else to pick him up."

"We could, but I want him with us. We're liable to need all the help we can get."

"Right. But what if Peter shows up before I get back?"

"Trust the K-9," Kyle said. "You know the commands as well as I do. He'll take out Peter if he needs to." She saw him grimace. "Even with three legs he's more threatening than I am like this."

"Okay." Leaving the motor running, she threw open the driver's door and took off toward her apartment. *Please, God*, she prayed, *let Kyle be all right*. The rest of her prayer was jumbled and confusing, yet she knew it included thoughts of love and devotion and the desire to somehow hold her impromptu family together. The fact that such wishes made little sense didn't bother her nearly as much as the possibility they might be pulled apart by circumstances beyond anyone's control.

"Father, help us," she whispered, meaning every word. "We can't do this alone."

When Stryker met her at the door, panting, tail wagging, eager to please, Rachel realized that part of her urgent prayer had been answered before she'd even asked. They already had capable help, ready and willing. Now all they had to do was get off the base and disappear.

Kyle was doing his best to keep his pain at bay. The only sign of suffering he could not control was the perspiration dotting his forehead. "Act calm when we're passing through the gate," he reminded Rachel.

"I wish you'd quit telling me to do that. This may be normal for a guy who's been in combat but it isn't to me."

"Then fake it," he said with a forced chuckle. "I'm glad you decided to do things your own way this time and came to pick me up. I was getting the worst of that fight."

"Probably because you were the only one bleeding," she said, grimacing and eyeing him.

He slipped his hand into the pocket of his jacket and began to apply pressure unobtrusively to hide his injury. With a wave at the nearest guard, they sailed through the gate unchallenged.

Rachel was shaking visibly when she eased her grip on the wheel and reached down to adjust the driver's seat to her size.

"I wondered if you always drove perched on the edge and clinging to the steering wheel."

"I was in a hurry to rescue you," she said with a touch of cynicism.

"Yeah. Thanks."

Kyle phoned a friend at the training unit. "That's right. I was attacked outside the BX. The airmen who came to my aid did *not* instigate the fight." He paused, listening, then said, "When I explained everything to Lieutenant General Hall, he gave me permission to do whatever was necessary to assist one of my techs. As I said before, trouble followed us back from San Antonio. At least two male civilians. Peter VanHoven and an unnamed assailant jumped me. I have no idea how they got on base, but there was dirt on VanHoven's clothing. Security should check perimeter fences. If there are any questions, I'll be available by cell."

When Kyle ended the call he relaxed back against the seat and briefly closed his eyes.

"Are you feeling faint?"

"No. Why?"

"You shut your eyes."

"If you must know, I was praying about our next move."

He checked his phone again. "GPS puts us seventeen miles from my cabin. That's where we're going."

"Your what?"

"Cabin. And don't give me any flack."

"What makes you think that will be any safer than holing up on base?"

"I owned the place before I reenlisted, and I haven't visited there in years."

"Really? Why didn't you sell it?"

"It's a long story," Kyle said. The cabin held poignant memories for him, memories he didn't want to let go of, yet didn't want to be reminded of, either.

He glanced into the side mirror. A passenger car was keeping pace with them despite their speed. Had his decision to pick up Stryker given Peter a chance to track them down? It didn't look good.

Rachel noticed Kyle's concern before he had time to tell her anything. "Are we being followed?"

"I'm not sure. Get ready to turn off the highway."

"Where?"

"It's coming up." He pointed ahead. "There. Don't slow down on the dirt road."

She complied, surprised at how rough the track was. "This bouncing must be hurting you."

"I'll live. Faster!"

She failed to see anyone behind them due to the brownish cloud they were raising. "They'll see our dust!"

"Can't be helped. Turn off at that pine with a gouge in its trunk. The cabin is just ahead on the right."

"I see it."

"Try to pull behind and get out of sight."

"Wow. It's sure overgrown."

Tense and perspiring, Rachel plowed through the undergrowth, hearing it snap, crush and scrape the sides of the SUV. Their stop was jarring. For a moment she just sat there, catching her breath.

The tiny cabin was pioneer log construction. Casement windows flanked a front door. There was no entrance in the rear. Kyle got out and led the way to a hidden key while Rachel fetched Natalie. Stryker followed.

When Kyle swung open the door the little girl gasped. The interior was a wonderland. Garlands were festooned from the ceiling. Tinsel hung from strings of tiny colored lights. Bright glass orbs twisted on invisible threads.

And in the far corner stood a miniature plastic evergreen tree with a manger scene at its base.

Christmas had been waiting for him for four long years.

TEN

Rachel didn't know what to say. Natalie was clapping her hands and jumping up and down. "Look, Auntie Rachel. Isn't it beautiful?"

"Yes." It was. Truly. Natalie made a dash for the crèche while Kyle checked the windows and reported no one else coming up the road.

"This is baby Jesus," the little girl said. "And these are the wise men. They brought birthday presents. Gold, common sense and fur."

Relieved to have escaped, Rachel smiled at Kyle. "Leave it to kids to put life in perspective. Did you learn about the wise men in Sunday school, honey?"

"Uh-uh. Maria told me. I miss her."

"We can go visit her after I adopt you."

"You're gonna be my mommy?"

"Yes."

The little girl giggled. "That's silly. Then you'd be Auntie Mommy." She paused. "Will Kyle be my new daddy? Please?"

He crouched next to the five-year-old. "I'll always be your friend," he said tenderly. "Your aunt works for me so I'm sure you and I will see each other a lot."

Joining them, Rachel added, "That's right. But there's a rule in the air force that I'm not supposed to date my boss, so Kyle can't be your daddy."

It took a few seconds for Natalie to process that information. When she had, she was totally candid. "Well, *that's* a dumb rule."

He ruffled her hair. "I agree completely. That is one very dumb rule."

"Maria says we have to be good and keep rules," Natalie told him. "Do we? Even if they're dumb?"

"I'll have to give that question some thought," Kyle told her. "Now you play over here while your aunt Rachel puts a bandage on my owie, okay?"

"Okay."

Rachel followed him to a section of the single room where he'd stored first-aid supplies.

"Use rubbing alcohol to clean the cut." He was taking off his jacket.

More aspects of their isolation began to occur to her. "There's no water?"

"We have fruit juice in cans and enough to eat for a few days. I'll phone the base and let Security know where we are after you patch me up. We'll go back as soon as they have your buddy Peter in custody."

"Do you think he was in the car that followed us?"

"Possibly. But we lost them."

Rachel's hands were trembling as she cleansed the wound. "I think a few butterfly bandages will take care of it."

"You just don't want to suture me."

"It's not something I've always dreamed of doing, no."

"What are your dreams, Rachel? Will they change now that you're about to become Auntie Mommy?"

That made her smile. "There was a time, long ago, when I wanted a family. Seeing what happened to my sister turned that dream into a nightmare but…"

Kyle touched her hand. Stilled it. Looked into her eyes as if he was able to see all the way to her heart's desires. "But?"

"Our time together has been extraordinary. It's hard to put into words without sounding sappy, but I've looked forward to almost every moment." She lowered her gaze to where his hand touched hers. "Especially to spending more time with you."

"I feel the same." He leaned closer. Rachel felt her cheeks flaming. She closed her eyes, hardly able to believe what she knew was about to happen. His nearness was palpable. A tender touch against her cheek, the whisper of his breath mingling with hers.

And then he kissed her.

Rachel was floating on clouds of intense emotion, yearning for the moment to continue. Kyle's kiss was everything she had hoped, and more. Walls that had stood between them crumbled to dust. Problems that had seemed insurmountable shrank into nothingness. Surrounded by love, she felt his arms encircle her, pull her closer, deepen the kiss until she was breathless, boneless, mindless.

He must love her. He simply must. No man could convey that depth of emotion without feeling the same affection she had been fighting ever since their trip to see Angela. She hadn't realized it then, but she'd started to fall for him almost as soon as he'd shown her his true self.

Kyle slowly released her, studying her expression

until she felt the heat rising in her cheeks. "I'm sorry," he said. "I shouldn't have done that."

"Yes, you should," Rachel said boldly. "And if you try to take it back I'll be really disappointed."

"You will?"

"Yes, I will." She stood her ground despite her spinning head and racing pulse. "Unless of course *you* didn't like it."

"Oh, I liked it. I liked it just fine."

It amused her to see high color in his face, too, so she grinned. "Okay. Good. What now?"

He grew even redder. "Um…"

Rachel laughed lightly. "I was referring to taking more precautions and notifying the base again."

"Um, yeah. Right."

"You're cute when you blush," she teased.

"I'm way too old to be cute," Kyle countered. "Besides, officers are not supposed to blush. We're supposed to be all the things that my being here with you negates."

"Would it help your case if I quit the service at the end of my current enlistment?"

"Let's not get ahead of ourselves," he said. "I did have permission to help you so we may skate through."

"Suppose we don't?"

Before Kyle could reply, Stryker sat up. A low rumble began in the K-9's throat and grew to a full growl.

Rachel jumped. Natalie began to cry and ran to her. Kyle strode to the window and scanned the otherwise quiet forest.

"They found us?"

"Not necessarily. It could be a nosy neighbor."

"You can't really believe that."

As she held the frightened child close, Rachel cast around for a safe place to hide her. A one-room cabin didn't provide a lot of options.

She watched Kyle barricade the door by upending a table. "You're not acting like you think it's a neighbor."

"That's because there's more than one person."

"Peter?"

Natalie began to sob against Rachel's shoulder and cling to her neck.

"Maybe. Call the police and tell them to hurry." Kyle displayed a shotgun and half a box of 12-gauge shells. "This is all we have for self-defense."

Rachel made the brief call and stashed Natalie behind the Christmas tree with Stryker, then joined Kyle. "How can I help?"

"You didn't happen to bring a rifle, did you?"

"Nope. And the local sheriff is busy at a multiple-vehicle wreck on the highway so we can't count on him. Do you think they'll attack?"

"Hard to tell. If they don't know we're sitting ducks they may try to wait us out. I don't intend to shoot unless they do." He looked past her. "Where's our girl?"

"Hiding with Stryker." Rachel shivered and rubbed her hands together. "I wrapped her in a blanket but that won't stop a bullet."

"I doubt they'll harm her," Kyle said. "You and I are another matter."

"I'm so sorry I got you into this." There was a catch in her voice.

"If anybody got me into anything it wasn't you," he countered. "I still see this as my second chance to do the right thing. I was absent by choice the first time, when I should have been there for my family. God gave me another opportunity to prove myself."

Was he trying to say he loved her, loved Natalie? Was that even possible? She and Kyle had known each other through work for a couple of years but that wasn't the same as dating. As for her niece, he'd barely met her.

Those facts definitely made them surrogates, she reasoned. This wasn't the only time that premise had occurred to her but it was the first time Kyle had put it into his own words. There was no doubt they needed each other. He needed healing of his spirit, and she needed protection from evil. That was for everyone's good, so how could she argue?

Because I'm selfish, Rachel concluded. When all this was over, perhaps Kyle would still be interested in her. If he wasn't, she'd have to accept it as an unwelcome answer to prayer. Just because she had worked out a pleasing solution in her mind, there was no guarantee God would agree with her plans. The Lord might just as easily see to it that they were separated by air-force protocol and hardly ever saw each other.

That notion brought tears to her eyes and made her want to throw herself into Kyle's arms. Well, she wasn't going to. He needed to be alert, not distracted.

She was searching the cabin for a makeshift weapon when banging on the door startled everyone. Stryker barked. Rachel gasped and froze. Kyle levered a shell into the shotgun.

Whoever was outside must have heard the metallic noise of the slide working, because they stopped pounding.

Rachel peeked through a gap in the curtains. "They're leaving!"

"Not for long, I'm afraid. Get my phone out of my

jacket pocket and bring it here. It's high time I called in reinforcements."

As soon as she delivered his phone, she went back to the window and watched four men searching the forest floor.

"Tell them to hurry," she shouted to Kyle. "I think Peter's making a battering ram!"

ELEVEN

"I'll leave my cell connected," Kyle shouted into the phone. "You can home in on it. Just hurry."

"Who's coming?" Rachel asked.

"As many of the K-9 unit as will fit into a small chopper. There's no clearance to land so they'll have to rappel down with their dogs and take the chance of becoming a target."

"It'll take too long for them to drive?"

"A few will fly in while the rest approach from the ground. It's an operation they've trained for."

"How can I help?"

"Stay back, out of the way."

"Not a chance—*Captain*."

"Forget rank and listen to me," Kyle insisted. "You're defenseless. If the bullets start to fly I don't want to worry about you." He jerked his head toward the rear corner. "Get behind the tree with Natalie and Stryker and make sure they stay down, too."

"Is that an order?"

Kyle rolled his eyes. "No, Rachel, it's not. It's a sensible suggestion from someone who cares for you in spite of himself, okay?" To his relief, her resistance gave way to shock, then acquiescence.

"All right. I'll get out of your way. But I won't promise to sit idle if I see you're in danger. Understood?"

Nodding, he figured that was the best he was going to get. Truth to tell, she'd bailed him out before by using her head and not panicking. If he needed help again it was good to know she'd be handy. His biggest problem was letting go of the notion that protecting them all was solely up to him.

Wrong. It's up to God, his thoughts insisted, pushing him to wordless prayer and reminding him of everything he had lost. How could he possibly reconcile those memories with the ones he was making at present? That was asking the impossible, leaving him with the need to place absolute trust in his heavenly Father's decisions. Much of life was beyond understanding for man. Either he believed and relied upon God or he didn't.

As soon as Kyle realized that he needed a different kind of help, he called to Rachel, "Pray. Hard."

He watched as she fell to her knees and pulled Natalie close. They bowed their heads. Kyle joined them in his heart and he gave thanks despite the risk of impending attack.

It was a lot easier to do so on a sunny Sunday morning in the safety of church, which was the point, he guessed. Faith without testing and proving was far too easy to take for granted. So was love.

Rachel let Natalie speak for both of them because the child's prayer was direct and heartfelt instead of being filled with the pat phrases so many adults fell back on when they didn't know what else to say.

"Thank you, Jesus, for saving me from Peter and hug my mommy for me. Please help Auntie Rachel and Kyle. Amen."

The little girl turned misty eyes to Rachel. "Was that okay?"

"It was perfect, honey."

"Good." Rachel let go and Natalie looped both arms around the three-legged dog's neck. "And thank you for Stryker. Amen again."

This was no time for smiles, yet the corners of Rachel's mouth lifted. What a precious little girl. Angela may have failed her in many ways, but the Lord had sent Maria into her life to plant seeds of faith. To take care of His child. Was He using her and Kyle, too? Undoubtedly. All Rachel had to figure out was how to assist without getting in God's way. That had been her error in the past, more times than she cared to count. She had tried to help too much, to do things her way. Listening to Kyle, however, was a different story.

And speaking of listening. She held her breath. Footsteps. Lots of them. On the porch? Yes!

"Brace yourself," Kyle announced. "We're about to be rammed."

Rachel reached for the child, including the K-9 in her embrace. Growls were rumbling, vibrating his chest. "Easy, Stryker. Easy."

Bang! The window panes shook. Dust filtered down from the open rafters. *Bang!*

"It's holding," Kyle shouted.

"What about…" Rachel stopped herself from mentioning the windows. They weren't very big but would probably allow a skinny guy like Peter to wriggle through. How many shotgun shells did they have? Would Kyle fire a warning shot if their attackers chose to come at them that way?

She cast about for a weapon. Anything would do. There was no poker in the fireplace but there was a blackened iron skillet on the woodstove. If she could reach that and place herself for a strike, she might save a shotgun shell.

Men were stomping around on the narrow porch, arguing and cursing. The moment she overheard one of them say "Window," she put her plan into motion. Cross to the stove, grab the handle of the pan, scurry to the opposite side of the small window without being seen, raise it over her head and wait.

In position, she glanced over at Kyle. He was furious. "Move! I can't shoot with you standing there."

Rachel merely shook her head and held out the pan for him to see, then raised it again. Just in time. The glass shattered. Someone ran a gun barrel along the edges to clear them of sharp points. A hat started to pass through the newly made access.

Every muscle tensing, Rachel forced herself to wait a few moments longer. Almost there. Almost time. *Now!*

Thwack! The iron pan glanced off hat and head, ending up at Rachel's side on the end of her straightened arms. People outside rushed to pull the intruder back and carry him away, all the while shouting and threatening retribution.

Her heart was pounding so rapidly she could hardly separate the beats. A tremor ran up her arms and raced along her spine, leaving her limbs weak and quivering. She met Kyle's astonished gaze. "I—I didn't mean to hit him so hard."

"Forget what I said about you being defenseless. And don't beat yourself up about hurting him. If they get to us they won't be gentle."

Tightening her grip on the handle, she said, "Yeah. That's what I figured."

Kyle got Rachel to back off by convincing her that their attackers wouldn't try the same approach twice. He still couldn't believe how brave she was. If she judged him in need of her help she was going to provide it, just as she'd promised, whether or not he agreed.

Watching through the unbroken window, he saw a man approaching. His hands were raised and empty, as if he wanted to surrender. That was too good to be true.

Kyle spoke aside to Rachel. "Peter's coming. He looks unarmed but I don't trust him."

"I knew you were smart."

A fist pounded on the door. "Hey, in there. I don't want anybody else to get hurt. Just give me the kid and I'll leave you alone. I swear."

The barrel of the shotgun remained aimed at the closed door. "Don't answer him, Rachel. Let him wonder."

"He should know better than to think I'd ever give up Natalie to him."

"Exactly. He's probably trying to divert our attention while his buddies do something else."

"What?"

"Beats me. I suppose we'll find out. Stay alert."

"Are those the only two windows?"

"Yes." As he scanned the side and rear walls an unusual odor caught his attention. He sniffed, then checked out Stryker. Ears perked, the three-legged K-9 was waving his head back and forth, making use of all his senses.

Apparently Rachel was, too, because she asked, "Do you smell smoke?"

"Yeah. But I don't see anything yet."

She was on the move. "Back here. Look! See it seeping between the logs?"

He certainly did. Soon it would be impossible to breathe inside, yet if they ventured out, Peter and his cohorts would grab Natalie. The situation was untenable. They couldn't hope to triumph without better weapons.

"I'm not giving up," Kyle declared. "If it gets too bad in here, I'll run out the front shooting so you can slip away with Natalie and Stryker."

"What good will that do? They'll just mow you down and come after us."

"It'll buy you some time."

"And cost you your life. No way."

"Do you have a better idea?"

"Yes. No. I don't know. How about letting them in and taking them on right here? It's cramped but we'd have better control. And Stryker can defend Natalie."

"You mean because they won't be able to sneak behind him. I get it." Kyle had kept the phone connection open. Now he pressed the cell to his ear rather than broadcast their plans. "Security, what's the ETA on that chopper?" His concerned gaze locked with Rachel's and he nodded soberly. "Copy. The sooner the better."

An unasked question lay between them. Kyle led Rachel away from the smoky wall. Stryker was on his feet, standing guard over Natalie while she hugged his ruff. "They're in the air," he told them quietly. "All we need is another five minutes or so. Stay put."

He saw unshed tears in Rachel's eyes as she bent to whisper to her niece. He had to get them out of this somehow. Even if it did cost him his life.

Flames licked up the inside of the logs at the base of the rear wall, leaving wispy fingers of soot. A layer of smoke filled the top half of the room and was slowly dropping lower. Rachel remembered the juice Kyle had mentioned and gathered up an armload of cans to pour over the visible fire. It did seem to help a little. The sound of the battering ram echoed again. Her head ached, her eyes stung and she started to cough. A second trip for more juice took her breath away. They were almost out of options. Almost done. Like it or not, Kyle was going to have to open the door and let in more air. And their enemies. Her duty, then, would be to defend the little girl.

Looking to Kyle and seeing him approaching the door with his shotgun raised, she held her breath. It was getting hard to see, hard to hear, hard to keep the faith.

He reached for the latch, released it and stepped back. In seconds the door burst open and four thugs rushed him. He got off one good shot before they plowed him down. Rachel stood between the child and the melee until one of the men came closer. Then she knocked him flat with her iron frying pan.

Men were shouting. Stryker was barking. The fire, fed by more oxygen, began to crackle and climb the wall. Rachel felt her pulse thrumming, the whoosh in her ears filling the cabin.

Wait! That wasn't her heartbeat; that was the sound of helicopter blades. Help was here!

Anticipation renewed her strength. She covered her

head and shoulders with the blanket, scooped up Natalie and ran. By bending over she was able to avoid the thickest smoke and make it to the door. So did Stryker.

The blanket was yanked off her from behind. Peter yelled. Natalie screamed. Stryker launched himself with his powerful hind legs and sank his teeth into their pursuer's shoulder, falling when Peter did but holding on as he'd been trained.

Men and women in full battle dress were rappelling down from a hovering chopper with their K-9 partners. The first pair passed her and burst into the cabin. The second stopped long enough to ask if she and Natalie were okay before joining the charge.

One of the later arrivals gave Stryker the release command and praised him. Rachel didn't care that Peter was bleeding from the bite. It was Kyle she wanted to see. As soon as Stryker hobbled up to her, she ordered him to guard Natalie and ran back toward the smoky cabin.

A simple prayer kept echoing in her thoughts. *Please, God, let Kyle be all right. Please, please, please.*

An airman guarding the space in front of the porch tried to stop her. "I'm sorry, ma'am, you can't come any closer."

"It'll take more than one air-force cop to stop me," she countered.

From behind him came a familiar chuckle. "Better let her by, Sergeant. She swings a mean frying pan."

Rachel had never heard a more welcome sound. "Kyle! I was afraid…" Her voice trailed off as she threw herself at him, wrapped her arms around his waist and held tight. Tears of relief fell freely. At this moment she didn't care who was watching or who might report them. All that mattered was Kyle. He was alive. And he was holding her as if he loved her as much as she loved him. More words could wait. They'd survived and so had the rest of their family: Natalie and Stryker.

Heart overflowing with thanks for deliverance, she clung to the man she adored and let the world go on spinning without further concern. Judging by the way he was embracing her and raining kisses down on the top of her head, Kyle was okay with everything, too. Very okay.

Nevertheless, she needed to hear the words so she took the lead. "I love you, Kyle."

To Rachel's delight he grinned, his eyes filling with emotion, and echoed, "I love you, too."

That was enough for Rachel. For now. And thank God, literally, they would have plenty of time to say a lot more in the future.

EPILOGUE

The annual Christmas party held at the K-9 unit head-quarters included several special guests. General Hall was there to award an official commendation to Stryker for his exemplary work in the field. The proud K-9 accepted his medal on four legs, one of them a cus-tom-made prosthesis. Although it was Kyle Roark who paraded the dog up to the general, little Natalie ac-companied them and carefully explained to all present what a hero her new best friend was. Applause rocked the building.

Rachel was so happy and proud she could hardly speak. If someone had told her a few weeks ago what was going to happen in her life, she wouldn't have be-lieved it. God had smoothed out the impassable road and was continuing to do so.

When General Hall followed Kyle, Natalie and Stryker back to the table where Rachel waited, he was all smiles. She mirrored his grin and swiped away a few happy tears as she stood tall and saluted. "Thank you, sir. Thank you for everything."

Hall nodded. "As you were. I'd say *it was my plea-*

sure if I hadn't had to pull so many strings to keep you out of trouble. You and the doc didn't make my job any easier."

"You went beyond the call of duty when you got Peter to sign over custody of my niece," Rachel said. "I can't believe he agreed."

"I can be very persuasive when I have to be," the general said.

Kyle laughed nervously. "I hope the same goes for me." He dropped to one knee and took Rachel's hand. "Will you marry me?"

"Yes!" Her eyes jumped to the general, then back to Kyle. "But, how can we? I can't marry my boss without getting us both in trouble, especially you."

"Don't worry. My enlistment is up soon and I'm planning to resume private practice. If you want to stay in the air force we'll just live off the base and you can commute."

So happy she could hardly believe it, Rachel leaned on Kyle's shoulder and sighed. "Okay, but are you sure? I know you love the air force as much as I do."

"I rejoined because I was running away from life," he said. "I had to have God's help forgiving myself and finding a way to move on."

"Sometimes we all do." She snuggled closer. "I wonder if I'll ever be able to forgive Peter."

"He did do two good things," Kyle reminded her. "He brought us together and gave us our first daughter."

Rachel knew she was blushing. "First?"

"God willing." Kyle pulled her into his arms and

kissed her under the mistletoe. "Merry Christmas, honey."

Thankful beyond her wildest dreams, she smiled up at him and said, "It certainly is."

* * * * *

Laura Scott is a nurse by day and an author by night. She has always loved romance and read faith-based books by Grace Livingston Hill in her teenage years. She's thrilled to have published over twenty-five books for Love Inspired Suspense. She has two adult children and lives in Milwaukee, Wisconsin, with her husband of over thirty years. Please visit Laura at laurascottbooks.com, as she loves to hear from her readers.

Books by Laura Scott

Love Inspired Suspense

True Blue K-9 Unit

Blind Trust

Military K-9 Unit

Battle Tested
Military K-9 Unit Christmas
"Yuletide Target"

Callahan Confidential

Shielding His Christmas Witness
The Only Witness
Christmas Amnesia
Shattered Lullaby
Primary Suspect
Protecting His Secret Son

Visit the Author Profile page
at Harlequin.com for more titles.

YULETIDE TARGET

Laura Scott

Beloved, let us love one another: for love is of God;
and every one that loveth is born of God,
and knoweth God.
—*1 John 4:7*

This book is dedicated to Vicki Lynn Christman and Sally Nowak, two wonderful women who love to read Love Inspired Suspense books. And of course, to their beloved Sophie.

ONE

Senior Airman Jacey Burke felt vulnerable without her K-9 companion, a Belgian Malinois named Greta, as she walked across Canyon Air Force Base toward her apartment. Shivering in the cold December air, she was grateful the darkness was relieved by the string of Christmas lights shimmering merrily up and down Canyon Boulevard.

The back of her neck tingled with awareness and she knew someone was once again watching her.

Curling her fingers around the panic alarm attached to her key ring and nestled in the palm of her hand, she did her best to act nonchalant. In lieu of a weapon, which dog trainers weren't permitted to carry, the panic alarm was the only way she had to protect herself. That and Greta, but unfortunately, rules dictated she kennel her K-9 partner at night.

Waiting at the corner of Canyon and Webster Avenue for the traffic to ease, she resisted the urge to glance back over her shoulder. So far, she hadn't caught anyone watching.

But that didn't mean someone wasn't back there, somewhere.

A large box truck rumbled down Canyon Boulevard, coming in from the south side of the base. As it approached the intersection, she wrinkled her nose at the rank odor of stale cigarette smoke and sensed someone behind her, a fraction of a second before a strong hand shoved her hard in the center of her back. With a muffled *oomph*, she stumbled forward, directly into the path of the oncoming vehicle.

Her heart lodged in her throat, her chest tightened, making it impossible to scream. It seemed like everything happened in slow motion; her arms pinwheeled as her keys flew from her fingers.

Then her hands slapped hard against the smooth surface of the box truck. Pain rippled up her arms. The force of the blow caused her to spin around like a top. The world tilted dizzyingly before she hit the asphalt with an ungainly thud. She felt the wind against her face as the truck rumbled past, missing her by less than an inch.

Dimly aware of the screeching sound of breaks and the scent of burning rubber, she felt pain reverberate through her body as she lay on the ground, trying to understand what had happened.

"Are you all right?" a deep male voice asked.

She lifted her head to peer up at the man who'd come to her aid, instinctively wary. The man leaning over her looked familiar, but she couldn't quite place him. She blinked, wondering how hard she'd hit her head.

"Jacey Burke?" The man knelt beside her and rested a hand on her shoulder. "Don't move—I'll call an ambulance."

"No, please, don't…" she tried to protest, but it was

too late. The man who'd come to her aid had already made the call.

"Did you trip and fall?" His gaze raked over her, as if assessing for blood.

"No." Ignoring his hand on her shoulder, she pushed herself up to a sitting position, wincing at the aches and pains radiating from her hands, arms and knees.

She knew it could have been far worse.

Swallowing the lump in her throat, she scanned the area. "Do you see my keys?"

"Here." He pushed them into her hand.

Fat lot of good her panic alarm had done, she thought with a wry grimace. At least it hadn't shattered to bits.

"Jacey, please. Don't move until the ambulance arrives."

The way he kept calling her by her first name bothered her. She stared through the dim light at his handsome, chiseled features and then belatedly placed him in her memory. "Sean? Sean Morris?"

He smiled and nodded. "It's been a long time, hasn't it?"

"Ten years," she agreed, her mind whirling. She and Sean had attended the same high school back in Branson, Missouri. Sean was a year older, the same age as her brother, Jake.

A wave of sorrow hit hard as she thought about her brother's death in Afghanistan nine months ago. This would be her first Christmas without him.

"What do you mean, no?" Sean asked, interrupting her maudlin thoughts.

She frowned, not understanding at first, until she remembered his earlier question. "No, I didn't trip. I was pushed."

"Pushed? On purpose?" The echo of disbelief in his tone grated on her nerves. She was tired of being treated as if she was losing her mind. Ever since she'd been sent back to base three months ago and reported the strange incidents she'd experienced, she'd heard the whispers.

Cuckoo. Crazy. Delusional.

And knew that's exactly what the person watching her intended.

Not just watching, she mentally corrected herself. Things had escalated beyond discrediting her. Being pushed into the path of an oncoming vehicle was far more serious.

He or she had escalated from trying to make her look crazy to attempting to kill her.

"Hey, is she okay?" A guy dressed as she was in a battle dress uniform came running over. She understood he was the driver of the truck. "I swerved to avoid hitting her."

A move that had likely saved her life.

"I'm Staff Sergeant Morris," Sean said. "I'm a cop, so I'll need to take your statement."

Sean held a rank one level above hers, and she squelched a wave of frustration at her recently denied promotion. She kept her gaze on the truck driver. "Did you see what happened?"

"It looked like you tripped and fell," the driver said.

Jacey swallowed a wave of frustration. "Neither one of you saw anyone behind me? Someone walking away from the corner?"

The two men exchanged a long glance.

"I'm sorry, Jacey, but I didn't notice anyone nearby," Sean admitted. "I was walking in this direction from the parking lot near the south gate, so I didn't have a great view. I only saw the truck swerve seconds before you went flying onto the pavement."

"When I noticed you at the corner, I was already in the process of moving over out of the way when you stumbled forward," the driver said, picking up his side of the story. "I yanked the steering wheel to avoid hitting you. Are you sure you're okay? No broken bones?"

"I'm fine," she insisted, although the bumps and bruises were making themselves known. Her entire body would be sore tomorrow.

"Staff Sergeant, I need to make a delivery to the hospital," the driver said.

"As soon as the ambulance arrives, I'll take your statement for the record," Sean said. "I'm off duty, but as the first cop on the scene, it's my job to make sure this gets reported."

Jacey noticed Sean wasn't dressed in his Special Forces uniform. He was a base cop? And hadn't seen anyone push her into traffic?

She shivered, a cold wave of despair washing over her. If she couldn't get an old high school friend to believe someone had lashed out at her on purpose, who would?

Reeling from seeing Jacey again after all these years, not to mention her allegation of being pushed into the truck's path, Sean did his best to stay focused on the task at hand.

While the EMTs examined Jacey, he nudged the box-truck driver aside. "Name and rank, please," he said, pulling out his notebook.

"Senior Airman Charlie Egan," the driver replied. "I really did my best to avoid hitting her."

"I know," Sean assured him. "If not for your quick reflexes, this could have ended much worse."

"Yeah." Charlie looked somber. "Do you really think she was pushed?"

"No reason not to believe her," Sean said. He fervently wished that he'd seen someone leaving the area where Jacey had been standing, but he hadn't. His entire being had been zeroed in on Jacey's body lying in a crumpled heap on the ground. "You didn't see anyone near her either, correct?"

"Afraid not." Charlie rubbed the back of his neck. "Is it okay if I leave now? I don't want to be late delivering these supplies."

"Sure." Sean tucked his notebook away. "I'll be in touch if I need anything."

"Okay." Charlie loped down the street toward his vehicle.

Sean turned his attention to Jacey Burke, annoyed when he noticed she was pushing the EMTs out of the way.

"I'm fine, see?" She stood and took a few steps. "If I thought I had broken bones, I'd go in for X-rays. But I'm fine."

"Ma'am," one of the EMTs started, but she cut him off.

"I'll sign a waiver. That way you can go help someone who needs it."

"Jacey, you need to go to the hospital," Sean said in a stern tone. "I won't take no for an answer."

Her gaze narrowed. "Really? How will you stop me?"

He glanced at the two EMTs. "Please give us a moment alone." The two EMTs backed off and Sean made sure to lower his voice so that their conversation couldn't be overheard. "You said someone pushed you into the truck's path, correct?"

Her gaze turned wary. "Yes."

"Then I need a hospital report to go along with your allegation so that your injuries are documented."

She appeared to consider his point. "Does this mean you believe me?"

"I have no reason not to," he said, repeating what he'd told the truck driver.

"Fine. I'll go to the ER."

"In the ambulance," he persisted.

She grimaced but reluctantly nodded. "I guess."

"Thanks." He put a hand on her back, gently urging her toward the EMTs. "Airmen? She's ready to go."

When Sean moved away, she grabbed his arm. "Wait. Aren't you coming with me?"

"I'll meet you there," he promised. "I'm going to look over the scene here one more time, then head over to get my car so that I can drive you home."

The warmth of her hand on his arm was distracting. He thought about the way he'd admired her from afar back in high school, then reminded himself that they were different people now.

Especially him. Staying away from his abusive stepfather had been his top priority. After his mother's death from cancer, he'd joined the air force and never looked back.

Besides, he wasn't in a good place. Recently, his confidence had taken a hit after the way he'd failed Liz Graber, a woman he'd promised to protect. Her death hung like a dark cloud over him.

The ambulance slowly drove away, and he forced

himself to jump into action. He swept the area for clues, but found nothing. He lived in one of the apartments on base but kept his car in a parking area several miles away. He preferred walking while on base but liked having a vehicle handy for those times he needed to get away. He'd moved his grandmother to a small house not far from Canyon and made weekly trips to see her as his schedule allowed. In fact, he'd just returned from a visit with Gram when he'd come across Jacey's collision.

Sean picked up his car and arrived at the base hospital roughly fifteen minutes later. He had to wait another five minutes before they allowed him to see her. Jacey was lying on a gurney, dressed in a hospital gown, her face pale and her dark brown hair falling out of its ponytail. She looked relieved when he stepped into the cubicle.

"They took X-rays and a CT scan of my head. I'm just waiting for the results." She lifted her hands, palms upward. "Just a few scrapes and bruises, nothing more serious. You really needed a hospital visit to go along with the police report?"

"Jacey, if not for the truck driver's quick thinking, you might not even be alive," he reminded her. "It's best to get everything that happened on record so that when we find this guy, we can press the appropriate charges."

She looked as if she wanted to say more, but at that moment, a doctor pushed into the room. "I'm Captain Grant Simons. I reviewed your X-rays and your CT scan—everything looks fine. I suggest you take six hundred milligrams of ibuprofen every six hours for the next two days."

"I will."

Dr. Simons did a quick physical exam, noting the

bruises on her knees and the scrapes on her palms. Sean was glad to see the thick fabric of Jacey's battle dress uniform helped protect the skin on her knees; it was obvious her hands had taken the brunt of the collision.

"Am I free to leave now?" Jacey asked.

"Yes. Don't forget to return to the ER if your symptoms get worse."

Jacey nodded and Sean stepped back out of the cubicle to give her privacy to get dressed.

He pulled out his phone to call his boss, Master Sergeant Doug Hanover, but before he could scroll to find the number, Jacey emerged from the room.

"Who are you calling?" she asked sharply.

He was taken aback by her terse tone and slipped his phone into his pocket. "I was going to call my master sergeant, Doug Hanover, but it can wait."

She brushed past him, as if anxious to get out of the hospital. It wasn't until they were outside and settled in his Honda Civic that she turned to look at him. "I'm sure you've heard about me from the other Special Forces cops."

"Um, no, not really." Probably because he'd been preoccupied with how he'd failed Liz Graber. He started the car and waited until she snapped her seat belt into place before backing out of the parking space. "Where do you live? In the base apartment complex on Oakland?"

"Yes, in the south building." She gnawed on her lower lip, as if mentally debating how much more she should tell him. "The report you're going to file tonight isn't the first one. There are a couple of other reports on file from me."

He tightened his grip on the wheel as a flash of frustration toward Jacey surged. "Are you telling me you've been shoved into the path of a truck before?"

"No, that's a first. The previous reports are nothing this serious. Tonight's event has escalated to a whole new level."

Sean tried to relax his grip. "Okay, so what has transpired before tonight?"

"Stupid stuff," she said, waving a dismissive hand. "Like moving my paperwork, hiding my keys, that kind of thing. But I've been trying to get the Special Forces cop I've been dealing with to take my concerns seriously." Her lips thinned. "Maybe after tonight, he will."

"Who have you been working with?"

"Senior Airman Bill Ullman." There was a brief pause, then she said, "I'll be honest—he never believed me. Thought I was making everything up as a way to get attention."

He frowned. "That doesn't make any sense."

"No, it doesn't. I even went over his head to his boss, Master Sergeant Hanover, but he brushed me off, too. And you should also know that I've heard rumors that people think I'm crazy."

"You're not," he instinctively protested.

"Thanks, but you'd be in the minority thinking that." There was a hint of bitterness in her tone.

He pulled up in front of the same apartment complex he lived in and put the gearshift into Park. "Why don't you tell me why someone is trying to hurt you?"

She shook her head helplessly for a moment, staring out her passenger-side window. Then she sighed and turned to face him. "I guess you'll find out sooner or later."

He nodded, waiting for her to continue.

"I've been back on Canyon Air Force Base since October, but prior to that, Greta and I were deployed in Kabul, Afghanistan. Greta is a bomb-sniffing dog and our job was to find IEDs before they could injure any members of the military. Greta and I worked tirelessly for six months, finding close to fifty buried bombs. I was called in to speak to Lieutenant Colonel Ivan Turks for what I assumed would be a promotion."

He inwardly tensed, sensing a promotion was not on the agenda.

"The time of the meeting was nineteen hundred hours, long after his office staff were gone for the day. The lieutenant colonel attempted to assault me." Her tone was flat, as if she were reciting from the air force handbook instead of an act of violence. "I managed to get away before he succeeded, and when I heard Greta and I were denied our promotion, I filed charges against him."

"I'm sorry to hear that you had to go through that," Sean said in a low voice. "I'm sure it wasn't easy, but I'm glad you filed charges. Too many women wouldn't have had the courage."

"Yeah, well I can understand why. Because it became a he-said-she-said scenario. My allegation was deemed *not credible*." She used her fingers to put air quotes around the phrase.

His gut clenched. "Why?"

"Because the lieutenant colonel was able to eliminate any evidence that he requested the meeting in his office. His story was that I came in uninvited and made a move on him in an effort to secure my promotion."

"That's ridiculous!"

"I know. But it doesn't matter. Greta and I were sent

back to base as if we'd done something wrong." She was silent for a long moment before she lifted her gaze to his. "I believe that being pushed into oncoming traffic was a way to silence me, forever."

Sean sat back, stunned by her theory. As a cop, he needed to consider all options. It didn't make much sense that a lieutenant colonel would try to kill a lowly senior airman over an allegation that wasn't even taken seriously.

But if this recent attack on Jacey wasn't connected to Turks, then what was it related to?

Who hated her enough to kill her?

TWO

Jacey hated reliving the moment when Lieutenant Colonel Turks roughly grabbed her and tried to force himself upon her. The stale scent of cigarette smoke was still enough to make her gag. If not for her older brother Jake's insistence on teaching her self-defense, coupled with her basic training, she may not have gotten away unscathed.

She swallowed hard, shoving the memory aside. At least Sean believed her, maybe because he'd known her back in high school.

Ten years that seemed like ten lifetimes ago.

"Who else knows about your allegations against Turks?"

"Who doesn't?" She did her best to hide the bitterness in her tone. "I'm sure the notification went into my file, flagging me as a troublemaker. I could tell because when I first arrived at the training center, Master Sergeant Westley James wasn't thrilled to be saddled with me. Thankfully, he's mellowed a bit since then, because I'm getting good results with the K-9s I'm training."

"Lieutenant Colonel Turks isn't on base, too, is he?" Sean asked.

She shook her head. "No, he's still in Kabul." It made her sick to think about how Turks may have already found his next victim.

Doubtful she was the first or the last. It only took a few bad officers to taint what most considered a noble profession.

Serving their country.

"Hard to believe that he could set up an attack on you from Afghanistan."

Her hopes of being believed quickly deflated. "I know." She unlatched her passenger-side door. "Thanks for the ride."

"Wait." Sean snagged her arm, preventing her from leaving. "I'm not saying I don't believe you, Jacey. I'm only thinking out loud here. Anyone sympathetic to Turks could be involved."

"Not just sympathetic to him," she argued. "It would take more than mere sympathy to attempt to kill me." And people thought she was nuts?

Trying to kill her—that was truly insane.

"You're right," he agreed. "I'll keep that in mind as I continue to investigate."

She glanced at him. "As much as I'd like that, you need to know Senior Airman Bill Ullman is the Special Forces cop assigned to my case. Master Sergeant Hanover wouldn't replace him."

"So you said. But since I was on the scene tonight, I'll pressure Hanover to let me take the case over. He'd have no reason not to."

She hoped he was right. Bill Ullman had made no secret of the fact that he didn't like her and didn't believe her. Then again, neither did Hanover.

No one did. Except for Sean.

"Any chance you'd be willing to stay in a motel off base for the night? I'd rather know for sure you're safe."

"I can't." It was odd, but despite the fact that she'd narrowly escaped harm from the earlier incident, she'd feel even more vulnerable off base. "I have to work in the morning, and besides, I don't own a car. Getting back and forth via taxi would be pricey."

Sean grimaced, then nodded. "Okay, I get it." He reached into the glove box and pulled out a small service weapon. "Stay put for a second. I'll walk you inside."

She knew that Sean was just being extra cautious, but it was nice to have him at her side as they approached the apartment building. The scent of his woodsy aftershave made her keenly aware of him.

Knock it off, she told herself sternly. Getting involved with Sean wasn't an option. He was putting his career on the line just by associating with her. Expecting anything more than friendship would be ludicrous.

They took the stairs to the third floor. "Do you live in the complex, too?" she asked.

"Yeah, but in the north building and on the fourth floor." Sean held the door at the top of the stairwell open for her. "Which unit is yours?"

"Three-ten." Outside her door, she pulled out her keys, but Sean took them from her fingertips.

"Stand behind me." He unlocked her door, then pushed it open. He entered the apartment first, weapon ready as he cautiously entered, making sure it was safe. She followed close behind, a little embarrassed at the small, crooked tree sitting on her kitchen table. No real trees were allowed due to the potential fire hazard.

And since Jake's passing, she'd found it difficult to get into the Christmas spirit.

"Thanks for the lift," she said, as Sean returned to the main living area, tucking his weapon away.

"You're welcome. Do me a favor and take down my number. Call me anytime for any reason, okay?"

Taking his phone number seemed a bit personal, but she reluctantly pulled out her phone and dutifully entered Sean as a new contact. "Got it."

He held his phone, looking at her expectantly, as if waiting for her number, too. She told herself to stop making such a big deal out of it and provided her number in return.

"Thanks." He entered the information, then scanned the room with a frown. "I don't like leaving you here, alone."

Truthfully, she wasn't fond of the idea, either. "I was thinking of calling my boss at the training center, Master Sergeant Westley James, to see if he'd give me special permission to keep Greta here with me 24/7. When the Red Rose Killer, Boyd Sullivan, was on the loose, K-9s were allowed special dispensation to stay with their handlers. After Boyd was captured and arrested last month, the rules went back to normal." She shrugged. "I figure Westley might grant me permission."

"I like it." He gestured with his hand. "Call him."

Bothering the master sergeant at home went against the grain, but remembering that moment when a hand shoved her in the back and directly into traffic had her making the call.

The phone rang several times, then went to voice mail. She left a message, then disconnected from the call.

"Do you think he'll get back to you tonight?"

"If he can, he will." She knew Westley's wife, Felicity, was about three months pregnant and suffering severe morning sickness. Westley was likely taking care of her. As he should. It was up to her to deal with her own problems.

"I'll stick around for a while," Sean offered. "I don't mind sleeping on your sofa. Or if you'd be more comfortable, you can sleep on my sofa."

"Not necessary." Just the thought of having Sean sleep on her sofa or vice versa was enough to wreak havoc on her concentration. He was clueless about the secret crush she'd had on him back in high school. He'd been cute then and had grown more handsome since. But her feelings were one-sided. Back then, he'd never seemed to notice her other than as the kid sister of his friend.

"Really, Sean, you've already gone above and beyond. I'll be fine."

He didn't look convinced, his blue eyes drilling into hers as if trying to read her mind. "There's nothing more important than keeping you safe."

She appreciated his concern. "I'm safe here. I'm going to take some ibuprofen and get some sleep," she said firmly. "Good night."

"Good night." He finally moved to the door. "Don't forget to call if you need something."

"I won't." She waited until he stepped into the hallway, then closed and locked the door behind him. Shooting the dead bolt home made her feel a little better. Then she toured her apartment, making sure each window was securely locked.

Good thing it was winter. In the spring and fall she preferred to sleep with the windows open.

Even with the Christmas tree, the apartment seemed hollow and lonely without Greta or Sean's presence. She set the phone near her bedside table, hoping Westley would call her back. She washed her face and changed out of her uniform into soft black stretch pants and a fleece shirt. Then she crawled into bed and tried to rest.

Images from the truck incident whirled around in her head, causing her to relive the moment over and over again.

It didn't take long to regret her knee-jerk reaction of refusing Sean's help. What would it have mattered if he'd slept on her sofa? She wasn't going to get any sleep this way, either.

She couldn't understand why someone wanted her dead. This all had to be related to her attempt to file charges against Lieutenant Colonel Turks. And it still irked her that she'd been denied the promotion.

Not just for herself but for Greta's sake. As with all dog handlers, Greta carried the same rank she did. Greta hadn't been given any recognition for the bomb-sniffing work she'd done overseas. They'd both put their lives on the line over and over again to keep their fellow airmen and other members of the military safe.

And as a result, not only were they denied a promotion, but now there'd been an attempt to kill her.

A faint sound had her bolting upright in bed, her heart pounding with fear. It was nothing—just the sound of an apartment door closing.

She couldn't seem to relax, tossing and turning relentlessly. The hours ticked by slowly: 2200, 2300.

At midnight, she gave up and rolled out of bed. She decided to head over to the training center to pick up Greta. She could explain everything to Westley in the morning. Surely, he wouldn't hold it against her, especially if she explained about the recent attempt on her life.

Spurred into action, she pulled on a quilted jacket and slipped out of her apartment, squinting in reaction to the brightly lit hallway. Taking the stairs to the first floor, she pushed through the heavy door into the darkness outside.

Belatedly, she wondered if she should have called Sean, then ruthlessly shoved the cowardly thought aside. The person who'd shoved her into traffic wouldn't find her such an easy target next time. And as an added precaution, she once again palmed the panic button. If she so much as saw anything suspicious, she wouldn't hesitate to make a lot of noise.

As she headed down Oakland, a shiver of apprehension rippled down her spine. This time, she purposefully glanced over her shoulder, letting anyone who might be watching know that she was on full alert.

But, of course, she didn't see anyone.

Stupid to be so afraid. Her schedule at the training center wasn't a secret. It wouldn't be difficult to figure out she reported each morning at 0900 and worked until 1800. No one could possibly know that she was making a midnight run to fetch her K-9 partner.

She squared her shoulders and picked up the pace until she was moving at a steady jog. *Just like being back in basic training*, she thought with a grim smile. Getting her blood moving also warmed her up, and she became even more determined to bring Greta back to her apartment for what remained of the night.

Fifteen minutes later, she reached the training center and the row of kennels along the back. She walked along the dimly lit hallway, refusing to let anything deter her from her mission.

As she moved down the corridor, she mentally counted the kennels as she passed by, knowing Greta was in number seventeen.

She approached Greta's kennel cautiously. Her K-9 partner was well trained, but she was also a warrior.

It didn't hurt to be careful.

Crouching beside Greta's kennel, she peered through the metal bars. The Belgian Malinois lifted her head, and her tail thumped with recognition, but she didn't seem to be her usual self.

"Greta?" Her tone caused several of the other dogs to bark. Ignoring them, she quickly unlocked the door and went into the kennel.

"What's wrong, girl?" She frowned as she noted a small puddle of green fluid staining the bottom of Greta's empty water dish.

Antifreeze?

No! She pulled out her phone and dialed the emergency veterinary service, surprised when Captain Kyle Roark himself answered the phone.

"Dr. Roark," he answered in a voice husky with sleep.

"It's Jacey Burke. Greta is sick—I think she's been poisoned with antifreeze."

"What? How did that happen? Never mind—I'll meet you at the clinic," he said, all traces of slumber erased from his tone.

"I'll bring her right away."

Jacey stuffed her phone in her pocket and then bent over Greta, who was struggling to stand. The dog weighed roughly seventy pounds, but that didn't stop

Jacey from hauling Greta up and into her arms. Surging to her feet, she staggered out of the kennel and hurried down the corridor.

Fearing for Greta's well-being, she prayed for strength as she carried her K-9 partner to the veterinary clinic. If she hadn't decided to come out tonight… She could barely finish the thought.

First someone tried to kill her, then they went after her K-9 partner.

She was afraid to think about what this guy might do next.

THREE

Sean's ringing phone instantly pulled him from a restless slumber. When he squinted at the screen and saw Jacey's name, his heart jumped into his throat. Levering upright, he quickly answered. "Jacey? What's wrong?"

"I-I'm at the veterinary clinic. S-someone poisoned Greta." Jacey's voice was thick with tears. "Dr. Roark is doing his best, but I'm afraid sh-she won't make it."

"I'll be right there. Don't leave, okay?"

"I won't."

Sean pulled on his uniform, including his utility belt and his weapon, just in case, before bolting out of the apartment. He wondered how Jacey had known that Greta was poisoned. It didn't matter, because he'd get a statement from the vet regardless, but there was a tiny portion of his mind that wondered if Jacey was blowing things out of proportion.

Maybe the dog was simply sick. And why was Jacey at the kennel at this late hour, anyway? He didn't truly believe she was crazy, but there was no doubt her behavior could be viewed as a bit erratic.

He debated waiting for a cab or just going on foot. Because the veterinary clinic wasn't that far, he opted for the latter. He quickened his pace to double time, heading up Oakland past the now-vacant children's playground toward Canyon Drive.

The lights were on at the clinic, but the door was locked. He rapped on the window and watched Jacey cautiously approach to answer the door. Her eyes were red and puffy, her cheeks damp with tears.

"Thanks for coming," she said in a husky tone, closing the door behind him.

Hating to see her so upset, he drew her into his arms for a brief, friendly hug. "Any news on Greta's condition?"

She leaned against him for a moment, the cranberry-vanilla scent of her hair teasing his senses, then straightened and shook her head. "Not yet. I can't believe anyone would be so cold and callous as to go after my dog."

"Why were you at the kennel tonight?"

She dragged a hand through her hair. "I couldn't sleep and thought it would help to bring Greta to my place for the rest of the night. I hadn't heard back from Master Sergeant Westley James, but thought I could ask forgiveness in the morning. If I hadn't gone to get Greta she may have died."

He had to admit her story sounded reasonable. But he continued, choosing his words carefully. "You mentioned something about her being poisoned?"

"I saw a small puddle of green fluid that appeared to be antifreeze in the bottom of her water dish." Jacey rubbed her hands over her arms, as if chilled. "Antifreeze tastes sweet so dogs and other animals are attracted to it, but it's extremely poisonous. I can guarantee there's no way even a smidgen of antifreeze got into the kennel by accident." Her gaze darkened. "Someone put it there on purpose."

"I'd like to see it for myself, maybe take pictures." He knew she wouldn't want to leave the veterinary clinic, but this was important. "Why don't you let Dr. Roark know we'll be back in twenty minutes? That should be long enough for me to get a sample of the antifreeze for my report."

She hesitated, torn between being there for Greta and helping to catch the person who'd done this terrible thing. She reluctantly nodded and moved over to the exam room. "Dr. Roark? Can you hear me?"

A pretty blonde poked her head into the room. "Is there something you need?"

"Hi, Airman Fielding. Just tell Dr. Roark I'll be back in roughly twenty minutes. The Special Forces cop wants to see the scene of the crime."

The woman nodded. "Okay. Don't worry, Kyle—er, Dr. Roark is doing everything he can for Greta."

"I know. Thanks again." Jacey turned away and faced him. "Let's go."

They left the veterinary clinic together. He was glad he had some evidence containers stored in the pocket of his utility belt. Having a sample of the antifreeze that had poisoned Greta would go a long way in proving her case that someone was trying to kill her and her K-9 partner.

Jacey didn't say anything as they hurried down Canyon to the training center. She used her key to access the building and then took him down a long corridor lined with kennels housing a variety of dogs. Several of them barked as they walked past, but Jacey acted as if she didn't notice.

"It's this one," she said, slowing to stop. She frowned, sweeping her gaze around the area. "That's odd. I'm sure I left the kennel door open. I was in a hurry to get Greta to the clinic so didn't bother trying to close it behind me."

He knelt down and peered through the thin metal bars of the kennel door to see inside. There was a steel water dish in the far corner but no sign of antifreeze.

"Are you sure this is the right kennel?" he asked.

"Of course I'm sure." Jacey used her key to unlock the kennel door and ducked inside. Then she stopped abruptly, staring in confusion. "The water dish has been cleaned up. There's no sign of the antifreeze in the bottom that I noticed earlier."

A sinking feeling settled in his gut. "You're sure you saw it?"

"Absolutely." She lifted her gaze to his. "Someone came in to clean up after I left with Greta."

He nodded, wondering who had access to the kennels. "Any way to track who has been in and out of here?"

Her shoulders slumped in defeat. "All the trainers and staff have keys. Unfortunately, there isn't an electronic trail. But Greta is trained not to take food or water from strangers, which makes me wonder if the person who did this is someone who works here."

"Is it possible someone followed you in and stayed hidden until you left with Greta? That would give them plenty of time to wash out the water dish."

"Maybe," she admitted, although her tone reeked of doubt. She slowly walked out of the kennel. "It's possible Greta drank the antifreeze because the dish was in her kennel. We can't always have the same staff providing food and water. Either way, I'm sure Dr. Roark will be able to verify the source of Greta's illness."

Sean followed her back outside, watching as she closed and relocked the kennel door. Hopefully she was right about that.

Because if the vet couldn't say with absolute certainty what the source of Greta's illness was, they only had Jacey's account of what she'd seen when she'd found Greta in her kennel.

And at this rate, Sean was concerned that no one would be willing to believe her.

If he hadn't seen her almost get run over by the box truck, he wasn't so sure he would, either.

But he did believe her. And not just because they'd known each other back in high school.

Jacey truly cared about Greta and wouldn't make something like this up.

Despite the efforts of someone trying to prove otherwise.

What they needed was a suspect. But who? Out of the thousands of airmen and officers on base, who would hate Jacey enough to attempt to kill her and her dog?

He wasn't sure but intended to find out. He couldn't bear the thought of another woman being attacked on base. Four weeks ago, he'd failed to keep Liz Graber safe from her abusive ex-husband. Liz's death was his fault. All because he'd gotten too emotionally involved and had let his guard down.

No way was he going to fail to protect Jacey Burke.

Jacey sensed Sean was struggling to believe she had seen antifreeze in Greta's kennel.

At this point, she was even beginning to doubt herself.

Worse, Sean only had her word about what she'd seen. By now he was likely wondering if the rumors about her being crazy were in fact true. She had to believe Dr. Roark would support her story.

"I didn't make it up," she said, finally breaking the tangible silence between them as they made their way back to the veterinary clinic.

"I believe you," Sean said, surprising her.

"Really?"

"Yes, really."

There was more she wanted to say, but they had already reached the veterinary clinic. She rapped on the door, grateful to see through the window that Airman Fielding had come over to let them in. The veterinary tech greeted them both with a weary smile.

"Dr. Roark has Greta stable for the moment. He'll be out in a few minutes to talk to you."

Jacey's heart swelled with hope. "That's good, right?"

"Yes, it's good. For now." Airman Fielding nodded, then disappeared into the back of the clinic.

Sean reached for her hand, and she gratefully took it, drawing comfort from his warmth.

He believed her. She wasn't sure why, but he believed her.

The relief made tears prick her eyes. Ridiculous, but hearing those three little words made her feel so much better.

"Senior Airman Burke?" Dr. Roark approached, eyeing Sean curiously.

She let go of Sean's hand and offered a quick salute.

"Captain Roark, this is Staff Sergeant Sean Morris. He's with the Special Forces."

Sean also saluted, as was required when facing a superior officer.

Captain Roark returned their salutes, then waved a hand. "At ease, both of you. No need to be formal here." The vet looked at her. "I've managed to stabilize Greta, but at the moment the biggest threat is to her kidneys. Depending on how much she took in, she'll need time for her system to return to normal."

Jacey asked, "But she'll survive?"

Captain Roark nodded. "Yes, her prognosis is very good. Most dogs can survive antifreeze poisoning if they get treatment right away. I plan to keep her here for at least twenty-four hours for observation." His gaze grew troubled. "It's good you brought her in when you did, Jacey—if this had waited until morning, she likely wouldn't have survived."

A cold fist squeezed her heart and she nodded. "I know. I believe God was watching over both of us tonight."

"You're right about that."

"Captain, may I ask a few questions?" Sean asked, pulling out his notebook.

Dr. Roark frowned. "It's the middle of the night. Can this wait until morning?"

"I understand. How about just one statement from you verifying that Jacey's K-9, Greta, was indeed poisoned by antifreeze."

The vet hesitated. "I can't say that with absolute certainty at this time. Jacey was the one who noticed the antifreeze—I simply treated Greta accordingly. She does have kidney failure, which is a key finding in antifreeze poisoning, but testing for ethylene glycol isn't as simple as doing a toxicology screen—it's far more complicated. At this point, all I'm willing to say is that it appears Greta was poisoned."

Jacey couldn't believe what the vet was saying. No way to prove for sure? No way to tell with absolute certainty that Greta was poisoned with antifreeze?

How was it possible? She couldn't bear to think about the person who'd tried to kill Greta actually getting away with it.

"But there is a blood test that can be done to prove it, right?" Sean pressed.

Captain Roark nodded. "There is, and I have drawn a sample, but need to send it out to the San Antonio crime lab for further analysis."

"I totally agree." Sean closed his notebook and stuffed it back in his pocket. "In fact, I'll swing by in the morning to pick it up to take it personally, if that's okay."

"Fine with me." Captain Roark yawned. "Good night."

"Good night." Jacey forced the words past her tight throat. She released Sean's hand and blindly turned toward the door.

"Jacey." Sean's voice was low and husky as he caught her arm. "Don't give up hope, okay? We'll prove what happened here."

"You can't be sure of that." She wrenched away, pushed open the door and stepped out into the frigid night air. Not only was she forced to return to her apartment alone, but there was once again the chance that her version of what happened to Greta wouldn't be deemed credible.

It was as if everything that had transpired with the lieutenant colonel was happening all over again.

And she couldn't help wondering if she wouldn't be better off leaving the air force for good.

Sean hated seeing Jacey so upset. He hurried to catch up with her, determined not to let her go anywhere alone.

"Jacey, wait." His sharp tone made her pause and glance at him over her shoulder. "We need a game plan."

"What are you talking about?" she asked impatiently. "There's nothing more to be done at zero two thirty in the morning."

"If you were followed into the kennel tonight, which is likely since we know someone cleaned up the antifreeze after you left, it's not safe for you to go back to your apartment." He took her elbow in his hand and steered her straight down Canyon, toward the small parking lot where he'd left his car. "You need to stay somewhere off base tonight."

"No, I don't." She dug in her heels. "It's too far away and I have to be at the training center first thing so I can explain all of this to my boss."

"You can do that over the phone," he insisted. "Are you willing to put the other K-9s in harm's way?"

That caused her to whirl around to stare at him. "You think my presence alone puts them in danger?"

He sighed, unwilling to lie to her. "I don't know— it's not likely. There are a lot of staff around, especially during the daytime hours. Still, why not call off sick for the day until we have a handle on what happened here?"

It was clear she didn't like that suggestion.

"Listen, my car is parked just up the block. Let's just

get off base and find a motel room. If you won't take off the whole day, at least tell your boss that you'll be in later, say around noon."

She narrowed her gaze. "But I'm not sick."

"No, but you were almost run over by a truck." Her stubbornness was starting to annoy him. "One late start isn't going to be the end of the world. I'm sure your boss will understand."

Her shoulders slumped as if she were abruptly slammed with a wave of exhaustion. "Okay, fine. But you're coming with me to talk to Westley. He'll want to know what you and your team are going to do to ensure the safety of all the K-9s. This is the last thing he needs right now, considering everything Boyd Sullivan did while sneaking on and off base. Boyd wasn't just the Red Rose Killer—he let all the dogs loose, along with attacking and killing personnel he'd targeted with a red rose. Not to mention killing people who simply got in his way. After months of havoc, Westley wants things to return to normal, especially with the upcoming Christmas holiday."

Sean nodded, relieved she'd finally given in. "Not a problem."

There was a lot of work he needed to do on Jacey's case. Two reports still had to be filed, one on the truck collision and the other on Greta's possible poisoning. Not to mention bringing his boss up to speed on everything that had transpired.

Lastly, he wanted to get copies of the other reports Jacey had filed with Senior Airman Bill Ullman.

Sean wanted to dig into the case immediately, but knew that he needed to start with a phone call to his boss first thing in the morning.

Right now, Jacey's safety was his only priority.

As they approached the parking lot, he slowed his steps, realizing that several of the streetlights were out.

The tiny hairs on the back of his neck lifted in warning. He reached for Jacey's arm and tugged her close. "I don't like this," he muttered. "The two lights on either side of the parking lot were working earlier. Now they're both out?"

"Maybe we should return to the apartment," Jacey whispered.

He wasn't keen on that idea, especially if they were being followed. "After everything that's transpired, I think getting off base is the better option."

The muffled sound of gunfire echoed through the night, followed by a burning sensation along his upper arm. Reacting instinctively, Sean grabbed Jacey and yanked her over toward the closest vehicle, dropped to the ground and used it for cover.

"Are you hit?" he asked anxiously.

"No. You?"

"I'm good." His arm felt like it was on fire, but he knew it was little more than a flesh wound. He looked around, trying to figure out which direction the gunshots had come from. Not directly in front of them, maybe to the north east? Using his body to shield Jacey, he fumbled for his phone, desperate to get backup to their location, *now.*

If the shooter had night-vision goggles, they were sitting ducks out here.

The next couple of moments could very well be their last.

FOUR

For the second time in a matter of hours, Jacey felt the rough asphalt against the palms of her hands. She held her breath, her heart thudding in her chest as fear cloaked her. What was going on? Sean had her pressed against the ground, his body covering hers. She listened as he spoke to the dispatcher, requesting backup to the parking lot near the south gate because of a shooter in the area.

Shooter? Gunshots? The sounds hadn't seemed loud enough for gunfire. While deployed in Afghanistan she'd heard plenty, all of it loud enough to make her ears ring for hours afterward.

"Backup is on the way," Sean said, his voice low and husky near her ear.

"You're sure someone was shooting at us?"

"Yes, I'm sure. I believe the gunman used a silencer."

Hearing the grim determination in Sean's tone made her stomach twist painfully.

Sean was in danger now, too. Because he believed in her.

She hated knowing that she'd dragged him into her

mess. Was this really all because she'd reported the lieutenant colonel?

It was hard to comprehend why someone on base cared enough about her allegation to try to kill her. That someone hated her enough to risk taking a Special Forces cop down, too.

"Do you think the shooter is gone?" she whispered.

"No idea, but we're staying put." The wail of sirens echoed through the night. Jacey thought that if the perp hadn't left by now, he or she no doubt would after hearing proof that help was on the way. "Once we have the scene secured, we'll look for evidence. I'm sure there are shell casings or bullets somewhere."

She nodded, wishing Greta was here. Her K-9 partner had a great nose for finding the scent of gunpowder. Bombs were her specialty, but during training sessions, Jacey had tested Greta with bullets, as well. Greta had been incredibly accurate with even the smallest-size bullet, like those from a 0.22.

Red-and-blue flashing lights grew bright as additional Special Forces cops arrived. Sean didn't let her up, though, until they were approached by two cops holding their weapons at the ready.

"Staff Sergeant Morris?" one of them asked. "You reported two gunshots?"

"Yes, I did." Sean straightened and then held out his hand to help her up. "This is Senior Airman Jacey Burke."

"Staff Sergeant Cronin," the cop introduced himself. "What happened?"

"This is the third attempt to harm Senior Airman Burke in less than eight hours." Sean's voice was terse. "Earlier tonight someone shoved her in front of a truck, then her K-9 partner, Greta, was poisoned with anti-freeze. I was planning to take her off base when I realized the two streetlights were out over the parking lot where I left my car."

Staff Sergeant Cronin glanced up to see for himself, and frowned.

"I suspected something was wrong," Sean continued, "but before we could move, I heard gunfire and felt a bite of pain along my upper arm. We dove for cover and called it in."

"You're hit?" Jacey brushed her hand along the side of his shoulder, appalled to find her fingers wet and sticky with blood. "Why didn't you say something?"

"I'm fine." Sean brushed off her concern. "The gunman used a silencer. I heard two distinct shots before I was hit. They came in from the northeast. We need to search the area, find the spent shell casings or bullet fragments."

"We'll take a look around," Staff Sergeant Cronin promised. "I'll call the EMTs over to provide medical attention."

"Don't bother," Sean said at the same time Jacey replied, "Yes, that would be good."

Staff Sergeant Cronin nodded at Jacey. "I agree with Senior Airman Burke. That wound needs attention."

"My arm doesn't matter—getting Senior Airman Burke to safety does."

"You'll both be safe enough in the ER for a while." The staff sergeant wasn't taking no for an answer. "You should call Master Sergeant Hanover to let him know what's happened. I'll get the EMTs over here."

"Your turn to make sure this gets documented by

the ER doctors," Jacey murmured. It was a lame attempt at a joke.

"I guess." Sean didn't look happy.

Twenty minutes later, they were in a different ER cubicle. Ironically, the same ER doctor, Captain Grant Simons, came in to examine Sean's wound. The skin was furrowed where the bullet had skimmed by, and staring at it made Jacey feel sick at how close she'd come to losing Sean. A few inches more, and he'd be lying on an operating-room table, or worse.

Jacey took a seat in the corner of the room and dropped her head into her hands. Then she lifted her heart in prayer.

Heavenly Father, thank You for sparing Sean's life, and I ask that You please continue to keep us safe. Please help Greta heal from her ordeal, too. Amen.

Another thirty minutes passed before a nurse came in to clean the wound and bandage it. Sean never uttered a complaint, even though she knew the jagged wound running across his biceps had to hurt.

At nearly five in the morning, Sean was officially discharged from care. They were getting ready to leave when Sean's phone rang. He pulled it out and grimaced. "My boss returning my earlier call," he said, before answering. "This is Staff Sergeant Morris."

Jacey wished she could hear the other side of the conversation.

"Yes, sir, I'm fine but Senior Airman Jacey Burke was the real target here and I need a safe place to go for the next few days. We both live in apartment housing and that's not secure enough."

Jacey didn't believe she was the shooter's only target; Sean had been the one injured, not her.

"A motel is one option. I may have another one. I'll keep you posted." He disconnected from the call and looked at Jacey. "I'm going to see if there's a vacant house we can use for a week or so."

"I thought base housing was only for officers and difficult to get?"

"It is, but I happen to know of a place where a family moved out rather unexpectedly. I know it will get reassigned, but I'm hoping we can use it for a limited time."

She narrowed her gaze. "You just happen to know this?"

"Yeah. I, uh, looked into alternative housing options when you refused to go off base to a motel."

She nodded, understanding his concern. If there was a house available to use, they should jump on it. It was far more preferable than a motel off base.

Sean made two more quick calls, then returned to her side. "Everything is all set. We can use the place for five days. Ready to go?" Sean asked, shrugging into his jacket. The sleeve had a rip in it where the bullet had torn through.

"Yes." She rose to her feet, feeling exhausted. "I need to shower and change before returning to the training center to talk to my boss about Greta."

"We'll take a cab to the apartment to pick up a few things, then grab a different cab to head over to pick up the key and take us to the house," Sean said. "I want to be certain we're not followed."

"All right," she agreed. "Let's go."

Jacey couldn't relax during the cab ride to the apartment complex. Sean sat sideways in his seat so he could keep an eye on the road behind them. Even at 0500 hours, Canyon Air Force Base had come to life. Military personnel started work early.

"Is there anyone behind us?" she asked.

"Too many," he replied glumly. He tapped the cab driver on the shoulder. "Will you circle the block?"

The cabbie shrugged. "It's your dime."

Jacey breathed easier once they managed to get into her apartment without incident. Sean waited for her in the living room, giving her time to shower and change. She quickly packed a bag, then rejoined him in the living room. "I'm set."

"Good." His smile didn't reach his eyes, and she knew he was troubled by the back-to-back incidents from that night. "My turn."

They used the side exit, avoiding the main areas, to walk over to Sean's building. He couldn't get his dressing wet, so he simply changed his clothes and packed a bag. He wore his official uniform, complete with the blue beret, and a wide utility belt that held a holster for his gun.

She thought he was handsome before, but wearing his full uniform he stole her breath.

Doing her best to hide her reaction, she kept her gaze averted as a different cabbie drove them to the small house off Webster, not far from the base apartment-housing complex. She could see the apartment building from the front window.

"Let me know when you're ready to head over to the training center," Sean said. "I'd like to talk to the staff who were on duty over the past twenty-four hours, see if they noticed anything unusual."

"Uh, sure. I'm ready." Jacey abruptly realized just how much time she and Sean would be spending together. He'd been nothing but professional, but ever since she'd seen the wound on his arm up close, not to mention seeing him in his full uniform, she'd found herself getting emotionally involved on a personal level.

She'd had a crush on him ten years ago, but that was then. This was now.

Best to figure out how to rein in her feelings before she made a complete and utter fool of herself.

Sean sensed Jacey was on edge as they took a third taxi to the training center.

"This is going to get expensive," Jacey muttered as he paid the fare.

She was right, but there wasn't anything he could do to change that right now. He didn't dare use his personal vehicle, but planned to sign out a jeep from the base motor pool.

"Did you call your master sergeant?" he asked as they entered the facility.

"Not since I left him a message about Greta's condition, but I'm sure he's looking for me." She led the way to the office area. "I hope he doesn't blame me for this."

"He won't," Sean said in an attempt to reassure her.

Jacey didn't look convinced, and knocked sharply on the door of the corner office.

"Come in."

Jacey grimaced and opened the door. She went in first and, while saluting wasn't required, stood at attention. Sean did the same, waiting until Master Sergeant James told them to stand at ease before relaxing.

"Take a seat. What happened, Jacey?" Master Sergeant James asked, his expression full of concern.

Sean listened as Jacey repeated the events surrounding Greta's poisoning. When he sensed she was going to leave it there, he interrupted.

"Sir? If I may interject here—" he paused and waited for Westley to nod "—there have been two attempts against Jacey over the last twenty-four hours along with the attack on her K-9 partner."

"Who are you?"

Oops. "Staff Sergeant Sean Morris with Special Forces, sir. I came to offer first aid to Senior Airman Burke after she was pushed into the path of an on-coming vehicle, then later, after we took care of Greta, someone took a couple of shots at us. All of these incidents have been reported to my superior, Master Sergeant Doug Hanover."

Westley James scowled. "I can't believe someone poisoned Greta," he said finally. He pinned Sean with a stern glare. "I need you to find the person responsible for all of this, understand?"

"Yes, sir. Believe me, I want to find the person who did this more than anyone."

"Staff Sergeant Morris was injured by the shooter." Jacey spoke up.

Westley's brows leveled upward. "You're okay?"

"Yes, sir. Just a flesh wound." Sean hesitated, then asked, "I'd like to speak to the staff who were working in the evening hours of the training center yesterday."

"Understood. Aiden Gomez was on duty, along with a few others assigned to shut down the kennel for the night. I'd start with him."

"Do you have a log of everyone who was here last evening?"

"Yes." Westley opened a file folder and removed a sheet of paper, then handed it to Sean.

"Aiden loves dogs," Jacey said. "He'd never do anything to harm them."

"I just want to see if he noticed anything unusual last night, that's all." That much was true, but Sean also knew that at this point in the investigation everyone was a suspect.

Even Jacey.

Not that he really believed she would harm her own K-9 partner, but he couldn't afford to overlook any remote possibility.

Getting personally involved is exactly what had gotten him into trouble with Liz Graber. Thinking her ex-husband had gotten the message, he'd asked Liz out on a date. The night they'd dined at a local restaurant off base, Liz's ex had followed them, and then he'd killed her. If Sean hadn't asked Liz out on a personal level, she never would have died that night.

No way was he going down that path again.

"Staff Sergeant Morris?"

He snapped his head up to find Westley James staring at him impatiently. "Yes, sir?"

"When would you like to speak to Aiden Gomez? He's here in the morning for four-and-a-half hours, then again in the late evening for three hours."

"If he's here, I'd like to see him now, if that's okay."

Westley nodded. "Very well. You can use the empty trainer office at the end of the hall. It's next to Jacey's."

"Thank you, sir."

Westley reached for his phone and gave a curt order for Airman Gomez to report to the office on the double.

"This way," Jacey said, leading him down the hall to the empty office. She opened the door, then hovered in the doorway for a moment. "I'm going to spend a few hours working with a group of puppies, so there's no need for you to hang around after you're finished with Aiden."

"I see." Despite his internal promise to keep his distance, he was disappointed. "Will you do me a favor?"

She eyed him warily. "Like what?"

"Call me when you're ready to leave. It's not safe for you to be alone, Jacey. I plan to sign out a vehicle, so there will be no need to take taxis back and forth."

She pursed her lips, then nodded. "Okay."

He let out a silent breath of relief. "Thanks."

Jacey looked as if she wanted to say something more, but then she glanced down the hall and smiled. "Hi, Aiden. How are you?"

"Not good—I just heard about Greta." The young airman was visibly upset. "I saw she wasn't in her kennel, but I didn't realize she was sick. What happened?"

"We don't know for sure but we think she was given something that made her sick," Jacey said, and Sean was glad that she'd glossed over the cause of Greta's illness. "That's what Staff Sergeant Morris wants to talk to you about."

"Come in, Aiden." Sean gestured the young man to step forward. "What time did you work last night?"

"From nineteen hundred to twenty-two thirty." Aiden glanced back at Jacey. "Greta was fine in her kennel when I left."

"I believe you," Jacey said.

"Aiden, I need to know if you saw anything unusual around any of the kennels. Any liquids or substances that aren't normally around."

Aiden frowned. "No, sir, I didn't. We have very strict

rules here because it's our job to make sure the dogs are safe."

"Okay, then, what about people?" Sean pressed. "Did you see anyone around who you normally don't see that late at night?"

Aiden's gaze turned thoughtful. "I did see someone wearing the usual battle dress uniform, but he or she had the collar turned up to hide their face, and had a hat on, so I didn't see who it was. The person was slender—made me think it was a woman, but I can't honestly say for sure."

Sean's pulse kicked up a beat and he pulled out the log, then glanced at Jacey. "Looks like both Misty Walsh and Reba Pokorny are on the log, although Misty left before twenty hundred." He found it telling that Jacey's name was not on the list, which proved it wasn't foolproof.

"Misty is a trainer, and Reba is a caretaker, like Aiden," Jacey said. "To be honest, it wouldn't be that difficult for someone to slip past without signing the log."

"You think the person I saw gave something to Greta that harmed her?" Aiden asked, his expression horrified. "I can't believe Misty or Reba would do something like that. Especially Reba."

Sean wondered if Aiden had a thing for Reba. "We don't know that for certain, so don't go around saying that, okay? It could be that the person you saw may have witnessed something, just like you did."

Aiden's expression cleared, and he nodded. "I understand. Everyone is considered innocent until proven guilty."

That was true in a court of law, but in police work, Sean tended to view it the other way around. Everyone was a suspect until cleared by either an alibi or evidence to the contrary.

And the glimpse Aiden had gotten of a person hiding behind a turned-up collar and hat was his first clue.

He only wished there was more to go on than a vague description that could include just about anyone.

FIVE

Jacey spent a couple of hours working with Aiden and three of four puppies that he'd helped to foster a few months ago. The mother had defended her pups against a coyote and, despite her serious injuries, had thankfully recovered. Aiden had named the four puppies after national parks; the two females were Shenandoah and Denali, the two males Smoky and Bryce. Shenandoah was the runt of the litter and hadn't taken well to training, so Aiden had been allowed to keep her as his own.

The other three pups were K-9 stars in the making.

"Good job, Aiden," she said when the three pups followed each of his commands. "You really have a great rapport with those pups. They respond to you very well."

"Thanks." Aiden ducked his head in embarrassment, but smiled at the praise. "I love working with them. I can't thank you enough for agreeing to teach me how to train them."

"My pleasure." She yawned and had to force her eyes to remain open. Every muscle in her body ached from the combination of hitting the asphalt and lack of sleep.

"You look tired," Aiden said with a frown. "Maybe you should try to get some rest."

She wanted nothing more, but couldn't leave the training center without calling Sean. And she wanted to head over to the clinic to check on Greta. "Soon," she promised.

Honoring her word, she called Sean. He answered almost immediately. "Jacey? Everything okay?"

She yawned again. "Uh, yeah. Other than being exhausted. Listen, I'd like to head over to see Greta at the kennel before heading back to take a nap. Do you want to meet me at the veterinary clinic?"

"No, I'll pick you up there. I have a hard-top jeep from the motor pool. I'll be there in ten minutes."

She was too tired to argue. "Okay."

Sean arrived within his allotted time frame, and she gratefully climbed into the passenger seat. Even walking the short distance to the clinic seemed an overwhelming task.

"Thanks," Jacey said when Sean came over to open her door for her. "Why don't you look as tired as I feel?"

"I completed my reports, then slept for a couple of hours this morning." Sean held open the veterinary-clinic door for her, too. "I need to drive Greta's blood sample to the state lab when we're finished here."

She'd forgotten about that, but knowing that Sean would personally deliver the sample was reassuring. "Good morning," she greeted the airman behind the desk. "I'd like to talk to Captain Roark and see my K-9 partner, Greta."

"One moment, please." The airman left, returning a few minutes later. "Dr. Roark will see you in exam room number four."

"Thanks." Jacey led the way into the exam room and dropped into the visitor chair, resting her head back against the wall. "I'm not sure having a few hours of sleep is enough to make a long drive," she said to Sean. "Maybe you should wait until morning."

"I'll be all right," he said. "I'm used to working long hours with little sleep."

She and Greta had done the same overseas, but apparently she'd grown soft while being back at Canyon.

The back door opened and Dr. Roark came in leading Greta by an office leash. Jacey's K-9 responded instantly to her presence and when Dr. Roark picked up the dog and set her on the stainless-steel surface, Jacey wrapped her arms around Greta's neck and buried her face in the animal's soft fur.

"It's so good to see you, Greta." Jacey lifted her head and smiled as the dog licked her face and thumped her tail on the table. Jacey lifted her gaze to Dr. Roark. "She looks so much better."

Dr. Roark nodded. "She's responded exceptionally well to the fluids I've given her." He gestured to the small bump beneath the fur on the animal's neck. "This is almost completely gone. See? We place the fluid under the skin and it slowly gets absorbed into her bloodstream. I think another small bolus will do the trick."

Relieved, she scratched Greta carefully between her ears. "I can't wait to bring her home."

"Actually, if you're willing to sit here for another hour, I think you can." Dr. Roark glanced at his watch. "I need to draw another blood sample to check her kidney function. If the numbers continue to improve the way they have been, then I can give another fluid bolus and release her into your care."

"Really?" The wave of relief pushed past her exhaustion. "Then I'll wait."

"We both will," Sean corrected.

Dr. Roark nodded and gestured to the two visitor chairs. "Make yourself at home. I'll take Greta back and get going on the blood work."

Jacey gave Greta one last kiss and stepped back so Dr. Roark could take her back. She sank into the chair and once again rested her head against the wall.

Sean dropped into the seat beside her. "I'm glad Greta is better."

"Me, too." She yawned again and closed her eyes. Maybe she'd just rest for a minute.

The next thing Jacey knew, Sean was softly calling her name. "Jacey? Wake up—Dr. Roark has Greta ready for you."

"Huh?" She lifted her head from Sean's shoulder and rubbed her eyes. Embarrassed at how she had used Sean as a pillow, she turned her attention to Greta, who was standing near her chair. "Hey, girl. Ready to go?"

Greta wagged her tail and licked Jacey's hand. There was a large bubble beneath Greta's fur from the second fluid bolus, so Jacey made sure to avoid that area as she gave Greta's coat a good rub.

Then she took Greta and patted Sean's arm. "Friend, Greta. Friend."

Greta sniffed him long and hard before wagging her tail.

"You'll need to take her outside frequently," Dr. Roark warned. "The more fluid she absorbs, the more she'll have to go."

"I understand." Jacey didn't care how much work was involved as long as she was able to take Greta with her. "Thank you for everything."

"You're welcome." Dr. Roark handed over the office leash and then provided a small square box containing Greta's blood sample to Sean. "I expect a copy of the results when they're ready."

"I will," Sean promised. They left the exam room. "I'm parked around the corner, so you and Greta should wait here in the lobby."

"I think we should stick together," Jacey countered. "All three of us have been under attack by whoever is behind this."

Sean's expression turned serious. "Yeah, you might be right about that."

They kept Greta between them as they left the clinic. The streets were busy at noontime with airmen and officers going out for lunch and doing Christmas shopping at the BX. The Christmas lights weren't as bright during the daytime, but wreaths decorated each lamppost providing a cheery atmosphere.

The drive to their temporary home didn't take long. Jacey walked around the back side of the property, which wasn't visible from the road, and allowed Greta to do her business. Sean watched over her and, when they were done, unlocked the door for her and Greta.

Inside, she took Greta around the house, familiarizing the K-9 with their temporary living arrangements. The place was only sparsely furnished, but she was pleasantly surprised to find a six-foot fake Christmas tree in the corner of the room, with a Nativity scene spread out beneath it. Greta sniffed at everything cautiously, then went over to drink water from a stainless-steel bowl Jacey had set next to her food dish in the kitchen.

"They must have left in a hurry to leave the Christmas tree and Nativity scene behind," Jacey said.

"I guess so." He watched Greta drinking from the water dish. "You seem to have covered everything."

"Yes, even Greta's vest for when she needs to get back to work." She yawned again. "I'll stretch out on the sofa for a while in case Greta needs to go out again."

"I hope to be back in a couple of hours," Sean said as he walked to the door. He glanced back with a frown. "I'd feel better about leaving if you were armed."

"Greta will watch over me."

Sean hesitated, then nodded. "Okay. See you later."

After he left, she locked the door and turned on some Christmas music for background noise, before stretching out on the sofa with Greta at her side. She thought she'd fall asleep instantly but found herself worrying about Sean driving all the way to the San Antonio crime lab on his own. Granted, no one other than his boss knew that he was driving a jeep, but still...

If not for Greta needing close monitoring, and frequent trips outside, she would have insisted on going along. Before drifting off to sleep, Jacey prayed that God would watch over Sean.

Bringing him back, safe and sound.

Sean kept a keen eye on the traffic behind him as he left Canyon. He hadn't signed the jeep out under his name, but had used his boss's instead and kept the paperwork out of the official file. Yet, that didn't mean he was willing to let down his guard.

The trip to San Antonio didn't take quite as long as

he'd expected. He handed over Greta's blood sample, then turned and headed straight back to base. He had taken his computer with him and planned to continue working the investigation from their temporary living quarters.

He'd gotten photos of both female training-center employees who were on duty last evening and had interviewed them both over the phone. Of course, both women denied having anything to do with Greta. Next, he decided to dig into their backgrounds, see if there were any red flags there. He'd also left a message with Staff Sergeant Cronin about what they'd found at the parking lot.

Jacey was still asleep on the sofa when he returned to the house. Greta met him at the door and he held out his hand, hoping she remembered him from the clinic. He needn't have worried; Greta was a smart dog and didn't hesitate to press her nose against him.

He took Greta out into the backyard for a moment, sweeping his gaze over the area. But he didn't see anyone, not even a curious face from a neighbor's window.

When he returned inside, he set up his laptop on the kitchen table, keeping his phone on Vibrate so as not to disturb Jacey.

If Cronin didn't call him back within the hour, he'd have to try him again. Granted, the guy had worked the night shift, but Sean had to believe they'd found some sort of evidence at the parking lot.

He pulled up the background he'd started on Reba Pokorny, but she was a relatively new airman, transferred over from basic training just four months ago.

Too new to get into trouble? Maybe.

He was about to switch gears and begin looking at

Misty Walsh when his phone rumbled against the tabletop. He swept up his phone, grimacing as he realized Jacey had woken up and was peering at him sleepily over the back of the sofa.

"Staff Sergeant Morris," he answered.

"This is Staff Sergeant Cronin, returning your call."

"Thank you. I'm interested in what evidence you were able to recover from the parking lot."

Cronin sighed. "Nothing."

Sean frowned. "What do you mean, *nothing*? Two shots were fired—there has to be something the gunman left behind."

"We waited for daylight and didn't find a single iota of evidence," Staff Sergeant Cronin said in a curt voice. "If not for the wound on your arm, I'd wonder if you didn't make the whole story up."

Sean's gaze met Jacey's, his chest tightening as he realized this was how she'd been treated by the Special Forces after reporting her incidents. It was awful to have someone in authority believing you lied about something so serious.

"There has to be something," Sean insisted. "The bullet that grazed my arm has to be there somewhere."

There was a long pause. "I guess we can try again," Staff Sergeant Cronin said without enthusiasm.

"We can use Greta," Jacey whispered from her spot on the sofa. "She has an incredible nose for gunpowder."

Sean nodded. At this point, he trusted Greta's nose more than the less-than-ambitious Staff Sergeant Cronin.

"Never mind," he told Cronin. "I have a better idea."

"Suit yourself." Cronin obviously didn't think Sean was going to find anything they'd missed.

"I will. Thanks for the call." He disconnected and set his phone aside. He supposed there was a remote chance the shooter had returned to the area and found the bullets on his own, but Sean didn't think so.

A smart gunman would have picked up the spent shell casings, then disappeared from sight. Returning to the scene of a crime was something to avoid at all costs.

Then again, some criminals weren't smart. That was exactly how the cops were able to catch them.

"Sean?"

He glanced up at Jacey's soft, questioning tone. "Yeah?"

"What do you think of giving Greta's nose a try?"

"I like it, if you think she's up to the task."

"Come, Greta." The dog instantly went to Jacey's side. "Sit."

The dog sat and stared up at Jacey with adoration.

"She seems fine," Jacey said. "It looks like most of her fluid bolus has been absorbed. I say we give her a chance and see how it goes. If she gets tired, we can always stop."

He wasn't about to argue. "I'm in. Let's go."

"Give me a few minutes." Jacey disappeared into one of the bedrooms, returning with Greta's vest. She strapped it over Greta's back and the dog straightened, looking as if she was on full alert.

"Amazing," he murmured. "She knows it's time to work."

"Yes, she does." Jacey gave Greta a small treat, then clipped on her leash. "We're ready when you are."

He slipped on his jacket as Jacey donned hers. Together they headed outside to where he'd left the jeep parked in the driveway. The south parking lot wasn't far, and he pulled into a slot on the opposite side from where the incident had taken place.

Jacey let Greta out the back, and the dog stood alert at her side. "You thought the shot came from the northeast, correct?"

"Yeah, but we shouldn't limit ourselves to just that area." He cast his gaze about the parking lot. "This way. Let's start where we were standing when we heard the shots."

They covered the distance, roughly thirty yards, and took the same position. Jacey was to his left and he'd been standing on the right. The shot had grazed his right biceps from behind.

Wait a minute. He turned in a circle until he was once again facing the direction they'd been headed last night. "We need to check the southwest, too."

"That's closer to the south gate, where two airmen are stationed 24/7," Jacey pointed out.

"I know—that's why I thought the shot came from behind. But I honestly can't say for sure, now in the light of day, so we need to check them both."

"Okay." Jacey bent toward Greta and held out a bullet for the dog to sniff. "Find," she commanded, releasing the leash.

Greta lowered her nose and began to sniff the ground, making circular patterns as she moved around the parking lot. Jacey followed close at her side, not saying much other than occasionally offering encouragement.

He was beginning to think their attempts to find evidence would be futile when Greta disappeared into some brush straight ahead of the spot where they'd started.

"Sean!" Jacey's voice held a note of excitement. "Greta found something!"

"What?" He jogged over to where the dog sat at attention. Nestled in the dirt was a brass shell casing. Only it wasn't a spent one, ejected after the bullet had been fired, but a full one.

"I don't believe it," he muttered, pulling an evidence bag from his pocket and using it to pick up the shell. "I can't believe the shooter actually dropped a bullet."

"I know, right? I think there must have been spent casings here, too, because Greta alerted in several other spots. But this was the only find." She hesitated, then added, "Look at this black spot here. I think it may be from a stubbed-out cigarette."

"Hmm." Sean rose to his feet. "This is evidence that someone was here, but it doesn't help our case. Anyone on base could have dropped a bullet and smoked a cigarette. We need to find the actual slugs that were used."

"We'll keep looking. Now that we believe the shooter may have stood here, we have a better idea where to look for bullet fragments." Jacey placed Greta back on leash and they returned to their initial location.

This time, Jacey faced Greta toward the area opposite from where the shooter may have been. Where there was a good chance the bullet may have landed. She repeated her command to find, and Greta went to work.

Again, he thought their efforts would be fruitless, when suddenly Greta once again disappeared into the brush. "Sean! She found one!"

He crossed the lot and peered over Jacey's shoulder. A somewhat mashed slug was lying in the brush. The fact that it was misshapen convinced him this was the one that had creased his arm. The one that had missed them completely could be in Timbuktu for all he knew.

"Greta, you're incredible," he said as he pulled out another evidence bag. He picked up the slug and tucked it next to the unspent shell. He looked at Jacey. "This is exactly what we needed."

"I'm glad." Her smile was hesitant, and he was once again struck by a wave of awareness. Before he could talk himself out of it, he caught her close in a warm hug.

She stiffened for a fraction of a second before wrapping her arms around his waist and returning his embrace.

Holding Jacey in his arms felt right, but it didn't take long for him to remember his secret promise to keep his distance. He loosened his grip and took a subtle step back, trying to force her cranberry-vanilla from overwhelming him.

He couldn't fail Jacey the same way he'd failed Liz.

Not just for her sake, but his own.

Because if anything happened to Jacey, he'd never get over it.

SIX

Bending over, Jacey rubbed Greta's glossy coat in an attempt to hide her reaction to Sean's embrace. She liked being held in his arms, more than she should.

For a split second she'd remembered being roughly and painfully grabbed by Lieutenant Colonel Turks, but quickly shoved the memory away. Instead, she welcomed Sean's strong arms cradling her close. The woodsy scent of his aftershave had provided a calming effect, until he'd abruptly pulled away, leaving her feeling empty, lonely and confused.

Logically, she knew he only saw her as an old high school friend, nothing more. And she wasn't interested in a relationship, either. Which was why she absolutely needed to keep her heart protected from the lethal impact of Sean's good looks and charm.

"Good girl," she murmured to Greta. "Even after being sick, you performed like a trooper."

"I'll drop you off at the house before handing over this evidence," Sean said. "Greta deserves some rest."

"That she does," Jacey agreed. She straightened and looked at Sean. "If you want my opinion, the bullet fragment and the shell should go directly to the state lab. I wish there was a way to prove the shooter had smoked a cigarette there, too."

He nodded thoughtfully. "I agree on both counts. It was clear from my conversation with Staff Sergeant Cronin that he wasn't very interested in finding this evidence."

"Oh, Sean." Jacey's heart squeezed in her chest. "I'm afraid that's my fault. I'm persona non grata within the Special Forces because of my allegation against Turks and now that you're stuck with me, the stink is rubbing off on you. I'd completely understand if you want to distance yourself from me."

"Not a chance," Sean responded without hesitation. "There's something going on here, and any Special Forces cop that doesn't do their best to get answers doesn't deserve to wear the uniform."

She appreciated his stout loyalty, but couldn't help thinking that he had no idea what he was facing. She shook off the deep sense of foreboding and walked over to the jeep. Greta kept pace at her side, and Jacey was impressed at how well her K-9 had performed today.

"In you go, girl." She opened the back of the jeep and Greta gracefully jumped inside. After shutting the door behind her, Jacey went to the passenger-side door and slid in.

Sean didn't say much as he drove back to the house. Her nap had helped a bit, but she still had a nagging headache and was famished.

She glanced at Sean. "Do you think we could pick up something to eat at Carmen's?"

He flashed a wry grin. "You read my mind. I'm starving. Besides, it's too late for another drive to the

San Antonio crime lab. I'll take the evidence in tomorrow."

Carmen's was an Italian restaurant on base with carryout service. Sean ordered a large spinach-and-eggplant lasagna to go.

"Here, I'll pay my share," Jacey said, digging money out of the pocket of her uniform.

"No way. This Branson Bulldog isn't going to make a fellow Branson Bulldog pay for a meal."

She rolled her eyes at his lame joke. Their old high school days seemed a long time ago, although she still remembered how cute Sean had been wearing his bulldog letterman jacket. He'd been a track star, and she'd loved watching him race.

He handed the white paper bag with their carryout order to her. The spicy scent of tomato sauce, oregano and cheese filled the interior of the jeep. Jacey noticed that he kept a close eye on the rearview mirror as he took a long winding path back to their temporary living quarters.

Jacey took Greta out back for a few minutes and when she returned to the kitchen Sean had the table set with the lasagna in the center. He'd gotten salads to go, as well, a small bowl at each place setting.

"Looks and smells delicious," she said as she filled Greta's food and water dishes. After washing her hands, she joined Sean at the table. Glancing at him beneath her lashes, she clasped her hands together and bowed her head. "Heavenly Father, please bless this food we are about to eat. Thank You for healing Greta so quickly and please continue to guide us on Your chosen path, amen."

"Amen," Sean murmured.

She was pleased that he'd joined her in prayer. He scooped out lasagna for her, then for himself.

"Thanks." She sampled the lasagna and wasn't disappointed. "Amazing."

Sean nodded, too busy eating to answer. She watched him for a moment, tempted to pinch herself to prove they were sitting here, sharing a meal after ten years had passed since they'd last seen each other. She felt bad about the way his fellow Special Forces cops were treating him but, at the same time, couldn't deny that God had brought them together for a reason.

She only hoped and prayed that they'd find out who was behind these attacks in time to salvage their reputations.

And before anyone else got hurt.

"This hits the spot," Sean said, breaking the silence. "My gram loves spinach-and-eggplant lasagna. I bring it out to her at least once a month."

She glanced at him in surprise. "I didn't realize your grandmother was living in the area."

"I moved her here two years ago. She was lonely back in Branson, Missouri, and I couldn't get out there to see her as often as I wanted. Having her in a small house close by enables me to visit on a weekly basis."

She was touched by the way he cared for his grandmother. "Is she your maternal grandmother?"

A shadow crossed his blue eyes. "Yes. I didn't know my father and didn't maintain contact with my stepfather's family."

She could hear the tension in his tone when he mentioned his stepfather and wondered what their relationship was like. Her parents had passed away several years go in a horrible traffic accident, leaving her and

Jake alone. They'd always been close, but losing their parents had bound them together even closer.

After Jake had died, she'd felt adrift, unable to find her own place in the world.

Reuniting with Sean had changed that. There was a connection between them, and not just because of their shared past, but because they shared the same values. The way he'd prayed with her at meals and his overall sense of decency. Not to mention the way he'd believed in her when no one else had. Her smile was wistful. "I'd love to meet your grandmother sometime."

Sean appeared startled at her comment, then quickly recovered. "Of course. Gram would love that." He ate the last bit of lasagna on his plate, then sat back with a sigh. "I'm stuffed."

She smiled, stood and stacked their dirty dishes together. "Me, too."

"I'll help," Sean protested.

"Washing dishes isn't women's work?" she teased.

"No, ma'am. Gram would flay me with the sharp end of her tongue if she heard me say anything like that." He carried the half-empty lasagna pan to the counter and covered it before placing it in the fridge. "My grandmother was an old army nurse. She didn't take attitude from anyone."

"That's amazing. Was your mother a nurse, too?" She filled one side of the sink with sudsy water.

"Yes, but she didn't keep working after getting married to my stepfather." The shadow was back in his gaze. "He insisted she stay home."

She glanced at him. "I get the impression you and your stepfather don't get along."

"We don't." Sean's voice was flat and hard. "I haven't seen him in ages and heard he passed away last year."

"I'm sorry." She'd obviously poked at a festering wound.

He blew out a breath and picked up a dish towel. "It's not your fault. He's just not a pleasant subject."

They finished washing and drying their dinner dishes in silence. She wanted to ask why Sean and his stepfather didn't get along, but could tell by the hard set to his jaw that he wasn't about to open up about his past.

Thinking back to their time at high school, she realized that Sean had come to their house often, but Jake hadn't gone to Sean's at all.

Had Sean been ashamed of his stepfather? She didn't know and couldn't ask Jake, either.

Sean alone was the only one who could answer her questions. And that wasn't an option at the moment.

As she dried her hands on a towel, her phone buzzed. She pulled it out, frowning at the unfamiliar number. Hesitantly, she answered, "Senior Airman Burke."

"This is Staff Sergeant Misty Walsh. I hope you don't mind me bothering you, but I was wondering if you'd have some time to talk. Privately."

Jacey's gaze clashed with Sean's and she covered her phone with her hand. "This is Misty Walsh," she whispered. Removing her hand, she added, "Yes, of course I'll talk to you, Misty. Do you have time tonight?"

"No, not tonight." Misty's response was swift and Jacey imagined she was hiding somewhere while making this call. "Tomorrow. In the daylight. Off base."

"Off base works for me. What time?" Jacey's heart thudded with anticipation and she kept her gaze locked on Sean's. "And where?"

"There's a coffee shop known as the Cozy Coffee Café, about six miles off base heading toward San Antonio. I'll meet you there at ten hundred hours."

"Ten at the Cozy Coffee Café," she repeated. "We'll be there."

"Wait, who's we?" Misty's voice rose with agitation. "Come alone or don't come at all."

"I meant me and my K-9, Greta," Jacey hastened to reassure her. "Misty, can you tell me what this is about?"

"You know." Her tone was full of bitterness. "Lieutenant Colonel Turks."

Jacey sucked in a harsh breath. "You've had experience with him, too?"

"Tomorrow, ten sharp." Misty disconnected from the line without saying anything further.

Jacey set her phone aside, trying to suppress a shiver. "I don't think Misty is the one who harmed Greta," she told Sean. "Seems as if she wants to talk to me about the lieutenant colonel."

"You're not going alone," Sean said in a tone that brooked no argument. "It's too dangerous."

She nodded, her mind swirling. "I know. You can sit in the back of the cafe to keep an eye on things. I'll have Greta with me, too."

"I hope it's not a trap," Sean muttered.

"It won't be." Jacey could hardly believe that Misty Walsh was another of Lieutenant Colonel Turk's victims.

Where there were two, there had to be more. Maybe if they all banded together, they could bring charges against the powerful commander.

They all couldn't be viewed as *not credible*, could they?

* * *

After Jacey and Greta disappeared into the bedroom to get some sleep, he stayed up at the kitchen table, combing through Misty Walsh's background.

It wasn't difficult to confirm she'd been deployed to Kabul, Afghanistan, under Lieutenant Colonel Turk's ultimate command. Sean stared at the roster, grimly wondering how many female airmen this guy assaulted.

And how many more might be next if they didn't find a way to bring him to justice.

Jacey had been one of the brave few who'd tried, and while her initial attempt may have failed, he was convinced she'd ultimately succeed.

The attacks on Jacey and Greta and the gunshots fired at the parking lot had to be related to her allegations against the lieutenant colonel. Nothing else made sense.

All he had to do was to figure out who on base might be doing the deed on the colonel's behalf.

Exhaustion finally caught up with him, so he stretched out on the sofa and allowed sleep to claim him.

The following morning, he woke up stiff and sore from sleeping on the sofa, but feeling better having gotten a solid nine hours of sleep. He stretched and padded into the kitchen to start coffee. He frowned, unable to remember if Jacey drank coffee or not. Just to be safe, he filled a red tea kettle and put it on the stove.

He'd brought a carton of eggs over from his place, so once the coffee was brewed, he proceeded to cook breakfast. Jacey joined him a few minutes later. "Morning," she said briefly before taking Greta outside into the backyard.

The teakettle whistled and he turned off the flame

beneath the burner. He watched through the window at the sink, admiring how pretty Jacey was, even first thing in the morning. It was too easy to remember how well she'd fit into his arms yesterday, and how difficult it had been to let her go.

Jacey and Greta returned a few minutes later. "Coffee smells great."

"Help yourself. The scrambled eggs are just about ready if you're interested."

"No complaints from me." Jacey gestured toward the teapot. "You drink tea?"

"No, but I wasn't sure if you did." He felt his cheeks flush with embarrassment. "Anyway, I thought we'd drive to the San Antonio crime lab to drop off the bullets prior to heading over to the Cozy Coffee Café."

"Sounds good." She dropped into a chair and cradled her coffee mug. "I can't believe Misty reached out to me. I wonder why she waited so long?"

"Good question. You've been back on base since October, right?"

"Yeah." She took a sip of her coffee. "Maybe I was wrong about Misty being involved in what happened to Greta. What better way to throw off suspicion than to attempt to form an alliance?"

He piled eggs on her plate along with toast and handed it to her. "You're starting to think like a cop."

Her lips quirked in a smile. "Comes from hanging around one."

"Or from having good instincts." He returned to the table with his eggs, then waited to see if she wanted to pray again. Sean had drifted away from his faith after Liz Graber had been killed by her ex-husband right under his nose.

But he couldn't deny liking the way Jacey had prayed before dinner last night.

She clasped her hands together and bowed her head. He followed suit. "Dear Lord, we thank You for this food we are about to eat. And we ask that You keep us safe in Your care as we start our day, amen."

"Amen," he echoed.

Jacey glanced at him, thoughtfully. "I don't remember seeing you at church services."

He inwardly winced. "No, probably not."

She looked a little disappointed, but then smiled. "You should see how beautiful the church is decorated for Christmas. It's the best way to get into the holiday spirit."

He reluctantly nodded. "Maybe I should."

She didn't push, but sampled her eggs. "Yum. Delicious."

"You seem to enjoy whatever edible items are placed in front of you," he teased.

She flashed a saucy grin. "I love any and all food I don't have to cook."

That made him laugh. When they finished breakfast, they worked together to clean up the mess, and he couldn't help thinking about how comfortable he was around Jacey.

So much so that he'd almost told her about his stepfather's physical abuse. Something he'd never told anyone, not even her brother, Jake.

She'd backed off, so he let it go. Besides, he didn't want or need her sympathy. Old history was best kept in the past as far as he was concerned.

An hour later, after they'd both showered and changed, they were on the road in his recently acquired jeep. As always, he kept a careful eye out for any hint of a tail, but so far, he hadn't seen anything suspicious.

The drive to San Antonio didn't take long, and they arrived at the Cozy Coffee Café ahead of schedule. He purchased them both large coffees, then took a seat a couple of rows behind Jacey's table, where he was able to maintain a good view of the door, Jacey and the street outside the window.

Jacey also sat overlooking the road, ignoring the curious looks the barista behind the counter shot toward Greta. Jacey had pointed out the K-9's vest that identified her as a working dog, so the barista didn't say anything about the animal needing to leave.

The minutes ticked by slowly.

At one minute past ten, Jacey straightened in her seat. Sean immediately saw what captured her attention: a redheaded female was standing at the street corner on the opposite side of the road.

His pulse quickened, but he attempted to appear nonchalant. He stared down at the sports section of the newspaper in front of him without reading a word.

"No!" Jacey shouted, jumping to her feet at the same instant he heard a distinct thud. Sean abandoned his newspaper and followed Jacey outside.

A crowd of people were gathered around the prone figure lying at the side of the street. Misty's bright red hair was unmistakable in the sunlight.

"What happened?" Sean asked, wishing he'd ignored the stupid newspaper to keep an eye on Misty.

"A black pickup truck sideswiped her." Jacey and Sean pushed through the crowd to kneel beside Misty. "Did anyone call 911?"

"I did," a kid with baggy pants answered.

Sean felt for a pulse, slightly reassured to find a fast and thready beat. There was a long laceration on her scalp, blood coalescing on her pale skin. Her left arm was bent at an odd angle, clearly broken.

"Did you get a glimpse of the license plate?" he asked.

"No, the plate was liberally covered with mud." Jacey's dark gaze was full of guilt. "I believe the driver of the truck was the same person who shoved me into traffic, poisoned Greta and shot at us."

Sean couldn't disagree. This hit-and-run convinced him that Misty had information that would help Jacey's case against Lieutenant Colonel Ivan Turks.

Whoever had done this was willing to eliminate any and all potential witnesses.

Without caring about the consequences.

SEVEN

There was so much blood, covering Misty and pooling on the road beneath her. Fighting nausea, Jacey put her hand on Misty's uninjured arm. Overwhelmed with guilt and sorrow, Jacey couldn't get the image of the truck hitting Misty Walsh out of her mind; it played over and over again like a stuck loop.

"It's okay, Misty. Help is on the way." The trainer was unconscious, but that didn't stop Jacey from talking to her. The rise and fall of Misty's chest was reassuring, but Jacey knew head injuries could be tricky. Especially since Misty's was bleeding like crazy.

Greta sat beside Jacey, sniffing at the female airman as if there was something she could do to help.

"I hear the ambulance now." Sean's deep voice was oddly reassuring. He rose to his feet and scanned the crowd of gawkers. "Anyone see what happened?"

"A black truck ran the red light and hit her along the left side." The kid wearing saggy pants spoke up. "It was bad, man. Really bad."

Jacey found no comfort in the fact that the kid's story mirrored hers. As she stared down at Misty's pale features, she kept thinking that it should have been her lying there.

Who knew that they were planning to meet today? Misty had called Jacey's cell phone directly to make the arrangements.

Was it possible one or both of their phones had been bugged? She knew her cell number was on file with the air force and that anyone with access could look it up. Or had someone close to Misty overheard her making the call?

Jacey didn't like any of the possibilities.

The ambulance arrived and soon the EMTs had Misty bundled up on the gurney.

"Wait." Jacey stopped them with a hand on the EMT's arm. "Which hospital are you taking her to? She's a senior airman from Canyon Air Force Base."

The two EMTs looked at each other and shrugged. "It's the same distance either way. We'll take her to Canyon if that's what you'd prefer."

"I would." She stepped back and glanced at Sean. "I'd like to meet her at the hospital, too."

"It will take some time before we'll be able to see her," he cautioned.

"I know." Logically she knew this wasn't her fault; Misty had been the one to reach out to her, not the other way around, but this had all started with her allegation against Lieutenant Colonel Turks.

Maybe she should have just kept her mouth shut.

The minute the thought crossed her mind, she inwardly rejected it. No, what the lieutenant colonel did wasn't right. She was fortunate enough to have escaped, but what if others hadn't been able to?

What if Misty hadn't?

The man was a menace, using his power as a weapon against women. No one deserved to be assaulted. Women could contribute to keeping the country safe just as well as men did. Even if she ended up being forced to resign from the air force, she knew she wouldn't go back to change the fact that she'd pressed charges against Turks.

She needed to believe that someday justice would be served.

Greta sensed her inner turmoil and pressed her nose against Jacey's hand. Jacey rubbed the K-9 between the ears and then crossed over to Sean. "We need to get out of here."

"I know. This way."

They walked back to his jeep in silence, each lost in their thoughts. When they arrived at the hospital, Misty was still being cared for in the ER.

"I'm the Special Forces cop who was on the scene after the crash," Sean informed the triage nurse. "I need an update on Misty's condition."

"I'll get the doctor for you."

Five minutes later, a man wearing scrubs covered by a long white lab coat came out to the waiting area. "Staff Sergeant Morris?"

Sean and Jacey both stood and approached the captain. They saluted and then went at ease.

"I'm Captain Robertson," the doctor introduced himself. "I understand you were at the scene when this happened?"

"Yes, sir." Sean briefly described what Jacey and the other young man had seen. "I'd like to understand the extent of her injuries."

"Her left side took the brunt of the damage. She has

a broken arm and leg. The arm has a significant compound fracture that will require surgery. She also has a collapsed lung on the left side that I was able to treat. I'm sure you noticed the laceration along the left side of her head."

"Has she woken up? Said anything?" Sean asked.

"No. She hasn't regained consciousness yet. I can have the nurse call you when she does."

"That would be great, thank you, sir." Sean handed the captain his contact information.

Awash in helplessness, Jacey watched the doctor walk away.

"There's nothing more we can do here," Sean said quietly.

"I know." That didn't mean she liked it. "Come, Greta." She followed Sean outside to the jeep. "Now what?"

"I'll keep digging for suspects."

Jacey put Greta in the back and then slid in beside Sean. As he headed back to the house, she considered their next options.

"We've assumed based on the log that the person Aiden saw in the kennel that night was female, but what if it wasn't? I think we need to broaden our search to men, and not just those employed by the training center."

"How would a man who didn't work there get access to Greta's kennel?"

She shook her head helplessly. "Steal it? Force someone to open it? Who knows? The fact is that we have to expand our pool of suspects."

"It's already a large pool, but I see what you're saying. I'll look into it—don't worry."

"We will." The stubborn glint was back in her eye. "I'm involved in this. After what happened to Misty…" She couldn't finish.

Sean pulled into the driveway and shut off the engine. He came around to open her door for her and for the second time in two days, she found herself cradled in his arms.

"She's strong. She'll pull through this," he murmured against her temple.

"I hope so." Her voice was muffled against his shirt and she breathed in his woody scent, then lifted her head to look up at him. "Thank you."

His brow levered up in surprise. "For what?"

"Being there for me." Keeping her gaze centered on his, she rose up on tiptoe and pressed her mouth against his.

He froze, and she feared he'd pull away, but he didn't. Instead he tugged her close and deepened their kiss. This was what she'd waited for. What she'd longed for. She reveled in his taste, the strength and warmth of his arms.

After several long moments, he finally lifted his head, breathing deep. "We can't do this. You're killing me, Jacey."

She couldn't help but smile. "Yeah? Well, after waiting ten years for you to kiss me, I figured it was time to take matters into my own hands."

His jaw dropped. "Ten years? You mean—"

"I've had a crush on you since high school." Seeing Misty lying on the gurney and hearing the extent of her injuries had convinced Jacey it was time to tell him the truth.

"I, uh, had no idea." He looked completely poleaxed by her declaration.

"I'm sure I was nothing more to you than Jake's annoying little sister," she teased. Greta poked her nose out from the back of the jeep, so she gestured for the dog to jump down.

He stared down at Jacey for a long moment. "Not exactly," he finally admitted. "I always thought you were pretty back then, but you're beautiful now."

"Really?" It was her turn to be caught off guard.

He nodded, then rubbed a hand along the back of his neck. "I— Things weren't good at home, so I pretty much stayed away from dating and friendships. Jake was the one guy I allowed myself to get close to, and even then, I never invited him to my house. I preferred hanging around yours, anyway."

"Because of your abusive stepfather?" she guessed.

His eyes widened in shock. "Yeah, but I didn't say he was abusive."

"You didn't have to. It was an easy assumption." She tilted her head to the side. "I'm sorry you had to go through that."

Sean let out a harsh laugh. "Me, too. But I finally convinced my mother to leave the jerk. But shortly thereafter, my mother was diagnosed with cancer and died within three months. After that, I joined the air force."

Her heart squeezed in her chest, and she placed a comforting hand on his arm. "I'm here if you want to talk."

"Thanks." His smile was strained. "But I think our time is better spent trying to figure out who is behind all of this."

She hesitated, then nodded. "All right. But just know, I'm here for you."

As they went inside, Jacey lightly touched her fingers to her still-tingling lips.

She didn't regret kissing Sean, but had the sense that he didn't feel the same way. His exact words were *we can't do this*.

Was it because of his abusive stepfather? Or something else?

Either way, Jacey was determined to get to the bottom of what was going through Sean's mind.

She'd planned to keep her distance, but that wasn't an option anymore. Certainly not after that toe-curling kiss.

They'd been given a second chance at a possible relationship.

If Sean had the courage to take it.

Kissing Jacey hadn't been part of his plan. But now that he'd tasted the sweetness of her lips, he wasn't sure he'd find the strength to stay away.

Remember Liz Graber, he harshly told himself. The image of how she looked lying dead on the floor was burned into his memory. Knowing that her ex-husband had taken the opportunity to kill her right under Sean's nose was a failure he'd have to live with for the rest of his life.

The only redeeming fact was that Sean had worked tirelessly to piece together the trace evidence needed to lock the guy up behind bars. At the time, he'd assumed he'd be demoted, but apparently bringing Liz's ex to justice had saved his reputation.

But it hadn't saved his heart.

And here he was, making the same mistake with Jacey. Getting too close and not keeping a professional distance.

If he was honest with himself, he'd say he'd already crossed the line by kissing her. Something he'd dreamed of doing ten years ago. And it rattled him to realize she'd felt the same way.

His emotions were tangled up in Jacey, no matter how hard he tried to unravel the hold she had on him.

Somehow, he had to keep his wits about him. No way was Jacey going to end up like Liz.

Not on his watch.

Jacey insisted on going to the training center for the afternoon, so he accompanied her and Greta, watching for a few moments as she put the animal through several training scenarios.

While Jacey worked with the K-9s, he did his best to stay focused on doing background checks of all the personnel on base who had even minor blemishes on their record in dealing with women. If the issue was Jacey's allegation against Turks, then someone must be holding a grudge against women who stand up for themselves against sexist behavior.

But there were so many, it was depressing. There were only two interesting items he'd uncovered. One was an allegation of inappropriate conduct against Bill Ullman, the cop who'd initially investigated Jacey's case, which had been filed just five months ago. The other was a formal assault complaint against his boss, Master Sergeant Hanover. The assault was two years ago, filed by a woman who Hanover had been dating. A lover's spat? Maybe. Regardless, he saved a copy of both incidents, although at this point, he was leaning toward Ullman as his primary suspect.

Then he switched gears to finish his report on the events of the morning. Less than ten minutes after he'd filed his report on Misty Walsh's hit-and-run, Master Sergeant Hanover called his cell phone.

"What's the connection between Senior Airman Walsh and Senior Airman Burke?" Hanover demanded.

"Misty asked Jacey if they could meet off base for coffee. She had something to tell her about Lieutenant Colonel Turks."

There was a long moment of silence. "You think she was assaulted, as well?" Hanover finally asked.

"We won't know for sure until she wakes up to tell us," Sean pointed out. It was interesting that his boss seemed very concerned about the assault. Maybe going through the issue with his former girlfriend had made him see how wrong he'd been to do such a thing. "But that's the working theory, yes."

"Hmm." Sean waited as his boss mulled over the information. "Do you believe her?"

"Jacey? Yes, I do."

Another long pause. "It's not easy going up against a lieutenant colonel without some hard evidence."

"No, sir. Yet it appears someone is trying to prevent us from doing just that."

"Be careful," Hanover said. "Oh, and be aware that Senior Airman Ullman isn't happy I transferred the case to you. I trust you to do a good job with it."

"Understood, sir." Maybe if Ullman had taken Jacey's concerns seriously, the airman would still have the case. Too bad for him.

Ullman had had at least one instance of attempted as-

sault of a woman. Were there more that hadn't been reported? Sean felt as if he were walking through a maze
blindfolded. The whole thing was beyond frustrating.
Lieutenant Colonel Turks was halfway across the globe
in Kabul, Afghanistan, while attempts were being made
on military personnel here, at Canyon.

Sean needed a break in the case, and soon. Before
anyone else was hurt, or worse.

He left the office Westley James had allowed him to
use and crossed over to wait for Jacey. She and Greta
joined him a few minutes later.

"You want me to pick up a pizza for dinner?" he
asked.

"Sure." Her smile didn't reach her eyes. "Any news
on Misty?"

"Not yet. We'll call the hospital for an update when
we get home."

She nodded, her expression troubled. "Even if she
wakes up, there's no guarantee she'll remember anything about the driver of the truck that hit her."

"I know, but we still need to know what she wanted
to discuss with you in the first place." It still bothered
him that Misty had asked for Jacey to come alone.

Why exclude a cop?

Sean had more questions than answers.

Jacey gave Greta food and water, then called the
hospital while he set the table. He set the pizza on the
table, pleased that Jacey had requested the works, exactly the way he liked it.

Stop it, he told himself harshly. Focus on the case,
not on the woman.

"Still not awake," Jacey said dejectedly as she
dropped into the chair across from him. "But they think

it's mostly because of her surgery. They had to place a rod and pins to align the bones in her left arm."

As horrible as it was, he knew it could have been much worse. He held out his hand, palm upward. "Let's pray for her."

She looked surprised by his suggestion but placed her hand in his and bowed her head. "Heavenly Father, we ask that You please heal Misty's injuries and help her wake up so we can seek justice against the person who did this to her. We also ask that You bless this food we are about to eat, and that You continue to guide us on Your chosen path, amen."

"Amen," he echoed.

She didn't remove her hand from his for a long moment. "I'm glad you suggested praying for Misty," she said, finally letting him go. "That was nice."

"Yeah." Truthfully, he'd surprised himself by making the request. Since reuniting with Jacey, he'd realized the importance of renewing his faith. "Maybe I should think about attending church services again, too. For more than just getting into the holiday spirit."

"That would be great." Jacey's smile was brighter than the lights on Christmas tree in the corner of the living room. "Have you ever spoken to Bill Ullman about the reports I made to him when the strange incidents started?"

He lifted a brow. "No, why?"

She shrugged and took another bite of her pizza. "I don't know, just curious."

"I figured there was nothing to gain by talking to him, since you mentioned he didn't take your concerns seriously. Although my boss did mention that he's not happy that I've been given the case." He didn't tell her what he'd found so far in the guy's file. One incident didn't make a murderer.

"That's interesting. Why would he care?" She lifted her head and stared out the window for a moment. Then her gaze narrowed and she abruptly leaped to her feet. "Sean! I think there's a fire over at the base-housing apartment complex."

"What?" He went over to see what she meant. Dusk was falling, but it was easy to see the dark cloud of smoke hovering over the building, obliterating the Christmas lights dangling from the light poles.

A coincidence? Not likely. Anyone looking at his personnel file or Jacey's would see that they both lived there.

Was this yet another attempt against them?

To silence one or both of them, for good?

EIGHT

"We need to head over there, see if they need help." Jacey bent over to fasten Greta's vest in place.

"We're not trained firefighters," Sean protested. "If this is an attempt to get to us, then we need to stay here where it's safe."

"You don't know that the fire is connected to us. Our military brothers and sisters need our help." Jacey secured a leash to Greta's vest. "I'm going to help them. They might need Greta's trained nose. You can stay here if you want."

"No way. You're not going alone." Sean's tone was clipped with anger. It occurred to her that this was the first time she'd seen him truly angry. "We'll take the jeep and if there is any evidence this is linked to us, we're out of there."

Parking would be a nightmare, but she decided to let it go.

The area around the apartment building was engulfed in chaos. For a moment, she wondered if Sean was right about this being a trap, but then she shook off the sliver of fear.

They needed to make sure everyone had gotten out of the building safely.

Greta sniffed at people as they passed by, and Jacey wondered if the perpetrator who'd started the fire used something that Greta could identify. The K-9 wouldn't pick up on scents like gasoline or fire-starter fluid, but if there was gunpowder or something similar, it was worth a shot.

This is what Greta trained for.

The firefighters were already on scene and not allowing any pedestrians to cross the perimeter. The scent of smoke was thick and heavy as the firefighters put out the blaze.

"Only the south building seems to be impacted," Sean murmured.

She nodded. "I noticed. They're soaking the north building with water to stop the fire from spreading, but it appears that they have it under control."

"I wonder where the fire originated?" Sean asked, staring at the third floor where it appeared the majority of the work was being done by the firefighters on scene.

Jacey shivered as the magnitude of the event washed over her. "My apartment is on the third floor."

Sean put his arm around her shoulders and gave her a quick squeeze. "Exactly."

The thought that this fire was set on purpose, maybe even in her unit, made Jacey feel sick. The person behind all of this obviously didn't care how many innocent people were hurt along the way.

Why had the perp set her apartment on fire while she wasn't there? To scare her?

Or was this all one big coincidence?

The fire chief turned to address the crowd of onlookers. "Has anyone seen Senior Airman Burke?"

Jacey swallowed hard and lifted her hand. "Here, sir."

He gestured for her to step forward, and she was relieved that Sean stayed close at her side. They both saluted the senior officer. Greta was on full alert, her nose sniffing constantly.

"Senior Airman Burke, your apartment has been deemed the source of the fire." The fire chief's gaze was stern. "Are you a smoker? Or did you leave candles burning?"

"No, sir." Jacey tightened her grip on Greta's leash. "I have never smoked. I don't have a real Christmas tree or wreath and do not burn candles. I'm aware of what is and isn't allowed on the premises, sir."

"Hmm." His stern expression softened. "Well, I'm glad you weren't home when this happened. Thankfully, the sprinklers worked well and the fire was put out quickly. Most of the damage was centered on your apartment and those adjacent and beneath it. And most of that is from water, not the fire itself."

Jacey sent up a quick prayer of thanks that no one was injured as a result of the fire. But it still bothered her that her apartment was used as the source of the blaze. "I'm glad to hear that, sir."

"Has the fire been deemed arson?" Sean spoke up for the first time. "I'm Staff Sergeant Morris, and I'm investigating several previous attempts to harm Senior Airman Burke. Hearing the source of the fire was her apartment gives me a reason to believe this event is connected to the others."

"Not yet. Who is your superior officer?"

"I report directly to Master Sergeant Doug Hanover, sir, but ultimately my CO is Captain Justin Blackwood."

"Fine." The fire chief nodded. "I'll let Captain Blackwood know when our investigation is complete. At this point, all I can tell you is that it appears that the fire originated on the sofa."

Jacey opened her mouth to protest, but Sean nudged her and shook his head. This was the part of the military she didn't enjoy, when brass would only communicate among lines of authority.

It was her apartment that had been torched. Sean was the key cop investigating her case. The bureaucracy was beyond annoying.

"Dismissed," the fire chief said, turning away from them. Jacey had to grit her teeth together to prevent herself from saying something she'd regret. The last thing she needed was another negative note in her file.

The one currently sitting in there was bad enough.

"Come on." Sean tugged at her elbow. "Let's get out of here."

"Where are these airmen who can't return to their apartments going to sleep tonight?" Jacey asked as she allowed Sean to lead a weaving path through the crowd.

"I'm sure they'll be ordered to double up—they won't be stranded in the cold." Sean brushed aside her concern. "We need to get back to the house. I don't like being out in the open like this."

"No one would be crazy enough to make an attempt on us with all these people around." Even as she said the words, she realized that wasn't entirely true.

Misty had been struck by a truck in the bright light of day on a busy street with pedestrians milling about.

The person behind this was growing bolder. Jacey would be a fool to underestimate him or her.

Him. Deep down, she knew the person responsible was a man. Who else would care about her allegation against Lieutenant Colonel Turks? Even if a woman didn't quite believe her, it was unlikely that a female airman or officer would go to such lengths to silence her.

Not just her, but Misty, too.

The perp had to be a man. Someone with a lot to lose if the truth about the lieutenant colonel came to light.

But who?

The strong stench of cigarette smoke made her wrinkle her nose seconds before someone shoved past her. The person making their way through the crowd was wearing a uniform, complete with a cap, and had the collar turned up around the face.

"Wait! Sean! This way!" She jutted around another person, trying to follow the guy weaving through the crowd. There were so many people, all dressed similarly and wearing hats because of the cold December temperatures.

"What happened?" Sean asked, joining her. "Did you see someone?"

"I did, but he's gone now." She sighed and glanced around. "I'm sure it was the guy we're looking for."

"A guy?" Sean asked. "You saw his face?"

"Not exactly." She glanced around, battling a wave of dejection. So close. The perp had been so close! "But can you honestly come up with a reason why a woman would do this?"

"No, but that doesn't mean a woman isn't involved." Sean anchored his arm around her waist, providing a sense of safety and protectiveness. "It's not smart to rule anyone out, Jacey."

She didn't answer, but the image of Misty Walsh's pale, bloodstained face wouldn't go away.

Then she remembered the scent of cigarette smoke. "It's the same guy who shoved me from behind that first night. I know it. He reeked of the same stale cigarette smoke. As if he'd smoked an entire pack within the past few hours."

"Yeah, okay, but that doesn't exactly narrow down our pool of suspects," Sean pointed out. "Almost half the personnel on base smoke."

He was right. She knew he was right.

But so was she. They were looking for a man who smoked and who didn't particularly like women. Or maybe liked them too much.

"Wait a minute." She stopped and looked at Sean. "Does Lieutenant Colonel Turks have family? Like a son?"

Sean shook his head. "That was the first thing I checked. He has a civilian ex-wife, and that's it. No other family listed on file."

"Does his ex-wife have kids?"

"No." She should have realized he'd check that, too, considering his experience with his own stepfather.

"Great." Her shoulders slumped with defeat. They were right back where they'd started two days ago.

No suspects, no way to narrow the list of airmen and officers living on base.

They were fresh out of clues.

Sean hustled Jacey through the crowd, looking over his shoulder at different time intervals to make sure they weren't followed.

He understood Jacey's frustration; in fact, he shared it. Just as they reached the playground located two blocks down from the apartment complex, a pretty blonde stepped in front of them. "I'm Heidi Jenks— I'd like to interview Senior Airman Burke about the fire that originated in her apartment."

"No comment," Sean said, holding up his hand so Jacey wouldn't respond.

"I was talking to Jacey Burke, not you," Heidi responded tartly. "I'm sure she can speak for herself."

Jacey didn't respond right away, as if weighing her options.

"Don't," Sean said in an undertone. "The last thing you need is to have your name splattered all over the base newspaper."

"Again, I think she can speak for herself," Heidi countered. "Jacey?"

"How did you know her first name?" Sean challenged, knowing there was no way to win the gender war.

Heidi looked taken aback. "I heard the fire chief mention her name."

"No, he only referred to her as Senior Airman Burke." Sean didn't like this one bit. "Not her first name. Which according to her file is listed as Jacelyn. So how do you know her nickname?"

"Okay, okay." Heidi lifted a hand in surrender. "If you must know, I learned about Jacey's allegation against the lieutenant colonel and thought it would be a good idea to do a story on it." She turned toward Jacey. "What do you think? Don't you want other women to be aware of what happened?"

"My allegation was deemed not credible," Jacey said

in a low tone. "Why would you want to do a story on something that hasn't been validated?"

"Because I think it's important that all sides of the story are told and women need to be encouraged to stand their ground and fight back against this kind of thing," Heidi responded. "Do you really want the lieutenant colonel to have the last word?"

"Why does it matter, if no one believes me?" Jacey asked.

"Whoa, Jacey. You need to take some time to think about the ramifications of giving an interview." Sean didn't necessarily think that Heidi Jenks was up to something nefarious, but at the same time, he didn't want Jacey jumping into something she may regret later. The lieutenant colonel already had someone on base attacking her; why stir things up?

Heidi was focused on Jacey. "I don't want to rush you into anything, but I am interested in hearing your side of what happened. You're not the only woman on base who's had to deal with this. Here's my card. Give me a call when you feel like talking."

"Thanks." Jacey took the reporter's card and offered a wan smile.

"I look forward to hearing from you," Heidi said as she turned away.

"Wait!" Jacey took a few steps toward the reporter and Sean curled his fingers into fists to prevent himself from reaching for her.

"Change your mind already?" Heidi asked with a grin.

"No, but I do have a question for you. Do you know Misty Walsh?"

Sean didn't think he imagined the flash of recognition in the reporter's eyes.

"Why does it matter?" Heidi asked.

"Because she was seriously injured by a hit-and-run," Sean said.

Heidi's eyes widened with horror. "No! What happened?"

He was a little surprised she didn't know, but then remembered that the hit-and-run had taken place off base. None of this was Heidi Jenks's fault. He was letting his personal feelings toward Jacey run amok, viewing Heidi as an adversary rather than an ally.

"Someone driving a black truck ran a red light and hit her on the left side," Jacey answered. "She has a head injury, a broken arm requiring surgery and a broken leg, among other minor wounds. Now it's your turn to answer my question. Did you talk to Misty? Did she tell you about having an issue with the lieutenant colonel?"

Heidi nodded slowly. "Yes, she told me that I needed to dig into the issue of abuse among ranking officers, specifically Lieutenant Colonel Turks, and she specifically mentioned you." Her expression filled with concern. "Do you think that's why she was hit by the truck?"

"I do," Jacey said before Sean could interject another *no comment*. "Because she called to set up a meeting with me off base. She was hit before she reached the café."

"Oh, no," Heidi whispered. "How terrible."

"This is why it wouldn't be smart for Jacey to talk to you," Sean said firmly. "Maybe later, but not now."

"Sean's right," Jacey said, her brow furrowed. "Things are too dangerous. Misty's life is hanging in the balance as it is."

"I'm sorry," Heidi offered. "I had no idea."

"It's okay." Jacey flashed a weary smile. "It's not your fault, but I think it's best if you leave this alone for a while. Bad enough that some of us are in danger. I'd hate to see anything happen to you."

"I can take care of myself," Heidi said. "And my fiancé, Nick Donovan, won't let anything happen to me, either."

"Nick Donovan?" Jacey repeated. "I worked with him a bit while training Greta. He's an explosives expert and Greta is a bomb-sniffing K-9."

"Small world," Heidi said with a wry smile.

"Yes, well—" Jacey cleared her throat "—I'm hopeful the truth will come out sooner or later, and if it does, I promise to give you an exclusive."

Heidi's eyes lit up. "Thanks. Please let me know when you're willing to talk."

"I will," Jacey agreed. "Where are you headed? It's not smart for you to be alone."

"I'm meeting Nick at Carmen's," Heidi admitted. "And based on what you've just told me, it would be silly to turn down an escort."

Finally, a statement Sean could agree with. As he walked between the two women, Jacey keeping Greta close by, he found himself hoping that Heidi wouldn't end up in the crosshairs the way Jacey and Misty had been.

The person doing all of this had to make a mistake sooner or later. And Sean planned to be there when he or she did.

NINE

Jacey and Heidi chatted a bit while Sean drove them to Carmen's. He parked nearby, and the three of them with Greta headed to the restaurant. Nick must have been waiting for them, because he came outside to meet them. Jacey and Sean each gave a quick salute in deference to his rank of captain.

"Jacey, it's good to see you again," Nick said.

"You, too. Oh, and this is Staff Sergeant Sean Morris with Special Forces. Sean, this is Captain Nick Donovan."

Now that the formalities were over, the two men shook hands. "Nice to meet you, Captain," Sean said.

Nick nodded and glanced at Heidi. "You're late," he chided gently with a private smile. "Because of the fire?"

"Of course!" She leaned up to kiss him. "Thanks for being patient."

"Always," he murmured, his gaze full of love.

Jacey couldn't help but sigh at how adorable they were together.

"Captain, you may want to keep a close eye on your fiancée over the next few weeks." Sean's serious tone brought the cheerfulness down a notch. "She's investigating a story that has attracted danger."

"The fire?" Nick asked with a frown.

"Not just the fire, but about allegations of assault against a high-ranking officer," Jacey said. She knew Heidi would fill him in anyway. "The fire is just one of the attempts against me, among others."

"Heidi?" Nick put his arm around the petite blonde. "Is this true?"

"Yes," Heidi admitted. "I didn't realize that one of the women I spoke to yesterday, Misty Walsh, was involved in a hit-and-run crash earlier today, before Jacey and Misty could meet. They both have experience with a particular senior officer. That, combined with the fact that Jacey's apartment is the source of the fire, makes it doubly suspicious."

"No more rushing off to cover stories alone," Nick said in a grim tone. "I'll go with you from now on."

"Good plan," Sean said with a nod.

"Do you have a list of suspects?" Nick asked.

"I wish I did," Sean admitted. "But so far there's very little evidence. There are a few items up at the San Antonio crime lab, but so far I haven't heard anything."

"Let me know if you need help." Nick's expression was troubled.

"I will. Excuse me." Sean pulled his ringing phone from his pocket and moved away from the other couple. Jacey went with him, curious about who was calling. "Staff Sergeant Morris," he said by way of greeting.

Heidi and Nick disappeared into the restaurant as Jacey strained to hear the other side of the conversation.

"She is? Great, we'll be right there." Sean slid his

phone back into his pocket. "Good news—Misty Walsh is conscious and able to talk."

"Thank You, Lord," Jacey whispered, knowing that God had answered their prayers. "That's wonderful. Can we go there now?"

"Absolutely. It's just a block away, so no sense taking the jeep, but stay close," Sean warned. "Keep Greta on your left, and I'll stay to the right."

Jacey wasn't going to argue.

Inside the hospital, the lobby was warm and brightly decorated for Christmas. Sean asked at the front desk for Misty's room number and was told she was on the second floor in room 228.

Jacey, Greta and Sean took the elevator up and found Misty's room without difficulty. Sean knocked on the door, pushing it open when Misty's feeble voice beckoned them to come in.

The woman in the hospital bed had a line of sutures along her temple and her left arm was completely bandaged, with pins and rods sticking out of it. The blankets covered her legs, but Jacey assumed the left one was casted, as well. Her heart went out to her fellow trainer.

"Misty? I'm Staff Sergeant Sean Morris and you know Senior Airman Jacey Burke and her K-9 partner, Greta."

"Oh, Misty." Jacey crossed over and lightly rested her hand on Misty's unbroken arm. "I'm so sorry this happened to you."

"Why did you bring a cop?" Misty asked, her gaze full of reproach. "I already told you I didn't go near Greta's kennel."

"Why don't you tell us what you remember about the vehicle that hit you?" Sean countered. "I'm not here to cause trouble. I just want the truth."

Misty reluctantly nodded. "I was waiting at the crosswalk. The sign indicated it was okay to walk, so I did, but a truck zoomed through the intersection, hitting me on the left side." Misty grimaced and tried to shift her position in the bed. "I don't remember anything else until I woke up here in the hospital. One of the nurses told me that the police would be here to take my statement. But I didn't think you and Jacey would be together."

"I'm so sorry," Jacey repeated. "But Misty, surely you don't think this was an accident? From where I was sitting in the café, it looked as if the truck hit you on purpose."

Misty closed her eyes and turned her head away, as if the news was unbearable. Jacey kept a light grasp on Misty's arm, hoping the physical contact between them would help keep her grounded.

"Misty, did you get a look at the driver?" Sean gently asked.

Misty finally opened her eyes, her lashes wet with tears. "No. I wasn't expecting the truck to be there. I had the walk signal. Did you get a license plate?"

"Unfortunately, the plates were covered with mud," Jacey said. "That's another reason I think it was done on purpose. Whoever hit you didn't want to be identified."

"Why?" Misty asked in an agonized whisper. "Because of Turks?"

"I'm afraid so," Jacey said. "I know you spoke to the journalist Heidi Jenks, as I have. He attacked you, too, didn't he?"

Misty winced and whispered, "Yes."

"How did you get my cell number?"

"From the training-center records," Misty answered. "In fact, I was in your office when I called you."

"My office?" Jacey glanced at Sean, who looked surprised. "Do you use my office often?"

"Sometimes, but only because I don't trust the phone in my office." Misty's voice was getting weaker. "I think someone is spying on me."

Jacey realized Misty may have been the one moving stuff around in her office. Interesting that they'd both experienced the same sense of being watched, too. Jacey wanted to ask more questions, but Misty's eyelids fluttered closed.

"Come on," Sean said in a low voice. "She needs to rest."

He was right. Misty looked battered, bruised and broken. The best thing they could do for her fellow trainer was to find the person responsible.

They left Misty's hospital room and took the elevator back down to the lobby. "She didn't give us anything to work with," Jacey murmured as they headed outside. "Other than to admit that she was attacked by Turks, too."

"Yeah," Sean agreed. "It's good to have confirmation about Turks. And I think it's interesting that she doesn't trust the cops."

Jacey had noticed that, as well. "Maybe she tried to file a report but was brushed off, the same way Senior Airman Bill Ullman did to me."

"Could be. I'll dig around to see what reports, if any, she filed." Sean placed his hand beneath her elbow. "The jeep is this way."

Sean took extra precautions so they weren't followed, and they made it back to the house without incident. When Jacey took Greta around to the backyard to do her business, Sean tagged along.

"Do you really think Heidi Jenks is in danger?" she asked.

He shrugged. "If the person doing this figures out that she's doing a story on abuse by senior-ranking officers, then yeah, that's a no-brainer."

Jacey shivered and nodded. Bad enough that Misty had been hit by a truck, the thought of adding other innocent victim to the growing list was disturbing to say the least.

"Come, Greta," Jacey called, when it appeared her K-9 was finished. "Let's go inside."

Sean unlocked the back door and held it open for her to precede him inside. In the kitchen, Jacey expected Greta to head straight for her food and water dishes, since the poor thing hadn't finished eating earlier, but instead Greta's nose went up and her entire body quivered.

A chill snaked down Jacey's spine. "Greta?"

The dog lowered her snout to the ground and moved in a zigzag pattern that was achingly familiar. It was the way Greta searched for IEDs in Afghanistan.

"We need to get out of here," she whispered to Sean, but it was too late.

Greta alerted at the stable of the Nativity scene at the same exact moment a man stepped out from behind the Christmas tree.

He was medium height, slim and held a gun. But it

wasn't Senior Airman Bill Ullman, as she'd half expected.

It was someone she'd never seen before.

TEN

"Master Sergeant Hanover?" Sean couldn't believe his boss was standing next to the Christmas tree holding a gun on them. "What's going on? Why are you doing this?"

"When you pulled my file, I knew you'd figure it out eventually," the man said in a snide tone. His boss was a few years younger than he was, and Sean had wondered how he'd risen up through the ranks so quickly. Now he knew it wasn't just because Hanover was good. Far from it. Greta stood frozen directly in front of Hanover and he glowered at the animal. "Call off your dog, or I'll shoot it."

"Greta, come," Jacey commanded.

Greta slowly backed up, keeping her dark eyes locked on Hanover.

"What's the link between you and Lieutenant Colonel Turks?" Sean asked, desperate to find a way to protect Jacey. "I mean, it's obvious he's greasing the way for your promotions, and you physically look enough like him to be his son."

Hanover's smile reeked of pure evil and Sean wondered why he hadn't noticed the underlying cruelty before now. "That's exactly why I knew you'd figure it out. You're smart, Morris—I'll give you that. Putting the jeep in my name and then finding this place without going through proper channels. You made me work to find you, that's for sure."

"Are you denying you're related to Lieutenant Colonel Turks?" Sean pressed.

"Not at all. Ivan never bothered to marry my useless mother, and I didn't blame him. It didn't matter, since I'm his son in every way that counts. Having different last names actually worked in our favor. And obviously I'll do whatever is necessary to protect my father." Hanover jerked the weapon toward Jacey. "Tie her up."

Every muscle in Sean's body went tense. He couldn't—wouldn't—allow anything to happen to Jacey.

Liz had died, but he refused to fail again.

"Jacey, run!" Sean shouted at the same time as he heard Jacey tell Greta, "Get him!"

He leaped toward Hanover. The distance was too far, and he braced himself for the gunshot he knew was coming. Greta moved swiftly, clamping her jaw around Hanover's leg.

"Owww!" Hanover fired his weapon and Sean felt the bullet skate along the side of his thigh but ignored the pain. Jacey's panic alarm shrilled loud enough to fracture his eardrums and everyone else's within a ten-mile radius.

Sean took his boss down and Jacey scooped up Hanover's gun. Greta clung to Doug's leg as the guy continued to shriek with pain. At least he appeared to be shrieking; all Sean could hear was the stupid panic alarm.

Finally, Jacey shut it off, the ensuing silence a true blessing.

"Master Sergeant Hanover, you're under arrest for attempted murder," Sean said, slapping handcuffs over his boss's wrists.

"Sean? We better hurry."

"Why?" He glanced up at Jacey, then realized that Greta was sitting straight and tall right next to the stable of the Nativity scene. "Are you saying there's a bomb in there?"

"Yes! Let's go!"

Sean winced as the muscles of his injured thigh protested when he hauled Hanover to his feet. Jacey grabbed Hanover's other arm and they rushed to drag him outside, with Greta keeping pace alongside. Outside, several airmen from nearby houses were milling about, rousted by Jacey's panic alarm.

"All of you, follow us! Hurry!" Sean said. "There's a bomb inside the house!"

Thankfully, the others joined them, and they didn't stop until they were more than halfway down the block.

"We need to call it in," Jacey said between gasping breaths. "Hurry!"

Sean was already fishing his phone out of his pocket when a loud *ka-boom* reverberated through the night.

"The neighbors!" Jacey shouted.

"I live on the west side of the place," one woman said. "My husband is currently overseas."

"We live on the east side," a young couple piped up. "That alarm was crazy loud—I couldn't figure out what was going on!"

Sean managed a smile. "You did it, Jacey. First Greta

found the bomb, then that ridiculously loud alarm of yours saved the neighbors."

"We did it," she said. "I didn't even know who he was out of uniform, but you did. I can't believe your boss is Turks's son. And you're bleeding again."

Sean couldn't care less about the wound on his leg. Knowing that Jacey was safe from harm and that he hadn't failed to protect her was all he needed.

Because he loved her.

The realization sank deep into his bones, and he knew that this was the real thing. More than what he'd felt with Liz, although he'd certainly cared about her.

But not the same way he loved Jacey.

He wanted to tell her, to see if she felt even close to the same way, but right now, he needed to stay focused on Hanover. His boss had to pay for his crimes.

"Misty Walsh talked to us just an hour ago," Jacey said, her gaze riveted on Hanover's face. "Between the two of us and any others we can find, we're going to drag your father down off his high-ranking-officer pedestal and toss him in jail where he belongs."

Hanover sneered and swore at Jacey. "You're all alike. Stupid women. You want to do a man's job, but then you're the first to crumble under pressure."

"Assault is not pressure," Jacey shot back.

"Don't waste your breath talking to him," Sean advised. "He's not worth it. Just imagine the two of them sharing a cell, father and son."

Before Jacey could say anything more, additional Special Forces cops arrived, along with half the firetrucks from the apartment fire.

"You again?" The fire chief did not look happy to see them.

"Yes, sir." Sean had to retell their story several times, forced to start over when a superior officer showed up. When Captain Justin Blackwood arrived, he took over the questioning, silencing everyone else.

Hanover tried to interject his side of things, claiming he was being framed and had only come to talk to Sean and Jacey about the case, but thankfully, Jacey had kept his weapon, and handed it over to Captain Blackwood.

"I believe we'll be able to match the ballistics of the bullet Greta found at the parking lot with Hanover's gun," Sean explained.

"Good work, Staff Sergeant," Captain Blackwood said, his expression grim. "I only wish you had escalated this to me sooner."

Sean frowned. "With all due respect, sir, I was keeping my immediate superior up-to-date on my investigation without having any idea he was the one responsible."

"True enough." Justin Blackwood scowled at Hanover. "So, we have Hanover on setting the bomb in the house and two counts of attempted murder. Anything else to add to the list?"

"Three counts of attempted murder, if he drives a black pickup truck," Jacey said. "I saw the truck run the red light and deliberately hit Misty Walsh."

"You can't prove I was the one driving," Hanover protested.

"But I'm sure we'll find traces of Misty's blood and tissue on your truck, won't we?" Sean countered. "Face it—we have you linked to everything."

"I didn't give antifreeze to the dog," Hanover whined.

"Yes, you did." Aiden Gomez stepped out from behind a tree, cradling a pup against his chest. "I saw you at the kennel that night. And Reba admitted to me that she lost her ID. You used it, didn't you?"

"Useless little punk!" Hanover tried to lunge upward, but Sean yanked him back down. "You couldn't have seen me from where you were standing."

Sean couldn't help but smile at how easily Hanover had walked into that one. Apparently being under pressure wasn't working so well for his former boss, either.

"Enough!" Blackwood lifted his hand up. "Hanover, I suggest you exercise your right to keep silent, as anything you say can be used against you in a court-martial. Let's go."

When the Special Forces cops took Hanover away, Sean finally allowed the EMTs to look at his leg. The injury wasn't serious, and only an inch longer than the gash on his arm.

"We'll give you a lift to the ER," the EMT offered.

"No, thanks. Just wrap it up and I'll be fine." The danger was over, but he wasn't about to leave Jacey alone.

The house was gone, her apartment was gone, which left his apartment, if she'd be willing to sleep on the sofa.

Or a motel off base, which didn't really appeal, either.

Then he had a better idea. "How about I take you to Gram's house for the rest of the night?"

"Oh, it's late and I don't want to inconvenience your grandmother," Jacey protested.

"Trust me, we won't be. I have a feeling she'll enjoy meeting the woman who helped bring down a lieutenant colonel."

"I haven't done that yet," she pointed out.

"You will." He had the utmost confidence in her.

"I have Greta, too," she added. "I think it's best if I stay in a motel. A dog-friendly motel."

"Gram loves dogs." He wasn't taking no for an answer. "Will you please trust me on this?"

Jacey hesitated, then nodded. "Okay. I'll trust you. But we'll need to stop by the kennel to pick up additional K-9 supplies. Everything I had in the house is gone."

"Fine with me. Let's go."

Despite it being close to 2200 hours, his grandmother was still up. She opened the door and greeted him with an enthusiastic kiss. "Sean! You're early—I wasn't expecting you until the end of the week!"

"Gram, I'd like you to meet Jacey Burke. Jacey, this is my grandmother, Maureen Morris. We'd like to stay for the night, if that's okay with you."

"Sure, dear," Gram agreed.

"It's so nice to meet you, Ms. Morris. Friend, Greta. Friend." Greta sniffed at Gram, then plopped onto her haunches. "Morris?" Jacey repeated. "Is that your mother's last name?"

"Yes. Thankfully, my stepfather never offered to adopt me."

Gram sighed. "I warned your mother he was no good, but she didn't listen."

Sean kissed her wrinkled cheek. "I know, and I'll always regret how he kept us away from you. But it's okay. Everything worked out just the way God planned."

"Oh, Sean." Gram hugged him close. "I'm glad to hear you say that."

"You can thank Jacey for bringing me back to my faith," he confessed.

Jacey's cheeks turned pink. "I have a feeling you would have come back on your own—I just gave you a gentle nudge."

He wanted so badly to tell her how much he loved her, but before he could think of a way to broach the subject, Jacey continued.

"Ms. Morris, I have to confess, I've had a crush on your grandson ever since high school." Jacey winked at his grandmother. "Despite all the adversity he had to go through, he has turned out to be an exceptional man and an amazing cop."

It was his turn to blush. His grandmother arched a brow.

"I like her, Sean. She's the first woman friend you've introduced to me and I can see why. Don't mess things up, you hear?" With that Gram turned and walked away. "Good night!" she called over her shoulder.

Jacey chuckled and shook her head. "She's something."

"Yes," he agreed, taking a step closer. "And so are you. I love you, Jacey Burke. If you must know, I had a crush on you back in high school, too."

"Oh, Sean." She slid her arms up and around his neck. "The way you kept pulling away from me, I thought you only liked me as a friend, nothing more."

"Far from it. I was only afraid I'd fail to protect you, the way I failed to protect another woman who I'd promised to protect. She was killed by her ex-husband because I let my guard down. I was convinced I needed to keep you at arm's length to keep you safe." He gazed into Jacey's beautiful deep-brown eyes. "When Hanover held the gun on us, I knew I'd readily sacrifice my life to save you. I love you, Jacey. I know it's fast, and we have barely gone on a proper date, but I hope you're willing to give us a chance."

"Done," she said with a smile. "Because I love you, too." She went up on tiptoe and kissed him.

He cradled her close, his gaze catching the bright star glittering on the top of Gram's Christmas tree. He reveled in her embrace, knowing that God had planned to bring them together all these years later.

For this moment right now.

Jacey had loved spending time with Sean's grandmother, but after three days was grateful to be assigned a new apartment back on base. She decorated the small Christmas tree, the third one, but who was counting? And silently reviewed her many blessings.

First and foremost, Sean. They'd attended Sunday services together and she loved standing beside him in church, listening to his deep baritone as he sang along with the choir. She never felt as close to a man as she did while worshiping God.

Sean filled her in on everything that had taken place when he'd returned to work the morning after the bomb had gone off. Over the next three days, Sean had collected the evidence needed to level charges against Master Sergeant Doug Hanover. When one of Hanover's fingerprints was found inside her old apartment after the fire investigation was complete, the charge of arson was added to the list.

The bullet fragment matched Hanover's gun, and the fingerprint on the dropped bullet was a partial match to him, as well. And a search warrant turned up Reba Pokorny's ID. Sean was happy to have a strong case against Hanover.

Jacey and Misty had renewed their respective formal complaints against Lieutenant Colonel Turks, and Jacey had heard from Heidi that a third female airman had come forward after Heidi's story hit the newspaper. Jacey was convinced even more women would be strong enough to tell their stories, as well, and this time, she was confident that her allegations would be taken seriously and that Turks would stand trial for his crimes, just as Hanover would.

A knock at the door pulled her from her thoughts. Greta let out a quick bark, her tail wagging as she stared at the door. Jacey peered through the peephole to verify Sean was the one standing there.

She unlocked the dead bolt and opened the door. "Hi, you're early."

"I know. Captain Blackwood sent me home and told me to take the next couple of days off." He swept her into his arms for a long kiss. When he finally came up for air, he added, "I bolted out of there before he could change his mind."

She laughed. "I'm always happy to see you. Check out my Christmas tree. Dinner won't be ready for a while. There's time to relax and make yourself comfy."

"Thanks." He shrugged out of his coat. "By the way, Gram insists on having us over for Christmas brunch. I tried to tell her to let us do the work, but she refused to listen."

"Your grandmother is one stubborn lady," she teased. "I can see where you get it from."

"Me?" His eyes widened with pretend innocence. "You're the most stubborn woman I know."

That made her laugh, but then her smile faded as she caught a glimpse of a snow-globe Christmas ornament that reminded her of Jake. "I'm glad you've invited me to spend the holidays with you," she said with a sad smile. "I only wish Jake could join us."

"I believe he's here, in your heart and in mine," Sean said, pulling her close.

"You're right." She did her best to push her feelings of melancholy away.

"Hey." Sean tipped her face up to meet his gaze. "After everything you've been through, I'm not going to wait until Christmas to give you your present."

"Oh, Sean, I don't need gifts," she protested. "Just being with you is wonderful enough."

His smile broadened. "I was hoping you'd say that."

She tilted her head to the side, confused. Then he slowly dropped down to one knee and held out a small red velvet ring box. Greta wagged her tail, sniffed him, and sat down beside him, but he never took his gaze off Jacey's. "Jacey Marie Burke, I know it's taken us ten years to find each other again, but now that we have I never want to let you go. Will you please marry me?"

Tears of joy blurred her vision and her heart swelled with love. "Oh, Sean, yes! Yes, I'll marry you." She tugged him to his feet and threw herself into his arms. He caught her close and spun in a small circle. Greta thought it was a game and jumped and barked around them.

He kissed her again, and insisted on sliding the beautiful diamond engagement ring on her finger. Then they stood together staring at the Christmas tree. "Gram is going to be so excited," he said, pressing a kiss against her temple. "She told me not to dawdle in asking you to marry me."

Jacey smiled. "I hardly think a week is exactly dawdling, but I appreciate her concern." She leaned her head against Sean's arm. "I love you so much."

"And I love you, too. Just don't make me wait too long for the ceremony. If Gram has her way, she'll have the whole thing planned before we know it."

"We wouldn't want to disappoint Gram," Jacey agreed. And even though this would be her first Christmas without Jake, she couldn't deny it was already the best Christmas ever.

* * * * *

SPECIAL EXCERPT FROM

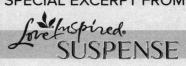

Love Inspired
SUSPENSE

*When her son witnesses a murder, Julia Bradford and
her children must go into witness protection with the
Amish. Can former police officer Abraham King keep
them safe at his Amish farm?*

Read on for a sneak preview of
Amish Safe House *by Debby Giusti,*
the exciting continuation of the
Amish Witness Protection miniseries,
available February 2019 from Love Inspired Suspense!

"I have your new identities." US marshal Jonathan Mast
sat across the table from Julia in the hotel where she and
her children had been holed up for the last five days.

The Luchadors wanted to kill William so he wouldn't
testify against their leader. As much as Julia didn't trust
law enforcement, she had to rely on the US Marshals and
their witness protection program to keep her family safe.
No wonder her nerves were stretched thin.

"We're ready to transport you and the children,"
Jonathan Mast continued. "We'll fly into Kansas City
tonight, then drive to Topeka and north to Yoder."

"What's in Kansas?"

Jonathan pulled out his phone and accessed a
photograph. He handed the cell to Julia. "Abraham King
will watch over you in Kansas."

Julia studied the picture. The man looked to be in his midthirties with a square face and deep-set eyes beneath dark brows. His nose appeared a bit off center, as if it had been broken. Lips pulled tight and no hint of a smile on his angular face.

"Mr. King doesn't look happy."

Jonathan shrugged. "Law enforcement photos are never flattering."

Her stomach tightened. "He's a cop?"

"Past tense. He left the force three years ago."

Once a cop, always a cop. Her ex had been a police officer. He'd protected others but failed to show that same sense of concern when it came to his own family. The marshal seemed oblivious to her unease.

"Abe is an old friend," Jonathan continued. "A widower from my police-force days who owns a farm and has a spare house on his property. He lives in a rural Amish community."

"Amish?"

"That's right."

"Bonnets and buggies?" she asked.

He smiled weakly. "You'll be off the grid, Mrs. Bradford. No one will look for you there."

Don't miss
Amish Safe House *by Debby Giusti,*
available February 2019 wherever
Love Inspired® Suspense books and ebooks are sold.

www.LoveInspired.com

LISEXP0119

WE HOPE YOU ENJOYED THIS BOOK!

Love Inspired® SUSPENSE

Uncover the truth in these thrilling stories of faith in the face of crime from Love Inspired Suspense. Discover six new books available every month, wherever books are sold!

LoveInspired.com

SPECIAL EXCERPT FROM

Love Inspired®

After returning to his Amish community after losing his job in the Englisch world, Aaron King isn't sure if he wants to stay. But the more time he spends training a horse with childhood friend Sally Stoltzfus, the more he begins to believe this is exactly where he belongs.

Read on for a sneak preview of
The Promised Amish Bride *by Marta Perry,*
available February 2019 from Love Inspired!

"Komm now, Aaron. I thought you might be ready to keep your promise to me."

"Promise?" He looked at her blankly.

"You can't have forgotten. You promised you'd wait until I grew up and then you'd marry me."

He stared at her, appalled for what seemed like forever until he saw the laughter in her eyes. "Sally Stoltzfus, you've turned into a threat to my sanity. What are you trying to do, scare me to death?"

She gave a gurgle of laughter. "You looked a little bored with the picnic. I thought I'd wake you up."

"Not bored," he said quickly. "Just...trying to find my way. So you don't expect me to marry you. Anything else I can do that's not so permanent?"

"As a matter of fact, there is. I want you to help me train Star."

So that was it. He frowned, trying to think of a way to refuse that wouldn't hurt her feelings.

"You saw what Star is like," she went on without waiting for an answer. "I've got to get him trained, and soon. And everyone knows that you're the best there is with horses."

"I don't think everyone believes any such thing," he retorted. "They don't know me well enough anymore."

She waved that away. "You've been working with horses

while you were gone. And Zeb always says you were born with the gift."

"Onkel Zeb might be a little bit prejudiced," he said, trying to organize his thoughts. There was no real reason he couldn't help her out, except that it seemed like a commitment, and he didn't intend to tie himself anywhere, not now.

"You can't deny that Star needs help, can you?" Her laughing gaze invited him to share her memory of the previous day.

"He needs help all right, but I don't quite see the point. Can't you use the family buggy when you need it?" He suspected that if he didn't come up with a good reason, he'd find himself working with that flighty gelding.

Her face grew serious suddenly. "As long as I do that, I'm depending on someone else. I want to make my own decisions about when and where I'm going. I'd like to be a bit independent, at least in that. I thought you were the one person who might understand."

That hit him right where he lived. He did understand—that was the trouble. He understood too well, and it made him vulnerable where Sally was concerned. He fumbled for words. "I'd like to help. But I don't know how long I'll be here and—"

"That doesn't matter." Seeing her face change was like watching the sun come out. "I'll take whatever time you can spare. Denke, Aaron. I'm wonderful glad."

He started to say that his words hadn't been a yes, but before he could, Sally had grabbed his hand and every thought flew right out of his head.

It was just like her catching hold of Onkel Zeb's arm, he tried to tell himself. But it didn't work. When she touched him, something seemed to light between them like a spark arcing from one terminal to another. He felt it right down to his toes, and he knew in that instant that he was in trouble.

Don't miss
The Promised Amish Bride *by Marta Perry,*
available February 2019 wherever
Love Inspired® books and ebooks are sold.

www.LoveInspired.com

LIEXP0119